T0129052

Tarsus

R. N. DECKER

Order this book online at www.trafford.com
or email orders@trafford.com

Most Trafford titles are also available at major online book retailers.

Printed in the United States of America.

ISBN: 978-1-4907-3389-0 (sc)
ISBN: 978-1-4907-3388-3 (hc)
ISBN: 978-1-4907-3390-6 (e)

Library of Congress Control Number: 2014907152

Trafford rev. 04/16/2014

www.trafford.com
North America & international
toll-free: 1 888 232 4444 (USA & Canada)
fax: 812 355 4082

Dedication

To Kelly, who stood by me through all the hardships in my life.
I'll always miss her. She left without seeing me finish the tale.

To Mike, who has been nothing but supportive. A brother
anyone could be proud of. He and Kelly were my staunchest
supporters through all my hard work and trials.

And to my family who has stood by my side through everything.
I love them all.

CHAPTER 1

"What?" roared the king.

"Father! Please! Listen," said Laura.

King Lionel of Musk was the Eighteenth Monarch in his line. And he wasn't happy. Not happy at all. In fact, he was livid. His only daughter, Princess Laura, was talking gibberish.

"No!" roared Lionel. "That's nonsense! You can't *be* a knight. You're to *marry* one! Are you mad?"

Princess Laura hung her head and sighed. This had been going on now for far too long. She had finally gotten her nerve to bring up the matter with her father, and all she'd gotten from him was platitudes and pompous posturing. This was getting old. She thought he hadn't taken her seriously since her mother, Queen Ely, had died. For every fight or disagreement between them, bigger and bigger gulfs widened under their feet. And this was just one more foot of that gulf.

"Father, please," Laura repeated. "Why won't you listen to what I have to say?"

King Lionel stopped his pacing and stared at his daughter. "Listen to you? That's what I've been doing. What I've heard is crazy."

Lionel couldn't quite get his head around what his daughter was saying. As far as he was concerned, it was just gibberish, nonsensical sounds spouting from her mouth. She hadn't been making much sense, since . . . since . . . well, since his Ely had died. It seemed he was constantly making excuses for her actions, her being young and not knowing what she wanted to do with her life, besides being a princess, of course. She needed direction. She had been like that for some time now. First, it was fashion: what dress was appropriate, what hair style, what jewellery, what shoes; he knew she must have a hundred pairs of shoes, and yet she only wore two. Two. What did anyone need with a hundred? Such things not only reflected on her, but also on him as a king. Then it was her trying to help every homeless person and vagabond in the kingdom, which, thank the gods, her duties as princess interfered with. She had to be reminded the church was there for that very reason. She couldn't do it alone. Laura had a big heart, which he loved about her, but she had to realize how the world worked and how to cope with her responsibilities. But this! This! Lionel had always known she was fascinated by the knights, since she was a little girl, but actually wanting to become one—no! Absolutely not!

Lionel continued, "I forbid it!" It was time she grew up, and for him to stop indulging her every whim. "I forbid it! No princess can be a knight. You are to marry one, not *be* one!"

"But, Father," Laura cried, "this is what I've always wanted."

"No! No! No! I forbid it!" Lionel roared again. "No daughter of mine, for that matter, no maiden, has ever been, or ever will be, a knight. And you'll not be the first."

With that, the audience was over, with Laura being no closer to her dream of being one of the knights of the king's guard.

$$* \quad * \quad *$$

That had been the scene in the throne room not two hours ago, just after Princess Laura's seventeenth birthday. No matter what she said to her father, the answer was 'No! No! No! You cannot be a Knight. You must marry one!' *Not likely*! But she just couldn't convince him to let her try for the king's guard.

Standing in the middle of her rooms, she fumed and grimaced. She wanted to start throwing things, have a good old-fashioned temper tantrum, maybe fling a piece of crockery, or the ugly handcrafted mug, love struck Jonathan had made for her when she was five.

Laura remembered the first time she'd seen the guard practicing maneuvers in the courtyard. She'd been seven. She remembered it vividly, couldn't get it out of her head. Through all the years, she'd known her father would hit the roof if she mentioned something like this, but she couldn't help it. It was all she thought about. Her forays into fashion or helping the homeless or anything else she'd done, through all of it, this had always come back to haunt her. She'd gone down to the kitchens to beg another small portion of food from the head cook and all around grump, 'Martha', and upon getting nothing but grief instead of food, she'd turned to storm back to her rooms, and a flash of light caught her attention from the gray-streaked window sitting off the pantry. She remembered clutching at the old weathered lintel staring at Sir Hook, Sir GuWayne, Sir Guy, Sir Dwayne, and so many others, marching in step to an unheard rhythm. Their swords flashed in the noontime sun, making sparkling fairies fly over the castle walls. Dust from their feet ballooned up behind them like a dust devil, covering their feet and shins with a light coating of brown. Sweat beaded along her brows as she tried to make sense of what she was seeing. It fascinated her. What were they doing out there? Why did they have all their armor on? Wasn't that supposed to be for show? From that day on, she knew only one thing, she had to be a guard in the king's knights, the most respected, renowned, and loved knights of all the five realms. She had to!

That was, until her father squashed her dreams.

But Laura wasn't so easily dissuaded. If she couldn't do it with his permission, she'd do it without his permission. Laura figured what her father didn't know wouldn't hurt him. All of her life, she'd been pampered and spoiled, doing anything she wanted, going where she wanted, and getting anything she wanted. Anything, of course, within reason, or what the queen mother thought was in reason. She'd everything a girl, being a princess, could possibly want: money, clothes, and fineries of every shape, color, and description. She went to all the right balls to meet all the right nobles, to have all the right connections, to make the perfect marriage. She even had her own carriage with foot soldiers to do her every bidding, but with all that, still Laura was unhappy. With all she had, she didn't have what she really wanted: a direction in life. But she did now. Laura wanted to be a knight, not just any knight, but a knight of the king's guard, the elite of all knight's of the kingdom. That was her dream.

The king, however, had other plans: wanting Laura to marry a knight, love having nothing to do with it. *Yeah, right!* She'd been forbidden! Forbidden! To follow what in her heart she knew to be true. She'd show him exactly what she thought of his plans; she'd show him she wasn't a little girl any more.

She was disappointed and miffed; her father wasn't listening or even considering what she wanted. Weren't kings supposed to be understanding? Weren't they supposed to help their people if they could? Encourage them? Support what they wanted? Weren't *fathers* supposed to encourage their children to do better things in their lives, to make something of themselves?

Turning towards the doors to her rooms, she could barely make out the peek of a shadow of the guards outside. She didn't have handmaidens like other princesses; she had footmen and guards. She'd often wondered if there had been a rule somewhere about royalty saying she should have maidens in her rooms instead of footmen. Thinking of that just made things worse. She stamped her foot, fists clinched tightly by her sides, getting no satisfaction out of it. If there was a rule somewhere, couldn't there be a rule, or maybe an unknown, unused law to force her father to at least rethink his stand?

Wait! He *was* the law. He was the king. He could make any law he wanted! She shook her head almost immediately after thinking such a thing. No, he was too stubborn, or pig-headed. He wouldn't listen.

Laura flung herself on her four-poster bed, burying her head in the pillows, sobbing. How on earth was she going to convince her father she was a grown woman who could make her own decisions? Well, close, she could make her own decisions about what to wear to a court hearing, or a court function; she just couldn't make the decision about becoming a king's knight. She knew what was best. Mother taught her to be independent.

'Oh Mother! Oh gods, mother,' the thought brought even more tears. Seeing her mother die in front of her eyes wasn't easy. Queen Ely had been sick for months, no one knowing why. Every healer in the five realms was called to help, but it was no use. In the end—at the end—it was horrible to watch. Queen Ely slowly deteriorated, wasting away: withered skin, stretched to breaking point over her cheeks and neck, red blotches showing on her hands, feet, and under the arms, which reeked so bad she couldn't stand it herself. She had to stay in bed for weeks at a time because she couldn't stand up for more than a few moments, the strain from trying causing her searing pain running down her thin, spindly legs. Blessedly though, when the end came, it was over in moments. Ely breathed in one final breath, and then it was over. That was the day Laura realized she was truly on her own. Father had nannies do everything he should have done himself. Laura realized she didn't need anyone for anything. Her mother taught her everything in her ten short years of life she needed to know.

For one: she wouldn't ever need healers. At one time, Laura thought healers knew how to do anything, cure any disease, what to say to make people feel and look better, anything; but after mother died, she'd realized she'd been but a child to think such thoughts. She wouldn't make such a mistake again. Father, by the gods, never understood. Her father never understood Mother. Her father never understood why Laura and her mother would take long walks in the garden, when the queen could do such things, or why at the end, Laura had taken it upon herself to feed the queen instead of letting a nursemaid do it. Father never understood anything. He didn't understand now.

That's why father couldn't understand why she needed this, why deep in her heart she had to be a king's knight. Mother could, but mother wasn't here to tell her she could do anything she wanted. She had to make that decision on her own.

Laura sat up, wiping tears from her cheeks, and nodded to herself, coming to a decision: she'd do it on her own. She'd be a King's Knight whether her father wanted her to or not.

* * *

As the palace guards were changing nightly shifts, Princess Laura snuck out of the castle. It was a pretty simple thing for her to do. All of her life, she'd been playing in the giant halls and rooms of the castle, roaming through every nook and cranny, and she knew all of the guards' routines: side step behind Sir Frederick's armor, a guard passes by without seeing her; step through the door to the library, around this corner, take two long breaths, watch a guard walk so near she could hear his breathing; go down the Hall of Tapestries, pull this handle to open a secret staircase, pass through to the castle gate unnoticed; watch guard change places with his replacement for the night, pass through the portcullis unseen while their backs were turned; there, she did it, outside.

Simple.

It took Laura three years to find all the nooks and crannies to hide in, and a lot of failures trying, but she was persistent. Until that night, however, it had only been a game. Now she used what she knew to get out of the castle for a purpose.

*   *   *

Squatting just outside the stables, in the corrals, Pip, the stable boy, watched as Princess Laura slipped out of the castle. He was impressed by the way she'd done it. He'd tried for the better part of a year to figure out a way to do the same thing. Mulch, his guardian, had told him no one had been able to slip in or out of the palace grounds in more than a decade, due of course to the training of the guards. They were always on the highest of alerts and always ready for any kind of trouble. *Ha! I guess he doesn't know everything after all. He'd have heart palpitations if he knew that a slip of a girl had bested his beloved guards. Ha!*

Pip hated his life. Well, not exactly hated it, but it certainly wasn't the one he'd chosen for himself. He was grateful to Mulch for finding him and getting him off the streets, but the work Mulch had him do to earn his way in the castle wasn't easy. Mulch, being the head stableman for the kingdom, had taught Pip everything he knew about running a stable and taking care of animals, most of which consisted of shoveling shit, feeding, watering, and rubbing down horses used by the knights. If it hadn't been for Mulch taking pity on a lost orphan wandering the streets, he'd probably have turned out to be a thief and scrounger his whole life. So, for most of his short stay in the stables, he'd done a lot of wandering at night, trying to find the best way out, this of course being only one of them. Not to run away exactly, but find something better—the grass is always greener as they say—but on this night, he'd seen something move in the shadow of the wall, long before he could begin his own journey.

Pip realized at once whom the shadow belonged to: Princess Laura. He knew who she was from the many posters around the town square announcing her seventeenth birthday just the week before. It was very unusual for anyone to see her outside the palace, and it was definitely unusual for anyone to see her like this. Princess Laura was supposed to be one of the most important people in the kingdom, and although he admired her bravery, and her quick thinking in figuring out how to do something he'd failed to do, he really didn't think she should be out without an escort of some kind. He thought about going and asking her, but no, that would look strange, a mere stable boy asking questions of the princess. He'd probably end up in a dungeon for his trouble. No . . . the more he thought about the princess outside the walls, the more he thought he knew what she was trying to do, the exact thing he'd been doing, trying to find a better life.

Pip nodded to himself. *Good luck, Princess. I hope you have better luck than I do.*

*   *   *

Laura looked about her trying to get her bearings: to the left and right the castle walls, running north to south—she looked above her and saw only faint glimpses of stars, wispy clouds blocking the rest from full view. *I hope it doesn't rain. That wouldn't do a thing for my disposition.* From memory and a lifetime of being inside the city and the castle, she remembered the walls continuing slightly east of west, completing an oval, rather than a complete circle, the whole structure spanning nearly seven leagues around a central town, which housed the castle in the center. The walls were four feet thick, made of native rock and sandstone, rising thirty feet above her head, taking nearly fifty years hard labor from the kingdom's best masons to complete. It was intimidating at first sight, which was the point. It didn't have a moat, which now she was grateful for, but it did have a stream running from the eastern ramparts through most of the town which supplied everyone with year-round water. The only problem with it was during spring thaw: mountain snow-melt usually causing flooding in the western part of Musk. Most inhabitants of the region could only put up with it, chalking it up to a trade off being safe inside the walls. Levies didn't stop the flooding, and dams were out of the question. A holding pond could've been built, but then where would excess run-off go when the next thaw came?

Although she'd been on the outside of the castle many times in her seventeen years, she'd never been out without her footmen or castle guards. She'd been told over and over it was dangerous to be out at night without protection; thieves and cutpurses abounded when the sun went down: this was only one of the many reasons the King's Knights were needed and wanted by the people.

The princess took a second to orient herself to her surroundings and then began tentatively to move towards the trees just thirty yards from the castle walls. She crossed the main road, running east from the giant portcullis. When she reached the trees, she took one last look back, took a deep breath, and then went in among the trees.

In an almost childish way, she figured she could find someone to teach her to be a knight. She didn't know who, or where, but there had to be someone who could teach her what she needed to know. Maybe she could get to one of the other four kingdoms and find a teacher, one that would be willing to teach a girl. She knew from past experiences traveling, as a Princess of Musk, which didn't happen as often as she wished, the nearest kingdom was Pate. And they always greeted her entourage with great fanfare, a great show of horsemanship, and a sparring from their own knights.

She took with her on this excursion only the basic necessities: a bedroll, some extra clothes, a cloak in case it got cold, and some food. She was scared, which she attributed to nerves, heart sick from her father's uncompromising morals, and determination to make her dreams a reality.

She felt sure her mother would have understood. Her mother also would have understood what foolishness she was doing.

Within days of (escaping?), she was hopelessly lost. She hadn't really thought of where she'd go, or in which direction. She simply wanted someone to help her. After two days, Laura found outside the city walls nothing but misery. Exhausted, frightened, hungry, and totally alone, she realized that she'd made a very big mistake. A mistake she hoped she'd live through.

The first night, when she'd left the castle, wasn't too bad, not having too long to wait until sunrise. To prevent anyone from catching her right from the start, she didn't stop, walking until she couldn't walk any longer. Her feet hurt, but she thought she was far enough away when the sun came up to stop for a short break. After walking in the woods for several hours, she realized the forest was completely different than when looking at it from the castle walls. Within moments of being on the outside, she also realized there was more to them than just trees. Strange sounds she didn't recognize came through the rustling trees: howls of strange beasts, buzzing, twittering, chirping, and humming. It was strange and frightening.

The provisions Laura brought didn't last nearly as long as she'd expected. Within the second day, her food ran out. She found wandering in the woods was a tiring and hungry job, and she'd nibbled all of her food away long before she planned. She thought she'd at least a week's worth. She didn't eat as much as a full-grown man. She'd always eaten like a bird, tiny bites of not much food. But she didn't take into account with any kind of strenuous activity comes a greater hunger. And how could she? Never being in this kind of situation before? She knew then she'd been an idiot. But it was also too late to go back. She looked around to find only trees and bushes; when looking up, she found leaves on the branches blotting out the sky. A tear leaked from her eye; *I was so stupid.* But there was nothing for it now; she had to keep going, for good or ill. She didn't know where she was, she didn't know how to get back, and she'd gone too far. How would she explain this kind of stupidity to her father? All she could do was hitch up her britches and take another step forward and pray she didn't die.

The second night was the worst. Laura didn't really know how to find safe shelter from the night or the animals that roamed in it, and by sheer luck, stumbled, literally—nearly cracking her head on a stone and found the hollow of a giant oak tree, burrowing in like a gopher in its hole. The skimpy blanket she'd brought along for warmth had done nothing to frighten away the cold of the night. When morning finally came, she found herself cold, hungry, and ready to admit she'd been an idiot.

Wandering in circles for over an hour after coming out of her oak burrow the next morning, a faint burbling sound came to her through a small stand of willows. It sounded as if a pot were bubbling on an open stove. She slowly approached what she hoped wouldn't turn out to be a wild animal in a fit of rage or a witch stirring a cauldron over an open flame. Her insides were churning, and her knees were knocking, something she didn't think could really happen, and found a most unexpected sight—just past the willows, the trees seemed to stop spreading in all directions making a forest, a clearing appeared. A clearing with a stream running down the middle of it.

Laura looked upon the open space with wonder and joy. She was finally out of the never-ending gloom of the forest. It wasn't particularly large, this space, but to her, it looked immense: wonderful. She could clearly see to the other side where trees began to take control again, in about sixty or so yards, and when she looked to the right, she could see the end about a hundred yards away. To the left, the woods didn't begin for some ways. It couldn't have been more than a couple hundred yards, but to her, it looked like a mile. She was at the top most part of the clearing. She didn't care if it were to the north, or south. The only thing she cared about was the stream. It flowed with a steady run of water heading to the left, gurgling and splashing over rocks and pebbles, and it was close, not even twenty paces from where she stood.

With a sigh of relief, she understood what she'd heard. In a matter of seconds, it was as if a new world were spread out before her; she no longer had to be cooped up in a never-ending sea of branches, twigs, and a canopy of leaves blocking out the sun. She took a deep breath and smiled, the first time in two days. If nothing else, she could take a bath and clean up, make herself feel clean again.

Looking upon the glade, she nearly forgot about being exhausted and frightened. Her troubles of being without food, worn to a frazzle, jumping at every sound, bedraggled and badly needing a comb through her messy locks faded out of her mind. Lush green grass sprouted up almost immediately from the overhang of trees; sunshine was beating down on her like a welcoming beacon. She wanted to run and jump into the water and splash around like a little kid in a wading pond. And the smells, oh gods, the smells were fabulous! In the forest, all she could smell was dampness and moss and the cloying odor of decay, but here, here there was fresh air, lilac, a hint of rose, and the clean fresh smell of water. Taking a gulp of clean air, she took a step towards her goal, but . . . before she'd taken more than two from underneath the canopy of trees . . . something stopped her. There was something . . . something about the place that made her itch all over. Her smile slid off her face. Looking around wearily, she got the oddest feeling: the clearing wasn't quite right. Nothing dangerous, at least she couldn't see anything dangerous, but something . . . something was missing . . . or something wasn't there that should be, or shouldn't be. She couldn't put her finger on it.

It was like looking out of the corner of your eye and only seeing a shadow, fleeting, fast.

It was there . . . but wasn't. If you looked at it straight on, it was gone all together.

Crossing her arms and rubbing herself as if she had a chill, although the sun shone down brightly overhead, Laura slowly crept to the stream, holding herself tighter the closer she got to the water.

What is wrong with me?

She only had a few steps to take and she'd be there, right there, nothing to worry about. She was being a goose! She took a deep breath, uncrossed her arms, and knelt down to get a drink but was as fidgety as a mouse being watched by a cat, nonetheless.

She lifted her head to look around again before her hand could cup a mouthful of clear water to her lips.

She froze!

Jerking her head to the right, then the left, she saw—something again not there—but was.

A flash of color? A flash of reflected light from the stream?

She didn't know. Couldn't tell. Trying to shake the feeling, or whatever it was off, she shrugged and bent to get that drink. But . . .

Her head came up for the second time . . . she was sure she saw something out of the corner of her eye. A sparkle? But . . . looking around her . . . saw nothing. Nothing but the breeze blowing the grass, only the breeze.

Had there been a breeze before? She couldn't remember.

Laura shook her head slightly to clear her vision. She couldn't have seen anything. There was nothing out there.

But . . . there was.

Color . . . flash . . . shadow . . .

Laura was tired and hungry. Needing a bath, she shook her head again, convincing herself she was only imaging things. Smiling, she got slowly to her feet, forgetting her drink. She walked down the stream a ways, thinking to find a suitable spot to bathe, then with a chuckle remembering she hadn't any soap. 'Oh well, maybe next time I do something this foolish, I'll remember to bring all my toiletries, including soap.'

'Next time! *What was I thinking?* There wasn't going to be a next time.' She was beginning to realize how stupid she'd actually been. She wouldn't admit it to anyone else, but she finally came to the conclusion that she was a little hasty in her thinking, and her actions. There could have been a better way to get her father to agree with her wishes. She'd been an idiot in the grandest way. She laughed out loud thinking of it.

Then she saw something monstrous . . . and wonderful.

Actually, she nearly ran right into it.

Ten feet in front of her was a dragon.

The biggest she'd ever seen.

Well . . . the only dragon she'd ever seen.

"Oh no!" she whispered, now frozen with fear. "Where did that come from?"

Laura decided this must have been what was wrong with the glade. This was what made her so uncomfortable when she fist laid eyes on the clearing. That, whatever it was, had been keeping her from seeing the dragon. Maybe magic? Had to be magic!

She slowly backed away, the dragon apparently not noticing her.

Then she stopped again. Was that even possible? She was ten feet from it. If she wanted, she could reach out and touch it. Its eyes, a beautiful orange flecked with red, were looking right at her. Well, right through her. The more she stood and watched, she noticed its eyes hadn't blinked, or moved, or done anything natural.

"This is crazy," she whispered, slowly taking another step.

Nothing happened. It didn't stir or move its head to follow her in any way. She took another step back, slowly letting our her breath. She wasn't even aware she'd been holding it until she heard air rushing out of her mouth.

Another step, never taking her eyes off the dragon. Then, another step. Another. One more.

She stopped. Something was wrong. But what? *It should have . . . I don't know . . . eaten me? Or something. But it hasn't even blinked its eyes.*

This was strange. Why hadn't the creature tried to stop her? It was as if it were asleep . . . or not able to move . . . or enchanted?

Laura's curious nature got the better of her. Cautiously—very cautiously—she inched her way back to the dragon, getting as close to it as she could without screaming her head off and bolting back to the tree line.

She didn't know why, but backing away didn't seem quite right any longer.

The dragon was a deep, rich, green color with its scales shining full of all the colors of the forest, as if its flesh reflected the colors and textures around it, like a mirror, but different somehow. The shadow, as she got nearer, was the reason she hadn't seen it when she first came into the clearing, it had misdirected her vision to look at what wasn't there, instead of what was.

He was quite obviously in plain sight, (always assuming it was a 'he,' of course), and he was very big, forty feet long if an inch. Circling the animal, looking for any kind of movement, she crept to its head and peered into one of its eyes.

Nothing. She could see her reflection in them, but that was all, a blank expression staring back. Quite beautiful eyes though, unusual, gold with red flecks.

Laura pondered what to do.

Run from it? (She was a bit nervous, actually more than a bit)—

Find a place to hide from it? (Like where? It was a field for the god's sake)—

Ignore the brute? (Yeah, like that could happen)—

Return home? (Which would constitute running)—

Try to help it?

As she pondered all the possible things she could do, she absently brushed against the dragon with one hand . . .

Then . . . it spoke to her. "Do you mind?"

Laura jumped as if someone had goosed her. She hurriedly looked about for the source of the voice.

No one there.

She shook her head as if clearing it of cobwebs. She touched the dragon again, this time on purpose, marveling at the feel of him, slowly letting her hand slide down its scales, smooth, but also rough in places, like sand, but not quite that either. Then she noticed movement from its body where her hand was, slowly rising up and then down, like a bellows from a forge. If she didn't know any better, she'd swear it was breathing.

But . . . that would mean . . . realization hit her like a rock, and she started to shake. Then froze with fear. Then she didn't know what to do. She removed her hand from the dragon hastily, slowly swiveling her head to look at the dragon's eye again.

It blinked. Her breath sucked in a rush.

Then . . . a massive snout, about the size of her head, was right in front of her. She blinked, tears slowly flowing down her cheeks, and then she started shaking all over.

Then again came the voice saying, "Do you mind?"

In a moment of unnatural clarity, Laura did what any sensible maiden would do: she fainted.

*   *   *

CHAPTER 2

The king was outraged. How could Laura do something like this? And more importantly, how could the guards have not seen her leave the castle?

"Granston!" Lionel bellowed. "Where are you?"

"Here, sire," said Granston running to the king's side. "What can I do for you, Sire?"

Granston, King Lionel's chief adviser, was a Gnome. The king and everyone in the palace didn't know this, of course, but it was true. The myths about Gnomes not being real had always been lies. He didn't know where they started, or when, but it made his life much easier. He and his kind didn't wear pointed hats and stand in gardens all day, and they were definitely not made of stone. His race was living, breathing, normally, working-class people. They just tended to hide in plain sight and be as unobtrusive as possible. He, however, aspired to greater things, much greater. He stood no more than five feet at his tallest. Short, he admitted, for a human, but tall in stature for his own race. One couldn't tell of course, from his posture; hunched over, feet shuffling. He had to constantly be on his guard if someone were to see him not at the king's side, to keep up the pretext. But he actually was quite tall for one of his species. He wasn't as tall as the Dwarfs, true, although he'd been accused of it more than once, but he wasn't as small as the faerie folk either. So far he'd not seen or heard or met another his height, except one, and he didn't know if he was still alive. And he'd been around for a very long time. He wore his long and lusterless hair hanging down in a braid, and his eyes shone with a brilliance that was disconcerting at first glance. His attire was simple, but functional: soft brown breeches ending in faded cow hide boots, which had seen many a season, and a brown tunic over a simple thong-hooked light gray shirt. In his right hand, he carried a walking staff, towering well over his head, At first glance, one would assume him to be either a simple page, with odd quirks to his nature, or an unassuming magician with little power. And everyone, even the sniveling twit of a princess, whom Lionel was so worried about, *may she drop dead in the forest and have ants feast on her remains,* thought him a toad. He liked it that way. He got great joy in reminding them all that he was chief adviser to their king, a position he'd worked towards for over twenty years. Twenty years of grovelling and crawling at the end of Lionel's rope like an animal on a leash. Bah! But his time for deception was almost at an end.

"Is there anything you can do to find my daughter, Granston?" the king asked. The strain of not knowing clearly getting to him. His forehead had a sheen of sweat on it, his neck red as a gourd. He thought his heart might jump out of the confines of his chest.

Yes. Drop dead right here, you lowly thing. Granston smiled knowingly, watching the pathetic wretch squirm with fear for his daughter. *It will make my wishes come true that much sooner. Things would be that much easier.* "No, Sire. I'm sorry. I've done everything I can. I've sent out patrols, but they've not returned."

Lionel's chin drooped towards his chest, thinking of his daughter outside the walls by herself. She'd no idea what it was truly like out there. If anything was to happen, he'd never forgive himself. If he hadn't been so hard on her, this never would have happened. But, didn't she realize it was dangerous out there? She could be hurt, brutalized, or killed. He had to find her. He'd bring her back for punishment, to be locked in her chambers, to be beaten within an inch of her life, to be . . . to be . . . to . . .

"Laura," the king sighed.

Granston smiled.

*   *   *

Laura woke by the stream. She jumped up remembering what happened. The dragon! The dragon spoke to her. It spoke! She looked frantically around, looking for the great brute, but it was nowhere to be found. All she saw was the clearing, a beautiful, lush, peaceful place, with a babbling brook running down the middle. She turned in circles, trying to look everywhere at once. She saw nothing. No sparkles. No shadows. And definitely no dragon.

She hadn't been dreaming. She wasn't crazy. She knew she'd seen a dragon! And he'd spoken to her! Spoken to her! A melodious voice that could have wooed angels from the heavens. But . . . it was gone now, just gone.

By all the gods, she'd been lucky. She took a deep breath, considering how lucky she'd actually been. The brute could have eaten her, or roasted her alive, or some other unspeakable thing dragons do to humans, or Elves, or Dwarfs, or whoever. Laura decided she couldn't just stand there as if she were going to grow roots; not only would she starve if she did, but she'd also be very foolish, and she'd been foolish enough already. After taking another deep breath, she slowly walked towards the end of the clearing, trying to figure out what to do next.

"This had to have been a dream. I was dreaming. Just a nightmare. That's it," she whispered, trying to convince herself it had been a dream, and having no luck. Her nerves were getting the better of her. "I need to calm down, get my head back to reality, and see what comes next, that's all. Calm down, figure out a way home." She chuckled to herself. If there'd really been a dragon, all she would have been would be a tasty little snack, a bit of underdone potato sprout that would have gotten lodged in his digestive track, and by all that's holy, dragons couldn't talk. Everyone knew that. All the stories said so. What she had to do was pull herself together. Get a grip. When she thought more about it, she'd come to the conclusion she'd been spooked, that's all, spooked. She was tired, worn out, and frustrated, that's all. She had a mission, a plan, and an ambition to fulfill. She still had to find a place for herself in the knights, after she found someone to teach her to be a knight, of course. How could she have thought of going back home, defeated before she'd even begun. She couldn't go back to the castle and her father and tell him she had run home like a maiden after seeing a mouse running across the floor. She wasn't that kind of princess. She was stronger than that, just needing to catch her breath and decide what and where to go next. Which way to travel to get out of these woods and back on track?

With a groan, she bent down and retrieved her belongings. What meager things she'd brought with her, and began again, one step and all that. She never realized traveling could be so arduous. 'Nothing for it,' she supposed. 'Time for the next step.' She hadn't gotten but a few short steps along the stream when she froze in her tracks.

A noise was coming from the trees. Actually, a tremendous crash was coming from the woods in front of her. As she looked in that direction, her heart skipping a beat out of terror, the dragon came lumbering out between two thick-trunked pines, licking fresh blood from his chops with a giant red serpent tongue.

"Oh my!" she gasped. "It wasn't a dream,." She screamed, rooted to the spot.

The dragon, slowly, step by step, lumbered its great bulk towards Laura, in no rush, to devour her. He stepped up, cocked his head inquisitively, and then put his great snout just inches from her own, literally nose to nose with the princess.

Laura's scream slowly faded away to incoherent wheezing sounds; she couldn't suck in enough air.

The dragon opened his mouth, his fetid breath gagging her. "That's better," he said with a lilt. "Now, where are you going in such a hurry? And who are you?"

Laura opened her mouth and took in a great gulp of air getting ready to scream again. The dragon saw this coming and stopped her by saying, "Don't do that. My ears are very sensitive and maidens screaming give me a headache."

Laura gave a little 'hitch', automatically holding her breath and the scream from escaping, and stood still, shaking.

"That's better," the dragon said. "Who are you? Where are you going?" he asked again.

Laura stammered, "I . . . I'm trying to . . . to . . ."

"Yes," said the dragon encouragingly. "Trying to what?"

"To get away from you if you want to know the truth," Laura finally blurted out in a rush, holding her breath, expecting the worst. Her words had come out in a squeak, squeezing their way out through her lips. Her knees were knocking, and she felt weak. She wished it would just eat her and get it over with before she collapsed. She didn't know how much more she could take.

The dragon lifted his head and cocked it to one side, eyeing her from his left eyeball, a quizzical look coming across his face. "Why? You have no reason to be afraid of me. I won't hurt you. I want to thank you for freeing me."

That stopped her. Free? She looked at the dragon as if it were the one about to become a snack. After which she started to calm down a bit and began to breathe, slowly at first, tentatively, and then with more regularity. It seemed to want to talk before a snack. If it kept her alive, she had nothing to lose, so, taking a small breath, she squeaked out, albeit shakily, "Free you? Free you from what?"

"My worst nightmare," the dragon said.

Laura watched him, still shaking on her feet. What could cause a dragon to have nightmares? It should be the one causing others to have them. She didn't answer, just stood waiting.

The dragon leaned close. When it did, it saw the girl actually flinch away. His head came away slowly, and he asked in a somewhat soothing tone, "Are you still afraid of me?"

Laura could only shake her head, not trusting to say anything.

"I said I wouldn't hurt you, girl. Why would you still cower like a cornered jackrabbit?" He eyed her suspiciously. Then he said with a little heat in his voice, "Do you consider me a liar? I'm in your debt."

This almost unnerved Laura completely. Cringing, she started to shake again. Everyone knew dragons were notorious monsters. The only things they cared about were killing and eating. Of course, they were liars! All the stories said so. Although none of them she'd heard said they could talk. That was besides the point—dragons were ruled by their emotions and their instincts, nothing more, and she didn't have the will or the energy to stand here in the sun and debate the issue. She was beginning to lose her patience and her nerves. If something didn't happen soon, she'd end up turning and running, like the jackrabbit he mentioned. She was tired of waiting for this creature to kill her, so to get it over with, she deliberately struck a defiant pose, chin out, and spouted, "Why shouldn't I be afraid of you? You're scary-looking, and with what I just saw, you coming out of the woods licking your chops, I thought I might be your after-dinner snack." She held her breath. Here it comes. She put her arms up in anticipation of being eaten. Like that would do any good.

That's when the dragon started laughing, a great growling belly laugh, smoke billowing from his nostrils.

Laura couldn't believe what she was hearing. She slowly lowered her arms and watched the dragon laugh, her mouth dropping open in astonishment. A dragon laughing? Not to mention the fact he was talking. Everyone knew dragons were killers: hungry, angry, evil, maiden chomping, and they didn't talk, couldn't talk. Dragons were dumb animals, useful for only one thing: killing, killing, killing, and more killing, vermin of all kingdoms the world over, killing whatever, or whoever got in their way, and at the moment, she was most definitely in its way. But here the brute was laughing.

The longer the dragon laughed, the more Laura began to feel foolish at the absurdity of the whole thing. The dragon's laugh becoming infectious, Laura's lips twisted into a half smile, forgetting for the moment all the stories she'd heard—which had apparently been wrong. His whole body seeming to breathe in happiness from the sound of his own merriment, and with it, he spread that warmth to Laura, like one would spread jam on a roll.

But then Laura realized something; this dragon was laughing at her. In an instant, she forgot about being afraid, or being nervous; instead, she got angry. Very angry. "What are you laughing at?" she demanded, crossing her arms, stomping her foot, and glaring at it.

The dragon looked down at her with a twinkle in its eyes and said, "You. You are what I'm laughing at, child, and it felt very good to do so. I haven't laughed like that in centuries."

Laura looked at the dragon askance. Centuries? She was still angry. How dare such an animal laugh at her. It had no right. She stomped her foot in agitation again. "What are you talking about?" She was a princess, and no one had the right to laugh at her.

"Dragons, my dear child," began the dragon, ignoring her temper tantrum altogether, "live for many centuries, and I haven't laughed in a very long time. For one thing, I couldn't. I couldn't laugh, cry, smile, talk, or even move under that spell, and I was starting to believe I never would again. To make it worse, I was getting a cramp in my big toe." He rubbed his right toe with a massive forepaw.

Laura thought this was getting ridiculous. How dare this dragon talk to her as if she were a child! It even called her a child. She was a princess, damn it! It should show more respect. She had to get to the bottom of this. She looked up at the dragon, who towered over her, and in her most haughty tone asked, "What spell? And stop laughing at me. Try to make sense. Tell me what's going on."

The dragon looked down at the girl and sighed, his laughter fading away. "If I must," he said, with a resigned look on his face. "I do owe you one after all for releasing me from that prison. Very well," he said sharply, "it's a long story, but the short of it, it was the work of a very angry, very determined little Gnome of a wizard by the name of Granston. He felt I was in his way and decided to get rid of me, and to do it, he put me under an enchantment. And the only way it could be broken was for one of pure heart to touch me."

Laura could only stare, her mouth dropping open in an 'Oh'. Her temper had all but dropped from her in the realization of what the dragon had said. *Granston? What's he talking about? How could my father's adviser have anything to do with this dragon?* Not knowing what else to say, she kept quiet, slowly closing her mouth. How could she tell this beast she knew the one who he thought did this to him?

After it was done explaining, at least as much as it was going to, Laura realized, it turned, opened its wings, which were very impressive indeed, and said without turning back, "Since you need no further explanation, it's time I get going. If you need anything, and I'm around, just ask. I'll be glad to help." Laura saw it was about to fly away. She needed help now. He swiveled his head around to look at her and offhandedly said, "By the way, thank you again for getting me out of that. And now if you'll excuse me, I've some pressing business with that little wizard, very personal business. I'm going to show him the error of his ways."

The dragon gracefully flapped its wings in preparation to leaping into the air, presumably to go after Granston.

Laura had to stop him. She couldn't let the beast roam across the country unheeded. So she said the only thing she knew would do the trick, "You'll find him at my father's castle."

The dragon slowly looked back at Laura, folded his wings, and said quietly, "How do you know that?"

"Simple," answered Laura, being almost coy, knowing she had its full attention. She looked down at her feet and scuffed her toes through the dirt. "Granston's my father's personal adviser."

The dragon didn't at first say anything, which unnerved Laura. She lifted her head to see what was going on and found one of the dragon's eyes staring at her no more than a foot away. Laura flinched back, her eyes going wide. The dragon ignored it and said, "Personal adviser? Why would he be an adviser to a young girl's father?"

After regaining her composure, Laura looked at the dragon with a smug expression on her face, not saying anything.

That's when the dragon started to smell something fishy. He leaned nearer and asked, looking at her more closely than before, "Just who are you, girl?"

"I," said Laura, with a smile on her face, "am Princess Laura McGinty, eldest daughter to King Lionel McGinty, regent of his Royal Majesty and Lordship, Sir Humphry of Musk."

The dragon sat down with a giant sigh. "That was quite a mouthful, child."

"It's the truth," Laura said getting upset again. "And quit calling me a child. I'm seventeen years now, a grown woman of legal age for a suitor, or a betrothal."

The dragon moved so fast Laura barely had time to register the movement until it was too late. Laura gulped. How can anything that big move so fast? He was nose to nose with Laura again, nearly gagging her with his breath, and said, "Still a child. Tantrums like you've shown aren't worthy of a woman, or a princess. And I don't doubt at all that you are a princess for, only a princess could be so arrogant and haughty. I've noticed, although I chose to ignore it."

The dragon eyed Laura for a moment longer and then lifted his head as if he suddenly remembered something. "Why is a princess in the woods alone? Where are your escorts? Servants? Guards?"

Laura shifted uncomfortably from one foot to the other, feeling as if the dragon were her father and he was asking her why she'd disobeyed him. How dare this beast question a royal personage. *I'm the one entitled to answers here, not it.*

"What are you going to do?" Laura asked. "And what's your name? I can't keep referring to you as 'you', or 'the dragon,' or 'beast,' or whatever. What do I call you?"

"Don't change the subject, child," the dragon cautioned her in an authoritative voice. It seemed all grown-ups knew how to use it, even ones that weren't human. "What are you doing out here alone?"

"I ran away," said Laura in a whisper, turning her head from the dragon.

Apparently dragons had excellent hearing. "You ran away? And why did you run away, child? Was it because Little-Miss-Spoiled-Rotten didn't get her way?" the dragon sneered sarcastically.

"I'm not spoiled," shouted Laura, becoming more angry by the moment.

"No? Then what was it?"

Laura looked squarely at the dragon with her fists on her hips and almost spat the words, "I want to be a King's Knight, and my father won't let me. So I've decided to find someone who will teach me to be a knight so my father will see I'm serious."

"Just as I thought, Little-Miss-Spoiled-Rotten couldn't get her way, so she figured she'd do it anyway," the dragon sneered right back.

Laura's chest heaved like a bellows. She was about to shout at the beast, when she realized just a short time before, she'd been thinking the exact same thing. Slowly, she got herself under control. No! . . . She shook her head. No! But . . . It can't be? Unshed tears formed in her eyes. She looked up to the dragon, and mouthed, 'No.'

But he was right. She'd been acting like a spoiled child. Crestfallen, Laura hung her head in shame, tears finally spilling onto her cheeks. She tried to speak, "That's . . . But . . ."

The dragon stopped her. "I know what you thought. You knew best, and your father didn't."

"But . . ."

"No buts about it," the dragon admonished. "And stop crying. No need for tears. What we have to do now is get you back to your father. He's probably frantic with worry. How long have you been gone?"

Laura wiped the tears from her eyes and said, "Two days. This is the third."

"Two days!" roared the dragon. "Holy Horde Mother of the Dragons," he swore. "Two days. Child, if you were one of my young, not only would my mate and I be frantic, but I'd be flaming every tree trying to find you."

Yep, no doubt about it, It was a 'he.' No one but a father could say such a thing in such a fit of anger.

"You have kids?" asked Laura in astonishment.

"Many, child, many. Now, come on, your father is more likely pulling out his hair, or making his subjects pull out theirs. Let's go. I'll get you back. Apparently, we'll be going the same way."

The dragon leaned down again, this time extending his right wing to the ground. Laura took it as it was meant for her to climb up on his back. She realized he was going to fly her home. She grasped his wing and started to climb, but before she got to his back, she stopped.

The dragon looked back at her inquiringly.

"What do I call you?" she asked again. "I can't accept rides from strangers."

"My name is Tarsus, my Lady." he said, smiling.

*   *   *

King Lionel was beside himself. He couldn't eat or sleep. Little catnaps and snippets of food he could take weren't making him any easier to live with. His most trusted adviser, Granston, seemed to be constantly at his side. After this was over, the king intended to give him whatever he wished for being so faithful. After two days of worry, he felt like pulling his hair out. If that didn't do any good, he'd start pulling out hair from his aids, except Granston. He'd wait until the last to do his, which was the least he could do.

As the king pondered the dilemma of his daughter, a messenger came running up to Granston, announcing there was something approaching the castle.

Granston looked at the page with a cold stare. He saw the man pale from his expression, and it made him glad. He rounded on him and snapped, "What do you mean something is approaching? What is it?"

The page, Duncan by name, took a tentative step back from Granston's gaze and said haltingly, "Word from the captain of the guard is they don't know what it is." Duncan had been in Lord Lionel's service for nearly forty years, and in all that time, he'd never had the occasion to be afraid of anyone. The king made sure his vassals were safe and well cared for, so they had nothing to fear. But he was loath to admit to anyone, even his beloved wife Martha, the head cook, he was afraid of the Lord Chief Adviser. In any dealings with the man, Duncan felt uneasy and out of sorts, his shuffling demeanor just an act. Duncan suspected simply delivering a message, the wrong message, could get you killed. It wouldn't happen in front of the king and his court, of course, but possibly in the middle of the night as you were abed. And the heavens help whoever stood in his way to try and stop him from doing it. The cold stare he just got drove that point home. He wanted to be done with the delivery as soon as he could, so in a rush he said, "The captain said to tell you whatever it was, was approaching from the west. On the wings of eagles."

The adviser never took his eyes off the man. He could feel him squirm, and he visibly saw him shaking. *Good! Everyone should be afraid of me. In time they will.* "Eagles?" asked Granston, nearly barking the question. "Are you sure that's what he said?"

Duncan withered again, sweat popping out on his forehead.

Granston smiled again. "Do you mean from the air?"

Duncan could only nod, his breath coming in short gasps.

Granston eyed the weasel for a short moment more then turned away saying, "Fine. I'll tell the king. But you also go back to that captain and tell him he'd better hold off whatever it is. That's his job." By this time, Granston knew the man was almost in a panic to get away from him, and he was giddy from the sheer pleasure of causing the man pain. But he had work to do, even if it was work he hated, so with a growl, he sent the man away.

Duncan was more than willing to leave. He'd fled almost before the adviser had finished telling him the message for the captain, knowing once delivered, he'd seek the solace of his wife in the kitchens.

Granston sighed deeply—of all the things to happen. He'd thought when he heard footsteps behind him, he'd have been greeted with good news of the whelp's death in the forest. This was totally unexpected. *What in the world is going on? What could possibly be flying into the castle? I better find out what it is. That stupid messenger may have misunderstood. It's probably a carrier pigeon coming from that idiotic kingdom of Pate.* He sighed again and spoke softly into the simpleton's ear, "Sire, something's happening at the west gate. I better find out what it is."

Lionel absently waved him away.

The Cretin! Granston fumed. *I'm not to be waved off like a simple servant!* Without saying anything else, he turned and stomped his way towards the main entrance to the throne room, a volcanic eruption of anger boiling just below the surface. *This had better be good!*

*   *   *

Tarsus unfolded his wings, and with a tremendous jump, sprang into the air, Laura holding on with all her strength. She didn't have much in the way of handholds, but Tarsus told her to sit in front of his wings where his neck met his torso, which gave her the advantage of sitting with her legs draped down, much as one would straddle a horse. When the moment came, she hugged him with not only her thighs, but leaned forward and wrapped her arms as far around his neck as she could. Good thing she did, although prepared, the powerful downward thrusts of his wings nearly unseated her.

Tarsus didn't know exactly where the princess needed to go, but he had to start somewhere, so he headed in a southerly direction. From high on his back, the princess hoped to see something she'd recognize to put them in the right direction. He knew it was a long shot, but it was all they had to go on for now.

The princess, having wandered through the forest for days, lost, lonely, frightened, and hungry, had no idea which way she'd gone. She'd been floundering around like a fish out of water. Tarsus felt she'd been very lucky not to have died.

He knew from his own past, if he was any judge, that a king or queen would go to any lengths to retrieve their offspring if they'd skipped out on their own as Laura had. Her father probably had his whole army out looking for her. Tarsus knew he wasn't the best of his kind, or for that matter, the best of sires—gods knew he'd done some very bad things in his long life, but he was certainly not the worst one either—but wanting to see your offspring safe and in good health, he could understand. This King Lionel was probably making every one of his subjects' lives miserable right now. He suspected what Laura had done wouldn't make things any easier between them, but she needed to realize she'd been irresponsible, especially for a princess. He didn't have to help her get back to her people, but he tended to do things without thinking, so he could relate. He just hoped flying in wouldn't make things worse. On the bright side, he'd be closer to that miserable little Gnome. Two birds with one shaft, or so the saying goes. Tarsus was very eager to show him the error of his ways. *I hope this doesn't go bad. I know I'm not the most temperamental being, but I'm in no mood to be pushed.*

Saddle sore didn't really cover what the princess was feeling. Riding a dragon was nothing like riding a horse. For one thing, the gait on a horse was a lot smoother. Tarsus had to flap his wings to remain in the air, and

Laura felt every downward movement. His scales, though smooth like a horse's hair, were very hard and uncomfortable against her thighs. Rash would be a sure thing. She suspected she'd be lucky if she could walk when this was over. Another thing, no horse alive could have a hope of keeping up with a dragon; the leagues flew by in a blur. She'd thought it had been hard to get her bearings on the ground; in the air, she was hard-pressed to figure out which was up or down and constantly looking down tended to make her dizzy.

After two hours of flying, three bugs swallowed, and a goose nearly colliding with Tarsus, the princess finally saw something she recognized. She thumped Tarsus on his neck to get his attention and pointed. "That big tree," she shouted. "It was my shelter last night." Just to the right of a small stand of junipers was a massive oak with almost half of one side carved out of it, gone from rot. She shivered remembering how cold she'd been.

Tarsus looked back at Laura and nodded. Thrusting his neck out as far as he could, he let a jet of flame roar from his mouth that would have left any building in cinders. *I'm coming for you toad. Beware!*

The flame was so unexpected, Laura was nearly unseated. When she regained her composure, she couldn't help but be impressed and frightened. *I hope I'm never on the receiving end of that. No one would have a chance of surviving.* She shivered. Then she pounded on his neck again. "We're going in the right direction," Tarsus grunted.

It didn't take long after that to come within sight of the castle.

Tarsus looked back at Laura and shouted, "We're almost there. I can see the castle ahead. Where do you want me to land? Inside?"

"No!" she screamed. "Don't do that! Sir Dwayne, the captain of the guard would have heart failure if you did. Please land outside the gates. Then I'll go up to whoever is on duty and tell them I've come home."

Tarsus grunted again. *Let's hope no one's trigger-happy down there. I'd hate to have to eat a guard or two to discourage them.*

*   *   *

Sir Dwayne, the captain of the king's guard, King Lionel, and the Chief Adviser, Granston, and fifteen other guards were waiting on the west parapet for whatever was heading their way. Sir Dwayne and all of his knights and guards of the castle were battle dressed, swords drawn, ready for anything. Lionel was wringing his hands, his nerves almost at the snapping point. After being informed something was coming towards the castle, from the air no less, he insisted he be present, his duty to his kingdom clear. But he fretted this could get in the way of finding his daughter. He didn't need anything between him and that goal right now.

Granston saw his duty to the simpleton clearly also. He had to be there to possibly wipe the idiot's nose or keep the simpleton's feelings in check, although he tried to convince the pathetic fool his guards and knights could take care of any trouble.

Everyone was very tense, you could've heard a pebble roll across the parapet, as if everyone were holding their collective breaths. Out of the sky, within moments, a winged shape appeared on the horizon. One of the guards pointed and said, "Look! Something approaches."

Lionel walked to the parapet and gripped the stone edge, staring at what was flying towards the castle. His mouth dropped open in shock and amazement. *What in the heavens?*

Granston had a bad feeling, already suspecting what was coming.

No . . . no . . . no . . . the shape looked *too* familiar.

A knot formed in the pit of the adviser's stomach. *By the gods! What happened? It can't be. It just can't. I got rid of that damn thing centuries ago. How did he get out?* He knew he had to do something fast. Fuming, while everyone's attention was focused on the shape in the sky, he slipped between the king and his guard, quietly making his way as fast as he could back into the castle and his private quarters. Once inside, he hastily began to pack some of the most important things he owned, knowing he wouldn't be there much longer. *Damn!*

*   *   *

As Tarsus got closer to the castle, he noticed quite a lot of activity. *Oh Great Horde Mother! I'm in it now!* He should have realized he'd cause such an uproar. He knew he was the reason for so much commotion seeing guardsmen scrambling to point cocked bows in his direction. He was afraid of this when he suggested he take the princess back to her father, but his judgment got the better of him, again. No self-respecting Monarch would've stood by and let a giant lizard land in front of their castle and not take action. This was his biggest problem. He tended to act without thinking, which had gotten him in this trouble in the first place.

You idiotic lizard! One of these centuries, you're going to get into serious trouble being so stupid.

This might be the time.

*   *   *

Everyone was amazed, scared, shocked, and/or awed, and mostly speechless, watching a dragon about to land, not only on the parapet looking down on the west gates, but all over the castle walls. Word had spread like wildfire. People thronged to see what the commotion was about, Pip and Mulch being only a few. There wasn't a space left for anyone to catch a glimpse, pushing and shoving, ensuring they got a good view.

A dragon was coming! A dragon!

A dragon hadn't been seen in centuries, maybe tens of centuries. Dragons were known the world over. Everyone told stories of dragons and heard stories of them from their fathers, mothers, sisters, brothers, relative of relatives or friends: everyone. There had once been dragons aplenty, living fire-breathing dragons. Once, but no more. Some said they still roamed the far northern part of the world where ice and snow always ruled the land, but no one had ever been there to prove or disprove it. Rumors all. Dragons and their kin were the stuff of legends. Long-lived people still told stories of them: Elves, Dwarfs, sorcerers of great age, the fairy folk, even Trolls, not humans. Yet, here one was landing in front of the castle, a big one. Rumor no more.

The most amazing of all: a rider was on its back.

"By all the gods,'" the stable master said, "a dragon."

"Gods protect us," another said reverently next to Mulch.

Mulch looked to see Tholed, the town's blacksmith—still dressed in his leathers, sweat beading off his massive brow, as if he'd come straight from the fires of his forge—one of many who came to see the miracle of a dragon. Tholed's hands shook with either nervousness, which was understandable, or fear of such a sight. Mulch suspected the latter. Mulch listened as he mentioned seeing a rendering of one of the great beasts in a book many years before, making a warding sign over his head and heart. He whispered, "I hope the stories about them aren't true. My Da' said they ate everything and everyone who got in their way."

Mulch looked at him and grimaced. *I've heard the same thing. My Da' told me too.* He turned back to the sight of the green monster landing outside the gates and shivered. A dragon!

Pip, on the other hand, grinned from ear to ear, standing just out of sight of the stable master and the blacksmith and was listening and watching intensely. He never had a Da' tell him anything of a dragon. The only way he found out anything was by hearing of it from Mulch or the other stable hands. Of course, he'd had friends tell him about all the fanciful creatures in the wide world, but those friends, and the strange creatures, were few and far between. How could he hear too much of anything the way Mulch constantly kept him busy with chores? Today, however, he'd been in the loft when the commotion started. He desperately wanted to see what was happening, so he bolted for the doors, right behind Mulch and the rest. He knew if he ran to the gates like all the rest, Mulch would send him back, so he made sure he was always behind the master, squirming his way between two other burly stable hands, getting knocked around by some frantic folks trying to get a good view also, and made it to his vantage point just to the left and behind the others. Pip could just make out the dragon glide in for a landing, and he could see quite clearly someone riding on its back. Seeing the princess get off the dragon was what brought on the smile he now wore. He'd wished the princess good luck, in his heart, on the night he'd seen her leave the castle. Now, here she was, right back where she started. *Apparently, she doesn't have any better luck than I do. Nice to know bad luck happens to everyone. Although bringing a dragon back wouldn't necessarily be called bad luck.*

Wow! A dragon!

*   *   *

As Tarsus glided in for a landing, his wings gracefully caught an updraft, which helped him in the many minute actions that prevented him from doing a nosedive in front of the gates. When he was down, he kept his wings outstretched, and his head held high. After taking a small step to help with balance, he looked back to his passenger and said, "My lady."

Laura nodded, took a deep breath, stood up, and carefully avoiding the dragon's ridge spines headed towards his wing. Tarsus leaned to the right, while the princess made her way along his membranous leather wings, finally to stand safely on the ground.

Above the princess, along a parapet that overlooked the courtyard right behind the gates themselves, stood a shaking figure with a crown of swords on his head. He looked at the sight of a flying lizard land on the outskirts of his castle and wasn't frightened, not even amazed by the sight of the creature; his whole attention was focused on the person who climbed off it's back. "My daughter. My Laura," King Lionel whispered, looking down upon the amazing sight. "My Laura." Tears were slowly sliding down his cheeks, and he didn't care, the only thing that mattered was his daughter. "Laura."

*   *   *

"Stay here, please," Laura cautioned the dragon. "I'll go tell them I'm back."

"I think they already know," said Tarsus, inclining his head towards the gates. Laura looked as the gates opened, not moving. Watching with Tarsus, the gates slowly swung wide enough for a figure to come out.

Tarsus chuffed, folding his wings against his body and settling himself, whispering to Laura, "This should be interesting. How is yon Knight going to handle this?" He smiled showing a healthy row of razor-sharp teeth.

Laura looked at Tarsus and chided softly, "Don't do anything to make things worse. I'm in enough trouble."

Tarsus didn't say anything, just chuffed again, allowing a few wispy tendrils of smoke to float out of his nostrils.

The captain of the king's guard, Sir Dwayne, came riding out on a stallion of purest white, holding up a lance with the king's pinions on it. He looked most regal. Laura couldn't help but be impressed. The knight's stallion, Champion, pranced closer to her and the dragon without complaining. One would think the smell of a dragon would cause him to balk at coming very close, but he'd been trained well and he did his duty. Laura thought the horse handsome and magisterial carrying Sir Dwayne. She held her breath, not knowing exactly what the knight would do or say.

Laura bowed her head to the knight as he approached, taking a few tentative steps towards him, and in the process deliberately stepping in front of the dragon. She wasn't going to let anyone hurt him. If they did, they'd have to go through her first.

The captain and his charger stopped just a few yards from Laura and the dragon, inclining his head slightly, dipping his eyes to the ground in deference to the princess, but not so much that he would have to take his eyes off the creature just behind her.

"Are you well, Princess?" asked the captain.

"Yes, thank you," she answered.

"Your father, the king, is most displeased with your conduct, my lady," he said, looking at Laura as if he wanted to scold her, or paddle her, which he couldn't.

Laura knew this was as close to a chewing out as she would get, but it was enough. She felt ashamed of herself for what she'd done. The king's captain was directly responsible for the welfare of the king's subjects, which most definitely did include the princess. She'd not only put herself in unnecessary peril by running away, but she'd put the captain's position in jeopardy. She'd been very irresponsible and knew it.

Before the princess could say anything else, the knight pointed to the dragon with his lance. "Who, or what, is this, my lady?" At the movement of the lance, Champion pranced and snorted, shaking his head. The captain gripped his reins to steady him.

Laura looked at the captain, and then back at Tarsus. Before she could introduce the dragon, Tarsus took it upon himself to speak.

"I," said Tarsus, lifting himself up to his full height, no longer waiting passively, anger welling up in him like a furnace, "am the one who just brought back your princess to you, you pompous ass!"

*   *   *

Everyone on the parapet gasped, but someone among them said what no one had the nerve to, "It can talk!"

All but Granston, who let loose an epithet under his breath. "By the gods! Tarsus! There is no mistaking that lizard. Damn him to all the fires of hell. How did this happen?"

*   *   *

"Oh boy," said Laura, lowering her head. "This isn't good."

The captain showed no reaction to the dragon's anger. Slowly backing his steed away, he said, "Do nothing untoward beast. My men have weapons trained in your direction. If you attempt to do any harm to our princess, you will immediately be executed where you stand."

Tarsus swore to himself and looked to the castle. Sure to his word, the captain's men had maneuvered weapons into place for their defense. He saw at least twenty soldiers arranged on the battlements of the castle with crossbows trained in his direction. Outside the gates, while the captain was keeping his quarry busy, his men had moved catapults into range.

Tarsus was secretly impressed and mad as hell for not noticing. *Keep the enemy busy, while you fortify defenses. Nice strategy. And stupid me for not noticing what he was doing.*

Laura jerked her head to the ramparts and then to where the catapults were being positioned. Sir Dwayne was doing exactly as he said. His men were aiming crossbows at Tarsus, putting two of the fearsome catapults outside the massive gates of the city. In her eagerness to be back with her father, she hadn't noticed what was going on until it had been pointed out. She shook her head in disgust. This whole thing was going terribly wrong in a hurry. This wasn't what she'd intended. If she didn't do something soon, blood would indeed be spilled.

Without much thought to her own safety, Laura took a few steps towards the captain and his charger, raised her hands, and shouted in a commanding voice, "Stop! This will not happen!" Her temper rose with every passing moment. She noticed out of the corner of her eye Tarsus had taken a defensive stand of his own, coming out of his patient waiting pose, into his full height and glory, his wings outstretched and a billow of smoke rising from his nostrils. His eyes blazed with the intensity of his emotions, not looking remotely like the same creature which had brought her home. He'd been threatened, and his anger aroused. Anyone with good sense could see a fight with such a creature would not be conducive to sustained good health.

Dwayne watched the dragon closely. From the countless times he'd tracked and hunted other fierce beasts of the forest, he knew the monster's posture was a defensive measure and nothing more. One animal was the same as another in instances such as these when threatened, and he without a doubt was threatening this monster. But he could do nothing with the safety of the princess in doubt. Whether the beast meant to or not, she could easily be crushed by its massive wings or shredded by its razor-sharp claws while it was defending itself.

In as calm a voice as he could manage, the knight forestalled her with, "Come, Princess, before there is bloodshed,.." This mirroring her earlier thought. "Our king wishes your presence."

"Stop!" Laura shouted again, not moving. "What are you doing? This is all a mistake. This dragon is trying to help me." Laura turned towards the dragon. "And you," she pointed at him, "don't be so arrogant. The captain's only doing his duty. He thinks he's protecting me."

Tarsus looked to Laura and then to the captain. He slowly relaxed his posture, lowered himself back to the ground, folded his wings, snorted in disgust in a very human-like way—acknowledging what the princess had said—realizing she was right. He looked at her and said very pointedly, "Make sure *he* knows that." He indicated the knight with a nod.

Laura said tight-lipped, getting her own anger under control, "I will."

When he saw the dragon's withdrawal, Sir Dwayne became visibly relaxed.

Laura then stepped up to the knight and said, "If anyone hurts this dragon, I will personally see to it they're brought up on charges, Captain. This dragon, Tarsus by name, has done nothing wrong. He's brought me here of his own will and my desire."

Sir Dwayne looked at Tarsus, not completely satisfied with the princess's explanation, but he was willing to let things stand as they were until he found out exactly what the situation was. "Yes, my lady," he said, bowing his head. Then he turned towards Tarsus and said, "If what Princess Laura says is true, we owe you much dragon, and I thank you." He bowed his head to Tarsus in acknowledgment.

Tarsus was even more impressed by the captain's graciousness. "And I you, Captain of the King's Guard, for I don't wish to be spitted over an open fire today like a roasting pig." He inclined his head towards the castle.

The captain took his meaning. He ordered his men to back off but stand ready.

Tarsus bowed his head to the captain. He'd hold judgment for the moment, as he knew the captain would, but only for the captain.

Granston was another matter all together.

*   *   *

Lionel had a tearful reunion with Laura in the throne room, the same room in which the problem between both of them started.

"Laura," said Lionel, "I'm sorry for not listening to you. I should've known better. But what you were saying wasn't what a princess would normally say. I was expecting something a little different: you wanting another horse or archery lessons or a new dress, not to be a knight. I thought it madness. Please, forgive me." He held her tight and sighed.

Laura hugged him hard and tears streamed down her cheeks. "I'm sorry, Father. I know I could have done things differently, and I don't spout nonsense. You should know that, just as I should know you want only the best for me." She released him, smiled, and wiped her tears away.

Lionel looked at his daughter with a critical eye. "You look quite different in those clothes." He crinkled his nose. "You could be a bit cleaner."

Laura laughed. "True, but I was a bit rushed. I couldn't exactly go in a dress."

Lionel laughed fondly at her and then hugged her again. Putting her at arm's reach, he asked, "I see you've brought home a stray."

"Actually, it's the other way around, Father. He brought me home."

The princess explained what happened and how she'd come upon Tarsus in the glade.

The king was amazed. A dragon! A dragon in his kingdom! "I suppose I should meet with this dragon," said Lionel. "If nothing else, to thank him for bringing you home."

"Oh yes," said Laura excitedly. "He's very smart and very gracious. He helped me when he didn't have to." She wasn't going to tell him the whole story. She'd never lie to her father, of course, but he didn't have to hear every detail either. She was definitely not going to tell him how Tarsus had scolded her for being so stupid. She had her father and Sir Dwayne to tell her that, she didn't need anyone else doing it. "Please, Father, you must. You won't be disappointed in him. I promise you."

Lionel agreed. He called his adviser, Granston. When he entered the throne room, Laura couldn't help but be leery of the little man. Even after all the years he'd been in the castle, she still didn't trust him. Maybe it was his shuffling gait or his constantly seeming to never take his eyes off her when they were in a room together or it was just him. The chief adviser always made her nervous, as if he had a secret no one but him was privy to. And after what Tarsus had told her about him, she didn't know what to think. Tarsus had called him a Gnome. A Gnome for the love of the gods! A mythological creature that didn't exist. But as he approached, all she could think of was the smug expression he always wore on his face. Laura watched him and smirked knowingly. *If Tarsus is right, your days are numbered. And the sooner the better.* However, she'd forgotten to tell her father what Tarsus had said and remembered only after Granston appeared.

"Yes, sire," said Granston, bowing slightly to the king, never taking his eyes off the princess. He hadn't failed to notice the smile playing across the little whelp's mouth as he approached. When he straightened up, he looked her full in the eyes and knew immediately that blasted dragon had told her the truth about himself. Without realizing it, his eyes became the size of saucers with fear.

Laura grinned an evil grin when he looked into her face. She realized he knew she knew, and in that realization, she knew also he was afraid. It showed in the size of his eyes and the shaking of his hands, which made her smile even more. From that moment on, she was never afraid of him again. Afraid because of him, but not of him.

"My daughter has brought us a guest," Lionel said to Granston while smiling at Laura. "Make preparations for me to meet with him, please."

"But, sire," Granston said, "it would be very dangerous for you to be near such a beast." Granston had to keep this simpleton away from the lizard as long as possible. His plans for leaving weren't complete. He had only time to pack a few essentials when the word had gone up about the lizard, and he couldn't just disappear. He needed to be sure before throwing twenty years of planning and scheming away. He needed more time, and from glancing at the kid again, he knew she hadn't said anything to the idiot yet. Maybe she hadn't had time with all the sick crying and weeping at their reunion. Whatever the reason, he needed more time.

The king looked crestfallen, but he knew that's why he had people like Granston around him, to keep him safe. He found by experience that advisers of Granston's worth were hard to come by, and they told him what he needed to hear instead of what he wanted to.

"No! Father," Laura said, coming to Tarsus's aid and giving the little man an angry scowl. *You will not keep my father away from him.* "You won't be in any danger." She sneered at Granston, gritting her teeth, not looking away. "Tarsus won't hurt you." *But I bet he hurts you, you*

35

little weasel. "He didn't hurt me. He helped me." She tried to convey her thoughts to the Gnome, *Keep your hate to yourself.*

"Yes, Princess, he did," Granston said, not taking his eyes off the girl. *Die like this miserable simpleton king, twit! I'll win this. Don't toy with me.* He also gritted his teeth and spoke in heat, "But that may have been a way for him to get close to our king. I can't allow such a beast near our sire. I cannot."

"You! You cannot allow it," repeated Laura angrily. "The king, my father, has the last word in this kingdom, *not* you!"

Granston sneered at the little twit. His eyes narrowed to slits. He thought that he had to do something fast. He had to placate her if he could so he could keep the king away from the lizard.

"Yes, my Princess, but . . ."

"Yes," said Lionel, interrupting again, "I do. Granston knows this, Laura," he said pointedly. "But Granston," Lionel turned towards his adviser, "this is also why I have guards and people like you around me, for protection. Laura's right. It's my duty and obligation to my daughter, not to mention my kingdom, to meet with this Tarsus. It's up to you to make it safe. Please see to it."

"But, sire . . ." he tried again, "it's dangerous . . ."

The king raised his hand, silencing any further discussion. "My mind is made up about this, Granston. See to it." He waved him away, dismissing him.

Granston almost snarled at the fool and his brat. He could always compel them, but then he'd have to compel everyone around the puppet king and that wouldn't work. He didn't have time. Then he realized he had but one choice: he could only bow and say with gritted teeth, "Yes, sire." He then turned and quickly walked out.

Smiling at Granston's retreating back, Laura looked at her father. "Father, I must tell you something about Granston."

But Lionel was already walking towards the door, hot on Granston's heels. "Later, Laura, I have a dragon to talk to," he distractedly said. "This is wonderful. I only wish your mother were here to see this day."

Laura could only sigh and follow. She knew her father better than anyone, and she knew he was tenacious and uncompromising, and like a child, when it came to wonders he couldn't explain. He was lost in the fact there was a dragon in his kingdom. He wasn't interested in anything else. Not even the return of his daughter. She'd get her turn to talk to him, but not until after he'd talked with Tarsus.

*　　*　　*

After the princess left the field, returning to the castle, the captain of the guard didn't move. He and all of his men atop the battlements and those outside with catapults watched Tarsus. They didn't say anything, only watched. Tarsus understood the knight's apprehension and duty, but knowing didn't make it any easier to swallow. So, to show them he didn't care if they watched or not, he made a great show of acting like it didn't bother him in the least. With great care, Tarsus settled down, sitting like a dog, getting as comfortable as he could, placing his forelegs under him, his wings folded at his sides, his tail wrapped around his great girth—not going so far as to lower his head in case of treachery, he wasn't that stupid—and watched his surroundings as if enjoying the day. Through all of this, he noticed the gates of the keep didn't stand open. After the princess disappeared through them, they'd slammed shut. He smiled at the thought. He'd no intention of going through the doors in the first place. His mission was to see the girl back to her father and kingdom and then take care of his own problem. Just by chance, the princess mentioned the name of his enemy. If he actually was here, Tarsus intended to have the satisfaction of killing him, and if these people knew what was good for them, they'd send him out so he could get on with it.

After a few minutes, Tarsus was actually beginning to enjoy the heat of the sun on his skin. He shut his eyes to block out the sight of the walls and his surroundings and stretched his neck out as far as he could, spreading his wings out along his body so he could feel the heat. He also slowly uncurled his tail to lie behind him. It had been a long time since he'd the chance to sun himself, and it felt marvelous. But it didn't last very long. After a time, he could hear the steps of someone approaching. His eyes sprang open to the sight of Sir Dwayne. He'd dismounted and was slowly edging his way towards Tarsus's head. The first thing Tarsus noticed was that he carried no weapons of any kind, no sword, no lance, not even a knife or dirk.

Tarsus swiveled his head to face the man as he came near. When he was ten feet away, he bowed, more of a gesture than a real bow from the waist, and said, "Dragon, I have been asked to convey our thanks for the return of our princess and ask if you would allow our king to speak with you?"

Tarsus considered this for a moment and then answered, "Thank you, Captain, that would be most agreeable." He looked towards the gates and found they'd been opened slightly, not enough for him to pass through, but enough for the catapults to be taken back inside the walls. He frowned, not at the knight, but at himself. He hadn't heard any movement of the weapons. He'd been so absorbed in his sunning, he hadn't heard a thing. He admonished himself for his lapse. To cover the fact, he inclined his head at the man and asked, "Do you not think me dangerous any longer, Captain?"

Sir Dwayne stood tall and answered, "I do. Anyone without good sense would be a fool." He looked at the dragon and smiled slightly.

Tarsus nodded with his own smile.

The knight turned and motioned for him to follow. "If you would."

Tarsus was surprised. He nodded again and followed the knight as he led him to another gate just along the west wall. It wasn't very far. It just took a couple of minutes to reach. When they arrived, he noticed that it was even bigger than the gate he'd landed in front of. Sir Dwayne, acting the gracious host, told him this gate was used when troops had to be moved in large numbers. They opened up not too far from the castle's stables, no more than thirty yards. The corrals were easily seen, being broken up into two main areas: one for the new horses being broke for riding, and the other for horses being put out for fresh feed and exercise, allowing cavalry to leave the city in great numbers. He learned later it was usually not manned but by a single sentry, there being no need for more. Upon closer inspection, as Tarsus slid through the gates, with room to spare for his massive size, he noticed there was quite a few more sentries than one at the moment. Tarsus spotted no less than twenty at fast count. He smiled again to himself. *This should be interesting. They aren't treating me badly, but they're sure keeping a wary eye on me. Good for them.*

As they approached the stables, a burly man in a leather apron and gloves opened the doors, who he found out later was Mulch, the stable master, who stayed as far away from him as he could manage. He merely nodded as the captain went through the doors but said nothing to Tarsus. He just looked at him, seeming to size the situation up. And from the look Tarsus was given, he didn't like it in the least. He probably thought the place for dragons was outside. Tarsus grunted as he passed through to one of the stalls. Fresh hay had been laid out and a bucket of water was in one corner; other than that, the place was empty.

Sir Dwayne turned to him and said, "I hope this will be adequate."

Tarsus stuck his head inside and sniffed. The space, which of course was built for horses, was too small, but Tarsus also knew the arrangements had been made in haste. And he couldn't exactly expect to be put up in the palace. He knew he was too big. "Yes. Thank you, Captain. It's most gracious of you."

"Not at all, dragon. You have the princess to thank, not I. She's the one who requested that we see to your needs."

"I must thank her then," said Tarsus.

"You'll get your chance. She and the king will be here shortly to talk with you."

Tarsus lowered his head in acknowledgment and lumbered into the stall assigned to him. When he was inside, it was a little cramped for his liking, but he accepted it nonetheless. Later, as it turned out, one of the neighboring walls was torn down to give him more room. But now, he could put up with a lot of discomfort to get his claws into Granston. It was only a matter of time before the Gnome of a wizard was where he wanted him. Then he'd have something to say. Oh yes, by the Horde Mother, he would.

*   *   *

CHAPTER 3

G ranston was in a fury. *How could this have happened? How is it, at this time, that lizard comes back?* He couldn't think straight. *How do I get out of this one?* He was babbling in his mind. *How is it, after all these centuries, Tarsus picks now to come back? I've been working on this idiot king too long, and in one move, it's gone to the dogs. Damn!*

Dismissed from the audience hall and leaving the spoiled daughter talking to the idiot king, Granston hurried towards his own chambers. He had to get out. He needed to make sure his escape was prepared. He couldn't let that damnable lizard see him. Not all of his possessions were in the castle, and he'd only stuffed a few essentials into a traveling bag.

Along one corridor, he found Sir Dwayne walking briskly towards him. He smiled. This idiot was as bad as the fool king. His duty as the captain of the king's guard was to protect his king and kingdom with his life, if necessary. He took his duty very seriously. Granston was going to take full advantage. Approaching the knight, Granston said, "You need to make arrangements for King Lionel to see and talk with the dragon."

"That's not my duty, adviser," informed Sir Dwayne in a voice that said more than words that he loathed Granston. This wasn't the first time the king's adviser had tried to impose his will on the knight. Sir Dwayne made it plain it wasn't wanted or needed. "It's your duty to do something like that, adviser. I've already seen to the dragon's disposition in the stables as I was commanded. My only duty now is to supply the protection for our king. Go fetch up the right people yourself. I'm the protection, so you've already done that part. Now you probably need to go fetch a scribe or someone to put the meeting down on parchment. Whatever it is, get to it. My duty is with the king." The knight went around the adviser, putting him in his place for the servant he was, his chin out not bothering to hide his anger.

Granston's mood was as black as a fireplace flue, but he couldn't do anything to this pompous ass like he so badly wanted. If he did, he wouldn't escape. Not only would blowing the ass to pieces call the attention of the other guards, but it would also cause that god-awful lizard in the stables to come stick his forked tongue in as well. Although the prospect of confronting the giant lizard didn't daunt him, just as it hadn't those many centuries ago, it wouldn't help him now either. So, he tried something else with the soldier. If he wouldn't do something for the king's adviser, maybe he'd do it for a king's order. "Sir Knight, do you understand the gravity of what's transpiring?" He followed the knight a few steps, trying to lure him back. Granston got him to stop, but not turn around. It was the fool's duty to listen to anything that might be helpful in the defense of his pathetic king. Granston walked back to him and in an almost conspiratorial voice said, "I'm scared for our king, Knight. And for his daughter."

Despite the contempt he felt for Granston, this statement got the knight's attention. Duty, honor, and kingdom were the only things in this world worth living and dying for, and questioning any of those virtues would always get his attention. "What do you mean?" asked the knight. "What do you expect from the dragon?"

"I expect the same as you," answered Granston. "The monster in the stables, at any moment, could attack the king and the princess." Granston stared into the knight's eyes without flinching, hoping it would give credence to his words. "The princess, in her naivety, may think the animal brought her back to help. But he looks to be cunning. What if he used her as a rouse just to get inside the gates? Without warning, he could easily take out all of your men. Then what do you think will happen?"

The knight said nothing, but his eyes told Granston he'd hit a chord. At every mention of the dragon, the knight's eyes darted to the outside, as if he could see through the walls at the dragon in the stables. Oh yes, he was ready for the finale. "Now, do you want that monster out there to kill your king and destroy your kingdom?" The knight's eyes smoldered. "I'm to make arrangements for the king's meeting, not his safety, yes, but I'm responsible for fulfilling his orders also. He's ordered me to take his most vital documents of the kingdom to safety. The documents and tomes are for future monarchs. The princess for one. They have to be protected. It's very important. I need your help so the king can assess the danger from the monster." *What claptrap! But it looks as if the idiot's going for it.* All Granston needed was time to make his escape, and it looked like the knight would be the perfect patsy.

"Fine," said the pompous ass after a moment. "I'll have the stables made ready for the king."

"Thank you," said Granston, making a mocking bow to the knight. "Make sure there are plenty of guards to help protect the king. I shall not be long. I'll meet you there."

The knight walked off. Granston watched and smiled. *Arrogant ass! I hope the dragon eats you!*

Granston turned on his heels and continued towards his quarters. He figured he had, if he were lucky, an hour. A very short hour.

Granston fled.

That was the last time Sir Dwayne saw the Lord Adviser in the castle.

But it definitely wasn't the last time the knight, the king, the princess, or Tarsus saw him. It was only the beginning.

*   *   *

Sir Dwayne was as competent and effective as ever. After Granston the weasel told him to make sure the dragon was to be made ready for an audience with King Lionel, he immediately made plans. Sir Hook, Dwayne's most trusted and second in command, was put in charge of the rest of the knights, placing them in a small circle around the whole barn. Two guards were posted at the doors, waiting for the king's arrival. He'd be ready for any untoward move by the monster if he decided to attack. A whole platoon of regular soldiers were put on standby, waiting just outside the stables in case he got further than expected if an attack actually happened. Then a page was sent to the king to inform him everything was ready.

A few short moments later, the page rushed back and told him the king was already on his way. Surprisingly, the page was carrying a chair. The knight looked at the man in puzzlement and then realized it was for the king to sit when he had his audience with the dragon. The knight nodded and the page went inside. In just a few short moments, he ducked back with sweat beading his forehead. His face turned a pale ashen color, as if something green and scaly had spooked him.

Lionel walked up to Sir Dwayne with Laura by his side. His eyes shone with the prospect of meeting the monster. Sir Dwayne said, "Sire, please walk slowly when you're inside the stable. If the monster attacks, you must move aside quickly so my men and I can take action in your defense." He bowed.

Laura scowled on hearing the knight's instructions, and came to the dragon's defense. "That's enough of that, Sir Knight. Tarsus will not hurt us." She put a comforting hand on her father's arm and said, "He will not hurt you, Father."

Lionel nodded, patting Laura's hand distractedly, not hearing either of them. Excitedly, he said, "Yes, yes. Come, let's meet our guest."

Sir Dwayne took a deep breath, nodded to the guards at the doors to open them, and both he and King Lionel walked inside. Lionel walked regally down the aisle as if he were going to his throne room. Dwayne stood slightly back a pace covering him with his sword. Laura stayed at the open doorway.

Please be gracious. This is very important to both of us, thought Laura.

Inside, Lionel noticed a high-backed chair positioned in front of one of the horse stalls, presumably where his guest waited. His aides were as efficient as always it seemed. He noticed, however, the doors were shut. He glanced around to see guards positioned around him with crossbows, lances, and battle axes, seemingly ready for any violent act on the part of the dragon. Then he slowly came to the realization who was there and who wasn't. Granston. *Odd. Granston should have been by my side. He was, after all, the one who didn't want me to meet this dragon. He should have been the first to make sure I was safe.*

Lionel walked quietly to the chair, seating himself very slowly, not realizing until after sitting he'd been holding his breath with anticipation. When he took in a deep breath to steady himself, to present the proper airs for a monarch, he nodded permission to Dwayne; the captain motioned for the doors to the dragon's stable to be opened.

A page shakily threw open a set of doors in front of the king, hastily scurrying out of sight. Inside, the king saw a wondrous sight: Tarsus, a dragon, was kneeling to him, his wings out as far as he could manage in the confined space and his head cocked slightly to the left nearly touching the straw of the stall. He was making obeisance to him, as any subject of the realm would. Lionel's mouth fell open in awe; this was unexpected to say the least, but most impressive. He closed his mouth after getting hold of his emotions and slowly stood up, lowering his head ever so slightly, acknowledging the courtesy.

Only when the king had been seated again did Tarsus lift his head and fold his wings, trying to get as comfortable as possible in his tiny space. As he waited for Lionel to speak first—knowing the etiquette of the court, one wasn't to speak until spoken to—he took the time to study the monarch. And as he did, he realized the king was afraid. Not so much that his nerve would break and he'd run from the stable yelling his head off, demanding the monster's head on a pole, but scared nonetheless. His posture was stiff. His eyes twitched from side to side, and his skin looked pale and pallid.

Tarsus waited patiently, smiling to himself. *At least he has the good sense to be afraid.*

Lionel merely looked at Tarsus.

Tarsus inclined his head inquisitively.

Although filled with people, the stables were very quiet. No chain mail or weapons rattled on the guards and there was no shuffling of feet from nervousness. No one spoke. An eerie silence had settled on the scene. King watched dragon; dragon watched king. Everyone was waiting to see what would happen. Laura stood just inside the open stable doors, smiling at Tarsus and then at her father, trying to silently communicate to both everything was all right.

Lionel ignored her.

Tarsus ignored her.

After a few moments, however, Lionel cleared his throat and finally said, "I wish to thank you for returning my daughter to me, dragon. Is there anything I can do or my kingdom can do to repay you for your actions?"

"Yes, sire," Tarsus said immediately, looking him in the eyes. "There is. First, you can stop calling me 'dragon.' My name is Tarsus, sire."

A gasp went up from everyone around. Even Laura couldn't believe what she'd just heard. *No. Don't do that. Not now. Just go with him, Tarsus. He'll get used to you eventually.*

Sir Dwayne stepped forward, advancing on Tarsus. "You'll not speak thus to our king, dragon. You'll show . . ."

The king raised his hand to stop him. He smiled and said, "You're right. I'm sorry." He inclined his head to Tarsus. "Being the monarch of this land has done nothing for my manners. Tarsus it is."

Tarsus nodded his thanks to the king, but he never took his eyes off Sir Dwayne. Although Tarsus knew the knight was merely doing his duty, he'd the most uncomfortable feeling they wouldn't get along well. Arrogance like his wouldn't win him any ribbons.

"You said first, Tarsus. That implies there's a second. What is it?" asked the king.

Tarsus slowly put a smile on his face and said with certainty, "I wish to kill the little Gnome Granston, sire. Bring him to me."

The king's jaw dropped open in astonishment and fear. Jumping out of his chair, he hastily moved away from the stall doors and the grinning jaws of the dragon.

Immediately upon hearing those words, Sir Dwayne unslung his battle ax and stepped in front of his king. Without saying anything to his men, each prepared to fight, crossbows leveled, swords unsheathed, and lances brought to bear. The king, backed against the far wall of the stalls, not moving, his twittering nerves doing a dance, waited for what would happen next.

"No one shall kill the king's adviser as long as I live, dragon," declared Sir Dwayne. "He and all of the king's subjects are under my protection as long as they're within these walls."

Tarsus didn't say anything, merely looked over the captain's head at the king.

The captain took a stand of defiance in front of Tarsus, ready as ever for battle.

Tarsus looked at the man, still not saying anything. The display of bravery he'd just witnessed—for no one could confront a dragon without showing bravery—hadn't fazed Tarsus in the slightest. But he was impressed. Not too many men of any realm could honestly say they'd looked a dragon in the eye and come back whole. He was beginning to like this little fellow, even respect him slightly, although he thought he'd never really get along with him, and he'd surely never admit it to anyone.

Tarsus decided to play it by ear. He bowed to Sir Dwayne, acknowledging his bravery and his honor. "That's why, sir, I haven't done so already. For I know he's here. Granston and I go way back. You could say we're old acquaintances. Very old. I merely wish to convey that to your king." He looked at Lionel again, talking to him alone, "I will put an end to that acquaintance. A permanent end."

Sir Dwayne said nothing, but he also didn't move either. Tarsus knew he wouldn't.

Lionel stepped closer to Tarsus and asked, "Why do you wish to kill Granston?"

"That, sire, as I've told young Princess Laura, is a very long story. Suffice it to say that Granston and I are no longer on speaking terms. Our enmity is long. He's wronged me, and I will extract justice for that wrong. And on that matter, I will say no more."

"You will answer what questions are put to you by our king, monster," Sir Dwayne snapped, advancing a step towards Tarsus.

Tarsus came to his feet in a fury, whipped his head to the captain's, at eye level, staring into his soul, and said coldly, "Who's the monster here, Captain? I'm not the one threatening you with spears and arrows or caging my dinner, fattening the sacrificial lamb, as it were. 'Monster' has many meanings. If you wish for me to show you what it truly means, I would advise you to step back from me."

The king abruptly came forward, coming between the two. "Stop!" he shouted, throwing his arms up as if to keep them separated. Laura dashed to her father's side, avoiding her own guards to try and help. She looked on as Lionel faced one and then the other.

Tarsus and Sir Dwayne never took their eyes off one another.

"This will not happen in my presence, or in my castle," the king commanded. "Each of you have a strong sense of honor. That's plain, but I'll not have you bullying one another in my presence. You, Tarsus, are a great and wondrous being in my kingdom, full of many great and terrible memories, as well as actions. And I've known Sir Dwayne for many a year. He's been my friend, my mentor at times, and my protector through my whole reign as king. Both of your honors are not at stake here. It's your lives. And I will not see them thrown away in a moment of heat. I, as king, command you both, since you are in my kingdom, to stand down. I want answers, and I'll have them."

Reluctantly, the captain slowly took a few steps back from Tarsus.

Tarsus slowly lowered his head almost to the floor never taking his eyes off the knight, again prostrating himself before the king. Then he looked up and said, "Sire, Granston isn't who you think he is. He's played you for a fool for as long as he's been here. This I can tell you.

I don't say these things to upset, hurt, or outrage you. I say them from experience. Centuries before, Granston and I fought more times than I care to remember. In the end, knowing he couldn't win, he put me under an enchantment Princess Laura broke."

The king was amazed. "What do you mean, centuries ago? Granston is no older than I. How can this be?"

Tarsus sighed, slowly sitting back down and composing himself. He really didn't want to go into this right now. "Granston, sire, is one of the most powerful Gnomes I've ever come across in my lifetime."

"Granston! A Gnome! That's impossible," said the king. "He's too big to be a Gnome, for one thing. And he has no power, for another. You act as if he were a wizard. He's never shown any of those tendencies."

"Forgive me, sire, you're thinking of Dwarfs when you think of size. A Dwarf is very different from a Gnome. Although Gnomes can be small in stature, many such creatures as Granston have as much size as Sir Dwayne. Only someone who has the experience can tell the difference." Tarsus knew this wasn't going to be easy to explain or to convince the king he wasn't lying to him. "Sire, trust me when I tell you this. Granston is very dangerous to you and to your kingdom. If you don't believe me, ask him yourself."

The king looked around as if he expected Granston to appear before him. But he was nowhere to be found.

"You see, sire, he couldn't show himself to me," said Tarsus also looking for the Gnome. "He knew I'd crumble his world around his ears. He'd be unmasked, and to him, that would be unthinkable. I fear, sire, that you may never see him again, as adviser, that is."

Lionel motioned for a page to find Granston.

"I'll get to the bottom of this, Tarsus. I assure you," said Lionel.

Tarsus bowed his head. "Yes, sire. Thank you. However, please believe me when I tell you Granston is long gone. He wouldn't dare show himself to me."

"Before this business with my adviser, however," said Lionel, asking Tarsus one other question, "there's still the matter of how we, I, can repay you for what you've done for myself and the kingdom. Is there anything?"

Tarsus thought a moment before answering. "Yes, sire, I believe there is."

Lionel inclined his head, waiting for what a dragon could possibly want.

"I'd like to stay, sire."

"That can be arranged," Lionel said. "I can have this place set aside for you as long as you like, for I fear you wouldn't be able to stay in the castle." He smiled sheepishly at Tarsus.

"Thank you, sire." He gave the king an understanding smile. "But there's a reason I'd like to stay. I may have brought the princess back to you, but she also did something for me I thought would never happen. She freed me from a fate I consider worse than death, frozen in a lifeless bubble, without time. I would like to help her as much as I can, and in the process, make my vengeance of Granston come to pass."

"Very well." Lionel sighed, placing his hands on his hips and looking at Laura. "Although I don't know how you may help her. So, if that's all, I will . . . ."

Tarsus interrupted the king before he could finish. "Sire? Please, if I may. I'd like to stay to help Princess Laura reach her dream."

"Dream? What dream?" asked Lionel suspiciously.

"To become a King's Knight, sire," answered Tarsus.

A hush came over the knights. Dwayne frowned. Tarsus merely smiled and nodded.

Before Lionel could make a reply, however, a page returned with news about Granston.

Tarsus was right.

Granston couldn't be found by anyone.

*   *   *

Granston was furious. *How could that lizard Tarsus have shown up now?* After all his years scraping to that so-called king, all his plans were ruined. All he needed was a few more years, and he knew he could have made the king's death look like a suicide. No one would have questioned a loyal adviser on the death of a worn down and broken king. No one would have guessed or suspected he, Granston, would have had the stupid simpleton murdered in his sleep, and then afterwards, put any puppet of his own on the throne, a puppet king that would take orders from him. He would have been in charge of the kingdom. It was perfect. Perfect.

But that stupid lizard showed up again. Again! The same lizard that ruined his chances at a kingdom all those centuries ago.

By all the hells!

He thought he'd gotten rid of Tarsus for good, but apparently not. The magic which imprisoned him had been very strong. He knew it had been. But by chance or fate or design or whatever the gods thought would be funny, he'd escaped it. Damn the luck!

Granston knew he couldn't show up at the audience with that damnable dragon. He had to make a hasty run for it . . . and hasty it was. After making sure most of the guards would be busy at the stables, he quick-as-a-wink, with a wave of his hand, and a burst of light, appeared in his private rooms. He then gathered up his most precious spell books and notes, clothes, in a small satchel he'd previously prepared, and a staff given to him by the Father of all Gnomes, Grundehl, and with another wave of his hands, he disappeared from the castle.

Damnation! Again I am put on the run by that soulless lizard. But I swear it shall be for the last time. Time to make some plans.

He was gone.

*　　*　　*

CHAPTER 4

"Pip! Pip! You son of a broken clod, where are you?" bellowed Mulch, the master of the stables. Mulch was responsible for tending to the horses of the King's Knights, and he wasn't very happy. "Where are you, boy?"

Pip grimaced. Whenever he heard Mulch yell for him, he'd either done something wrong, or he had something disgusting for him to do. Usually, it was the latter. Pip turned from the loft window and slowly made his way to the ladder. He'd been watching for the dragon again. He was fascinated by him. He'd never seen a dragon before. Come to think of it, he supposed no one had, but that wasn't the point; the point was he wanted to see him, at least see him, everyone else had. The only other time he'd gotten a glimpse of the dragon was when he'd shown up the day he carried Princess Laura back, which had been weeks ago. Dugon, another stable boy, told him the dragon had flown out early that morning, supposedly to get something to eat, so he was watching for him to return when Mulch bellowed. He never imagined such a wondrous thing would stay in the stables he helped clean. Every chance he got, he climbed into the loft and stared at the skies, waiting to see even a glimpse of him. But, like every other day, he was called to do more chores, an endless amount of chores, which kept him from getting that glimpse. The closest he came was replacing the hay in his stall, which wasn't fair. Every night, he'd fall into his bed, exhausted and out of sorts, as if Mulch didn't want him to go anywhere near the dragon. On the days when he was cleaning the loft, or forking hay from it, he could see some green color, at least a little bit, on the practice fields. The princess was always with him, of course, but he saw her almost every day roaming the town and giving orders to everybody. But the dragon was something else. He was worth watching. And this is where Mulch found him.

"Here I am," Pip said meekly.

"What have you been doing up there?" asked Mulch, eyeing Pip as he climbed down. "You know you have chores."

"Yes, sir," said Pip, looking down at his feet, trying to assume an innocent look.

Mulch scowled and then cuffed the boy on the back of the head. The blow wasn't all that hard, but anything from Mulch felt like a hammer hitting an anvil. Mulch was about five feet ten inches tall, nearly two hundred fifty pounds, and mostly muscle. You couldn't tell from the belly hanging down, but he was stout. Mulch used to be a knight himself, until he became the master of the stables. No one really knew why he quit the knights, and no one was foolish enough to ask him. He was tight-lipped about it.

"Don't give me that innocent look, boy," Mulch admonished. "You've been spying on the dragon again, haven't you?"

Pip gave Mulch a severe look. "I wasn't spying. I was just watching."

"Same thing," said Mulch. "And don't look at me like that. If it wasn't for me, you'd be out on the street, just another gutter urchin."

Pip hung his head, looking at the toes of his shoes. He knew Mulch was right. If Mulch hadn't accepted him as an apprentice stable boy, he'd probably be living in an alley or dead in a gutter by now. Pip knew it, and Mulch never let him forget it.

"Go, do your chores, and remember to clean Master Tarsus's stall."

Pip scurried away before Mulch could help him along with another cuff to the head.

One of these days, I'll do that to him. Then he won't think it too funny.

Mulch looked at Pip menacingly and then stalked off. *Ungrateful gutter Urchin!*

Pip hurried to finish Tarsus's stall, the last thing in a long list of chores he had to do just like every other day, when he was reminded of what day it was: his birthday, his fifteenth to be precise. He knew no one would think of it, but the day always brought a smile on his face, realizing he was one day closer to when he could do what he wanted and go where he pleased. Being a stable boy was OK, but it wasn't what he wanted to do for the rest of his life. Mulch saved him, and he owed him, but servitude like this wasn't what he had in mind. He knew the day would probably end like all the others, with him saying a prayer for the day he'd been saved by Mulch in an alley; and a prayer for him finding his own way in life, all be it with a little help of course; and a prayer to not always be a stable boy; and the most important, a prayer for the master of the castle—not much, but something to be thankful for. He'd never be more grateful for that. He took a deep breath and started in.

His mind wandered when he did chores, as they were repetitious and boring. He thought of all the things he'd most likely not be, a knight of the guard, for instance, which was highly unlikely, since he was most assuredly low born and couldn't possibly compete for such a high status in life, a mere page, one's life spent in the service of a king, or queen or even a princess, maybe, if he was lucky enough. But to be noticed by Princess Laura? About as unlikely as her noticing who cleaned the dirt from her shoes each day. She was too worried about her own life to be interested in anything else. Deep down in his heart of hearts, he knew he was undeserving, especially of Princess Laura noticing he was alive. Why would she? He was merely a stable boy. He was just someone else she could command, someone to pity, and someone to loathe because of his station in life.

He lost track of time and of what he was doing when he dreamed of a better life for himself. He wandered in a world of his own choosing, a world unpopulated but for himself.

"Why are you standing there?"

Pip nearly had a seizure when he heard the voice. He turned so fast his head creaked on his neck, giving him a sharp pain. He instinctively grabbed his neck and ducked his head waiting for the cuff that was sure to come.

Nothing happened. What the . . .

"You find anything worth looking at?" the voice said above him.

Above? *Wait . . . That can't be . . .*

Pip slowly raised his eyes, still holding his neck in his hand, and found the dragon staring back at him.

"Well?" said the dragon again. "Did you find anything worth looking at?"

Pip only gaped, his mouth frozen open, showing teeth and a slimy drool running down his chin. He'd usually finished with the stall long before the dragon needed it. He realized he'd been standing in the straw, in the middle of the stall, daydreaming. And looking down at him now was a five-foot long head with two baleful star speckled eyes.

He was wide awake now, drooling, but awake. This is what he'd wanted, to see the dragon, but he'd never pictured it happening like this, and he'd certainly never imagined the dragon talking to him.

Tarsus craned his neck to look around Pip, scanning the area around the stall, and then looked back at him.

Pip tried to speak. Nothing came out.

Tarsus looked Pip over from head to toe. *Scrawny looking thing.* "You gonna stand there all day drawing flies with your mouth, or are you gonna talk, lad?" Tarsus asked him.

Pip blinked.

Tarsus blinked back.

Pip did the only thing a sensible boy could do when faced by a three-ton dragon who could squash a horse's head with one swipe of its paw: he fainted.

"By the Horde Mother," Tarsus swore. "Not another one!"

*   *   *

Pip woke with the sight of Mulch bending over him. "What . . . what happened?" he asked sheepishly.

"You scrawny little urchin, you keeled over like a frightened maiden," said Mulch sneering down at him.

Pip looked around him to discover he was still in the dragon's stall. His bucket was beside him, with the wash water still inside. "Ugh!" groaned Pip rolling over to get on his hands and knees. Mulch did nothing to help. He simply watched and waited.

"Get up and finish, you louse. The dragon needs his stall," Mulch sneered. "Then get your weak bag of bones to that flea trap you call a bed. I'll need you on the morrow to muck out the other stalls." Then he turned on his heels and walked away.

Typical. The only thing I'm good for is shoveling shit. Well, at least I'm used to it. I've been shoveling enough of it from Mulch over the years. This is simply more practice.

Pip crawled to his feet. He found he was shaken, but he could stand. He looked around, wondering what had happened to the dragon.

Tarsus was nowhere to be seen. *Great! Even a dragon couldn't stand to be around me.*

Nothing was left for Pip to do but finish what he'd started and return the bucket to the supply room off the last stall. "Gods!" Pip mumbled, running a hand through his hair after finishing. "I must have gone out like a candle flame. What in the two levels of hell happened to me?"

Pip turned from the closet and came face to face with Tarsus again. He froze. *Where the hells did he come from? How could such a big lizard sneak up on him like that?*

"Can you speak now?" asked Tarsus, eyeing the boy up and down.

Pip opened his mouth . . . closed it . . . opened it again . . . closed it . . . Nothing.

Tarsus looked at him and chuffed.

Pip realized the dragon was laughing at him.

"Still drawing flies I see."

Pip's mouth shut with an audible clack.

"That's better. Now, can you get over the sight of me to tell me your name?"

"Pi . . . Pi . . . Pip," Pip finally squeaked out.

"Pip?"

Pip bobbed his head.

"OK, Pip."

Tarsus craned his neck behind to look over his shoulder and then looked over the top of Pip's head, as if he were searching for something or someone. Then he leaned close to Pip and whispered in his ear, something Pip never would've believed if he hadn't heard it.

"Could you scratch behind my ears?"

Pip nearly fainted again. Did he hear right? Did this gigantic lizard just ask him to scratch behind his ears?

Tarsus looked over his shoulder again and then back at Pip. "Can you? Can you? I'm going crazy. That spot's been driving me insane for ages."

Pip could only nod his head.

Tarsus leaned close and cocked his head expectantly.

Pip slowly reached towards Tarsus's head.

"Come on, Pip," growled Tarsus.

Pip shrank back, jerking his hand away, thinking very seriously of bolting for the door.

"Easy, Pip," Tarsus said soothingly. "I didn't mean to frighten you. It's just that—that damn spot is making me crazy. I won't bite you in half, or gobble you down, or tear you into tatters, or any of those other colorful things you may have undoubtedly heard about me, or dragons specifically. I just have an itch I can't scratch. Nothing more. I'd really appreciate the help." Tarsus looked into Pip's eyes almost pleading.

How could Pip refuse? Especially when the lizard was obviously in pain.

Pip reached up and slowly, cautiously scratched behind Tarsus's ears.

"Harder," urged Tarsus.

Pip did as instructed.

"By the Horde Mother," breathed Tarsus, "That feels good." He laid his ears to one side so Pip could get easier access to where he wanted the teenager to scratch, fairly enjoying Pip's machinations. Slowly he unwound his tail. He slumped towards the floor, his whole body relaxing.

By the gods! This dragon is like unto a pup when it comes to his ears being scratched.

As if reading the boy's mind, Tarsus whipped his massive head to Pip's. He looked at him straight in the eyes, stopping him in mid-scratch, and growled, "Don't get any ideas, boy! If I wanted, those rumors you heard were nothing compared to the truth."

Pip gulped. *Holy Saint Sebastian!* . . .

"But," Tarsus said, eyeing Pip, his face going back to a more natural pose. "I thoroughly enjoyed what you were doing." Then he smiled at Pip, a long, toothy smile, spreading from one side of his rather large face to the other.

Pip relaxed . . . Phew!

"Now then," said Tarsus, "don't go belly up on me again. I know you can talk. That's why the gods gave you a mouth. Use it. I didn't mean to frighten you. It was strange even for a human, to be standing in the middle of the floor. I was curious, that's all."

Pip found his voice. "Curious? You?"

"Yes, me," growled Tarsus. "That's one of the rumors about dragons that's true. Dragons are, by nature, curious beasts. What would you have thought if you'd seen me in that situation?"

"You have a point," admitted Pip.

Tarsus nodded his head once sharply. Yup! "What are you doing here, boy? I mean, in this castle? Do you do anything besides muck out the stables?"

"I don't know what are you doing here, dragon?" Pip shot back.

Tarsus leveled an eye at him, but Pip glared right back. Somewhere between scratching and queries, Pip had found his backbone right along with his voice. *Lad has spunk. I like that.*

Tarsus nodded sharply again. "My apologies, Pip. After being under a spell for so long, my manners have suffered."

This time it was Pip who nodded sharply. "Mine also, Master Tarsus. I, like you, have suffered much over the past ten years being here."

Tarsus looked at Pip quizzically. "Ten years? Surely you are older than ten years?"

"Yes," answered Pip. "I've just turned fifteen summers today."

"Ah, so you haven't always been here. Where are your parents? Where do they stay? What do they do?"

Pip looked down at his feet, embarrassment coursing into his voice and a little bit of sadness too. "Gone. Dead. I know not which. Mulch found me in an alley and brought me here. He's the closest thing to a parent I have."

"I pity you," Tarsus said.

Pip went livid. "I need no pity from anyone! I can . . ."

Tarsus poked his snout squarely against Pip's nose, which had the desired effect. He gulped loudly and shut up. "I meant for having Mulch as a father, not for being a foundling. I, like you, knew not my sire or dam. I was brought up, as you humans might say, on my own. It wasn't easy at times."

Pip calmed down, realizing he'd been an ass, but it took some effort. Over the last couple of months, it seemed nothing was going right. If it wasn't one thing, it was another. Today was just an example of bad things always happening to him, his nerves suffering for it. Mulch had constantly been at him for no apparent reason. The other pages and workers in the castle had been standoffish, and he wasn't eating or sleeping properly. All of this added up to one messed up and confused Pip.

Tarsus returned to his original queries. "What else do you do around here?"

"Mostly," said Pip, "what you found me doing: cleaning, sweeping, mucking out stalls. Shit work no one else will do."

Tarsus thought a moment, and then he seemed to come to a decision. "Not any more. From now on, you'll be my squire. Whatever I or the princess may need, you will supply it for us."

Pip was stunned. "Me? What about my duties here?"

"Don't worry. I'll take care of that by the morn. You just be ready when I call." And with that he turned, went to his stall, and closed Pip and the rest of the world out.

Pip stood in the middle of the aisle for a moment thinking about what just happened, then he smiled to himself and went in search of his own bed. *Mulch isn't going to like this.*

Pip was right. Mulch didn't.

✳   ✳   ✳

"Pip! You scoundrel! Pip!"

Well, here we go. Pip turned over on his pallet. Morning hasn't even been born yet, and Mulch has come.

Before Pip could climb down from the loft, Mulch poked his head up from the ladder. "Pip!" Mulch screamed. "Get your scrawny backside down here." Then he was gone.

Well, nothing to do but face his wrath. Better to get it over with quick. Maybe then it won't hurt as much. Wiping gritty sleep from his eyes with the back of his fists, he hastily pulled on his shirt, britches, and shoes. Running his fingers through his ungainly shoulder-length hair, he hurried as quickly as he could to the ladder and dropped to the ground. As he turned from the ladder, Mulch stuck his nose to Pip's, reminding him of Tarsus. *Whoa!*

"What did you say to Master Tarsus?" Before Pip could reply, Mulch answered for him, "Probably that I beat you, right?"

Pip tried to say something, but again Mulch interrupted. "Or that I thought you were worthless: you are by the way! Or you told him you were miserable being in the stables. No one cares, boy! No one! It's your lot in life, boy." Mulch put his fists on his hips, raising up, emphasizing each remark by little jerks of his massive body. Pip thought he may have a seizure of some kind if he didn't calm down. The only other time he'd seen Mulch this red in the face and upset was when a page, quite by accident, had left a stall open and one of the knight's horses had taken a midnight stroll. It had taken nearly four hours to finally coral the animal and every hand to do it. Then to make matters worse, Mulch found out all one had to do to get the knight's horse to come back was whistle for it: a mighty piercing whistle to be sure, but that's all it took. The animal came trotting back to his stall like a lost kitten to its mother, and why a former knight like Mulch didn't know that was still a mystery. "Without me, you'd be just another gutter urchin, a snipe waiting for the executioner's block, a miserable worm wallowing in the trash of the city, scrounging for food and shelter, a walking cesspool of disease! You have no gratitude! None! Why you little . . ."

Just then, as Pip was becoming more and more angry—

"Pip! Where are you?" roared Tarsus, finally shutting Mulch up.

Pip's head whipped towards the dragon's stall and then back at Mulch. Mulch simply glowered at him.

Who do I answer first?

Pip looked back towards Tarsus's stall and then back at Mulch. But Mulch was no longer in front of him. He'd simply walked away. Pip got a glimpse of his massive backside striding for the doors.

That answered that question.

"Pip!" roared Tarsus again.

Pip hastily went to see to the dragon's needs.

*   *   *

CHAPTER 5

"Thrust! . . . Parry! . . . . Thrust! . . . Don't expect a riposte! . . . Thrust! . . . Over . . . Down stroke! Thrust! . . . Up!"

What was I thinking? Why would anyone want to be a knight? This is damnable hard work. Will this never end? Laura gulped air as she sparred with Sir Hook. Ever since Tarsus came along, he'd been training her to be a knight. An art form, for it was an art, which for a dragon, he knew quite a lot about. And he wouldn't talk about how he learned the things he taught her. He was very tight-lipped. But Laura had to admit he was an excellent teacher.

Each day, for the past fortnight, for nearly five hours, Princess Laura wore breeches, a light shirt, knee-high soft leather boots, and a short jerkin, clothes any man would wear for training. If she was to play the part of a knight, she had to dress the part, this being the first of many lessons. She must be able to move without any hindrance, with easy flowing grace, or she'd wind up dead in a real fight.

And today was another of many real lessons. Today she was learning about sword fighting. Tarsus seemed to know maneuvers the captain said were unorthodox. But as far as she could tell, they worked.

"Thrust! Parry! Thrust!" shouted Tarsus. "Use your legs more for balance. Now thrust! Thrust!"

Tarsus sat back from the training and watched Laura go through the motions. He was trying to pick out her flaws so he could teach her how to overcome them, and to help him do this, he'd asked the captain for the loan of one of his men. And as Tarsus expected, after much grousing and complaining, he'd agreed. He'd sent, he said, one of his best swordsmen, Sir Hook, but after two or three minutes, he was hoping the captain had a sense of humor. Hook was anything but the best, and if he was, the captain had serious problems. If Hook had been in a serious fight, with a competent fighter, he wouldn't last but a couple seconds, but for the purposes of sparring with the princess, he was an almost perfect match.

Tarsus heaved a sigh. "That's enough," he called. "We'll start again in the morning."

The two combatants put their swords away, and Sir Hook bowed to Tarsus and the princess and left the practice field. Laura walked to Tarsus with her sword almost touching the ground, sweat beading on her brow, and exhaustion written on her face.

"Will it ever get any easier?" she asked.

Tarsus didn't say anything. He simply stared at the princess. Laura knew she wouldn't get an answer because she already knew the answer.

Laura walked to the castle, head bowed, more tired than she'd ever been. Tarsus merely watched, more concerned about the performance of Sir Hook than of Laura. He desperately needed to talk to Sir Dwayne about his training, it couldn't wait.

*   *   *

"You're treading on dangerous ground, dragon!"

Sir Dwayne wasn't happy. Tarsus knew it the moment he broached the subject of his training tactics, and he knew Sir Dwayne wasn't going to calm down any time soon from the way he was shouting.

"What right do you have coming in here?" Tarsus was listening to the knight rant and rave, not saying anything. The knight felt the dragon was trying to interfere or usurp his authority over his guards. Training was under the purview of the captain of the guards, not Tarsus.

Tarsus's head, the only part of his body small enough to fit in Sir Dwayne's quarters, through a window, of course, bobbed in agreement. "Yes, yes," he tried to say, "but . . ."

"No, dragon," screamed Dwayne. "You will not tell me how to train my men!"

"I'm not trying to tell you how to train your men," yelled Tarsus right back. "I'm simply saying if that's the best swordsmen you have, then you better find better training methods. The one's you're using aren't working."

"Listen, dragon . . ."

That was another way to get under Tarsus's green scaly hide, by the use of the term 'dragon'. It was infuriating. Sir Dwayne wouldn't like it if he constantly called him 'human' or 'shorty' or 'dinner'.

"When you get your own position as captain of the guard, then you can decide how to train men. Otherwise, keep your nose out of my business," shouted the knight. "I went along with King Lionel on your training Princess Laura, a fanciful dream I might add, because it was my duty. Whatever the king wants, he gets, but that doesn't mean I have to like it or help you do it." Sir Dwayne came closer to Tarsus while his head was in the window, making his point by pointing his finger at the dragon, (which didn't help, by the way). "Get out, dragon! Now! And take your new training with you!"

Tarsus backed out the window disgusted with himself for even trying to help the arrogant man. After taking a few paces, he snorted, turned back, poked his head back inside, and said before Sir Dwayne could bellow anything else at him, "Give me two days. If Laura can beat Sir Hook in a fair fight, you have to listen to me."

Sir Dwayne was taken aback. His mouth opened and closed like a dying fish out of water. His fists clinched at his sides. After what the dragon had said dawned on him, a slow smile played over his face. He looked at the monster and said, "Two days? Two? Sir Hook against Princess Laura? Right?"

"Right," Tarsus agreed, smiling himself. *Got him!*

Dwayne's smile never left his face. "Agreed. But, in the wild, unlikely chance that Hook wins?"

Tarsus didn't hesitate. "I'll leave the castle."

"And never come back."

"Agreed," said Tarsus.

*   *   *

"Have you lost your mind?" Laura demanded. "Can you possibly be serious about what you're suggesting? I can't do it."

"No. Yes. And yes, you can,." answered Tarsus.

Laura was dumbstruck. Tarsus actually expected her to fight Sir Hook in two days, in a fair fight, and win. She could barely walk into the castle after sparring for a couple minutes; to be able to keep up, let alone beat, Sir Hook, a seasoned warrior, she had to be able to do better than that. She wasn't ready and knew it. Tarsus was a raving lunatic.

"Are you mad? I'm not ready." She put her fists on her hips, adopting an irritated pose, reminding him of her father. Lionel had done the same thing on numerous occasions when he was thinking hard or deeply. He smiled.

Laura rounded on him seeing his smile. "What's so funny?" She didn't let him answer; instead, she asked the question bothering her the most. "Why did you agree to leave if I lost?" She was fuming now. "If you leave, I won't stand a chance of becoming a knight."

Tarsus merely looked at her. He didn't know if she could handle the truth, at least not all of it. His agreement was to ensure a fair assessment of her abilities by those whose opinions mattered the most: the knights, especially the captain of the knights. If he didn't see her potential as a valuable asset to his men, then no matter what he or she did wouldn't matter. The other thing was she needed more confidence in herself. In the time he'd been working with her, he'd seen many aspects of her personality: anger, envy, sloth, even petulance, but never confidence. Not even while dealing with her own subjects, including the knights. She always deferred to Sir Dwayne or Sir Hook when it came to giving orders to her own guards, as if she expected them to tell her 'no'. She needed confidence of her own for him to continue with her training. And the most important reason: he knew it was the only way for him to stay in the kingdom. Eventually, Dwayne and he would clash, the outcome inevitable: the death of a knight and banishment or death for him. Plus he needed to be close to the other, just as much or more so than for her.

Finally, he answered her, "Because you need confidence in yourself. And this will do it."

Laura shook her head, still not understanding, and repeated, "But I'm not ready."

"Yes, you are," said Tarsus. "You're more than a match for Sir Hook. With my help, I'll prove it to you."

"How?"

"Just listen to me. Listen and learn a little bit, and I'll show you how to beat him. I've watched him sparring with you. His style is barbaric. He's unconditioned, slow, sloppy in his swordsmanship, and his movements are jerky at best," explained Tarsus. "I've talked to Sir Dwayne about his training techniques, and he's made it abundantly clear training is no concern of mine, which will be his undoing and Sir Hook's. If he's the captain's best, you have nothing to worry about." Tarsus nodded and smiled.

Being around Tarsus as much as she'd been for the past fortnight, Laura had learned very quickly to trust Tarsus in many things, things which he seemed to know a great deal about, which she thought he shouldn't know, but was quite good at anyway. Fighting a seasoned warrior and knight like Sir Hook was quite another matter. Fear was motivating her actions at the moment; she could get hurt.

Tarsus seemed to read what was on her face. "Don't fear, child. That's one thing that will defeat you before you even try. And don't worry about me. If you lose and have done your best, I will leave here with an enlightened heart and a great understanding of castle protocol." This last he said smiling.

Laura groaned watching the dragon. His smile was a toothy grimace, sporting four-inch long fangs and razor-sharp eye teeth, not the prettiest sight for anyone. He looked more like the castle cat who got into the morning cream barrel.

She'd do it. Tarsus knew it and began to laugh.

*   *   *

Pip hadn't seen the princess in the whole fortnight in which he'd been a squire for Tarsus. For some reason, the tasks which Tarsus had set him had taken nearly all day, every day. He didn't know whether that had been planned it that way or it was merely a coincidence on the dragon's part, but it was awfully frustrating. He desperately wanted Princess Laura to know he was alive, or the very least know he was around. But it seemed as if that wasn't going to happen. Not only was he not around the princess, but he wasn't seen around the stables most days either. Tarsus wanted things the castle's resources couldn't provide: a specially made saddle. Tarsus didn't say why it was needed or why it was being made by an outside shop. The hostelry of the castle couldn't provide enough raw leather for the whole saddle, so Pip ended up scrounging the rest from the city proper. It took nearly a week for that one errand, and every night, he'd end up collapsing in his bed from exhaustion.

Another errand was finding a rune-carved fighting blade—the sword handle made of bone which was rune encrusted, supposedly giving the wielder of the blade magical awareness of where one's opponents were at all times—whatever in the two corners of hells that was. Tarsus insisted Pip find one. He had no idea where to go until Tarsus put him on the right track of an unsavory merchant off the beaten path. How the lizard knew where to send him he didn't know and eventually didn't care, simply retrieving the sword, which took another four days. Gold had to be passed between them, and then Pip hotfooted it back to Tarsus.

The rest of the time was pretty mundane stuff, but it took time to do it: gathering and or making the princess's battle armor, stitching rent clothing from previous training exercises, and of course mucking out Tarsus's stall. By the time he ate, cleaned up, threw himself in bed, it was well past time for Princess Laura to be anywhere around. This was definitely not what Pip had in mind when he was recruited by Tarsus. He began to think he'd have been just as well off staying in the stables with Mulch. Tarsus was just as demanding as Mulch had ever been. Pip was still weighing one against the other when Tarsus announced one morning, "Princess Laura and Sir Hook are to meet in single combat on the morrow. I want you close by, just in case I need you."

"Princess Laura and Sir Hook are going to fight?" Pip asked Tarsus, his mouth falling open in surprise. "Does she have a death wish?"

Tarsus rounded on Pip. "No!" His long snout came inches from Pip's nose. "If you would have seen what I had when they were sparring, you would have set a match between them too."

"What did you see?"

"His weakness!" snapped Tarsus. "The one reason I know the princess will win!"

"But Tarsus," Pip argued, "Sir Hook has no weaknesses in battle. He's said to have bested all of the King's Knights. All of them. He is the best."

"Then," said Tarsus smiling, "after tomorrow, Princess Laura will be!" At this, he clicked his teeth together, making them sound like a bear trap snapping closed, when for the briefest moment, Pip thought he saw a starburst bloom over the lizard's head.

Pip's eyes went round with amazement.

"How did you do that?" He pointed to the place over the dragon's head.

Tarsus played dumb. "What?"

Pip was in no mood for games. He wasn't only exhausted, but frustrated. "You know exactly what I mean. That burst of light when you clicked your teeth together." *Young, I may be lizard, but stupid I'm not!*

Tarsus clicked his teeth again. "You mean . . ." The burst of light appeared over his head again, but only for a split second: blues, greens, reds, and purples collided in a kaleidoscope of colors. The effect was short lived, a mere eye blink, but wondrous and beautiful to behold.

Pip watched in fascination, realizing something no one else had before. "You're a wizard," he said, looking at the dragon in a new way.

Tarsus smiled. "No," he said. "I merely do tricks of light and sound. I can throw my voice. Do other things. Make others hear what they want or don't want to hear."

Tarsus studied the boy for a moment, debating whether to tell Pip what he knew of him since the day he'd seen him in the stables. But, after a moment, he shrugged and walked back to his stall. No sense in getting him too excited. He'd only worry. Before he closed the doors, he said, "Be close. I may need you tomorrow. Be sure to bring the Rune Sword. I haven't given it to Laura yet. I've been waiting for the right time." Then he closed his doors, leaving Pip standing in the aisle.

A wizard! Damn! The dragon's a wizard. Why hasn't he told anyone?

"When am I gonna meet the princess?" he said to no one.

*   *   *

The day of the contest dawned bright and sunny. Tarsus was almost chipper, humming to himself as he watched Laura prepare to do battle with Sir Hook. First, she put on the new set of armor that had been custom designed for her. It had been specifically crafted for a woman, a lightweight breastplate made of tough cowhide leather, instead of steel, fire-hardened to withstand a substantial blow, with nothing encasing her arms except a patch of leather on her forearms, strange looking but effective, to ensure a wide range of motion. And surprisingly, there was nothing to protect her legs but a shin guard, buckled at the back, which she approved. They'd allow her free movement which was critical. Satisfied, she then picked a sword from the sword-rack, hefted it, swung it experimentally to get used to its balance, looked it over from hilt to top of the blade, and brought the tip to the opening of the scabbard. Just before she plunged it home, Tarsus stopped her with a cough. She looked at him quizzically.

"Try this one instead," he said, stepping out of the way of the jeweled sword. "This may serve you better than any the castle armory."

The princess was awestruck. Standing upright in a cradle was a sword, the like of which she'd never seen before. She slowly walked towards it, mesmerized, automatically reaching for it. She slowly put out her hand, and it seemingly jumped into her palm. Breathing heavily, Laura studied the sword, turning it over and over again. It had small, very imperceptible jewels encrusting the hilt-guard, small as grains of sand, but not the grip. Diamonds? Sapphires? She knew not which. They looked shiny, but muted at the same time. She tried focusing on one aspect of jewels, but they turned her gaze away, making her look somewhere else: like the glade she found Tarsus in but smaller. The blade was no wider than the palm of her hand, more rapier than glaive-like. Its length was about three feet. Short for a true blade, but small and light enough for her to handle easily. A perfect match and balance for her hand. There was no doubt the sword was enchanted.

Laura looked down at the practice sword still clutched in her other hand. Shaking her head, without ceremony, she discarded it, throwing it towards the sword rack, not caring where it landed. Her sole attention was on the new one Tarsus had just given her. Upon picking it up, a glow infused the hilt for a split second. She couldn't be sure she'd really seen it, but . . . she knew she had. "Where did you get this?" she asked wonderingly, her eyes glazing over.

"I have my ways, child. Just use it. It's yours. This is my gift to you for getting me out of the pickle I was in," said Tarsus, grinning from ear to ear. It wasn't a nice sight. No one could have said a smile from a dragon was a good thing.

Laura looked at the sword with a frown. "Thank you. I think. I'll cherish it always, but using it will be a violation of your agreement with Sir Dwayne, won't it? It's supposed to be a fair fight after all. Using an enchanted sword . . . It's an enchanted sword, isn't it? . . . would put me at an advantage."

"Oh, it's enchanted, all right, but not how you think." The dragon grinned mischievously. "The sword will grow and learn right along with you in the coming months and years as you train. The longer you wield it, the more it will adapt to your fighting style, and eventually, no one will be able to match your prowess with a blade."

"Thank you, Master Tarsus," said Laura, bowing. "It's beautiful, and unnecessary on your part. I wished for no reward." She straightened, looking him in the eyes. "Your teaching is enough."

"Let's just say," said Tarsus, "I felt teaching wasn't enough."

"Thank you again."

"Now," said Tarsus, "since we have that out of the way, let's go kick some Hook butt."

That brought it all back to the princess, why she was in this get-up in the first place and why she'd been about to vomit on her boots. "Why are you so happy, you great blithering lizard?" asked the princess irritably, getting over the gift of the sword. "This is probably the day you get kicked out of the kingdom."

"Be civil, child. We'll see about that," he answered and walked into the courtyard.

*   *   *

The king wasn't happy. His daughter was about to go up against one of his best guards. A guard who'd been fighting for nearly twice the number of years Laura had been alive. She could get hurt, or heaven forbid, killed. What in all the hells was Sir Dwayne thinking, agreeing to this madness? Sir Dwayne's job, and duty, was protecting the court and all its subjects, not promoting senseless brawling and not with a member of the royal family. Good thing I ordered Sir Hook to take it easy on Laura. There would be all kinds of hells on Earth if she were to be injured. The only reason he'd agreed to this crazy notion was to appease Tarsus. Having his own daughter train to be a knight was just ludicrous. If he'd have had a son, that would have been a different matter, but Laura? *Tarsus must be mad. Tarsus, damn that arrogant animal. His blood must be diluted with water: cold water.* He vowed to personally use an axe to his serpentine neck if his daughter were to even receive a scratch.

*   *   *

After two days of intensive training, Tarsus felt Laura was the equal to any guard Sir Dwayne was to throw her way, be it Hook or not. Laura was an apt pupil, had fast reflexes, and was straight as an arrow when it came to common sense. Tarsus was confident Sir Hook was in for a surprise or two from her.

He'd also shown her a daring maneuver intended to stop anyone in their tracks, a desperate ploy Tarsus hoped she wouldn't have to use. It was an ace thrown from a dice cup.

Laura, however, wasn't too sure. She remembered all of Tarsus's lessons, but implementing them was totally different. Against Sir Hook, one of the best knights of the guard, no matter what that crazy lizard said to the contrary, sword or not, she wasn't sure of anything.

*   *   *

The king stepped out on his balcony overlooking the practice field, the same place he'd stood for the past fortnight, watching every move Laura made. He was quite impressed with her skill as a swordsman, but he was equally impressed with Sir Hook and his competence as a guard. At the back of his mind, Lionel remembered all the days he'd spent as a youth on this same field, training with Sir Dwayne. Over and over again, he'd seen it happen, where the new comers of the knights had been injured, some quite severely, in the midst of a training exercise just like the one his daughter was about to participate in. It would be interesting to see how this played out. And it wasn't only he who was interested in the outcome; looking around, he thought he saw most of the castle watching. The practice field was surrounded by staff, servants, and apparently the rest of the guards who weren't at their posts.

He noticed one particular young man who was watching with avid interest: the stable boy.

*   *   *

Pip watched the proceedings with avid interest. It seemed the whole castle and most people of the town were at the practice fields today. Apparently word had spread about the match between the princess and the realm's best fighter. Tarsus told him not to be seen, which he didn't understand, but on hand if needed, which made no sense: he wasn't fighting Sir Hook. When asked why, Tarsus said the princess didn't need any added distractions before the match. From what Pip had seen so far, one lone stable boy the princess didn't even knew existed was the least of her worries. So, he tried to be as small as he could, not making much noise, which he doubted could have been heard anyway with so many people milling about, and stayed well out of the way. Sitting on a small basket of cloth, which had covered her new armor, he'd tried to make himself as inconspicuous as possible. But he didn't think he would

68

have been noticed anyway. Her eyes were unfocused and looked far away as she prepared. He smiled anyway at the sight. The armor she was admiring was one of the many things the dragon had him commission outside the castle. At first glance, it looked as if a swipe from a dull dirk could cut the 'armor' in two. But first-hand experience told him otherwise. The master craftsman who made it demonstrated its strength before Pip brought it to Tarsus: a full blow from his sword didn't even scratch the chest plate. The only thing left for him to do was sit back and watch what transpired.

He had no idea at the time that the king had noticed one lone boy, sitting just behind the dragon, avidly watching his daughter.

✸   ✸   ✸

The princess and Tarsus came onto the field, and they didn't have to wait for Sir Hook. He was already prepared and waiting for them, standing beside Sir Dwayne.

Laura and Tarsus moved towards the center where both knights waited. Laura hadn't even noticed the crowd of people who'd assembled to watch the contest. Her attention was focused on not throwing up and making a bigger fool of herself than she thought she was going to make. Her nerves were in such a mess. She didn't know if she could do this or not. That was until Sir Dwayne started to speak, and Sir Hook eyeing her raiment and sword sneered.

Without ceremony or preamble, when the princess and the dragon approached, Sir Dwayne addressed Tarsus. "The rules are simple, dragon," he hissed, enjoying the grim look on Tarsus's face. "This contest is over only after one of the contestants yields."

Tarsus looked at both men and said, "Agreed. But also, no one may stop it, short of actually killing."

Sir Dwayne said, "Agreed."

Tarsus continued, "And anything goes. In a real fight, there are no such things as rules or honor."

Sir Dwayne: "Agreed."

The princess wasn't about to let either of the three, dragon and two knights, decide her fate for her. With a bit of heat showing herself, she joined in, "And there's no holding back. I don't care if father is watching or not. Knowing my father, he probably gave you an order to do something like that to protect me. If I even suspect Sir Hook is holding back, I'll have both of you thrown in the dungeon and then banished."

The captain hung his head.

Sir Dwayne said, "Agreed, but you have to tell the king. My orders were very clear, my Lady, nothing was to happen to you, not a scratch. You must take full responsibility, not I. I shall not disobey my king."

Laura said, "Agreed. I thought as much before I came out. A sealed letter is at this moment being delivered to father with those same provisos. You and Sir Hook are absolved of any and all responsibilities for my welfare until after this contest."

Sir Hook went on one knee and bowed his head to the princess, acknowledging what she'd done for him and the captain. She returned the bow with a nod.

Sir Dwayne said, "Agreed."

Tarsus said, "Then let's get on with it."

*　　*　　*

One of the many messengers of the castle knocked at the door of the king's balcony. The king waved to an attendant who opened the door. The messenger, who was quite nervous, simply placed the sealed envelope in the attendant's hand, turned, and hurried from sight.

"Sire," said the attendant, placing the envelope in the king's hand. "This just arrived."

Lionel looked at the sealed missive bewildered. Written on the front of the envelope was simply: 'Sire'. It was sealed with the sigil of the royal court, his royal court.

The king turned from the attendant and looked back at his daughter and Sir Hook. He then looked down at the sealed message in his hand.

"What in the name of all the gods . . ." Lionel whispered.

And before he'd opened it, he realized what it was.

"By the gods!" he roared. "No!"

*　　*　　*

Laura stepped towards Sir Hook with her sword drawn. The jewels surrounding the hilt of the sword swirled with the light of the morning sun, making a kaleidoscope of colors form on the ground at her feet. It was beautiful, but ominous at the same time. If she could just read what the shapes and colors meant, she may have a hope in hell of coming out of this without a scratch. Wishful thinking, she knew, was useless, but . . . maybe the rules for cunning would make up for that, especially after she saw the small smile on Hook's face. Coming within only feet of him, she bowed, a great, courteous respectful bow, bending from the waist, nearly putting her head at stomach level.

Sir Hook was momentarily taken aback. It was unseemly for a princess of the realm to bow to a lowly knight. Honor dictated he must lower himself past the point in which Laura had postured herself. No member of the royal family shall be seen, in any pose, below the level of eye contact by a servant. It was a matter of honor and duty to his crown.

As the knight lowered himself almost prone in front of Laura, she didn't stand on ceremony. She struck with a swift move of her sword arm, cutting at an angle to Sir Hook's head. Quick reflexes from years of training saved him from losing it. Sir Hook brought his sword up to meet hers. The resounding clang of metal on metal was heard throughout the courtyard. The move was intended to block, not cut. In an instant, he was on his feet in a fighting posture, facing the princess.

A gasp went up from the watchers.

"Bold move, my lady," said Sir Hook.

Laura said nothing. She merely smiled at the knight.

They came together. Sir Hook lunged for Laura's right side. She stepped out of the way lightly, backhanding the sword thrust. At the same time, she came in close and delivered a kick to the knight's groin.

Hook went down on one knee, clasping his hands over his privates in pain.

Laura didn't think twice. As Hook went down, she delivered another blow with her fist on his cheek, rocking his head back.

Hook spit blood, but wasn't out. He was a seasoned veteran. He smiled. This after all was what he'd trained for most of his life. As Laura advanced again, he rolled with the punch, kicking out with his left foot, solidly connecting with Laura's mid-section, sending her reeling, gasping for breath. He immediately took advantage of her pain. He jumped to his feet. Planting his left foot behind him and spinning on the toe of his right foot, he delivered a round kick to the left side of Laura's head.

Laura spun to the ground spitting blood herself.

Hook saw the princess spit blood and was indecisive on what to do next. Although he'd been cleared from any wrongdoing in the face of this contest, the princess was, after all, only a mere girl. He'd not intended any harm to come to her. He looked towards Sir Dwayne for guidance, but received none. Sir Dwayne merely looked back at him.

Laura saw what was happening. She came to a crouch, wiping blood from her face and upper lip. She looked to Tarsus. Tarsus was looking at her like Sir Dwayne was looking at Sir Hook. No help there.

"Do you yield, my Lady?" asked Sir Hook.

In answer, Laura lunged at Sir Hook again, this time swiping at his legs. Hook jumped over the sword and then ducked immediately, presuming Laura would complete a well-known maneuver: leg swipe, turn, and head swipe. But she did the unexpected; when Hook ducked under the head swipe that didn't come, Laura brought her knee straight to Hook's nose, connecting with a resounding crunch.

Hook reeled back gasping, spitting more blood.

Laura rushed in, not letting him get his balance, flinging herself at him with all her strength, knocking him to his back. As he hit, he lifted his sword arm, anticipating a downwards thrust with a sword. Nope! She did the unexpected again: kicking the knight's hand holding his sword, hoping to dislodge it from his grasp. It didn't work. Hook feinted down with his sword as he saw the princess pivot from her waist for the kick and jammed the hilt into her thigh.

Laura screamed. The pain was intense. While she was unbalanced and feeling the effect, Hook rolled to the right and knocked the princess on her backside. She hit the ground with a thump. Pain radiated up her spine. She automatically rolled to her left, away from him, giving her the small amount of time to come to her feet. Ignoring the pain, she stood face to face with Sir Hook again, grimacing with the effort.

Back to square one. Both bleeding and in pain.

Each was laboring to catch their breath. Sir Hook knew this was taking too long. Not only would the heat get to him if this lasted much longer, but the princess was better than he'd given her credit for. If it had been any of the other guards sparring with him, he knew it would have already been over, him being the winner. It was time for him to do something to end this now. He'd underestimated her, and he wasn't going to do it again.

They both circled each other like caged lions, each trying to take advantage of a perceived weakness.

Laura also knew this was taking too long. One of the main things Tarsus had stressed to her while she'd been training was that in each individual combat, there was always a factor involved that did the other opponent in: time. The more time one kept at a fight, the more time one's opponent would find a weakness. So she had to do something fast. She knew her weakness very well, her youth, which in most instances made for an advantage: faster speed, greater endurance, but also weaker strength because she was so young. Also the male chauvinist in Hook would see being female counting against her. The fairer sex and all that trash. She had to admit though, most males had an advantage over the fairer sex, because they were the fairer sex, but, you can't have everything. It was time to take that into account. She took what Tarsus said was her secret weapon and used it against him.

Before the knight could make any move against her, Laura knelt in the dirt before him, propping up on one knee, as if praying, her sword in front of her as if offering it to him. This gave the impression she was giving up, yielding to the superior swordsman.

Sir Hook straightened up from his crouch with a bewildered look on his face. He cautiously asked her, "Do you yield?"

The princess didn't say anything. She waited, with her head pointing down to the ground.

Sir Hook cautiously advanced until he was standing in front of the princess. "Do you yield?" he asked her again. His breath came in great gasps like a bellows feeding a smith's furnace.

Still she said nothing. She merely looked at the ground in front of his feet.

Sir Hook started to get upset. If she were finished, she was to say she yielded, which was the only way to end the competition. He put his sword to her throat, but before he could ask her again if she yielded, Laura struck. She brought up her left forearm and swept aside his sword and then stabbed her own sword (the hilt of course) into the knight's gut, which produced a satisfactory grunt from him and doubled him over. Then she sat down completely on her backside, rolled on her back, and jammed her feet straight up with all her strength, soundly connecting with his jaw. The resulting backward thump of his back hitting the ground made the rest of his breath eject from his lungs in a tremendous 'whoosh'. Laura came to her feet in a heartbeat, stepped on Sir Hook's arm holding his sword so he couldn't move it, and put the tip of her sword to his throat.

The crowd grew quiet.

"Do you yield, Sir Hook?" she asked, standing over him, gasping herself.

Sir Hook blanched.

Princess Laura was panting, fighting for every breath, when she asked him again, "Do you yield?"

With blood dripping from his nose and mouth, he said simply, "I yield."

Laura stepped back, still fighting for breath, her exertion nearly being her undoing. Although she was in good physical condition, once the adrenaline rush of battle had been expended, she found she was exhausted. Her sword arm slowly lowered the blade. She then looked at Tarsus, who nodded to her. His face split with a wide grin.

The crowd around her was silent.

Sir Hook came slowly to his feet, blood running in trails down his weathered face. He also was grinning. He went in front of the princess and bowed formally to her. "My Lady, I am your servant for life. My life is yours to command."

Although it seemed to Laura the sword fight had taken a lifetime to end, in reality, it had taken a mere seven minutes. Later in the day, Sir Hook would complement her on the only person to have ever bested him in so short a time.

Laura went to him, dragging her sword, placing her hand on his shoulder and began, "Thank you. Now I . . ." and promptly collapsed in front of him without another word being spoken.

Tarsus hung his head. "Damn! Not again."

*   *   *

CHAPTER 6

*O*f all the things to happen, why did it have to be that damnable lizard? I was so close to having what I wanted out of this miserable kingdom. Just one more year, possibly two, and I'd have been running the whole thing. Damn the lizard!

Granston paced across a narrow, fifteen by thirty room, in a hideout he'd reserved for an occasion as this. He thought he'd never have to use it, of course, especially in such a backwater place as Musk, but nonetheless, here he was, all due to a miserable lizard he should have killed all those long years before. Who would have thought he'd come back?

Damn!

Granston stopped pacing and faced the small window. Through the narrow slit, he could barely make out clouds lazily drifting by. His so-called hideout was situated on the top of a mountain peak—the only mountain for hundreds of miles—in a mountain range over five hundred miles from Musk. It was doubtful anyone could find him there, but then it had been doubtful at the time, anyone could ever awaken Tarsus.

Blast!

The small room in which he was in was one of only two. This one housed his bed, clothes, and a few items which he used on a daily basis. The other was his workshop, where he conducted his many acts of wizardry. It also contained his many tomes of ancient spells—beakers of boiling alchemy (some of which had never stopped boiling). Alchemy and wizardry went hand-in-hand, but the problem he found with either was sometimes neither one worked as planned, and of course, there was his most prized possession: the Staff of Talsoun, the only truly magical article he possessed. Thinking of it made him nostalgic. Grundehl, the Father of all Gnomes had given it to him personally, not merely as a gift, but for his heroic conduct in the heat of battle.

Some heroism on his part. Ha!

If Grundehl would have known the truth, he'd have been executed instead of revered. It was the battle between the Gnomes and the Trolls, two factions fighting over the same piece of muddy ground—which wasn't worth the effort if anyone would have bothered asking him—for centuries.

You couldn't have planted rice in the soil (marsh ground?). Worthless!

A veritable army of Gnomes was dispatched to rout the Trolls from the land once and for all. He'd been an apprentice then, to the Great Wizard Shimmer. His duty was to observe the master at work. Bah! What he'd done was far easier. As Shimmer routed a great flood of Trolls to their deaths by blasting them with fierce lightning strikes, he simply nudged Shimmer over the edge of a precipice. It was fairly simple to do, being distracted as he'd been, concentrating on the Trolls and what he was doing, Shimmer failed to notice the enemy in his own ranks. Nudging Shimmer over the edge of the cliff was the simplest of things, and the old fool Shimmer didn't have wings. It was believed he'd overtaxed himself in the fight. After that little piece of work, one of his best, he thought, he became victor and savior of the Gnomes, through mighty wizardly deeds, single handedly smiting the enemy. Of course, no one was left alive of the almost five thousand enemy soldiers and eight thousand Gnomes who'd come together that day, except him. When Shimmer the Great toppled over the edge, Granston the Wiley took possession of the Mighty Staff of Talsoun, the only remaining Staff of the Five, all others being destroyed throughout the ages. With the Staff held aloft, he commanded a great rift in the earth to open and swallow them all. No one ever questioned, or suspected, his treachery. Fools! Grundehl being the biggest of all. Eight thousand Gnomes wiped out at one time nearly took his entire people, and he, the fool, proclaimed Granston their savior. Toady fools all! It would take many generations for Gnomes to repopulate the world, and while they were doing it, Gnomes became that which legends are made of. Because of this, they were a people rarely seen or heard. Legends sprouted up all over the world concerning the fate of such a rare people.

No one ever suspected the truth.

In great pomp and circumstance, Granston was hailed as hero to the Gnomes and keeper of the Great Staff of Talsoun, which was exactly what he'd wanted from the moment he'd laid eyes on it. Shimmer was a fool, deserving the death he'd met. He knew not what he had possession of; the Staff of Talsoun was a mighty talisman of power. With it, one could learn the secrets of the gods. Shimmer never used it to its full potential: parlor tricks, healing the sick, making rain for crops, all the same old nonsense the peasants wanted from a wizard. Doddering old fool was what he was! He could have had the Gnome Kingdom itself for his own, or the world. But he was weak, used up. It was time for a change. Granston had seen this from the first moment Shimmer used the Staff. It was an awesome power not being used to its full potential. He could use it. Oh yes, by the gods! He could and had for centuries.

The Gnome Kingdom was almost decimated. Grundehl had delivered the Staff into his hands, and he could do almost anything . . . but he found there was a catch: the Staff could be used but once every thousand years with such might. Once! And Granston had already done that, tapping the power, opening the Earth to swallow both armies. Blast! Blast and damnation!

The power from the Staff wasn't completely severed, but it could only do mundane things now. It still had power for transportation, for protection spells, for rain making, for healing minor injuries or healing the sick, and for things which any good wizard could do anyway. There was one advantage: the aging process slowed to a crawl. Being a wizard in itself almost certainly implied immortality, but with the Staff, he was assured it, which made Granston immortal by any standards. Since the time he'd taken possession of it, he'd lived nearly nine hundred years, a mere eye blink in the scheme of the world. And he wanted nine thousand more if he could get it.

Thinking of the Staff, he smiled. He thought how Shimmer must be rolling in his grave all these many years, thinking his precious Staff was in the hands of a mighty wizard, who wasn't afraid to use the power when the time came around again. But thinking of the Staff also brought to mind how that infernal lizard nearly killed him and stole the Staff.

Blast that damnable lizard!

* * *

CHAPTER 7

King Lionel paced his throne room. How could he have been so stupid as to agree to let his daughter participate in such an undertaking as fighting a knight of the guard. A princess, especially his own daughter, wasn't meant to be a knight. His Laura was meant to marry a knight or another prince from a foreign land, maybe, but not go traipsing off on a steed fighting the gods knew what. Somehow he had to stop this nonsense. He had only agreed to let her do this to appease the princess's whim. He'd found since his wife, the beautiful Kayli, Laura's mother, had died, he couldn't refuse her anything. On almost every occasion, Laura got what she wanted. How could he refuse to give her first horse? Or her first fine satin evening gown? Or her first Ball? How could he refuse her those things? How? Only Queen Kayli really knew, she with her beautiful smile and outstanding sense of the appropriate. Lionel remembered his wife saying, "Laura isn't made of glass, dear. She needs only to be shown what and how to do things properly, even at such a young age. Don't try to fix things if they aren't broken. You may come to find, you'll fix them till they are."

Ah, my Queen, how I wish you were still here to show me how to take care of such a precocious child as we have. And not such a child, a seventeen-year-old young woman whose flights of fancy could get her killed. I fear I may not make the right choices in this matter. How I wish you could have left me instructions to go with the building of such a woman. My Queen, my love, I miss thy council greatly.

Lionel strode from his throne room, long cape trailing behind with his King's Guard immediately falling into step behind. Up until now, he tended to forget about them. After all the years he'd had them in his service, he'd never have wished them to be gone. They were a great comfort and boon to not only himself, but also the kingdom as a whole. The people of Musk revered them as the only true honorable, steadfast commodity to be proud of. Their fighting skills were known far and wide throughout not only his kingdom, but many others as well. So how, by the gods, could one lone girl manage to defeat one of the best of them, in so short a time? Sir Hook was well known for his prowess with the sword and hand-to-hand combat, yet a seventeen-year-old slip of a girl had bested him in a fair fight.

The presence of the guard reminded him of this and much more, as he strode purposefully towards Laura's bed chamber. After collapsing on the field, she had been removed to her rooms where the best physicians in the land were caring for her. As he approached, the guard protecting Laura's door bowed and opened it for him.

"My Laura," Lionel whispered, silently shedding a tear going to her bed. "Please forgive an old fool such as I. I love you, child."

*   *   *

Pip's day to meet Princess Laura dawned two days after her match with Sir Hook. It was a day to remember indeed, one which both would never forget. And it didn't go well at all.

The morning started like others: Pip scrambling out of his loft, hurriedly putting on shirt, breeches, and boots and combing his mop of hair with his fingers after hearing Tarsus scream for him.

"Pip! Pip! Where are you?"

Pip came sliding up to Tarsus, out of breath, disheveled and looking as if he'd been running a foot race with a thoroughbred.

"Do you ever take a bath?" asked Tarsus, eyeing Pip up and down, sniffing the air like a hunting dog, and crinkling his long nose. "You look and smell as if you've been sleeping in those clothes, and your hair is a fright. You need to start taking better care of yourself." *Just as well start this off right. Later, I'll have to apologize, but I need to know.*

Pip merely stood there seething, his face contorted in a scrunched up ball, his eyes peeking out through tiny slits. "You arrogant lizard!"

he finally exploded. "When have I had the time to do anything but your bidding?"

Tarsus stepped back a pace. *Wow! That didn't take much doing. He must have been at the boiling point for some time.*

"For the better part of a fortnight," continued Pip, "all I've done is tasks you've set for me." He was really working up a head of steam. The more he thought about all the nasty jobs he'd been doing for the lizard and all of the chores that needed to be done in the stables and the many chores the lizard had him do besides gave him the perfect opening to let fly his grievances. And since this would probably put him in hot water with Mulch besides, he'd just as well get everything off his chest now. He may not ever get another chance.

Pip put his finger in Tarsus's nose, poking him with each word he said, trying to get his point across. He knew it wasn't a good idea to piss off a dragon, but he'd had about enough.

"Give . . ." Poke!

"Me . . ." Poke!

"Half . . ." Poke!

"A . . ." Poke!

"Chance . . ." Poke!

"And . . ." Poke!

"I . . ." Poke!

"Will . . ." Poke!

This was going too far for Tarsus's nerves. Leaning closer, moving Pip's finger out of the way, and growling low in his throat, he said. "Move thy finger before it becomes my breakfast."

Pip slowly put his finger away, but he didn't do anything to relinquish his anger. "Of all the things to start with me this morning, you chose my appearance? Why? I look fine for the jobs I've been doing, and besides," he put in smugly, "when have I had the time? Every night I fall into bed exhausted, and every morning, I wake at sunrise to your bellowing at me. I could have gone through this with Mulch. I don't need this from you!"

As Pip ranted on, Tarsus sat down, knowing he'd eventually wind down. He knew he'd been tough on the lad these past weeks, but after ten minutes, Tarsus was beginning to think it wouldn't end.

"And another thing," Pip continued, not bothering to catch his breath, "why haven't I been introduced to the princess? Am I to be kept on the outside looking in, while she trains all day? I may be your squire, but I'm not a slave or an indentured servant." He punctuated this last with lifting his hand and poking Tarsus in the nose again.

"That's about enough!" roared Tarsus. "Mulch was right. You are high-spirited, open-mouthed, and exasperating to the point of annoyance."

Pip didn't stop. He'd had enough of Tarsus being so arrogant. Let him be the one who mucked out his own stall, mend all those torn garments, and do all that crap. He didn't need a squire, he needed a slave. And he sure as hell wasn't that.

"Why don't you go build a nest with the grouses?" Pip shot back.

"If I did, you'd be cleaning out their shit as well," retorted Tarsus.

"Maybe Granston could help!"

"Maybe your backside needs paddling!"

"Not by you!" screamed Pip.

"Oh yes, little one, by me." Tarsus took a menacing step towards him, as if to do just that, but it didn't quite have the effect Tarsus wanted. Pip merely glared at him, defiantly looking him straight in the eyes.

"Why you little . . ." Tarsus began, leaning close to Pip. Smoke curling up from his nostrils.

This is when Laura came in.

"Having a bad morning, guys?"

Pip looked down at Laura. "This is none of your business. Beat it!" He turned back to Tarsus.

Tarsus glared at Pip, then looked down at Laura, and then back up at Pip.

Up! By the Horde Mother! Up! Tarsus realized Pip was floating seven feet off the ground, looking him straight in the eye. Straight in the eye! *By the Horde Mother!*

Tarsus smiled, which nearly sent Pip into another fit of rage.

What the hell was so funny? No part of this is funny. None!

Laura took this moment to speak again. "Could you possibly come down so I can scream at you properly? Doing it like this will make me strain my neck.'"

Pip rounded on the girl again, his fury not yet spent. He needed to find a release somewhere, and it might as well be on her. "You don't hear so well, do you? I told you to beat it! This isn't any of your . . . ." Pip stopped in mid-sentence, knowing his anger shouldn't be directed at this girl. He was originally going after the lizard. He needed to stay focused.

He took a deep breath, slowly floated closer to the ground, and then began again. "Sorry, miss, I was telling this giant lizard what I thought of him, and you opened your mouth at the wrong time. I apologize for yelling at you. Now, if you'll excuse me, I'll continue with the big green dog." He then turned his back on Princess Laura and floated back in front of Tarsus's nose.

Tarsus blinked at him.

Pip stared hard at Tarsus and began once again. "Oh, you'd just love for me to walk out, wouldn't you, you overgrown lizard? So you and precious little Laura could be alone together. But, you know what, I'm not going anywhere. I'm staying right here till you introduce me to the princess like you agreed. Then you can go play with the other lizards in the moat for all I care." Pip gulped air, catching his second wind. "And another thing, I'm not . . ."

"Excuse me," interrupted the girl again louder.

Apparently, she wasn't going to leave as Pip had told her. This wasn't making him any happier: first the lizard, and now this girl. Plus, waking up with the big green lizard talking down to him hadn't been the best thing to happen. "Why can't you just stay out of my business?" shouted Pip down at her. "Just don't say anything, Keep quiet, shut . . ."

Pip realized something was wrong and stopped again. He looked at Tarsus over his shoulder. Tarsus cocked his head at him. No help there.

He looked back down at the girl. Down? Holy Mother. Down! That's what's wrong!

That's all it took. Pip came down hard, landing unceremoniously on his ass in front of the princess (girl?), which gave her the perfect opportunity to commence screaming at him.

Pip ignored her and looked to the green dog for answers. Tarsus simply smiled.

Pip took that moment to faint, again.

Damn! He's got to quit doing that.

Laura didn't seem to mind Pip could no longer hear her. She kept right on screaming at him.

*   *   *

What the . . . was the first thing Pip thought when he finally came to. He opened his eyes to find Tarsus bending over him. This wasn't the kind of sight Pip would prefer to wake up to. Although Tarsus was probably a handsome specimen of his species, Pip preferred human females any day, and thinking of females brought to mind the one who'd interrupted his tirade on Tarsus. She'd looked vaguely familiar, and although he'd only gotten a glance at her from his vantage point, he had the unsettling feeling he'd blundered somehow.

Maybe my height advantage over her had disoriented me? Height advantage? Height? Wait a minute. Height! He turned to Tarsus, realizing what he'd been doing. He'd been floating in the air. Holy shit! From above! Above! Holy crap!

"Hold it, boy, hold it!" Tarsus said, seeing panic in Pip's eyes. "Yes, you were floating, but it isn't anything to get excited about, at least not yet."

Pip looked into the dragon's large face and saw he was still grinning. "But on a more serious note, I really wish you'd stop fainting, it's rather undignified, especially in front of royalty."

Pip shoved Tarsus out of his way and jumped to his feet. Brushing himself off, Pip asked, "What happened?"

Tarsus snorted, turned, and walked away. Pip could only follow. He had to find out what happened. He came beside Tarsus as they walked out of the stables. "Why did you do that?"

"Do what?" answered Tarsus with his own question.

"Make me float in the air? I could have hurt myself when I came down."

Stopping and cocking his head to one side, Tarsus looked at Pip and said, "I didn't. You did." He resumed walking.

This stunned Pip. *What does he mean by that? The lizard had to have done it to me. He has to be a wizard. And if he isn't, that means . . . Oh boy!* For a moment, being caught up in his own thoughts, he realized that Tarsus had got ahead of him, and after his wool-gathering, his feet moved him unexpectedly in front of the dragon.

Tarsus put on the brakes as quickly as possible, but being as big as he was, he nearly rolled over the teenager.

"Only a wizard could do something like that, and I'm no wizard." Pip insisted.

Tarsus just looked at him, harrumphed, and then continued on.

Pip's feet didn't seem to get the message the first time. They seemed to want to get him squashed like a grape in a press. He found himself right back in front of the big green lizard, but this time, he was yelling at him. "Hold it! Stop!"

Tarsus groaned, and then stopped. His eyeball swiveled to look at Pip squarely. He studied the boy for a long moment and then only snorted. How could the lad be so dense?

"This is crazy," exploded Pip. "I couldn't have done something like that. I don't have any powers. Wizards are said to have been born, not just one day be able to do it. Don't you think I would have been using something like that if I'd known I had it?"

Tarsus snorted again, this time moving Pip out of his way with his head. The lad *was* dense.

Pip wasn't getting anywhere. He decided to try something else. He simply changed the subject. "When do I get to help you with the princess? I'd like to at least meet her?"

Tarsus smiled. This tactic he knew well, changing the subject was a time-honored method of not facing what you know was the truth. Youth was wasted on the young. He decided not to rock the boat any more than Pip could handle. He went along without missing a beat.

"You already have," answered Tarsus.

"What do you mean? I already have what?"

"Met her," said Tarsus, not quite stifling a chuckle.

"Why are you laughing? Met who?"

"The princess, young lad, the princess. You've met the princess already," said Tarsus, articulating every word slowly, to be sure the boy understood.

"No, I haven't," argued Pip. "This is why we've been having this conversation. You don't want to seem to stick with your bargain."

"Yes, lad, you have." Tarsus disagreed with him. "The young female you yelled at this morning was Princess Laura. And she's not too happy with you at the moment."

Pip groaned. *I knew she looked familiar.*

Tarsus chuckled again.

Pip didn't appreciate his attitude. "You could have warned me."

"How?" asked Tarsus. "You were too busy making wind."

Pip could only groan again. He did have to admit he'd been awfully angry at the time. If the king had been there, he still would have done the same thing. Then he'd probably be in the dungeon cooling his temper on rations of bread and water. But . . . he probably still would have done the same thing.

Damn! Another stupid stunt. When am I gonna learn? You really are gonna wind up on the gallows, you know. One too many times at the post and BAM! End of Pip. Now what do I do? How do I get out of this one? Is there any getting out of it?

Pip slowly turned and walked away, without saying anything else, mumbling to himself. Tarsus just let him go, chuckling.

*   *   *

Laura was furious.

How dare that wizard yell at her? Didn't he know who she was? Didn't he realize she could get her father to put him in the dungeon for a hundred years? *Could I? Come to think of it, I don't know. But I could have him flogged at the least. He'd deserve it too.* Or could I? Laura knew she had to tell her father. For one thing, she couldn't ever remember seeing the kid before—yes, he was young, the more she thought about it—and for another, Tarsus should have said something about employing a wizard, young or not.

The past week had been very trying for the princess. Her whole body was aching from the training Tarsus had put her through. The match with Sir Hook left cuts and bruises that were still healing. She was in no mood to be treated like a common chamber maid, although she'd never treated her maids like that.

She'd gotten up that morning feeling fairly good, beat up and bruised, but good. Her aches were slowly fading away, and her strength was coming back in small doses. A few good nights' rest had done wonders. She'd donned a plain linen blouse, a loose fitting pair of trousers and soft boots, not having the energy to waste on frilly dresses, lugging that amount of silk around. She'd planned to go to the stables and speak with Tarsus about the match and her continued training. When she walked into the stables, a most unexpected sight met her eyes: a young boy about her age, sixteen or so, was berating the dragon. It wasn't so much he and Tarsus were arguing. She'd done that plenty with Tarsus since he arrived. It was the fact the boy was floating in the air to do it. That's what surprised her. Not meaning to interrupt, she listened for a moment; it was becoming funny. The boy was giving Tarsus 'what for' on his chores, his clothes, the dragon's attitude towards him, and many other things. She'd walked in finally to ask him if he'd like some help, but instead walked in to him turning his wrath on her, which upset the apple cart. The worst part wasn't him turning on her. The worst part was she didn't think he'd recognized her, which made things worse. And even if he didn't know who she was, he was being rude, which made her furious. Good manners should be instilled in everyone. Tarsus ended up getting between the two, telling her to go away till he could straighten things out, which brought her back to where she was headed now.

Laura stomped up to the massive doors of the throne room, flinging them open before the guards could do it. Her father, the king, was sitting quietly on his throne trying to read a communique from a neighboring noble. He wasn't alone, of course. His ever-present guards were with him. Ignoring them all, stomping up to the throne, she exploded with, "Father! I want you to do something with that obnoxious boy wizard."

"What?" asked Lionel. "What did you say?" he asked, looking over the top of the parchment he was trying to read before being interrupted.

"I said, Father," Laura stated again, more slowly this time, as if she were talking to the town's idiot, "I wish you to do something with that boy wizard Tarsus has brought into the stables."

Lionel looked dumbfounded. "Laura dear, what are you going on about? Can't this wait? I'm busy you know. The kingdom doesn't stop for you," he shook the parchment in his hand at her, "or for me."

Laura stomped her foot, frustration making her cross. "Father, Tarsus has employed a young wizard. He was impertinent and rude to me. He should be punished!"

Lionel put the scroll aside and looked at his daughter just as defiantly as she was looking at him. "Who was impertinent?"

"That young . . ." Lionel cut her off by clearing his throat. Then cocking his head, he looked at her askance.

Laura blinked, opening her mouth as if to say something else about the boy in the barn, and then just as fast closed it again, realization dawning on her face. She took a deep breath to calm herself, relaxed a bit, and then bowed to her father. "Forgive me, Father. Maybe I should first know what impertinence is, and not show it myself. I didn't mean to be rude. Please forgive me."

Lionel nodded. "Very good, child. You're forgiven." Under his breath, he said, "Till next time."

Laura stood in front of him with her cheeks flushed with embarrassment.

"Now, begin again, please," said Lionel. "What's this about? I see you're upset."

"It's Tarsus," said Laura calmly, going slow. "He's employed a young wizard. He needs to be punished."

"Tarsus needs to be punished?"

"No, Father. The wizard."

"Wizard, you say?"

"Yes, Father."

"What wizard?" Lionel asked, now interested. *There isn't a wizard here. At least not that I know of.*

"I don't know his name, but he was rude and impertinent. You should punish him,." Laura said again.

"I see," said Lionel, watching his daughter closely. He knew her temperament better than anyone, and if she felt someone had been rude to her, it was more than likely someone hadn't listened to her. It had always been that way. She'd once demanded, when she was seven, that he imprison her nanny for making her eat vegetables. He asked her innocently enough, "And what would you have me do to this wizard?" He cocked his head waiting.

"I don't know," Laura said, shrugging her shoulders. "Can't you throw him in the dungeons for a couple days to teach him some manners?"

"Uh huh," Lionel grunted. Always the dungeons. "Don't you think being thrown into the dungeon for being rude is slightly excessive?" he asked.

"Maybe, Father, but I think some form of punishment is due. I was upset when I first came in here, so that may be an overstatement on my part, but something should be done."

Lionel agreed with his daughter, just not to the extent that Laura was thinking. Master Tarsus absolutely needed to explain himself, if it were true about a wizard. He knew of no such wizard being in the castle, especially one employed by him. This had to be dealt with as soon as possible. He clapped his hands, and immediately, the doors to the throne room opened, with Sir Edward peering in. "Yes, sire? May I be of service?" he asked, bowing.

"Send for Master Tarsus. I wish an audience."

"Yes, sire. At what location, sire?" the knight asked.

"Here. Now. I have matters to discuss with him," Lionel pointed out sternly.

Sir Edward didn't immediately move, seeming to be thinking something over. Before he could say anything, however, Laura saw the look on the knight's face and came to his rescue. "Father, Tarsus can't fit in the throne room, remember? He's too large."

Lionel thought it over a moment. "Ah, yes, quite so." Lionel looked to the knight. "Forgive me, Sir Edward, for putting you in such a pickle. Of course, you're both right. Please inform Tarsus I shall meet him in the courtyard, just outside the stables."

"Yes, sire," said Edward, bowing. He then turned to the princess and bowed to her as well, thanking her for her insight. He immediately turned on his heels, breathing a sigh of relief.

Laura turned back to her father and asked, "Are you going to punish him, Father?"

Lionel didn't say anything. He was thinking about the unknown wizard in the stables.

*   *   *

Tarsus was informed of his meeting with the king while he was sunbathing in the courtyard. He was lounging flat on his back, his feet sticking straight in the air, when Sir Edward found him. This had been one of the few times in the past month in which he'd time to relax. He figured he'd give both Pip and Laura some time to cool off before he went at it again with their training. Pip's also, now that he had a wizard to train as well as a knight. He'd been musing over the events of the past month when Sir Edward interrupted his thoughts.

"Master Tarsus?"

Tarsus rolled his head to look at the knight. "Yes," he said. 'What do you want? I've finally had the chance to relax for a while, and you come barging in on my time. What's so important?" He snorted a smoke ring out of his left nostril in irritation, watching it lazily drift away in the breeze.

"Master Tarsus, I have been sent to summon you to an audience," answered the knight, not even blinking at the dragon's bad mood.

Tarsus eyed the man, beginning to have great respect for these King's Knights. Not too many men could stay calm in the face of a dragon's wrath. He supposed he'd have to rethink his opinions of them when he had the time, but, still, Tarsus took notice at the word 'summon,' not request. His ire was rising. In a deep rumble, he asked, "Who would have the authority to do this? I know of no one who has the audacity to throw out such a command to me, not even the princess. She knows better. I'd give her the scolding of her life, and then the spanking to go along with it."

Sir Edward merely listened patiently through his tirade but said nothing afterward.

"Well? Who's summoned me, Knight?" demanded Tarsus.

"Thy king, dragon!" said Sir Edward and walked away.

The king? That flopped Tarsus over in a hurry.

*   *   *

Pip had slunk to his bunk in the loft over the stables like a dog caught in the garbage bin. He figured if he couldn't do anything right, he should go back to bed. He'd done enough that day.

How could you have been so stupid? Couldn't you for once keep your mouth shut? Just once? Do you always have to go off half-cocked? The princess probably wants me boiled in oil, or put in a tower wearing an iron mask for the rest of my life. And she'd be right to do it. Pip! You idiot!

That was his last thought before falling into bed, slumber claiming him.

*   *   *

Tarsus sat in front of the stables and patiently waited for King Lionel.

The place was a flurry of activity: squires, surfs, waifs, helpers, and knights were making preparations for the king's arrival. It was as if he never came out of the castle. A small shade was erected in front of the doors so his Majesty wouldn't have to be in the sun like all the common folk: this included a red carpet approximately twenty feet square he could sit on, in a chair, of course. A very nice, plush, antique high-backed chair that a common man couldn't afford in two lifetimes, in which the king had probably never seen before. He, after all, couldn't be undignified. Oh no, he was the king. Guards were positioned around the carpet for his protection. There was a waif of a girl holding a pitcher of water in case his

Majesty needed to wet his throat from so much exertion and another girl holding a glass inlaid with jewels for him to drink from. Then he noticed something strange: Sir Dwayne, the captain of his Majesty's guard came to stand beside him. Tarsus eyed the knight suspiciously. He wasn't necessarily concerned seeing the man. It was his duty to protect the king's person in case of trouble after all, but it was very unusual for him to stand so close and be so aloof.

Tarsus acknowledged him and bowed slightly.

"Dragon," said Sir Dwayne. Before he could say anything else or before Tarsus could ask what was going on, trumpets sounded the king's arrival.

Lionel walked stoically towards the hastily put up shade, neither looking right nor left. His attention was focused solely on Tarsus. He was surrounded by his guards, with the princess immediately behind him; before he'd taken a full step under the canapé, he began to speak.

"Tarsus, what's this I hear about you having a wizard in your employ at the castle? I have heard of no such wizard, and this troubles me very much."

Holy Horde Mother! Here we go already. That didn't take long. I need to stop this now if I can. Tarsus knew he had to do some fast talking. "Your Majesty, may I ask who has told you such a thing?"

"My daughter, Master Tarsus," he answered, looking back at Laura.

"I see," said the dragon, thinking fast. (As the Horde Mother says, flattery never hurts anyone, but honesty always does.) "Your Majesty," began Tarsus, looking towards Laura instead of the king; he knew the only reason this charade was going on was because of another tantrum by her ladyship. Apparently even what she'd gone through in the past few weeks hadn't gotten rid of her little girl's attitude: 'Daddy will take care of it.' *Well, little girl, this is one time he won't.* "Your Majesty, you're well informed of what's happening in your castle. Most monarchs could care less, as long as their dinner isn't late being put on the table." Tarsus looked to Laura and scowled. Then smiling, he turned to Lionel again. "The princess is misinformed, however. I don't have a wizard in my employ."

"So, let me get this straight," said the king, looking Tarsus straight in the eyes. "You're saying, my daughter, the one person in the whole realm I would move heaven and earth for, the one in whom I trust the most, lied to me?" He placed fisted hands on his hips.

At these words, a gasp went up from the assembly. Sir Dwayne immediately drew his sword, placing himself between the king and the dragon.

Tarsus took a step back. This was definitely not going well. He eyed the knight and his sword before speaking. He needed to be careful. Although he couldn't afford to offend anyone, he wasn't going to be bullied into anything either, now being as good a time as any to prove it.

"Your Majesty, before I fry Sir Dwayne to a cinder, have him put away his toothpick. My honor says all that which needs saying here. I haven't threatened anyone, and I shall not, but I shall not, on the other hand, put up with *being* threatened. You, your kingdom, and most assuredly, the princess are safer with me than with your own guard." He then placed his head barely two inches from Sir Dwayne's sword tip, billows of smoke beginning to climb up between them both from Tarsus stoking his mighty furnaces deep within his gullet.

Sir Dwayne didn't budge a muscle.

Laura, however, did. "Stop!" she shouted. Everyone looked to Laura: King Lionel with amazement, Sir Dwayne with admiration, and Tarsus with amusement. "That's enough! If I'd known this was going to be a pissing match between all three of you, I would have kept my mouth shut." She faced the king. "Father," she said, "I just wanted to find out about this wizard. I know my temper can get the best of me, but I also know you can find out things I can't. I thought you, being who you are, could do it for me. I'm sorry for that now. I'm not accusing Tarsus of anything." She turned to Sir Dwayne and Tarsus. "And you two." She placed her fists on her hips as Lionel had, frowning at them both. "This has to stop between the two of you. My honor isn't always at stake, Sir Dwayne, and your honor not in question, Tarsus. Each of you needs to stay clear of the other for a while, so your honors can get some rest." Laura's voice rose with frustration. "Now, both of you, back down, before I put each of you in a separate cage!"

Sir Dwayne slowly put away his sword, but he rested his hand on the hilt. This wasn't lost on the princess, nor on Tarsus. The dragon slowly released the pressure from his furnace, refreshing his air passages, clearing away the soot. He waited.

Lionel began again. "Yes, now then . . ." but that was as far as he got. Laura wasn't done. Facing the king again, she stabbed at him with her finger. "And you, Father . . ." the whole assembly took a collective breath,

"I just wanted answers. I know you were trying to get them, but you've got to try and be more diplomatic. You didn't have to do this in front of the whole castle." She planted her fists on her hips again. "Yes, you are my father. You are my king, and I love you, respect you, adore you, and would willingly follow you to the two hells and back, but you are embarrassing me."

Lionel couldn't say anything. He had a lump in his throat. *My Laura's growing up.*

Laura positioned herself between Sir Dwayne and Tarsus, pushing the knight and dragon away from each other, ensuring neither would go against what she'd said to them and each kept their distance.

"Tarsus," Laura asked, pointing her finger at him, "do you, or do you not, have a wizard at your disposal?"

Tarsus looked down on the princess, slowly blinking at her, stalling for time. He said nothing.

"Answer her, lizard!" bellowed Sir Dwayne, drawing his sword again. "Thy princess has asked you a question."

Tarsus's head whipped towards him, eyes going flat, smoke rising from his nostrils once again.

Laura rounded on Sir Dwayne before it went any further, pointing her finger at him and saying heatedly, "That's enough from you. Keep out of this. Your time for answers will come soon enough. I'm getting tired of you two going at each other like kids on a play field."

Sir Dwayne blanched, bowing and acknowledging his princess's right of command.

Laura turned back to Tarsus, pointing her finger at him. "Now, answer the question please. Do you, or don't you, have a wizard at your disposal? And if you do, why haven't you told anyone?"

He looked at Lionel, then at Sir Dwayne, and finally back at Laura, who was the one he was actually answering. "Yes, and no, Your Highness."

"Yes, and no? What do you mean?" demanded Sir Dwayne, stepping forward, not able to keep out of this after all. The knight's eyes shone with anger. His breath came in great gasps. Almost shouting at Tarsus, he said, "Just answer the question, dragon!"

"That's enough!" shouted Laura, turning back to Dwayne. Her eyes were showing flame now. "I've told you once, Sir Dwayne. I won't tell you again. One more word and I'll send you away from this place. Then how will you do your sworn duty to protect me and my father?"

The knight didn't say anything, simply staring at Tarsus with a murderous look in his eyes.

Tarsus did the same. The knight was definitely getting under his hide.

"Please answer the question, Tarsus," asked the princess, still standing between them.

Tarsus bowed slightly and said, "Yes, I have one at my disposal, just as everyone in the castle does. And no, Your Highness, because at the moment, I believe he's nowhere around."

Lionel watched his daughter with pride. She'd finally come to the realization she did in fact have authority. He wouldn't interfere, so as to not embarrass her again, unless it became absolutely necessary. A small smile played across his face. Just then however, Tarsus said something he couldn't ignore.

"Explain yourself, Tarsus. Either you do, or you don't. I don't believe it can be both."

"Yes, Your Majesty, it can," Tarsus said, looking at Lionel over Sir Dwayne's head. "For you see, everyone has at his or her disposal the services of the court magician or wizard. And no, Your Majesty, because if my information is correct, he isn't here at this time."

"That, Master Tarsus, is sophistry," said the king, eyeing Tarsus suspiciously. "But even if it weren't, that isn't what was meant and you know it. Granston was never mentioned here. Plus, there's still no proof to what you've told me about my adviser. Even if he's a wizard, he never showed it."

"Not Granston, Tarsus," said the princess, interjecting herself, trying to get the questions back on the subject. "The other one."

"What I want to hear from you is the answer to my daughter's question, please,." said the king. "I know for many years you've been in a trance or spell or whatever you call it, but you're avoiding the issue. I don't believe even you've forgotten how to answer a direct question. And I don't believe you'd want to test my patience in that regard," warned the king. "So, if you don't mind, please answer the question. Do you have a wizard at your disposal in the castle? And not Granston, for everyone can see he's not here. That's obvious. We, being myself and my daughter, are talking about the other one. Why didn't you notify anyone in authority, namely myself, about him?"

Laura looked quizzically at Tarsus. *What's he playing at? Why won't he answer the question?*

Tarsus knew he couldn't keep this up. Prevarication wasn't his strong suit and lying surely wasn't. He took a deep breath and started again. He just couldn't tell anyone about Pip until the time was right, and the time was definitely not right. "Your Majesty." He bowed again to Lionel. "I don't have a wizard at my disposal in the castle or anywhere else," answered Tarsus. *Well, at least not right now. When I train him, maybe, but not right now.*

The princess's mouth fell open. *You have got to be kidding? Why are you lying?* "You know exactly who I'm talking about, Tarsus," said the princess. "The young wizard in the stable with you this morning."

"My lady," said Tarsus, "the only ones with me this morning were you and the stable boy, Pip. He's been here many years from what I've gathered. Mulch, the king's stableman, has taken a shine to the lad and taken him under his wing—so to speak—and he offered the boy to me for the duration of my stay here."

"The stable boy?" said Laura. "If he's the stable boy, why was he floating in the air?"

Oh, boy, Horde Mother help me, here goes the big lie. I hope I can pull this off, and I hope one day you'll forgive me, my lady. "'That was me, my lady. I made the boy float in the air because he was annoying me. We were getting eye to eye, so to speak."

"You did that?" asked the princess, with a note of doubt in her voice.

"Yes, my lady."

"Then you're a wizard?" asked the king.

"No, sire." Tarsus shook his head.

"Then you have magic?" asked the princess, stepping in again.

"Then again, yes and no, my lady,." answered Tarsus.

Sir Dwayne stepped forward again, but before he could say anything, Princess Laura stopped the knight by planting herself in front of him, making good her threat. "Sir Dwayne, I told you about that. I wasn't jesting. You may leave the area now."

Sir Dwayne looked stunned, as did everyone else. Tarsus cocked his head at her and smiled.

Laura saw the smile and pointed a finger at Tarsus, saying menacingly, "And you, I told you also, you'll not make light of these proceedings or Sir Dwayne. Even with his gruff tones and manner, he's my sworn protector. One more word of contention from you, I'll have you in chains and put in a dark place."

Tarsus saw the look in her eyes and knew she was serious. He had to be very careful. He lowered his head in acknowledgment.

"Good! Now then," Laura looked at the knight. Seeing he hadn't moved, she said, "I believe I just told you to leave the area, Knight. Do it."

Sir Dwayne looked to his king for guidance. The king looked at Laura, then back at the knight, and then back at Laura again, who stared back, expecting him to command the knight to leave. *So much like her mother.* He made his choice. "Sir Dwayne."

"Sire," the knight bowed.

"Please do as my daughter said. I will not gainsay her here. You may rest assured I've enough protection. I shall speak to you after this is over."

"Yes, sire." He bowed to his king and sheathed his sword. Straightening, he looked at Laura and said, "I do this under protest." He then turned and left.

The king looked at Laura and said, "Continue, I want to be done with this."

Laura looked at Tarsus and said, "Please answer the question asked, before we got sidetracked."

Tarsus bowed his head. "Yes, my Lady."

"Do you have magic?"

"As I said before, my lady, yes and no. Yes, I do have some magic, but very little. And no, because dragons are part of magic, our very nature allows us to control, to a certain extent, some magic. It's only parlor tricks: a gust of wind at the right moment, a sparkle in the eye of someone you look at amorously, a sparkle of lights in the air, even floating objects in the air, be it man or rock."

Laura planted her fists on her hips again, scowling at the dragon. She had a feeling this was hogwash. From what little she knew of Tarsus, training with him, he didn't have any magic. Something was up, and it was not just the stable boy. She made up her mind right then to find out exactly what he was hiding and why.

Lionel looked at both the princess and Tarsus. Then he said to one of the other guards, "Please go find Sir Dwayne for me."

"Yes, sire," said the guard, turning and rushing away.

The princess looked at him sharply, but Lionel stopped her with a gesture, saying, "There's a reason, my daughter. I'm still the king after all."

"Yes, Father," she said meekly, controlling her anger.

Within moments, Sir Dwayne appeared, apparently not having gone very far. The princess took note of that fact. When he showed up, Laura scowled at him and Tarsus grunted. He immediately bowed to the princess and then turned to the king, doing the same. "Yes, sire, you sent for me?."

"Yes, Sir Knight. I want you to bring me the stable boy Tarsus has been talking about."

"Sire?" said the Knight wonderingly.

"I'd like to hear from him what made Tarsus do what he did. Maybe he needs some looking into. Apparently I'm not as informed about what's going on around here as Master Tarsus purports," explained Lionel. "I'd like to meet the person who can get a dragon so excited and come out alive. I'd say not too many people have the nerve to do so,." the thought mirroring Tarsus's own not long ago, "except maybe yourself. Find him and bring him out here, please."

Sir Dwayne started to protest, but the king waved his objections away, saying, "I know it's your sworn duty to be by my side, which you have done for many years, but I don't think Tarsus is going to do anything. I trust him." He looked at Tarsus and then back at the knight. "As I do you. Laura's right, one day you two are going to have to patch things up between you, but for now, just please do as I ask. I'm sending you instead of anyone else because I trust Tarsus with my life. However," he looked back at Tarsus with a small smile playing across his face, "I altogether don't believe everything he may say. He may not lie to me outright, but I think he could withhold valuable information, or at the least, not volunteer any that may be useful." At this, Tarsus smirked . . . Lionel only grinned wider showing he knew all too well. "And, if by chance, this young boy does possess power in some form, I want someone who can protect themselves. I believe you're the best man for the job."

"Yes, sire. Thank you. I'll return as quickly as possible." He bowed to Lionel. Before leaving, he turned to Tarsus. "We're not done yet, dragon."

"That, Sir Knight, is plain. I look forward to our next bout." Then Tarsus bowed to him.

Sir Dwayne simply walked away.

Laura watched him go, turned to Tarsus with a scowl on her face.

Lionel admonished Tarsus when the knight was gone. "Tarsus, do you have to antagonize him so? He's a loyal and trusted vassal."

"Yes, sire, I know," sighed Tarsus answering. "That's probably why I get on his nerves. I don't mean to infuriate him like I do. He simply rubs me the wrong way."

"Yes, I see that. Can't you at least make an effort to get along with him? I don't want either of you injured from something as stupid as a fight. Both of you have honor. Try using some of it."

"Yes, sire. I'll try," Tarsus nodded. "But you know, a good healthy fight once in a while could save his life."

"How so?" asked Lionel curiously.

"Well," said Tarsus, "if he doesn't stop pointing his sword at me, I may have to roast him in his armor. A fight may prevent that." Tarsus's smile wasn't pleasant.

"Tarsus . . ."

"Yes, sire." Tarsus bowed again. "I know. I'll control myself."

"Please do," said the king.

Tarsus was impressed. Even monarchs know when to use a little flattery. Tarsus knew also he could be in a lot of trouble if Pip couldn't keep his mouth shut. He needed time to train him, and so far, he hadn't found that time. But of course, it had only been since this morning when Pip found out he was a wizard. *Please let the boy be a good liar. Please.*

✶   ✶   ✶

CHAPTER 8

Mulch grumpily stomped into the stables looking for that street urchin Pip. The captain of the King's Knights couldn't find the boy. It seemed the boy had gotten into some kind of trouble again. From the looks of it, it seemed to be serious trouble this time but the captain wouldn't talk about it. The man's sole purpose was to find the lad and bring him before their king. Mulch wasn't too happy about the gutter snipe doing the dragon's errands and acting like his personal page, shirking his duties in the stable, but he didn't feel the boy needed a knight to fetch him for a wrong he may or may not have committed. And Sir Dwayne didn't look too happy about the job— maybe he felt it was beneath him, which Mulch could understand. A page should have been sent instead of the captain of the guard, but, here he was, demanding Mulch's help, only after he'd searched the stables and the loft without any luck.

Mulch, along with all his other hands, was industriously cleaning the stalls when Duncan, the king's house page, came running in with news of the upcoming meeting between Lionel and the dragon. Mulch was to make sure the space outside the stables was clear so a small canopy could be erected. He'd grumped and blustered about being interrupted during his busy day, but knew it wouldn't do any good to take it out on the messenger. When orders came from the castle, one jumped to it and liked it. He immediately stopped what he and his crew were doing and took control of preparing the space for the audience. Afterwards he dropped back to the stable doors and waited. He, like everyone else, was curious, but he couldn't do anything but wait. Only after watching the guard assemble before the tent did he think something important was happening. Then, moments before the arrival of Lionel, the dragon lumbered up to make himself comfortable, and not long after that, the show really began.

Mulch watched as Sir Dwayne hurried towards him and his stables. He looked at the knight curiously but didn't ask any questions. The knight offered none. He simply brushed past and entered. After a few minutes, he'd stalked back and confronted the Master. With his hand on the hilt of his sword, Dwayne demanded, "Where's the boy?"

Mulch looked bewildered. "What boy?"

Dwayne grimaced and then barked, "Pip, the stable boy?"

Mulch shrugged, not minding his harsh attitude. He always had an attitude lately. "He's around somewhere, probably running another errand for the dragon. Why do you want him?"

"That's no concern of yours, Stable Master," snapped the knight. He never was strong in the patience department.

Mulch shrugged again. Nothing to him.

Dwayne said slowly, his temperature rising even more, "Can you help find him?"

Mulch thought it over a moment and then shrugged for a third time. "If the king needs him, I guess I could find him. It shouldn't be too hard."

Mulch knew he could find the boy, for he was hiding again. Pip always wanted to shirk his responsibilities in one way or another, feeling he had too many things to do in one day. Pip had been hiding for years, but when he couldn't be found by anyone else, the stable master could usually root him out. But he had to admit, even if just to himself, it was unusual for the boy not to be in the stables or in the loft or in one of the stables sleeping with a horse or with the dragon, never too far from the dragon, that boy.

Where is he? He has to be here somewhere.

Sir Dwayne was right behind the stable master, sword in hand when Mulch began his search.

Mulch looked to the knight and pointed, "What's the sword for?"

"The boy," answered the knight.

"Pip!" squawked Mulch, blanching. "What did he do to deserve you looking for him with a sword?"

"He's a wizard," said Sir Dwayne through gritted teeth. "If you must know. I'm not taking any chances."

"Wizard!" scoffed Mulch almost choking. "You must have been dunking your head in the ale barrel to believe that, knight. Who told you such a fool thing?"

"My king and yours. Do you not believe now?" asked Sir Dwayne, smirking.

"No!" Mulch spat. "I don't." Lord Lionel should know better of me. He should have realized I would inform him of such a thing. He should have more faith in his vassals. "That boy has no more power in him than the palace mule."

"We shall see, Stable Master. We shall see," said the captain holding up his sword.

"Pip, you scoundrel, where are you?" yelled Mulch. He was getting tired of this upstart captain, wanting this nonsense over with, and him gone. "The captain wishes to speak with you." Nothing.

"Where are you, boy? Pip!"

Still nothing. He started his search: the loft, just hay and grain sacks, each stable, no Pip. Then the tack room, still, no Pip. "Where are you, lad?" Mulch shouted, sweat popping out on his brow.

Sir Dwayne stood in the middle of the stable with his sword in hand looking around nervously, as if expecting the lad to jump out at him with a wand, or a staff, screaming a spell.

"Where could the boy be, Stable Master? Can't you keep up with your ward? What kind of guardian are you?"

Mulch stepped out the door to the tack room and planted his fists on his hips, eyeing the knight dangerously. "If you think you can do better, knight, you're more than welcome to try. I've been looking after the lad since he was barely out of his clouts. He's always been impetuous and headstrong, but he's never been outright disobedient. He's here somewhere, and I'll find him."

"No," disagreed Dwayne with a shake of his head. "We'll both find him. The king wanted someone who could take care of themselves if the boy really did have any kind of power. That's me." He thumped his chest with a cocked thumb. "I just need you to point him out."

"I'll do just fine by myself, knight," said Mulch. "I don't believe the lad has any kind of power anyway, that's silly. Don't you think if he was a wizard I'd know by now?"

"Anything could be hidden, Mulch. Even from you."

✱   ✱   ✱

The makeshift pavilion for the king's audience was quiet for the moment while Sir Dwayne went to fetch the stable boy Pip. While they waited, the king decided to amuse himself with his favourite pastime, harassing his daughter. Actually, he considered it constructive criticism; she considered it harassment.

"You've been spending a lot of time with Tarsus, my dear. Wouldn't you rather be inside the castle, instead of sweating on the practice field, day in and day out?" asked Lionel. He couldn't understand what she got out of putting on all that armor, although he went through the same thing in his younger days. His father, the king before him, thought training would improve his skills in protecting the kingdom.

"No, Father, I like exactly what I've been doing lately." Laura wasn't as naive as her father believed, knowing exactly what he thought of her choices lately. She shook her head while walking towards him, her hands on her hips. "I've told you for as long as I can remember I wanted to be one of your knights and I'm going to do it." She grinned at him.

Lionel scowled at her, choosing to ignore the comment. He did know better than to say anything, for he also knew her temper; then he thought of something else, a smile twisting his lips. Maybe he could bribe her out of the guard. It had always worked when she was younger. "You know, you've been very good today," he said with a hint of pride, "and we're not done yet. Being the king, as I am, I could make you the kingdom's negotiator." Then he dropped a rock on her head, so to speak. "At least until you wed."

That brought Laura up short. Although being the kingdom's negotiator was a very highly prestigious honor, the part about getting wed was a knockout punch as far as she was concerned. She'd no intention of getting married. What she most worried about was getting through the next couple of weeks, hell, the next couple of days would be nice, unless Tarsus worked her to death. Marriage? She was only seventeen. She had plenty of time to think along those lines, if ever. "I don't think I'll be getting married any time soon," she told her father calmly, which she wasn't, but she didn't let it show. "I have some time before I have to think of what will happen or won't happen in the future."

R. N. Decker

Lionel smiled, but groaned inwardly, that didn't work. So he nodded agreeably enough and said, "Yes, you have time." He held up a finger to emphasize his next point. "But not too much. You do realize you're my only heir. You'll be the one to produce the next king or queen for the kingdom since I don't have any boys to do it."

"Yes, Father, I know. I know. It'll be my duty. But, I hope you also realize I won't be married to someone I don't love." Laura looked at her father and smiled, one which her father knew quite well. "And you will not be the one to pick my husband for me." She waggled a finger at him. "I'll do that for myself."

"Yes, yes, I know, but you can't wait forever. And you know, once you do get married, you can't be a knight," explained the king. "You'll have obligations, as I do now, and traipsing around in a suit of armor won't be one of them."

Laura bowed her head, sadly. She said softly, "Yes, I know." She'd done nothing but dream of becoming a king's knight for so long. The thought of giving up that dream, although she hadn't made it yet, was almost too much to bear.

Tarsus sat placidly waiting for Dwayne and Pip, and while he did, he listened to Laura and her father discussing her future. He didn't consider it eavesdropping if no one knew he could hear better than any human. He smiled to himself, remembering what dreams he'd had so many years before and the reality his Dam had explained to him about things to come. Not everything in life could be planned out like Lionel was suggesting, and not everything could go one's way like Laura was hoping. Living tended to get in the way. Then he grinned openly with the time-honored ways of the young—no matter the species—changing the subject.

Laura had to get her father off the subject of marriage, and to do it, she brought him back to the present. "Father, are you really worried about this stable boy?"

Lionel was shocked out of his reverie of possible grandchildren. "You're the one who informed me he was a wizard. Do you not think I should be worried? Even you, being so young, should understand my concern."

"Yes, Father, I do understand. But don't you think Tarsus would have informed you if the boy was dangerous?"

Lionel looked at the dragon sunning himself before the pavilion. "Like I said, I trust Tarsus completely with my life and kingdom." Laura watched as his eyes shone with the wonder of a little boy who oftentimes dreamed of dragons, even after having one drop into his kingdom. She also watched as he brought those memories back to the present and the safety of his family and kingdom. "But I don't altogether trust he would tell me everything he knows. And I would be remiss in my duties as king if I didn't check out this stable boy for myself."

*   *   *

Tarsus watched the king and princess slowly do the dance known by every parent and child who has ever been born: back and forth, back and forth, step, turn, and step again. It seemed to be a time-honored thing even among the two-legged animals. He smiled. He'd had many such dances with his own offspring, although he had to admit, his mate, Aranea, was the one who did most of the dancing. He seemed to always be too busy or on one quest or another.

That had been many long years ago, and he didn't know if his offspring were even alive. His many young had spread throughout the whole earth, and he didn't know where they'd gone or if they'd found mates of their own. He mused that he must have had some grandchildren; at least one of his offspring must have had the forethought to keep his line going. Dragons were one of the most fierce creatures in any kingdom when it came to survival. If they hadn't been killed, he knew he must find out one day.

He didn't know how long he'd been in that state of uselessness either, so long his ability to gauge time had been somewhat skewed. But Granston was still alive, so he knew he couldn't have been gone more than a couple of centuries at most. Even a wizard as powerful as Granston wasn't immortal; he'd eventually grow old and die. One of the benefits of being a wizard gave one the innate ability to slow down the aging process, not stop it altogether, which was just one of the many benefits of being a wizard. But on the other side of the coin, he couldn't stop it all together. The oldest wizard in the world had a finite time on the Earth. All he knew for sure was someday he'd get the chance to make Granston pay for what he'd taken from him, what was most important: his mate. Aranea was the one he longed for the most; without her, he didn't feel whole. He may have been a fool in many things in his long life, but he wasn't a fool in that. He'd one day get his turn at the Gnome, and when he did, it would be a great day indeed. The rivalry between them would be at an end, a very bad end for Granston.

But, no matter, at least not today. Today, his worry was for Pip.

*　　*　　*

Pip came back to the barn with water dripping from his body and a soft towel wrapped around his waist. He'd awakened and decided to take the advice Tarsus had given him and clean up a little bit. The river water had felt wonderful. The main thing he'd wanted to do for the past fortnight had been to take a bath and clean his hair, but like he'd explained, or rather shouted, to the large scaly critter, he hadn't given him the time. He'd scrubbed his body so many times he'd come out looking like a lobster, not a mere lad of fifteen, running his fingers through his now clean hair. *I possibly could use a bit of a trim too.* He'd been so strung out from the past couple of weeks, he'd neglected to take care of himself. Although this had been pointed out to him by Tarsus, he couldn't be upset about it. Oh, he'd flown into a fit when Tarsus called him on the carpet, but that had been from exhaustion, not from real anger. He liked the lizard just fine. He couldn't remember how he'd gotten along without him all his life. He'd never admit it to him. The lizard's head was already too big. Pip didn't want it to swell out of proportion. What Pip had been doing for him hadn't been anything that he wasn't already used to; he'd been doing it after all, all his life. Pip knew he'd been cranky over the fact he hadn't been introduced to the princess. *Well, not like I wanted to be introduced to her. I was expecting more of a 'hello'. If I'm lucky, when I do see her, she won't throw me in a dungeon and throw away the key.*

Coming into the stable, Pip went straight to the loft to put on some clothes; it wouldn't do to be seen half-dressed by Mulch. He was in too much trouble as it was, and he didn't need, or want, more. Pip also knew he'd better find Tarsus and see if he could get him to talk to the princess to explain to her it had all been a mistake. She'd come in at a bad time, and he didn't know what he'd been doing. After all, it's wasn't like he wanted to be a wizard.

A wizard? That was something he'd have to get used to. He didn't even know how to use any powers. Hell, he didn't think he *had* any powers. How could he be a wizard and not know it? He had to talk to Tarsus about that too.

In the loft, he put on his cleanest shirt and trousers from his pile in one corner. He then slipped on his boots and headed down the ladder to find the dragon. As he put his foot on the floor, a voice behind him said softly, "Don't move."

Pip froze, not knowing who had spoken. Then he felt a point touch the back of his neck.

"If you move, lad, I will cut your head from your shoulders."

✱   ✱   ✱

Laura had just about enough, looking around at the many faces in and about the pavilion, when she realized she'd been a little hasty in her anger. This was getting out of hand. She sighed, watching Tarsus, who wasn't making it any easier. *If he'd only tell the truth.* Her father was right in many things, but she didn't think he was in this. He didn't have to do this in front of the whole kingdom, and Tarsus, along with Sir Dwayne, didn't have to be so damn stubborn. She should've known better. She had to talk to Tarsus by herself and see if she could straighten this out before things really got ridiculous.

"Excuse me, Father. I think I'll talk to Tarsus for a moment. Maybe I can talk some sense into him. He might be more cooperative with me."

"That's a good idea, Laura," Lionel agreed. "But do try to be respectful with him, would you? I don't wish this to be more unpleasant than it already has been."

"Yes, Father," she said, bowing. Then she turned and headed towards Tarsus who was waiting patiently in the sun. She didn't quite make it to him before a page rushed under the canvas and talked excitedly into the king's ear. *That's strange.* She stopped and looked back. *I wonder if something happened.* She saw her father wide-eyed, standing suddenly, peering towards the stables, just beyond where Tarsus lay. When she turned, curious, she gasped.

What she and the rest of the assemblage saw nearly thunderstruck them all.

Tarsus had a smile on his face when he heard Laura coming his way. He knew she wouldn't get anywhere with him but the game would be fun to play. Then he noticed Laura stop and look back for a moment at the king. He watched as Lionel jumped from his chair and peer behind him, away from the pavilion. He turned his head. His smile vanished, and he jumped to his feet with a roar.

Sir Dwayne, Pip, and Mulch, the stable master, were slowly walking towards the king and the pavilion with all its onlookers. Pip had a pole over his shoulders with his hands tied out at the ends of it, crucifixion-style. Laura noticed Pip's movements had to have been painful. His head was lowered in such a way he couldn't see where he was going. His breathing was labored. She clearly heard his tortured gasping. All Pip could see was his boots. Sir Dwayne was holding his sword at the back of his throat.

Tarsus had wisps of smoke rising from his nostrils, fire and brimstone in his heart.

Laura looked to her father and gaped.

Lionel stood with his mouth hanging open.

The crowd around the pavilion didn't say a word. There were no words for what was happening.

When the three finally reached the pavilion, holding tight to the crucifixion pole, his sword savagely pressing into the boy's neck, Sir Dwayne bowed to his king and said in his matter-of-fact way, "Here is the stable boy, Pip, your Majesty."

Tarsus slowly walked towards the knight with fire in his eyes and flame licking his lips.

Sir Dwayne saw the dragon drawing near and smiled, savagely tightening his hold on Pip, putting his sword to Pip's throat, lifting his chin, drawing a thin line of blood, and said in a not so matter-of-fact way, "If you take another step, monster, this boy will be the first to die."

"No, my lord," pleaded Mulch. "The boy has no power. He's but a stable hand. I've known him all his life, don't you think . . ."

The look Sir Dwayne gave Mulch shut him up.

"What are you doing?" demanded the princess, drawing nearer.

"*Why is Pip being treated like this?*" roared Tarsus, fire licking the air.

"I . . . ca . . . n't . . . bre . . . athe . . ." Laura heard Pip choke out, his face slowly turning blue.

"You had no right . . ."

"Stop!" A voice rang out.

Sir Dwayne looked from Laura and the dragon and saw his king heading towards him.

Before he got there, Sir Dwayne stepped slightly to the side of Pip, not removing his sword from the boy's throat, and made a cursory bow. "Sire."

"What is the meaning of this, Sir Knight?" Lionel demanded, coming to within feet of one of his most trusted knights acting like a bounty hunter. Lionel's anger showed in every line as he pointed at Pip. "I didn't tell you to truss him up like a hog going to slaughter. I told you to bring him before me, that's all." Lionel began to shake with frustration.

Tarsus looked at the knight in a new way: with distaste. He looked at Pip with sympathy. Pip didn't deserve such treatment, and it was his fault. It was time for this so-called knight to realize when he gave his word to the throne, it wasn't to be misconstrued as anything more than what it was, his honor. The king was right in the fact he may hold some things back, but he never intended for young Pip to take the brunt of this ongoing feud between himself and Sir Dwayne. Because of him, Pip may have been hurt and that wouldn't do at all.

"Sire," the knight said, "it's my duty to make sure you and the kingdom aren't in danger. I felt also it was my duty to be sure. You sent me to bring the boy to you. I felt it should be in such a fashion there would be no mistake he could do no harm."

"Release him. Now!" Ordered the princess, stepping towards the knight and his captive.

"I cannot, Your Highness." His words stopped Laura as surely as pole axing her. Her mouth fell open in amazement.

"Yes," spat the king angrily. "You can." His voice rose in volume. "This isn't what I had in mind. There's no danger here in front of my guard and the whole castle."

"I'm sorry, Your Majesty." Bowing yet again to his king, his face showing the first real emotion since coming before the pavilion with his captive, Sir Dwayne said, "I regret I can't release the boy."

A gasp went up from the assembly. Many of the guards surrounding the king took up arms. The sound of metal hissing out of scabbards was deafening in the quiet.

"Sir Dwayne, explain yourself, now! I am your king," Lionel demanded yet again. No knight had ever refused a direct order from their rightful monarch. *I may have the beginnings of a war on my hands.* "I've given you an order to release the boy." Lionel opened and closed his fists in frustration, sweat popping out on his forehead. His breathing was becoming as labored as poor Pip's.

Sir Dwayne looked flushed but held his ground, shaking his head. "I'm your sworn protector, sire. As such, it's my duty to hold my office to the best of my ability. This boy is said to be a wizard, to have powers or abilities of as yet unknown origins, and it's my contention as such, he's to be treated as an enemy until proven otherwise." His eyes pleaded with his king for forgiveness, but his next words didn't. "Therefore, I'll not release him."

"Knight . . ." Laura began . . .

"No!" spat Sir Dwayne, interrupting the princess, his own eyes blazing now. "This is my purview, not yours. Until I know this lad is not a danger to my king, I shall do what is necessary. Even if it costs me my station, I'll not allow anyone or anything to stop me."

Tarsus had never taken his eyes off the captain, looking at the knight with disdain. He said in a low rumble, "Mark my words very carefully, knight. If at any point in the next few moments the young lad comes to any more harm, I'll take that as a personal affront to my honor. I've given my word to King Lionel this boy isn't a threat to him or his kingdom. *My* honor is at stake here, and *you* shall not take that from *me*."

Pip looked as if he may collapse at any moment, but Sir Dwayne held him up.

"That, monster," the knight said just as menacingly, "isn't for you to say. I'll do as I see fit in this instance. My king and my kingdom are at stake here as is *my* honor."

"No, your honor isn't at stake here, Sir Dwayne," said the king, mastering his anger and speaking in a normal voice. "Your honor has never been in question. And Tarsus," he looked to the dragon, "I have said, and I mean it, your honor is not at question here either.'

Tarsus looked at the king, then the princess, and finally back to Sir Dwayne holding the sword to Pip's throat, small plumes of smoke still rising from his nostrils, knowing he could trust Lionel and Laura to be true to their word, but Sir Dwayne was making it almost impossible for him to believe anything he may say. All he knew for sure was if Pip got seriously injured because of what this knight has done, he'd make true on his promise: boil the man alive in his armor.

Tarsus stretched his neck towards the hated knight and hissed at him like an attar.

Laura shouted, "No!"

Lionel shouted, "Do not!"

What stopped him, however, was not the king or Laura, but Dwayne pressing his sword to Pip's throat harder, blood welling from underneath it.

The rest of the guard had been watching the proceedings with some interest. It had been conveyed to them by Sir Dwayne they must not take anything the dragon said at face value. In small groups, they slowly worked their way closer. Sir Edward and Sir Hook, with pikes in their hands, were making their way to a more advantageous position, being told specifically if anything untoward were to happen, their first priority was to protect the king and princess. Sir Dwayne would first take care of the boy and then all would take care of the dragon. This would go no farther. It was time to make sure the kingdom took the appropriate action.

Out of the corner of her eye, Laura noticed Sir Hook coming closer to the proceedings holding a pike. Looking around as calmly as she could, she saw others doing the same, advancing with weapons. She saw this was definitely escalating in the wrong direction. She had to do something, but as usual, Lionel was faster on the uptake.

"This will not go any further," said Lionel looking at the knight. "Sir Dwayne?"

"Sire."

"I will not have fighting in my presence." He turned to his guards, Sir Hook, Sir Quint, others, and then back to Sir Dwayne. "I've been watching my guards coming closer with mayhem in their eyes." He waved them away with a flick of his hand, noticing some didn't stop, however. Those he faced squarely, and without a word, put them in their place, and then facing Dwayne again, said with a smirk, "And I know it's your duty to protect me. But this will not happen. I give you my word, as your king and liege lord, and as your friend of many years, if anything happens while in my presence, you will bear the brunt of my wrath. Your honor and your bravery in the face of danger is unmatched, but I believe from what I see of the boy in front of me that you've no need of this. And the enmity you feel towards Tarsus is unwarranted and beneath you. You've nothing to fear from him."

"That's yet to be seen," rumbled Tarsus, fire spitting above their heads.

"No!" shouted Lionel, rushing forward to stand in front of the dragon. "That will not be seen, not here, not ever, as long as I have something to say about it. And I believe I do," exclaimed the king.

Tarsus didn't bother to look at Lionel. He was more and more worried about Pip. His senses were quite a bit more heightened than humans, and Pip seemed to be having trouble breathing. The rope tying him to the pole and Dwayne's blade were cutting off his air. If this didn't stop soon, Pip wouldn't make it. He'd die in front of everyone. And if that happened, no matter what he told the king, Sir Dwayne would die next to the lad.

Laura watched both Pip and Sir Dwayne. She didn't think Pip could hold out much longer. She could clearly hear his breath laboring in his lungs. To look at him, he'd have fallen over if Sir Dwayne hadn't been holding him up. It was time to do something. "Sir Knight, I believe it would be better for Pip if you'd loosen the restraints around him. If he collapses, he may injure himself. Please, for the sake of these proceedings, I think you could remove them. With you so close, I don't think anything will happen." She spread her hands to him as if pleading.

Sir Dwayne looked at the boy as if seeing him for the first time. He nodded. He'd been so focused on what the dragon would do, he'd completely forgotten about the boy, although he'd been gripping the lad's arm. He hadn't wanted to injure him, even though it looked like it, he'd merely wanted to make sure he couldn't do anything, if per chance he did have some kind of power. He studied the boy's face and then nodded again, as if coming to a decision, surely, with the boy's hands trussed up in the air, it would be almost impossible for him to do magic.

Sir Dwayne, like so many others, wrongly thought magic could only be done with grand hand gestures and chanting.

Sir Dwayne slowly removed a dirk from his tunic, never taking his eyes from the dragon, and cut the rope trussing Pip to the pole. Immediately, Pip collapsed at the feet of the princess choking, trying to draw breath.

Laura stooped to help him, but just as her hands were about to grab his arm, the knight stopped her by placing his blade between them. "No, Your Highness. Please leave him be. Until I know he's safe, you may not touch him." He then unceremoniously yanked Pip to his feet with a hand under his armpit.

Tarsus growled menacingly at the treatment. Dwayne ignored it.

Pip rubbed his neck. Blood smeared over his fingers. Crouching, he finally took a lung full of air. Hearing his breathing ease and knowing he'd be all right, Tarsus lowered his head, sighing. Being treated as he was by Sir Dwayne wasn't making it any easier for the lad, however. Tarsus never let his eyes stray from the knight.

"Talk, boy," said Dwayne, shaking Pip. "What powers do you have?"

"That's enough, Knight!" barked the king. "I believe you've done far too much already. Let the boy talk without making his teeth rattle."

"Yes, sire," said Dwayne, bowing slightly. "But I stand ready if he does something." He nudged Pip with the point of his sword in his back.

Pip looked at the king and almost fainted again. He knew he'd made a few mistakes, but he didn't think it had been that bad. He looked only at the princess. His eyes showed relief as well as fear. Haltingly, then with more strength, albeit hoarse from his treatment, he began. "I'm sorry, Your Highness."

"For what?" asked the princess, surprised.

"For speaking to you with such disrespect this morning." Pip looked at Tarsus and then to King Lionel, a flush coming to his cheeks. "I didn't realize who you were when you came into the stables while Tarsus and I were arguing." He massaged his throat trying to get the words out. "I know it was wrong of me to do, and I apologize." He then bowed to her, wobbly, almost falling face first in the courtyard's dirt. "I'll do as you command to make up for the affront."

That caught the princess off guard. "Oh! That. Yes. Well . . ." That's what got this whole mess started, and she didn't want it going anywhere else. She was going to have to learn to not only keep her temper under control, but her mouth as well. "We, uh, can talk about that later."

Laura looked down at the ground sheepishly, the young man making her feel petty.

"Yes, Your Highness,." Pip answered, not fully understanding. The more he stood in front of all of them, he was coming to think that wasn't the reason he'd been trussed up and brought before her.

"Never mind that now, boy. Talk! What powers do you have?" Sir Dwayne emphasized his question by poking Pip in the back with his sword again. And each time he'd done it, Tarsus's nostrils plumed smoke. Noticing this, the knight smiled. To make his point to the dragon, he poked the boy yet again, getting a satisfied grunt from the lad.

This didn't go unnoticed by Tarsus either. He smiled right back. It wasn't a friendly smile.

Lionel raised his hand, commanding, "Stop!" He looked at the knight. "That's enough! There's no need for you to antagonize Tarsus," he gestured to the dragon. "Or terrorize the boy in my presence." He gestured to the sword poking Pip in the back, lifting his eyes to the knight's, making sure he understood he knew exactly what was happening between them. "Do not do so again."

The knight nodded, his smile slowly fading, but said nothing.

Lionel turned his attention to Pip. "Just answer a few questions lad. This won't take long."

"Yes, sire," squeaked Pip, rubbing his throat.

Tarsus held his breath. *Here we go.*

"I understand your name is Pip? How long have you been here?" asked the king. "I don't recall ever seeing you before."

Mulch started to reply for him. "He's been here, sire . . ." The king looked his way and Mulch abruptly stopped, his face going ashen. "Sorry, Your Majesty." He bowed.

"Yes, I'm Pip, Your Majesty." He looked towards Mulch standing just to his left and smiled, thanking him for trying to answer. Then he returned his attention back to the king. "I've been here as long as I can remember, sire."

"What have you been doing here?"

"Mulch has been taking care of me, sire. He's given me a place to stay and given me a job. He's teaching me to work the stables. If it weren't for him, I'd probably be living on the streets, stealing for my supper." Pip realized at that moment how much Mulch actually had done for him. Over the years, he'd complained a lot about what he does and what Mulch made him do, but when it came down to it, Mulch had really taken care of him. He was sorry now he'd said anything against the man. He looked down at his feet, not able to look the king in the eyes. Pip wasn't afraid to admit he was frightened as he'd ever been in his life. One minute he'd been coming down from the loft after a bath in the river and the next being taken by Sir Dwayne, trussed up like a hog. He thought he'd be in trouble after what happened this morning, but he never expected this. The most he thought would happen was Tarsus being obnoxious to him, or Mulch thumping him upside the head for being stupid, but this! Pip cleared his voice and continued, "I know, Your Majesty, that I haven't always been the most dependable. But I also realize now that without the help of Mulch, I wouldn't be here now. I guess I owe him my life. I just didn't realize it until now. I'll probably never get along with him as well as I should." He smiled at the stable master again, "but, I do realize what he's done for me. And he's never explained why he did it."

Lionel looked to Mulch with affection and grinned. "I think I do, young man." Lionel had known Mulch longer than anyone in the palace or the stables. At one time, he was the premiere knight, one of renowned skill and horsemanship and beloved by all. But by design, or misfortune, he renounced his knighthood, dedicating himself to the care of his beloved horses. Lionel's father had been the only person who truly knew the reasons for Mulch's actions, and it was on his deathbed those actions not be questioned. "He may look and act like an old goat, but he's got the heart of a lion and the stubborn streak of a mule." He nodded to the stable master.

Mulch turned red, chagrin on his face, and simply bowed to his king, his friend. The king's family being the only ones who really knew why he'd given up being a knight. "Thank you, Your Majesty."

"Master Tarsus has been explaining to us that he's been using you for a page while he's been with us." Lionel continued with Pip. "Is this true?"

"Yes, Your Majesty." Pip nodded.

The princess stepped in, wanting to get back to the original subject and get this over with. "So, why were you arguing with the Lord Dragon this morning?" She gestured to Tarsus.

Pip looked to Tarsus. Tarsus looked back without saying anything. "I . . . um . . . I was upset with him, Your Highness," was all he could manage to say.

"That was pretty obvious," Laura said, getting frustrated. She wanted a straight answer from him, and he wasn't cooperating. If she didn't know any better, he'd been taking lessons from Tarsus. "I don't believe I'd ever seen anyone scream at a dragon before." It didn't seem to matter Tarsus was the first dragon anyone in the kingdom had ever seen. "You must be very brave to do something like that," said Laura.

"Well . . . I . . ."

"Or very stupid!" finished Laura.

Tarsus chuckled. Laura looked at him and gave him a very intense stare, which didn't seem to bother him, which bothered Laura quite a bit.

Sir Dwayne stared at Tarsus as if he had two heads and wanted to cut one of them off. That didn't seem to bother him either. With eyes smoldering, the knight barked, "Monster! This is no laughing matter."

Tarsus whipped his head towards the knight, with no laughter evident. "That's the third time you've called me monster," hissed Tarsus, eyeing him. "I believe when we first met, you referred to me by that term. As I said then, I say now, I don't believe you know the meaning of the word. Let me explain it to you one last time." Tarsus positioned himself to be standing straight in front of the knight and Pip, his eyes wandering to Pip, making sure he really was all right, but his attention solely focused on Sir Dwayne. In the background, gasps and grunts could be heard from the other knights moving into better positions to defend their king if necessary. Tarsus ignored them all, focusing solely on the man threatening his young charge. "I've done many things in my long life, ones in which I'm not very proud, but I've never been a 'monster.'" He looked at Laura and Lionel trying to gauge their reactions, but saw nothing from them. He looked back at Dwayne. "You, being the humans you are, can be very monstrous to one another, hacking and stabbing until there's no one left. Dragons have never done such a thing. We, as a species, find a different solution to our problems unless there's no other way. We don't exterminate our own kind. Yet . . ." he paused to look around the assembly, noting the knights and guards slowly inching closer, ". . . who's the monster here? You seem to be the one who's tied up a boy from fear. I don't recall ever having to do that. But I'll tell you I can be a very fearsome monster if I choose to be." He smiled a toothy smile.

The assemblage around the pavilion took a collective step back.

"That's enough!" snapped the princess. "Sir Knight," she pointed to Dwayne, "your only job here is to guard your king and myself, not get the animals stirred up." This had the effect she was looking for. It shut him up, but it also drew a small chuckle from the crowd. Then she turned to Tarsus. "And your job here today, Dragon, is to answer our questions without all this flippancy." This got the attention of Tarsus, and the crowd chuckled even harder.

Smart kid: redirection. Maybe there's hope for her yet. Tarsus ducked his head.

"To get back on the subject," said Laura, looking at Pip, "why were you upset with Tarsus? What happened?"

"Well, Your Highness, I thought what he was making me do was pointless."

"How so?"

"Well . . . I . . . um . . . Maybe not pointless, but I thought I could have gotten the same kind of treatment from Mulch." He hung his head in shame, thinking of what he'd said only a moment ago about what Mulch had done for him. He snuck a fast peek at Mulch, ducking his head, expecting a thump to the back of it. "It wasn't fair. I hadn't had a moment to myself, or for myself, in over a fortnight, and I thought he should know. I just sort of . . . um . . . got carried away when I told him. I guess I lost my temper."

"That's an understatement. Like I said, brave or stupid. When I walked in, you were screaming at him eye to eye, seven or eight feet off the ground." She placed her hands on her hips and looked at him quizzically.

When Tarsus let out a laugh, Laura's heart nearly stopped. "Shut up!" she snapped at him. Then she looked abashed herself.

"See what I mean, Your Highness," Pip said quietly.

The crowd chuckled again. Laura looked around with a stern face, shutting them up quickly. Dwayne was right about one thing, this wasn't funny.

Dwayne poked Pip in the back again, giving another grunt.

"That's enough of that, Knight," the princess told him. "Father's already told you. I asked him a question and he answered. I don't want him to be split down the middle. I don't believe he's going to do anything untoward here."

Dwayne didn't say anything. He merely nodded, looking towards his king, hoping for him to give the orders and not her, but there was no help there. In the king's eye, all he saw was disappointment.

Lionel asked the next question, however, that took Pip totally by surprise. "Are you a wizard?"

Tarsus held his breath. *Don't say anything, boy. Just keep your mouth shut. I'll explain things to you after this is over.*

Pip looked at his king and said very distinctly, "I don't think so, Your Majesty."

"Don't think, or don't know, or no, you're not?"

"I don't think I am, Your Majesty. I can't say for sure because I don't feel like one. And I figured I'd know if I was. If someone is a wizard, wouldn't they know?" He cocked his head as if asking confirmation.

"I don't know, young man," Lionel admitted. "He or she might know, but I'm not sure myself."

"So, how is it," the princess asked, "that you were floating in the air while arguing with the Obnoxious One?" She lifted her chin indicating Tarsus.

Tarsus looked hurt. *I? Obnoxious? Doubt it. I have a wonderful disposition.*

115

The king admonished the princess. "That's enough from you also, Laura. I know I taught you better about being respectful. Didn't we ourselves have this discussion just recently? Try remembering it." He looked at his daughter sternly. "This will not become a pissing match. It has already become something it shouldn't."

"Yes, Father," said Laura ashamed, remembering what transpired in the throne room just hours before.

"Humph!" humphed Tarsus. *That got her. Looks as if she isn't quite what she makes out to be herself.*

Lionel then looked at Tarsus and said, "And you, Tarsus, should definitely know better. You've more years than anyone here. Good manners should be ingrained in you, if not good sense and honor. I'm getting very tired of these games." He looked squarely at the dragon and scowled.

Tarsus looked ashamed himself, bowing, knowing he'd been part of the problem.

This made Sir Dwayne smile wickedly. It wasn't lost on the king. He saw what was going on. "And you, Sir Knight," going after Sir Dwayne now. "You should be the one most ashamed. You're no more innocent than these two." He indicated Tarsus and Laura. "From the moment Tarsus entered the grounds, you've been like a cat in the cream. You find any slight you can throw in Tarsus's face. And the way you've conducted yourself in my presence . . ." Lionel looked to Pip for emphasis. ". . . It's not worthy of my knight's captain. You above all others should know better. I don't know what's come over you lately, but it will stop, or someone else will take your place. No one is irreplaceable."

Sir Dwayne's mouth fell open. *My King?*

No one said a word after Lionel's admonishments. Each was watching what the other was doing, looking around as if they'd lost something. Lionel peered at them all. *Kids on a play field Laura called it. Maybe a little humility will do them all some good. Nothing else has worked.* "Go ahead, young man, how was it that you were floating in the air when my daughter came in the stables?"

"I don't know, Your Majesty. I thought I'd broken something when I finally came down. It scared me nearly to death."

"Didn't you ask Tarsus about it?"

"Yes, sire, but he wouldn't say anything. I nearly got trampled trying to get him to talk to me."

Tarsus didn't comment, just kept watching Dwayne next to Pip.

"I can believe that," said the princess. "He can be very stubborn."

"Yes, Your Highness," answered Pip, smiling for the first time, looking at Tarsus.

Tarsus sighed deeply. He was getting tired of this himself. His main problem was getting Dwayne away from Pip, not going over what he'd already said. But he had to say something, so he looked at Laura, then to Lionel, abruptly sat down, and then turned to Lionel. "I have told you, Your Majesty, I can do simple things. That's all," explained Tarsus slowly. "I felt it was necessary to calm the young whelp down. It just didn't have the effect I was looking for."

"I see," said Lionel, eyeing the dragon. *I know he's holding something back. I just can't prove it right now. Apparently he's going to keep his own council. He keeps things too close to his chest. That was nearly his undoing once. All I can do is wait.* "I guess I can't fault you for your efforts, although, I can fault you for your actions." He stared at the dragon hard.

"Yes, Your Majesty," Tarsus said, ignoring the look.

"As for the rest of this nonsense," he looked at Dwayne still standing next to the boy, sword to his back, at Tarsus, sitting calmly, never letting his eyes stray from Dwayne, at Laura, shaking her head in exasperation, not knowing quite what to say; and then looked around at the assembly of castle guards and knights holding weapons, Lionel was tired of it all. "Let's be done."

Lionel looked to Mulch. "Stable master, I wish to thank you for your service and your caring of this young boy while he's been here. You don't need permission from me to do something as noble as what you've done. I not only commend you for it, but I thank you for it. You do me and the kingdom proud with such deeds. I've never doubted your heart was that of a lion, although as I've said, you're stubborn like a mule." At this last, he smiled affectionately at him.

"Thank you, Your Majesty," Mulch said, his voice thickening with emotion, bowing.

Lionel then addressed his knights and guards, looking from one to the other as he spoke, "I thank you all for your service and your stewardship, but I think you can lower your weapons. This little circus is over for now. You've done your duty and your kingdom proud." *Flattery never hurt anyone. I need to cool down tempers while I still can.* "But, remember, until I, your king, say to bear arms in my presence, don't let me see you do otherwise." He warned them. He wouldn't have bloodshed in his kingdom. "Is this clear?"

The knights and castle guards put away their arms and yelled in unison, "Sire!" The message was loud and clear to them. Lionel nodded.

Then the king turned his attention to the main players. He addressed Sir Dwayne first. "Sir Dwayne?"

"Yes, Your Majesty," answered the knight.

"Are you satisfied this young man has no power?"

Sir Dwayne looked at Pip and shook his head. "I don't know, Your Majesty. It hasn't been proven whether he does or not." He stepped hesitantly away from Pip and sheathed his sword. "All I can do is keep an eye on him and hope the word of the dragon is as honorable as you believe it is."

"Very well," Lionel sighed, not wanting to believe otherwise himself. "I guess that's the best I can hope for, for now." Then the king looked towards the dragon. "Tarsus?"

"Yes, Your Majesty." Tarsus never took his eyes from Dwayne while answering.

"I expect you to inform me if this young man shows any kind of power in the future. You know it's my right to be informed, as your king, while you're here, of any developments."

"Yes, Your Majesty." Tarsus understood quite well: say something, or else.

Pip looked at Sir Dwayne and shuddered, realizing he'd come very close to dying. The dungeons were definitely no place for a kid like him, but dying would have been worse. He massaged his neck again, remembering the feel of the rope and of the knight's sword at his throat. Ugh!

Laura watched Dwayne put away his sword and sighed with relief. She stepped to Pip and gently laid a hand on his arm. "Are you OK? I think we can go now." Laura looked into Pip's eyes and saw fear. At her touch, he flinched, looking as if he wanted to run. She really couldn't blame him. She said gently, "I don't believe you have to stay any longer. We just wanted to find out what happened between you and Tarsus." She looked at the knight. "Sir Dwayne simply got carried away."

Sir Dwayne looked hurt but knew she was telling the truth. He really hadn't meant it to go so far with the boy, but he seemed to overdo things when it came to that damnable dragon. If he was involved—be it a boy or training his men—he had to outdo the critter at every turn, to his detriment apparently. He didn't know why and didn't care for some reason. One-upping the lizard was all that mattered. But he knew he better get his head back into his station. He couldn't always be put on the spot because of being reckless and narrow-minded. He was better than that. He was better than the Lord High Damn Lizard. He was the captain of the king's guard, and it was time, he started acting like it. He ignored the rest of what the princess and the boy were saying.

"Come on, let's get you cleaned up," said the princess, pulling on Pip's arm softly.

"That's what I'd just done when Sir Dwayne got me, Your Highness," he said, letting her lead him away. "I'm sorry for what happened this morning. I really didn't realize who you were. Tarsus can have that effect on people." He felt he still had to apologize to her so she wouldn't think badly of him. He didn't know why, but it was important she knew he was sorry.

"Yes, I think I know what you mean." She looked at the dragon with some interest. She was definitely going to watch him closely. He was hiding something, and after what happened here, she was more determined than ever to find out what.

The princess led Pip away from the pavilion. With a look at Mulch, he fell in beside them when they left.

"Sir Dwayne," Lionel said, coming to his knight and standing before him.

"Your Majesty."

"I want to see you in my throne room right after you disperse the guard. We have a few things to discuss. Not the least of which is how you behaved today." The king looked at him and knew what was coming wouldn't be easy. "And you, Tarsus," he looked at the dragon, "you've some explaining to do also, in private, about your actions. Don't think you've gotten away with it either." He turned on his heels and left without saying anything else.

"Yes, Your Majesty."

"Yes, Your Majesty."

CHAPTER 9

Granston was fuming.

How on earth could that blasted dragon gotten out of the trap he'd set? It was one of the best traps he'd ever devised, and it had gone off without a hitch. Something had gone wrong, was the only thing he could think of. Over the centuries, the magic must have worn at the edges or faded into the ground. Some magic was like that: it would simply dissipate after a certain amount of time. Something! But for now, that wasn't important. He had plans to get back what he'd been working on for the past two decades.

The first stop on his unplanned getaway had been to a very remote outbuilding he'd set in the Faraway Mountain Range in the Northern continent. It was secluded, no one knowing its whereabouts. It wasn't much to look at, simply a square building made of logs, sitting on top of a snow-covered peak surrounded by pine trees and willows, which obscured anyone's view of it, but anyone had to look awfully hard to even spy the top.

Granston slowly walked around his self-imposed cell. It didn't look too impressive: a small stove for cooking and warmth, a few basic utensils for eating on one small shelf over the stove, a cot which had seen better days, two threadbare covers thrown over it. In one corner was a pot for his necessary business, and one stool in the opposite corner, meager possessions for someone who'd at one time a whole kingdom to plunder at his whim. Also with him were his Dwarf Staff and a tome of such bulky proportions that he could barely lift it. But this was one thing which he was glad to have, a reminder of days in which he'd had so much. It wasn't only his life and soul, but his power and heart all in one: his grimoire, the book of spells he'd amassed over the many long centuries he'd been practicing magic. He couldn't do what he did without it. It was in this tome he'd found the spell to put Tarsus away for so long.

Now? Why now? Was it just blind luck? Or bad luck? The spell he used on the lizard should have lasted forever. So how did the contemptuous little snot of a princess find him? The day he found his way out of that trap became the worst day of Granston's long, long life. The only thing he could possibly say good about it was both he and Tarsus were approximately the same age. In the bubble, Tarsus didn't age . . . unfortunately, he had.

The Gnome wizard took a deep breath, trying to calm down and to stop feeling sorry for himself and do something about his problem. He had to make plans to finally get rid of that blasted lizard once and for all. He wasn't going to go through that again. It was too hard the first time. He nearly got his head bitten off. So, it was time to do something about his biggest scaly problem.

*　　*　　*

Laura slowly walked with Pip towards the stables. Master Mulch following quietly. When they entered, Mulch made his apologies and said he'd duties to perform and continued on his own. Pip didn't acknowledge him leaving, his eyes glassy, walking where Laura led him, not caring where. He looked as if he'd lost his last friend. His head hung down to his breastbone, and he tended to weave when he walked, not looking where he was going. Laura had felt something like it when her mother had died: lost, alone, not knowing what to do or who to talk to.

"Pip, it wasn't your fault," she said softly, touching his arm again.

Pip looked up at the princess and said softly, "I know, but I feel I did something wrong, besides what I did to you, I mean. If it hadn't been for me, this wouldn't have happened in the first place."

Laura tried to put the blame on herself by saying, "If it hadn't been for me saying I'd seen you floating in the air, I doubt this would've come about." She made as if to touch his throat, reminding him again of the rope and sword.

Pip flinched away, stopping her. Then, confronting her face to face, his eyes brimming with unshed tears, he said huskily, "That's where you did right. It was your duty to say something to the king." Pip tried to smile through his anguish. "It was my duty also, and I didn't."

Laura didn't say anything, she didn't have to, knowing Pip was right. Both of them had done something they were ashamed of today. "Maybe," she said. "But I could have done it differently, just as you should have. If there's blame to be put anywhere, I guess we're both to blame. It's time we admitted it and just moved on. What say we start over? OK?"

Pip nodded, not trusting himself to say anything else.

"Go get some rest. I'll see you later,." Laura told him.

Pip walked away without a word, heading towards his hayloft and bed. Although it was only past noon and he had more chores to do in the stables, he didn't have the strength, or the courage, to finish them, they could wait a while. Maybe a little rest would do him good. His neck hurt like he'd been strung up on a gallows.

Laura watched Pip go. *Blast! Why did this have to happen? One of these days I'm going to have to learn to keep my mouth shut. But right now . . .* Laura headed back the way she'd come, determination in her steps, time to confront the lizard again. *This will be pleasant.*

Laura found Tarsus where they'd left him, in front of the pavilion, what was left of it. The King's Guard were arrayed around the grounds watching the castle's servants take down the canvass that made up the tent, and she noticed they never quite kept their gaze from straying too far from what Tarsus was doing.

But the dragon wasn't doing anything at all. He merely watched the activity around him, or seemed to, but when she said his name . . . "Tarsus?" . . .

Tarsus jumped slightly, startled out of his reverie. "Huh?"

"Are you OK?" asked Laura, coming to stand in front of him.

"Huh," he said again, his eyes clearing of the faraway look he had.

"Are you OK?" the princess asked again, looking at him worriedly.

"Yes," the dragon slurred slowly, seeming to finally clear the fog from his mind. He said gruffly, looking down on her, "What do you want?"

This got the princess's ire back up. His seeming irritation for interrupting his musing had reminded her why she'd come back to talk to him. She didn't want him to be hurt, but she sure as all the blazes wasn't going to take his attitude. "That's about enough of that, dragon!"

"Dragon!" Tarsus growled dangerously, his head rising farther above the princess, looking down at her, puffs of smoke slowly streaming out of his flared nostrils.

The sound of Tarsus's bellow got the attention of the guards. All of them, who weren't many, only four, took stock of what was transpiring between the princess and the dragon. Sir Edward slowly drew his sword from his scabbard, taking a tentative step towards the encounter, and as he did, the knight noticed out of the corner of his eye the others had already done the same.

"That's right, dragon!" Laura said, ignoring everyone and everything except Tarsus. She looked up and her mouth quirked into a slight smile. "If you're gonna act like an animal, I'll refer to you as one," she said not backing down, planting her hands on her hips.

Tarsus lowered and cocked his head to one side so he could peer at her with one baleful eye. "I thought better of you, Princess," Tarsus growled, smoke still billowing from his nostrils.

"And I, you, up until a few moments ago," countered Laura, not backing down.

Tarsus snorted, relaxed, and then sat on his haunches. He shook his head to clear away the remaining fog clouding his thoughts, smiled slyly, and then winked at her. *Smart girl. I just can't be upset with her for long. I was wrong, and she knows it. Blast!*

Sir Edward saw where this was going and relaxed a bit, even showing a slight smile himself. He put his sword back in his scabbard, signaling to the others to do the same. He knew the relationship between the princess and Tarsus was at times volatile, but he'd also seen over the past month it was usually more pomp and circumstance than actual violence. Shaking his head, he turned away.

Tarsus took a deep breath. "Forgive me, Your Highness. What can I do for you?" he asked trying to make amends for his behaviour.

Laura scowled at Tarsus, dropped her hands to her sides, and confronted the dragon before she lost her nerve and her composure again. She wasn't really mad at him, just slightly disappointed in the outcome of today's events. Although she'd been partially at fault for what happened to Pip, she knew it was also born of stubbornness, and pride, of failure to protect Pip that had sparked the madness that ensued between himself and the knight. If not for that pride and stubbornness, Sir Dwayne probably wouldn't have acted as he had.

"Why do you always have to antagonize the captain so?" asked Laura.

Tarsus sighed and blew out a puff of smoke from his nostrils. "I don't mean to do it. He simply rubs me the wrong way, that's all," said Tarsus, repeating what he'd already told Lionel.

"That's enough. You know he's loyal and a faithful vassal to my father and the kingdom. What you and the knight have done to Pip, putting him in the middle of your feud, was intolerable. There was no honor in it. You don't have to goad him into such actions."

"Goad him?" Tarsus snorted. "He needs no excuse to do what he does, or how he does it. What he did to Pip was not only dishonorable, but also the most un-knight-like deed I've seen."

"But what you did wasn't honorable either," she argued. "I don't condone what he did to Pip, but I can understand it. He felt if Pip had powers, he could use them to injure someone."

"Do you honestly think Pip could have done such a thing, if he had any power? Even you must know that he's not made that way. You or anyone else in this kingdom never knew he was alive, except for Mulch, until just recently when I showed up." The more he spoke about Pip and Sir Dwayne, the more agitated Tarsus became. His enormous tail swished back and forth, creating a small dust storm behind him. "And I don't forget my role in Pip's pain. It will forever be a source of my own pain. But I tell you now, Princess," he put his head close to Laura's again and hissed, "I will not forget the knight's role either."

Tarsus, Please. Don't do this. "Please, Tarsus. For my sake, if not Pip's. My father is right. You and Sir Dwayne must stop this enmity. I don't wish to see either of you injured."

Tarsus didn't say anything.

*   *   *

After leaving the princess, Pip went to the loft and lay down. Maybe some sleep would help. But sleep wasn't easy to find. He was too wound up from the happenings of the past couple of hours. All he could think about, staring at the poorly thatched ceiling of the stables, being trussed up like a pig for the slaughter, had unnerved him more than he wanted to admit. If what Tarsus had said of him was true, he was in more trouble than he could imagine. He didn't want to be anything but what he was, maybe not a stable hand, but definitely not a wizard. All of those dreams he had of becoming a knight, or even a mere page, those were the dreams of a kid. The kind of dreams which make a boring life more bearable; nothing more. But a wizard! A wizard! *By all the gods. Why did this have to happen? Now of all times when my life had finally become interesting. I'm working for a dragon. A dragon!*

Pip decided he wouldn't get anywhere with just laying in bed, so he got up and headed down the ladder to finish some of the chores he hadn't got around to before Sir Dwayne got him.

He really didn't have any specific chore, so when he saw a pitchfork leaning against one of the stalls, he got it and headed into Gwyneth's stall. Gwyneth was Sir Dunn's mount, the only mare in the knight's stable. Pip heard Sir Dunn tell Mulch, "A mare is more gentle towards the rider and more fierce in a battle situation than all the stallions in the world." Pip couldn't comment on the gentle part of his statement, but he could surely attest to the fierceness. She'd nearly kicked Budge to death, Mulch's second in command, when her fetlock had been inflamed from a mulberry sticker.

Pip literally dug into his work after removing Gwyneth and putting her in another stall. Pitching the used hay out of the way, into a pile by the door, he began methodically mucking out the waste. Dung from the horses wasn't wasted. It was either used as fertilizer for the king's garden or the dried pieces were used as heating supplements. Pip used a wheelbarrow to load the dung and then spread out new hay. He then put some of the hay into Gwyneth's feed tray that was hanging from the stall wall, afterwards pitching the used hay into another wheelbarrow and wheeling it into the 'old' hay pile; this was used as mulch for the orchard trees and gardens. Usually, he'd scoop the old hay first and then clean out, but his mind wasn't completely on the job. He worked at a steady pace, and never cursed himself for being so dense, doing some things more than once, trying to sweat out his frustrations.

After the third stall, he heard something thumping at the stable doors. He turned in time to see Tarsus moving into his own stall just off the entrance, his having been converted to fit his great size. Two walls on either side had been removed by Mulch to accommodate his great girth. Seeing him, Pip was glad he'd already done his. He may not like being without fresh hay to sleep on. Pip didn't head towards the dragon right off, standing in the aisle staring at the door opening and wondering if Tarsus would even talk to him. If it hadn't been for him, Tarsus wouldn't be in trouble with the king and Sir Dwayne.

As Pip debated whether to go and talk to him, Tarsus took the decision out of his hands and called, "Pip?"

Oh boy! Here we go. I hope he's not too mad. I don't know how much more I can take today. Pip walked to Tarsus's stall doors. "Yes," he said quietly, not daring to talk over a whisper. He didn't go in. There wasn't very much room with Tarsus in it, but that wasn't why he'd stopped at the threshold. He didn't know whether the dragon would want to be near him at the moment. And, to put it plainly, he was frightened, not of Tarsus himself; Tarsus wouldn't hurt him, but afraid of what the dragon would say.

Tarsus had settled himself as well as he could in the new hay put down, his head pointing towards the door where Pip was standing. He said quietly, "Pip, are you all right?"

Pip stared at the dragon not knowing what to say. As far as physically, yes, he was OK. His neck hurt, sure, and blood was still smeared around his shirt collar from the cut; mentally however, he didn't think his mind would be altogether right. He may not have been some kind of head doctor, to succor the ills of the mind, but he wasn't stupid. So instead of saying something that didn't matter to either of them, he kept quiet.

Tarsus looked at him. *I guess I can't blame him.* He nodded his head. Then to Pip's amazement, he apologized, "I'm sorry, Pip, for everything I've put you through. For causing you pain, and for putting you in the middle of the knight and myself."

"You're sorry?" Pip was stunned. His mouth fell open in shock. Why would he say such a thing? *I was the cause of the problem, not him.* "You're not the reason for what Sir Dwayne did. I am. If it weren't for me being a wizard, I wouldn't have gone through that. And if I hadn't yelled at the princess, it wouldn't have happened in the first place." Pip took a tentative step into the stall. "I'm the one who's sorry. If it hadn't been for me, I wouldn't have gotten you in trouble, or Sir Dwayne coming after me."

"No, Pip, that's where you're wrong," said Tarsus, shaking his head and looking down at the lad. "I knew from the moment I met you standing in the middle of the stables, you were a wizard." Tarsus looked into Pip's eyes and saw his stunned reaction from the statement. "And one who has the potential to be the most powerful mage that has been seen in the past thousand years. And that is where I made my mistake."

"You? But . . ."

"Pip, listen to me," Tarsus interrupted.

Pip closed his mouth, holding his breath for the anticipated scolding he was going to receive. He'd been on the receiving end of enough of those from Mulch. But that's not what happened. Surprisingly, when Tarsus began again, he was calm. At some points, Pip had to strain to hear what was said.

Tarsus snorted and looked away before beginning. He looked at Pip with eyes almost pleading for understanding. "My arrogance put you at risk. I made a mistake by not telling you who, and what, you are. By making that mistake, I laid the groundwork for what culminated in Sir Dwayne's deed. I didn't mean for you to be hurt by my actions." He shifted his great bulk, scratching in the hay like a dog fluffing his favorite place to sleep. He then looked back at Pip and said, "That's my arrogance, Pip. I tend to jump in before truly thinking out my next move. That's how I ended up in this time without my mate or my kin: my arrogance and stupidity. I should have realized what was going to happen when I first met the knight and especially you, history repeating. It seems I don't learn from past experiences." He chuffed to himself, small puffs of smoke leaking from his nostrils.

Pip realized what was happening, all be it by accident, Tarsus was talking about himself. He'd never explained what happened to him, or how he'd gotten in that spell which trapped him for so long, so while his loose tongue lasted, he wasn't going to stop him. Maybe this would not only help him understand the dragon, but explain why he kept so many secrets.

Pip held his breath, but Tarsus didn't say anything else about his past. He stopped and went in another direction instead. "I wish to beg your forgiveness, Pip," he said, bowing his head.

Pip stood in front of the dragon not knowing what to say. Tarsus wanted forgiveness from him. But he had nothing to forgive. Pip blamed himself, not the other way around, and when all was weighed against what happened, Pip came out as the loser, not Tarsus.

"But, Tarsus, you've nothing to be forgiven for," Pip finally managed to say. "If anyone should be asking for forgiveness, it's me. I didn't want this."

"No, you didn't, lad," said Tarsus looking up. "But I put you there anyway. I'm sorry. I make you a promise . . ."

Pip felt tingly all over at Tarsus' words. Something was happening. He didn't know what, but something. Tarsus' words themselves were invoking magic. Tarsus had a faint glow about his body, and his eyes shone. The flakes in his pupils resembling stars now shimmered and melted together, forming a solid line across his whole eye.

"I'll never put you in such a position again. From this point on, I'll make it one of my missions in life, for however long, to protect and teach you everything you need to know, to help you become a mage. Whatever happens to you will also happen to me. This my solemn vow."

Pip stood in front of the dragon and shivered not knowing how much longer he'd stay on his feet. His knees knocked, and his teeth literally chattered in his mouth. "What . . ."

Tarsus smiled at him. The first Pip has seen for a while.

"What was that?" asked Pip. "What did you do?" The tingling sensation slowly faded. It was like having a goose walk over your grave. Then, as swiftly, it went away.

Tarsus smiled broadly at Pip and then said, "You got your first lesson in real magic. Not the fake stuff you'd see in a show, but real magic."

"What do you mean?" asked Pip.

"I mean," said the dragon, still smiling, "the feeling you experienced was the result of magic. You'll find as a wizard, the words you say will have power. You'll have to be careful how you phrase your sentences and even what you say, as your feelings and emotions affect how magic is performed. That's why the promise I made was formed of magic and not an empty promise as most people would casually speak. From this point on, your fate and mine are sealed, and it can't be broken. This I've done for you."

"But, what have you done?" Pip asked, not fully understanding. "I thought you weren't a wizard. You told the king you weren't."

"Pip," Tarsus sighed. "You and I are sealed together for the rest of our lives. I'll not allow you to be hurt in any way. The promise I made has been sealed in magic, and it's unbreakable." He took a breath, wisps of smoke rising from his nostrils again, delaying talking for a moment, giving him time to think of how to explain to Pip what he needed to know and what he needed to hear. "And I'm not a wizard. I told the truth to the king. But dragons are inherently magical. It's our nature and part of our lives. All dragons control some magic, and all are part of magic. If we weren't, we couldn't be who and what we are. That's just the way of things. As you grow and learn, you'll find other beings who have the same inherent magical abilities."

After a moment, when Pip didn't say anything, but only stared back at Tarsus. Tarsus asked, "Do you understand?"

Pip nodded. "I think so." He couldn't believe it. What Tarsus told him was frightening. Pip felt light-headed. He didn't know whether he was going to faint again. He shook his head to try and chase some of those strange feelings away, but it only worked a little. So, to distract himself, he said to Tarsus, "But it's strange knowing there are other people or things or beings, as you put it, out there that have magic too. Or are part of magic." He shook his head in wonder. "I have a lot to learn I guess."

"Yes, you do. But I'll be teaching you what you need to know, so you won't be alone. This is another reason I did what I did. You don't have to be watching your back any longer. I'll do it for you. What we have now can never be broken, Pip."

"But, Tarsus, what happens if it ever is?"

"That's just it, Pip. It can't. The only way to break it is for you and I both to die. The only thing I can tell you for sure is that if you die, I die also."

"But, Tarsus," Pip said, excitement and anger showing in his voice, "I don't want you to die for me. I don't want anyone to die for me."

"I know, Pip. That's why I did it," said the dragon, trying to explain.

"I don't understand. Why would you seal your fate to me? Someone who isn't going to live as long as you."

Tarsus grinned. "That's where you're wrong again, Pip. You'll live as long as I. Probably, the same goes for me, I'll live as long as you. That is, as long as you don't die in a wizard's dual or something."

Pip had to sit down. He slid down the wall and stretched his legs towards the dragon, looking at him. He didn't know how to feel. From all the stories he'd ever heard about dragons, they'd all said the same thing: dragons lived for centuries. Tarsus mentioned he'd been around for a couple centuries already. *Me, live for centuries. Gods!*

"The pain I caused you will haunt me for the rest of my life, Pip. I didn't intend for you to be put in such a position. It reminds me constantly of my own pain. So, therefore, I'll meet it with you, sharing the outcome." Tarsus couldn't look into Pip's eyes any longer. Guilt filled him to the point he couldn't talk about it any longer. He'd been guilty of many bad and stupid things in his long life, and he hoped, with this one act, he'd make some form of amends to his conscience. "For now, let it stand as it is. In time, I'll tell you other things which won't make much more sense to you than this has today, but I'll try to make it as plain as possible and go as slow as the need arises to teach you the proper way to do things, and in the right sequence. It'll be painful, sometimes frustrating, and especially irritating for you, but, if you aren't taught in the proper way, you could end up killing yourself and me in the process. So please, Pip, try to learn from me and my actions so you won't make the same mistakes as I."

Pip could only nod. Unshed tears were in his eyes.

"I'll try," he finally croaked out.

*　　*　　*

Two days later, Tarsus woke with a sour disposition. When it came to sleep, dragons could do a lot of it—sleeping for two weeks straight was nothing unusual, especially after gorging on fifteen or twenty deer at supper. For the past fortnight, however, he hadn't gotten much; his nerves wouldn't let him. At odd hours of the night, he'd wake not knowing why, his thoughts wandering to times and places in his life he wished to forget, he couldn't quite get it together. But last night . . . last night he'd come to the conclusion he had to take control of his emotions and life again. The talk with Pip had energized him to stop feeling sorry for the way his life had gone, for Pip's sake if not his own. There was still time to make amends and ease his conscious. To start with, he had to begin training his two charges: Princess Laura and Pip the Wizard. Plus, if he didn't do something, he'd go crazy. Heaving himself from his mat, he went to wash his face in the stream just outside the corrals. Dragons, like humans, do morning ablutions too. He, being the sentient being he was, usually had business to do in the mornings, disgusting as it was. At least something was keeping to a schedule. Afterwards, however, his thoughts wandered back to his training schedules; Laura had to keep training, and he had to find time to start Pip's schooling in magic. But he had to figure out how to do it and keep both away from each other at the same time, which wasn't going to be easy. He told Pip to keep a low profile, do his chores, get some rest, and above all stay out of the way of Sir Dwayne until the knight calmed down. He didn't feel it was time to push Pip into the knight's face, at least not yet, wanting Pip to catch his breath and think about their talk. Tarsus knew it would be a lot for him to process, and he most assuredly needed a clear head for the trials of wizardry, and the knight not to see the boy as a threat, a threat not only to himself, but also to his kingdom in general; from what he'd seen of the lad in the past couple of days, he didn't think he had too much to worry about in that regard, he'd barely seen him himself. Although Pip hadn't done anything to merit the knight's attention, Tarsus knew he'd been keeping an eye on the boy. Pip noticed also. It seemed every time the lad took a step, or turned a corner, a knight was watching him. It made for a very nervous and conscientious Pip, which was good and bad. Good, Pip did no wrong; Bad, Pip didn't do much.

But all of that was for later. He headed back towards the stables to find the princess. Time to get this going. With his head held high and a quick step, Tarsus, with his renewed sense of purpose, was determined to see the princess become a knight, and Pip survive long enough to become a wizard. His only problem was trying to figure out how to do it. He absolutely had to talk to Pip about his training and his future, but he knew it had to wait a few more days. The princess came first, at least for the moment, but he had to figure out how to keep her and Pip away from each other. The problem was twofold: one being he didn't want Pip, even by accident, to tell the princess what he really was; two, he didn't want the princess to find out about him, which Laura was making increasingly difficult to do. It seems every couple of minutes, she was 'checking up' on him, turning up almost as often as the knights. This made Pip feel that much more pressure not to do anything he shouldn't, which in turn gave the dragon fits, and made Pip more jumpy. Tarsus thought he'd be pulling his hair out if he had any.

Tarsus couldn't tell the princess, or anyone else for that matter, about Pip, quite yet; the main reason was because of the lie he'd already told. He didn't know how she'd react to Pip indeed being a wizard, since he already told her he wasn't. His second biggest mistake. He didn't know how to break the news without being sent to the equivalent of a dragon dungeon or dragon execution, or even worse, banishment from the castle, which would leave Pip to fend for himself, which in the end would be an execution. Since he had magically promised Pip that this would never happen, this meant banishment breaking the magic, therefore killing not only himself—for breaking the enchantment—but Pip as well for breaking it. Tarsus knew the rock he was hiding behind wasn't big enough for himself and his self-inflated ego.

Tarsus didn't think circumstances could get any worse. His life had become a scene in a court jester's tale. Shaking his head, thinking how wrong that was, he ambled into the stables. Laura was probably around someplace she usually was. He knew he had to begin her training again. It wasn't necessary to bellow for her like he would for Pip. Not only would it be unseemly to 'call' a princess, it may bring on the 'wrath of Laura' as the servants called it. And that was one reason he was in the predicament he was in. She was a princess after all, and she made sure everyone knew it. Tarsus shook his head, chuckling, spoiled children being the same no matter their species. He couldn't have one of the servants go 'fetch' her either, no one would. They were too frightened of him to come near enough to give the order. It seemed there wasn't too many who weren't afraid of him or her. So, there was only one thing for it, to look himself. Sighing, he stuck his head into one of the stalls . . . nope . . . another . . . nope . . . another, behind him while his head was in the fourth . . .

"Tarsus? May I have a moment?"

Tarsus jumped slightly, not hearing anyone approach. He swung around as fast as his great girth allowed in such tight quarters, ready to fry whoever it was, and found Lionel behind him. Tarsus gulped down the flame in his mouth. A smell of smoke escaped from his clinched teeth. "Sire!" he exclaimed. He berated himself, his head definitely not in the game, or anywhere near the field for that matter.

Lionel looked at the dragon calmly. "Something wrong?" he asked innocently. "You jumped like I poked you with a sword."

Tarsus scowled at the monarch, ignoring the comment. Turning completely around to face Lionel, Tarsus looked at the man, studying him from head to foot. He wasn't dressed in royal robes, but plain brown jerkin and soft suede boots that came to mid-calf. And he was alone. Tarsus was wrong, it just got worse. How much so he didn't yet know.

Tarsus sat down and huffed. To buy some time to think, he said, "Your Majesty, you've got to stop sneaking up on me."

Lionel grinned at him. "Haven't we had this conversation?"

"Yes, we have. My tongue is burned from my flame." He stuck out his tongue to show him.

"Good thing it wasn't mine," Lionel said, still smiling.

Tarsus sighed, "Yes, Sire." He let that pass. Then he snaked his head above the king and looked behind him, and then looking back to Lionel, he cocked his head without saying anything.

"Yes," said Lionel, nodding, understanding the dragon's actions. "My guards are here, just outside. I told them not to come in unless I called. They didn't like the idea of me being alone with you, but I have some pull around here."

"Yes, I suppose you would, Your Majesty," said Tarsus, dipping his head, smiling himself. "And if I were them, I wouldn't let you alone with a dragon either. I bet Sir Dwayne is having a stroke."

Lionel let out a long sigh. "I didn't give him the chance to do anything. I sent him away to get him out of the castle grounds so I could talk with you."

Tarsus grunted. He knew better than to laugh, but it took an effort. If the king had to manipulate his own vassals, he knew it must be important. "Thank you for your trust, sire. So what may I do for you?"

Before he started, Lionel looked around the stables, his eyes seeming to soak in his surroundings. He hadn't been here in quite some time. The last being the day Tarsus came to the castle, that the first time in years. Duties as king kept him from doing the things he'd loved when he was younger. He took a deep breath and grinned. Tarsus noticed and smiled.

"You don't get out here much, do you, sire?"

"No," said Lionel looking up at Tarsus. "Not nearly as much as I'd like. In my youth, this was my second home. I loved, and still do, the smell of the stables and horses. It seemed I couldn't do any wrong here. Plus, it kept me from being underfoot."

"Underfoot, sire?"

Lionel smiled again, seeing memories of long ago. "Oh yes, I was definitely underfoot." Grinned the Monarch. "Seemed my father thought I could get into more trouble by being in his way and then in the knight's. He made sure I was out of sight so he could run the kingdom without my interference." He sighed and took another deep breath. "But, those days are long gone. I can't think of them without some regret, and remorse, for those who are no longer with us." Then he took another deep breath, and Tarsus realized he was about to say why he was there.

"Tarsus? Why must you always antagonize Sir Dwayne?'

Tarsus looked at Lionel and sighed himself. He'd gone through this more than once. But, upon looking at Lionel, he saw something deeper than mere wondering and decided flippancy wasn't the way to go. He had to be very careful not to alienate the only person he felt he could truly trust. "Sire, I believe I've already answered that question."

"Yes, you have," said Lionel nodding. "But, you really didn't explain much. Just getting on somebody's nerves doesn't explain why you go out of your way to upset him. Or him you. I don't understand, Tarsus, why you do it."

Tarsus was in a pickle. He couldn't outright lie to him. He'd done enough of that already. From the moment of their first meeting, Tarsus knew Lionel to be an honorable and honest man. He wouldn't be prone to violence, or hastily assume anyone or anything else was either, plus he greatly respected him. Sir Dwayne, however, was altogether different. With their first meeting, it was a totally expected military response. He was honorable, yes. Honest, somewhat. Loyal, fiercely. Trustworthy, maybe. Capable, absolutely. Rigidly strict in his methods, without question. And that was the problem. Tarsus could understand everything the knight did at the castle gates. He could anticipate it, but the incident with Pip two days ago told him all he needed to know about Sir Dwayne. He had to be in control: his way or nothing. The trouble he found was he couldn't control a dragon. So, he did the next best thing: he took control of a boy the dragon cared for, who couldn't do anything about it. At least for now.

Watching Lionel, Tarsus decided it may be time to start telling the truth, at least part of it. He sighed again and brought his head closer to the ground, making it easier for Lionel to see his eyes and maybe see his sincerity when he said, "I'll try to explain, sire, but you may not like what you hear."

"Let me be the judge of that, Tarsus. Whatever you say to me will be in confidence, and I'd greatly appreciate the answer."

Tarsus nodded. "Very well, sire. I see in Sir Dwayne the same thing I saw in Granston so many centuries ago."

"Granston?" Lionel said, shocked. "But don't you want to kill Granston?"

"Yes, sire."

"Does this mean you want to kill Sir Dwayne?"

"No, sire."

"Then what? What do you mean?" Lionel said, excitedly. He was becoming quite agitated with Tarsus not coming to the point.

Tarsus took a deep breath, knowing this wasn't going to be easy. "Sire, Granston, in those long ago days, was a different person. He was honorable, to some extent honest in how he treated people, but power corrupted him. Not only wizardry power but also the power to manipulate men, and with that power, he felt there was more he could accomplish. Arrogance and pride taught him he was immune to the effects of such rigid strictures. Or at least that was what he thought. He used that arrogance and confidence to further his goals. Many years went by before I realized exactly what he wanted and how he meant to achieve them. By the time I went to do something about it, it was too late. That is how I ended up here. Sir Dwayne . . ." Tarsus stopped a moment to get his thoughts in order.

"Yes, go on," said Lionel impatiently.

"Your Majesty, Sir Dwayne has the power to command, somewhat like yourself, but he sees it as the power of authority. There's a difference, as you know." Lionel nodded. "Authority breads intimidation. If one is not intimidated by his authority, such as myself, he sees it as a threat. That's why he's acted the way he has from the moment we met and why he did what he did to Pip. He sees me as a threat, and because of that threat, he took his anger out on an innocent lad. His threat came across loud and clear to me. That's why from this point on I'll not allow him to harm Pip or anyone else."

Lionel thought a moment before replying. Tarsus noted his face contorted into a grimace at some of the things being said, but in the end hadn't disputed them. Tarsus could smell the distaste coming from Lionel, but he was the one who wanted a truthful answer. "I guess I can understand that. I didn't want to believe it of one of my most trusted vassals, but I fear it's true," Lionel reluctantly admitted. "Authority does bread a form of intimidation in some people. But I also know he's very competent in his duties and fiercely loyal to myself and the kingdom." This is where the king stopped. He seemed to be trying to convince himself rather than Tarsus. "I also know he's the man for the job. There's no one who could possibly do it better. At least not at this moment."

"Yes, sire, I think you're right," the dragon agreed.

"You do?" Lionel was shocked.

Tarsus looked at Lionel with a smirk on his face. "Yes, sire, I do. Just because I think he's an ass and he can't intimidate me like he would anyone else, I don't doubt he's the right man for the captain of the guard. Because I don't particularly like him doesn't mean I don't know why you picked him for his post."

Lionel looked perplexed.

Tarsus went a little further, seeing Lionel struggle with his explanation. "Sire. Sir Dwayne is definitely a man of honor. I just don't like the methods he employs to carry out his duties. He needs to temper his actions with compassion and understanding, not barge in with fists full of swords yelling of trolls killing the common people. Pip did nothing to deserve what was done to him by Sir Dwayne." Tarsus grunted, a small puff of smoke drifting up from his nostrils at the memory. "I believe you saw this." Lionel nodded but said nothing. "That's another reason he feels threatened by me. Being in the position he's in, he feels he should know everything about what's happening around him, which is true to an extent, but one can't know everything. Just because he doesn't know, doesn't give him intimidation rights to make someone talk. I think you'd agree with me, different circumstances call for different methods. As far as I can tell, he has only one: speed, and rushing in will someday get him roasted in his armor." Tarsus smiled his toothy smile, which made Lionel shudder.

Lionel said, "That's much the same thing he told me about yourself before I sent him out on patrol. He feels the same about you. He doesn't trust you. He thinks the only reason you brought Laura back was to get inside the castle. And because you don't tell the whole truth," this is where Lionel looked at Tarsus askance,—"he thinks you're hiding your true intentions. Therefore, he can't do his duty of protecting myself and the princess to the full extent of his abilities."

Tarsus snorted.

Lionel scowled. "He has a point you know. You haven't been very forthcoming with us since you arrived. My patience has been taxed to the extreme with the both of you."

Tarsus cocked his head and dipped it slightly, faintly acknowledging what Lionel said. "Yes, sire. But if I told you all I know, or think I know, I'd not have time for anything else. I've lived for many centuries, and probably will for many more. In that time, I've gained much knowledge and experience. If we're talking about not being forthcoming, Sir Dwayne didn't happen to mention our little talk, did he?"

"Yes, he mentioned something," the king said. "But he didn't go into any detail. He hinted of you trying to interfere with his method of fighting and his knight's skill with the sword."

Tarsus snorted again, this time letting flame leak out his nostrils. "Before I say anything about that, I'll ask you a question. Did he say anything about our little wager?"

"Wager? What wager?" Lionel looked shocked. "What was it about?"

"Princess Laura and Sir Hook's fight in the training yard."

"What about it?" asked Lionel suspiciously.

"I made a wager with him that if she could beat Sir Hook in a fight, he'd have to listen to what I said about his training tactics. That's what our talk was about. If she lost the fight, I'd leave the castle and never return." Tarsus had an evil grin on his face, dragon feasting in the goat-yard look. "He's yet to honor our bet."

"That wasn't told to me," said Lionel.

"Before there's an accusation of secrets, he should look in a mirror. That's just one example I could name, sire." Tarsus looked at Lionel and smiled. It wasn't a very nice smile. "Everyone has secrets, or things they don't want to come to light. Everyone. Even you I suspect." He cocked his head, not expecting an answer. "I'm no different. The difference between him and I is that I don't care about those things. They're in the past and long gone, or most of them. What matters is the here and now!"

There was silence between them as they both considered what had been said. Then Lionel said, nodding, "I guess I can put that to rest, but there's still the matter of both of you trying to get along. I still don't want either of you to be injured because of distrust. I trust and respect both of you."

"Thank you, sire," said Tarsus, bobbing his head in a small bow. Then he came to a decision which in the long run came and bit him in the butt. He said, "I can't guarantee we'll get along in the future, sire, but I won't be the one to start anything between us."

"I guess that's all I can hope for," answered Lionel, edging towards the stable doors.

"But . . ."

"But, what?" Lionel said, looking back.

"But, sire, I also won't allow Sir Dwayne to harm Pip again. That you have my solemn vow on."

With those words, a small tingle traveled up and down Lionel's arms. It was as if a goose walked on his grave. He shivered, but said nothing, leaving Tarsus to his own thoughts.

*   *   *

CHAPTER 10

Granston was dressed as a peasant and wasn't happy about it.

He knew he couldn't just roam around the country like nothing was wrong. There were too many people in the kingdom who knew who he was and what he did or used to do. He'd get to his kinsmen in the Gnomish Mountain Range, and to do that, he needed supplies and a mount. It was a long and tedious journey, so the first thing he had to do was find supplies and a horse, because he sure as the two hells wasn't going to walk carrying his belongings on his back like a pack mule. He couldn't 'flash' himself to where he wanted to go either. It was a trick he used to get out of the castle and away from that blasted dragon, but the trick didn't work as well as it should, if a wizard didn't set it up to do what he wanted. Not only was it draining and dangerous, it had to be practiced so the wizard doing it didn't wind up popping into a tree, or at the bottom of the ocean, or in solid rock. The wizard first had to know the area as well as they knew their own living space to hit the spot aiming for when they 'flashed'. It took many years and many tries to do it right and not get killed in the process. Start small and end big, many years down the line, trial and error. The next thing: get to the mountains and see his kinsmen. So the disguise was necessary and distasteful.

A short distance from his mountain retreat, he came upon a small village nestled in a wooded valley. Not much to see but pine trees and a few spruce, and of course, the village. The name of the village was unimportant. He needed only supplies and a mount. Running through the village proper, he found shops on both sides of the dirt track of the village. Surprising, nodding to himself, he knew he'd come back, but first, he had to see about a horse. The village wasn't very large. There was a central road or track running between the buildings, but for lack of anything else, it seemed at first glance to have everything he'd need for his journey. At the end of what had to be the main road in or out was a livery stable, a rickety building which looked as if a stiff mountain breeze could blow it down. A three rail fenced in area about twenty feet across was just to the side, presumably for horses, but there were no horses present. Posted on a board just outside two swinging doors was a sign that read 'Web's Horses'. Granston walked in, but no one was about.

The place may have looked rickety and worn down, but inside looked like any stable area he'd ever seen: two rows of stalls, one on each side of the other. At the end of the stalls, there was a small room, presumably for tack and feed. The place smelled of hay, dung, old sweaty leather, rotting wood, old wet hounds, and hundreds of others he couldn't or didn't want to identify. Granston called out, "Anyone here?"

There was a noise to his left, and out of one of the stalls came a very portly man dressed in farriers bib-alls and nothing else. His hair was tangled and shooting out in all directions, with a mustache and beard that looked as if crows could nest in it. Granston felt sick at the sight of him. He had rags tied to his feet, to keep them out of the muck in the stall, and his demeanor was one of indifference. He looked as if he hadn't bathed in a month and smelled as if he hadn't bathed in a year.

As much as Granston was eyeing this fellow, he was doing the same thing to him. The man took a step closer, and Granston took a step back.

"Are you the owner of this place?" asked Granston, wrinkling his nose, wanting to hold closed his nostrils because of the smell.

The man merely nodded, his mouth opening slightly to show missing, rotting teeth.

"I need horses and supplies. Do you have anything?" demanded the Gnome.

The bibbed man looked at Granston for a moment before speaking. After a short pause, he said in a gruff voice, "Yep."

Granston waited for him to say something else, or do something, but all he did was look back strangely.

"Where?" Granston asked looking around. The sign outside may have advertised horses, but there was no evidence of them—the stalls he was close to, which he could peer into were all empty.

"In back," the man said, nodding his head over his shoulder, still not moving.

"Show me,." Granston barked irritably. He wanted this over with.

For a moment, the man didn't move, merely staring at Granston, or through him, and then he slowly turned and headed down the aisle. Past the last stall on the left, there was a door. He pushed it open. It led to the back of the stables. Outside there were two horses: one a speckled roan, the other a mare that wasn't good enough for dog food, having been ridden hard and put away wet too many times. Even Granston, who hadn't had too much experience with horse flesh, could tell the horse was on its last legs. It's belly was hanging low, and it appeared the weight at any moment could make it collapse to the ground. Its withers were almost bald from apparent whippings the owner had inflicted, its hooves caked with mud and cracked from lack of nutrition. The roan wasn't in such bad shape, however, but still not in the best shape or the best possible he could have wanted; it would do in a pinch. Its coat was dusky and matted from not seeing a curry comb in a while, and its mane was a lackluster shade of black, but it appeared to be in better shape physically than the other.

Granston walked to the roan and held out his hand. The horse merely looked at the offered digits with disinterest. Then he sniffed, snorted, and finally looked away. This was the one. With a little help from his magic and a decent combing, he'd make this animal far better than he was now. He desperately needed the beast for his journey.

"How much?" Granston demanded.

The grubby man watched the exchange between horse and perspective rider without saying anything, but now that he had a potential buyer, his demeanor changed. Granston saw it, recognized it for what it was: greed. For a moment, he said nothing, and then he quoted a price:

"Three crowns."

"One half crown," countered Granston.

"Two crowns," the man re-countered.

"Half crown three."

"One crown five."

"One crown with saddle and bridle," Granston said, becoming perturbed at the man. He knew from the way the man was looking at the horse, he hadn't had an offer in quite a while, if ever. Throughout the haggling, the grubby fellow had been looking Granston over trying to gauge his money situation. Granston had done the same thing many times to others. Although he didn't look much cleaner himself, dressed as he was, he knew the fellow would eventually sell. It was getting to the price each would agree on making them both impatient.

"One crown nine with all," the man countered again, eyes going flat, chin sticking out.

"One crown three," Granston said, not being intimidated. *This grubby little man will be lucky if I don't turn him into a toad for my trouble here.* This was becoming a barter session which Granston couldn't afford to lose. He could have done better somewhere else, but he didn't have the time to walk another two or three leagues to the next village. That's assuming it had a stable and horses for sell.

"One crown five." The man put his fists on his hips, squinting at Granston, that being his final offer.

Granston thought a moment and then nodded. *Seems I better take it.* He sighed.

The man smiled with a mouth full of crooked, missing teeth and held out his hand. Deal done.

After leaving, Granston headed straight to the next building over, a clothing store. The only sign of anyone was a light shining in the dirty front window. When he went inside, a small tinkle accompanied as the door opened. A small bell attached by a string to the door frame tinkled when the door opened announcing anyone walking in. When he shut the door, the first thing he noticed was a used pickle barrel overflowing with clothes right in front of him. Then he saw there were actually quite a few of the barrels in the small shop, plenty of clothes to pick from.

When his eyes adjusted to the poor light, he turned to a small desk set just off to the right of the door. A small portly woman of perhaps forty was looking at him. "What can I do for you?" she said not looking up from an assortment of leggings she was going through.

"I need extra clothing for a long journey ahead of me,." Granston answered.

The woman looked up and on her face was the same as the stableman's: greed. The transaction didn't take long. Apparently, the village didn't get very many customers. Granston could see why: the shabby run-down hamlet was a hole in the valley of the mountain with almost nothing to offer. But, he had to make do. Before he walked out with the bundle of extra clothes, he asked, "Where do I find a place to get supplies? I need at least a month's worth."

The woman looked at Granston, eyeing his money pouch more than his eyes. After a moment, she said with a grin, "As it happens, I can help you there too. The shop across the way is owned by me. I can't fill a month's worth, but you can get as much as I can spare."

"Very well." Granston had no choice. He'd need as much as he could get.

This was getting ridiculous and tiring. He could easily take what he wanted and not haggle or pay for any of the things. He knew this, but coming in with lightning bolts and blazing fireballs and killing the locals would announce his whereabouts. The lizard would surely have been on his trail then. So, as much as he hated it, he was forced to deal with these shop-owners. It didn't sit well with him at all. *When this is over, I may have to return and level this dump. The mountain gods would probably approve.*

After spending over two hours getting what he needed, more time in the town than he wanted by far, he rode out on the roan. Avarice was the only consistent sin permeating this slimy village, the stink alone enough to make it unforgettable. He was more than willing to leave. What the woman could spare wasn't enough to get him to the Gnome Mountain Range. It was only enough to last a week. He could either hit another town or village to resupply or steal what he needed.

Either way, a means to an end.

Two days after leaving the no-name village, he got his chance to make good on his plan to steal what he needed. More than a few of the hovels lining the way, which one couldn't really call towns, didn't have, or wouldn't part with any of their supplies, no matter how much money he offered. Most of the people in that part of the kingdom were farmers or merchants who traded for food or goods needed, and on a day which had been particularly bleak and rain soaked, he'd had a run-in with a farmer who thought he was stealing supplies from one of his storage rooms, which he had been. He barely got away without losing a piece of his arm to an axe. Afterwards, when the dust settled, anger had been the cause of the farmer's demise. Lizard or no lizard, he wasn't going to be chopped to pieces by a commoner. When Granston finished, there wasn't much to bury, gobbets of flesh scattered over the storeroom. Buffoon should have known better to bring a blade to a wizard dual.

The traveling was wearing on Granston's nerves: tedious and tiring. The one thing he wanted more than anything was a nice warm fire and a dry place to rest. Anywhere was preferable to the ground to sleep on and a fire in the open where the wind whipped the smoke in his face. The weather was turning bad fast for this time in the season. Granston realized he was getting closer to the mountains which he'd called home for so many years. He also realized after a miserable three days trudging in the rain, why he'd escaped.

As he traveled, his thoughts spiraled in and out of focus to the years in which he'd lived with his family. The years in which he had nothing, wishing for everything. In some ways, they prepared him for what was coming in his later years. In some ways, they were nothing like what finally transpired. Living in a small one-room cave for so many of his younger years taught him a lot about wanting what you couldn't have. His father slaved his whole life working in the mountain mines, for a small portion of freedom for himself and his family. In the end, all it got him was a shortened life. Cave-ins were a natural part of mining, but cave-ins that are deliberate to prove a point to the one's holding the purse strings are quite another. Split factions of a clan can be more devastating than any cave-in. Doing the right thing was apparently not always the right thing to do. His father proved that with his dying. His mother proved that when she forced him and his siblings to move into another one-room cave owned by the one's holding her purse strings. Leverage on a mountain scale. And when the time came for him to make something of himself, he found he could only do one thing: mine. And it wasn't as easy to not get trapped in the same position as his father. He'd been so naive. The purse strings went too deep. He couldn't compete with the ones at the top of the money pile. So he did the only thing he could at the time to get away from it all: he ran, which nearly killed him. But it also put him in the most unlikely position to run into a mangy old man who saved his life and taught him what he was.

No . . . not what he was, but who he was: a wizard, a wizard with great power. The kind of power that can make a difference. After years of learning to control his powers and train under the tutelage of the old wizard—he couldn't remember his name after so many centuries—he knew what had to be done. He went back to the mountain, his home, and schooled the 'money makers' in life and campaigned his people to name him leader. It was a tragic mistake. In his enthusiasm at winning

143

over 'the powers that be', he'd forgotten the Gnome empire was a kingdom. Grundehl didn't appreciate the fact that another Gnome was trying to usurp him. The king couldn't simply throw away a power like his arbitrarily, so instead commanded him to aid in the Troll war. For centuries, Trolls and Gnomes had been fighting over one silly thing or another, and Grundehl commanded him to apprentice with the Great Shimmer, master magician of the Gnomes, a doddering old fool who was on his last legs. Parlor tricks were the most he could do without aid. Through betrayal and the death of Shimmer at his own hands, and fancy footwork with the Staff, he became known as Granston the Wiley, hero of the war.

Fools! Afterward, Grundehl was so impressed with his power and mastery, he awarded the Staff of Talsoun to be kept by him for safe keeping, the only truly magical object he possessed. But the flaw it carried was enough to make Granston scream with frustration.

Granston remembered all of this and more and cringed at the thoughts, for he'd been ultimately banished from his home, all because of one little flaw of his own: Tarsus. A flaw that was his undoing. A simple thing really, so simple it took him by surprise. He learned to trust a being with the same mindset as himself: kill all in your way and let the gods sort them out. But his flaw turned out to be not only false, but a thorn in his side, a deadly magical thorn that could kill with a breath and call an army of his kind with a roar of his mighty lungs. And that had nearly been his undoing too. From one instance to the other for many generations of the frail humans, Tarsus had been an open weeping wound in his side that wouldn't close and heal. Until he'd finally—he thought—taken care of the lizard. But in that, also, there had been a flaw, an obscure flaw in his magic. Twice in one lifetime was enough to be humiliated by any animal; this time he was going to make sure it didn't happen again. His allies of long ago and his kinsmen were his last chance at redemption, and he wasn't going to fail again. No matter what it took or what the consequences, this would be the end for that blasted lizard.

*   *   *

The closer Granston got to the Gnome Mountain Range, the more he felt the cold. In the higher elevations, the cold seeped into one's bones, slowly but assuredly gnawing at one's very marrow until you thought you might scream to be released. Twenty feet of snow was not uncommon for this region of the mountains, and every year, lowlanders who wandered up got lost, hunting for big game, found the next spring frozen to death. Death was a way of life here; one wrong turn or step could mean your life, the mountains unforgiving. Being frozen to death was common among the valley people who inhabited the many villages surrounding the mountain range, but every year, their transgressions, and deaths, were blamed on wild men. Gnomes hadn't been seen in the world for centuries. Their deeds had become legends, stories townsfolk told at night around a cook stove. What had come out of the mountains to explain the many deaths were tales of wild hairy men living on the slopes of the frozen mountains, superstitious nonsense—it was Gnomes, of course—to perpetuate the wild man legends, rumours, which kept the locals away from areas of the mountains the Gnomes didn't want known. But every once in a while, maybe twice a season, mountain folks went missing, and every year, search parties were sent out to find them and inevitably the search parties never made it back either. Gnome representatives were dispatched to make sure of it. Gnome representatives? There was a joke if ever spoken: part of the Gnome army was sent out to make sure no one made it back. What Grundehl really wanted to do was kill everyone in the valleys to protect what was his. He'd meant to do just that centuries before, but he also knew if he did, he'd be in another conflict with kingdoms with more resources and more warriors than him. He couldn't afford the trouble or the loss of any more Gnomes.

The highest point of the mountain range was well over 13,000 feet, and where he had to go was pretty close to the summit. A cave obscured by outcrops of rock was the only marker to finding his way to his people, and if you didn't know how to find it, you could wander in the mountains your whole life, lost and disoriented. The Gnome people had too many enemies, so after the troll war, Grundehl decided it best to hide away from society and rebuild his kingdom. Unwanted intruders caused too many problems. So he isolated himself and his subjects from the rest of the world.

*　　*　　*

After traveling nearly a month, being wet, miserable, going through wilderness, sand, mud, accosted by commoners, enduring extreme weather conditions, and putting up with a saddle literally chafing his backside, Granston sighted the Great Gnome Mountain Range. A sight he hadn't seen in centuries. If he was lucky, when he finally got to the cave mouth, no more than a week away, he'd convince the Gnomes to help him. Hopefully, Grundehl will have been killed by a rival, and he wouldn't have to put up with that fat slob to do it. Convincing his people to join his cause would be hard enough without having to go through Grundehl.

Going farther than he intended in the night, Granston finally stopped to set up camp, a mere five miles from the cave mouth. He needed to fix something to eat, which would give him time to think about what he'd say to his kinsmen the next morning. When he ran, he didn't exactly leave on good terms. Convincing them to help him wouldn't be easy. But he hadn't planned on playing fair either, maybe mind control or intimidation or just plain threats, he didn't know. He was strong enough by himself to do considerable damage to the king of the Gnomes and his people. He'd need some time to think about the best way to go about it. He didn't get very long though, only a few short moments after he'd started a fire, a gruff voice floated out of the dark, "I see you've come back."

Granston looked in the direction of the voice and saw no one. He wasn't really surprised. The fire he'd built wasn't very big, and the light only reached a few feet away. After a few moments, he said, "I didn't have much choice."

A figure slowly stepped out of the dark, as if materialising out of thin air, the light illuminating a hulking figure nearly seven feet tall. "Everyone has choice," he rumbled with a deep gravelly voice.

As the hulking figure came closer, Granston recognized him, although he hadn't seen the giant in over a century. The wizard noted that he hadn't changed much, his shaggy hair a little thinner, his paunch of a belly hanging farther out maybe, but all in all, the same as when he'd left.

"Hello, Raulch. You haven't changed much over the years. You're still the biggest Gnome I've ever seen."

"You, Granston, are not so much as you used to be. From talk by others, you the biggest Gnome around. I guess people don't get out much, aye?" the giant Raulch guffawed.

"Gnomes don't, you mean," said Granston wearily. Raulch was a dangerous fellow. Granston had to be careful. He knew although the giant may sound slow-witted, he was anything but. "Grundehl wanted it like that." He took a few steps away from the fire, giving himself room to maneuver. "What are you doing so far from the cave? I thought I'd have a while before I had to show myself. You're a little far out, aren't you?." The galoot still hasn't learned to talk right, even after all the centuries. Interesting.

"Na," said the hulking Gnome. "We been going out more. Two or three leagues isn't bad. Too many strangers in past couple years." Raulch looked over the shallow fire pit at Granston's belongings and then without a care, took a few steps towards the other end of the fire, halving the distance between them. "You alone?" he asked, making a show of looking for a possible companion. "That not like you. You usually have couple lackeys.' "From his great height, he looked down his massive nose at Granston. "And a lot more stuff." The monster looked at Granston's meager bundle of supplies, kicking over his bedroll and saddlebags. "You get thrown out of your place?"

"Something like that," answered Granston, putting a smile on and stepping a few more paces away from the giant.

Raulch smiled back with a toothy grin of his own and then began to laugh. It was a booming guffaw laugh, and it wasn't from mirth. With a shrug of his massive shoulders, he turned, stepping out of the camp light. His voice came wafting back to Granston out of the gloom, "We'll be here in the morning for you. Grundehl will want to talk. He has lots to say."

"I bet," Granston said in a faint voice, listening as Raulch's steps faded away. He watched for a few moments before taking a deep breath. He hadn't realized he'd been holding his breath.

Damn!

*   *   *

CHAPTER 11

After his talk with Lionel, Tarsus got back to work with the princess. He had to teach her how to control her movements with the sword. Oh, she knew how to swing one, but finesse wasn't one of her strong suits. To be able to beat any opponent that came her way, she had to learn the fine points of fencing. Although fencing and swordplay wasn't necessarily the same thing, the finer points of one was used in the other, and her use of the one could be measured by the use of the other. So, what he had to do was get her to develop her skills in fencing so she could apply them to her techniques of swordsmanship. And it wasn't going to be easy.

"Now," said Tarsus, "you need to pare, then thrust. Not thrust and hope for the best."

"I'm trying, Tarsus, but you're not telling me how to do it," complained the princess.

Tarsus had Laura dressed in a long shirt, soft leather britches, and knee-high leggings for greater movement. According to his theory, if she could move faster than her opponent, she would have a better chance of success. But he also knew he was going to have to do some more thinking on the protection aspect of the outfit. The more he saw her move, he realized the configuration was right, but the overall safety was wrong. He wanted her to have a greave like in the suit of armor she used in the contest with Hook, but in this instance, it would be too heavy and bulky. So Tarsus had Laura wrap a piece of dried leather around her left forearm, not only to protect her arm, but to redirect downstrokes of an opponent's weapon. It wouldn't stop a mace or a lance, but it would protect her from a rapier strike. It wasn't much, but for now, it would have to do.

This time around, Tarsus used Sir Edward as her fencing opponent. He was wire thin and fast as a snake. The perfect opponent for this type of exercise. When Tarsus first approached him, he was somewhat leery. He'd been in the court the day the princess confronted Sir Hook and wasn't too eager to go through the same thing. Tarsus could understand. But Tarsus assured him he was only interested in a short practice session to teach Laura the basics in fighting with a rapier instead of a heavy sword. He was still reluctant, but agreed, on one condition, of course: both Sir Dwayne and the princess release him of all responsibilities concerning any untoward mishaps. Tarsus talked it over with the princess and Sir Dwayne. After much argument on the knight's part and a commandment from the princess, the bargain was struck.

"I'm telling you how to do it. You just have to listen and watch Sir Edward and his movements," admonished Tarsus. "You must first learn the fundamentals of using the rapier. Swinging a sword is different. The finesse with fencing is more to the style of your framework and speed. Sir Edward, show her one more time. This time watch what he does, Laura, how he moves."

"Yes, Master Tarsus," said Sir Edward.

"OK, but I don't see the point," Laura said, sighing in frustration.

Sir Edward began again, this time slower, so the princess could see exactly what he was doing. His first position was the riposte, then the pare, and then the thrust. His feet were in motion as he moved from one position to the other, in a straight line.

As the knight went through the moves, Tarsus had a running commentary going. "See how he positions his feet? He at no time lets them get tangled together. Always apart, moving in a line, never shoulder-length apart. See his stance? His rapiers always in front, in a position to block or parry anything to come."

Laura nodded.

"Now, you do it," the dragon commanded. "This time, think of it as a dance. From what I understand, you've been to many dances or balls. Any princess worth her salt has been a diplomat, dancing her way to a husband."

Laura flinched. She'd been to many dances all right, but catching a husband wasn't the sole reason to go. Her father may have wanted her to catch the right man, but all she ever thought of them was as a welcome relief from the tedious grind of palace life.

A dance? Well, maybe. What kind? If she could picture herself in a gown, moving to the feel of music, maybe she could learn the steps. She walked towards Sir Edward lifting the rapier, putting herself directly in front of the knight. Looking down at her feet, positioning them as Tarsus said, mimicking Sir Edward, she lifted her rapier. Their blades came together in a small clink, and . . . within moments, the knight had his blade at her throat.

Laura moaned. Tarsus hung his head. A small chuckle came from Sir Dwayne a few yards away.

Tarsus whipped his head to the sound and found Sir Dwayne smiling at him, still chuckling faintly. "What do you find so funny, Knight," asked Tarsus, smoke billowing from his nostrils.

"You, dragon," answered the knight stepping closer. "Your prowess with a sword, I'll give, albeit reluctantly, but your teaching skills when it comes to finesse leave something to be desired."

Before this little squabble could escalate into something dangerous, Laura stepped between the two. "That's enough from both of you. I didn't come here today so you two could have a showdown."

"Yes, Your Highness," Sir Dwayne said, bowing. "I merely wish to make it plain to the dragon he needs to tailor his teaching to you, not to the style of fighting. Everybody learns at his," he bowed to her again, "or her own pace. And teaching a different form of fighting to one who's learned another isn't always the easiest thing to do. One doesn't necessarily go with the other."

"Yes, I understand that," said the princess. "You don't have to be so arrogant in your explanation. I merely wish to learn the style of fighting that's best for me. That's why, I presume, Tarsus," she emphasized his name, "is trying to teach me the rapier. Fighting with the rapier is different than a sword, yet some of it will undoubtedly play a part in the other."

"Yes, Your Highness, that's true, yet fighting with a rapier is different than swinging a sword. With your permission, I'll attempt to instruct you in that fact."

Tarsus cocked his head. "You, Knight?"

"Yes," said Sir Dwayne, smiling at the dragon. "Who do you think taught Sir Edward the art?'

Sir Edward bowed, acknowledging the truth of what he said.

Laura bowed also, impressed despite herself. For Tarsus, this was a revelation unto itself about the knight. He'd been impressed with Sir Dwayne from the moment of their first meeting. He just wasn't going to tell him. This was merely another part of Sir Dwayne.

The knight went to the princess and said, "I may not agree with what you're doing, and who's teaching you, but I don't wish you to fail, Your Highness. Not only duty, but honor compels me to help you succeed." He then whispered something into her ear for more than a minute. Then he stepped back and smiled encouragingly at her. The princess opened her mouth to say something, but the knight simply wagged his finger to stop her. He pointed to Sir Edward. She shrugged, took a deep breath, and took up the stance again.

Sir Edward also took his stance. When their blades touched, it began again. This time however, it took longer for Sir Edward to beat her. Sir Dwayne knew he would, but the contest wasn't as one-sided as before. The knight was noticeably winded and sweat beaded on his forehead. Sir Dwayne smiled.

After a few more whispered instructions by Sir Dwayne, the contest began yet again. The outcome was the same, yet it was apparent Sir Edward didn't have the upper hand in the match. This time, the princess made it plain she was a contender for even Sir Edward's skill.

The more Tarsus watched, even he couldn't doubt the skill level of the captain of the King's Guard. He was patient in his instructions to the princess and helped her develop her own style of fighting in a few short lessons.

After the third round, Tarsus called a halt for the day. He said to the princess, "Go clean up and get some rest, you'll need it for the next round of training." Laura looked as exhausted and sweaty as Sir Edward. "And get something to eat. It looks as if you could use it." She nodded, smiled, and then walked towards the castle. When he saw she was on her way, he turned his attention to Sir Dwayne. Watching him, he thought he may have figured out why he was so against him. If he were careful, he may be able to end the feud between them. As Sir Dwayne turned to follow the princess off the practice field, Tarsus called to him, "May I have a word, Sir Knight."

Sir Dwayne stopped and looked back. From the look on his face, it was apparent that he was deciding whether to talk to him. After a moment, he merely nodded his assent. Tarsus lumbered to him and said quietly, "May I talk to you this evening about the princess?"

The knight said nothing; he merely looked at him and then said, "If you like. I shall be in my quarters after supper."

"Thank you," said Tarsus. "I shall call when I'm ready. As you know, I can't fit inside the castle, but if you would, we can meet in the stable yard."

Sir Dwayne simply nodded and then continued into the castle, following his ward.

*   *   *

After lumbering his big bulk back to the stables, Tarsus sat in his stall waiting for Pip. He knew the boy wasn't very far away. He always showed himself when chores had to be done. While he waited, his thoughts turned to Granston. As he'd told Lionel, when he'd first met the little Gnome, he'd been a different person. It was a time in Tarsus's life he thought the world didn't have anything to teach him. He had no cares, although his mate and offspring were waiting for him. All this time later, he knew he'd been used; through his own arrogance and self-righteousness, he did what the little Gnome wanted without thinking of the consequences. That was only one of the reasons Tarsus was going to make him pay. But the act he couldn't forgive was the little wizard taking his family away. Tarsus had a lot to be ashamed of and even more to make up for, with Granston dead, out of the way for good, he could finally find some peace and put some of his conscience to rest. For his soul's sake he hoped so. But he also knew vengeance wasn't the same as justice.

While he was going over the many acts in which he had to atone for over his long life, Pip showed up. Apparently he didn't know Tarsus was in his stall, because when he opened the doors, he was pushing a cart with a pitchfork hanging over its edge. "Oh, hi," said Pip, dropping the cart, spilling the contents and the pitchfork.

"Sorry about that," apologized Tarsus. "I didn't mean to startle you."

Pip said, as he began picking up the mess, "That's all right. I'm kinda used to doing dumb things. I just didn't know you were here. I was going to get your stall done before you needed it again." As he picked up the pitchfork and put it back in the cart, he asked, "How's it going with the princess? I saw both of you in the practice field, looked to me like she was doing pretty good." His faced turned a shade of red when he mentioned the princess. Tarsus took it for embarrassment. If he didn't know any better, he'd think the boy was sweet on her.

"Oh, it's going OK. It was time for a break. That's why I'm back so early." For a moment, he watched as Pip continued his cleaning up. The he said, "Why don't you stop picking up that straw for a moment and sit down. I think we need to talk."

Pip stopped and looked at the dragon, but didn't say anything. *Oh boy, here it comes!* "Talk about what?" he finally asked, fidgeting.

Tarsus looked at the boy and smiled. "You know what. We have to talk about your training. And what happened to you?"

Pip didn't say anything at first, scuffing his feet in the straw and shuffling his feet back and forth, not knowing what to say. Tarsus didn't say anything either, just watched and waited, giving the lad time with his thoughts. Then, Pip slowly got out, "What can I say?" He looked at the dragon, unshed tears filling his eyes. "I don't know what to do or what to say. Even if I did, I don't know who to say it to. I don't know what I did wrong."

"You didn't do anything wrong, lad,.." Tarsus told him softly.

"No?" Pip burst out. "I must have. I was trussed up like a criminal and put on display because of what? A mistake? A prank? A tantrum from the princess? A remark from you? What did I do?"

Tarsus snorted and then swung his head to look out the stable door at the courtyard. His thoughts wandering to the first time he'd come upon this strange lad, staring at nothing in this selfsame stable. A lad with the light of a wizard in him, although no one but he could see it, entranced in what he was doing, not knowing what he was and not so long ago. And although the dragon had known what the light meant, and why it was shining, he didn't realize what kind of light it would be, until now. "All of those things, Pip. All of them led you there. I'm sorry."

Pip looked at Tarsus, tears forgotten, his face scrunching into a knot, his cheeks turning a dark red, his eyes blazing with fire. In a nutshell, he got mad. Very mad. Normally, Pip was a very mild young man, but his nerves were frayed almost to the breaking point, his patience seeming at an end.

"Sorry? You're sorry?" Pip almost barked at Tarsus. "What happened to me wasn't an accident. I'll tell you what happened. A dragon who has an attitude problem happened! A knight with a grudge against that dragon happened! That's what happened!"

Tarsus wasn't surprised by the outburst, he was expecting it, and although he was the object of Pip's rage, this was a good sign. If Pip didn't vent on someone, he'd implode from the pressure. Tarsus knew a wizard with a mad-on wasn't a safe person to be around. Magic did strange things to those who performed it. If not careful, a wizard can lose control and start killing anyone or anything in their path, the most dangerous kind, one who isn't in control. Pip shook with his emotions. As he did, Tarsus looked around the stall, seeing the pitchfork the boy had dropped floating some two feet off the floor.

That wasn't good. Tarsus had to do something quick or even he wouldn't be able to stop what was undoubtedly coming. If Pip got a lot of steam going, he'd conceivably tear the stables apart and not know he'd even done it. So Tarsus took the direct approach: meeting the new wizard with power of his own. With a great roar, Tarsus pitted his own power against Pip's. Before the echo of the roar faded, the dust settling from the rafters, Pip was stunned into silence and immobile with fear instead of anger.

For a moment, nothing else happened. "I'm sorry, Pip," Tarsus said in almost a whisper. "You've got to get a hold of yourself. You, being a wizard, can't get so angry. If you do, things happen, not in a good way. If you don't believe it, think of the first time you got angry at me." Cocking his head, he smiled ruefully.

Pip's eyes widened, realizing Tarsus was right.

Tarsus nodded. "Until you learn to control your powers, you'll have times like that. It happens to all wizards. You have to learn control. The one's who don't learn that basic rule go mad, not a very pleasant or pretty sight."

Pip hung his head, letting out a sigh. "Just another thing for me to worry about."

"No," said Tarsus. "Just be aware of it. I'll be here with you. I'll help you through everything."

"I didn't ask for this, Tarsus." Pip jerked his head up to stare at the dragon. "What if I choose not to be a wizard?"

It was Tarsus who hung his head when he said, "I wish it were that simple."

"What do you mean?"

Tarsus looked at Pip, at first saying nothing, but Pip encouraged him to go on. Reluctantly Tarsus said, "Remember, I said you had to get a hold of your emotions or . . ." (Pip gulped, nodded, not sure whether he wanted to hear what was coming) ". . . well, the same thing will happen if you try to ignore it."

"That's just great! You mean I'm stuck with this whether I want it or not?" Pip exploded again.

Tarsus nodded. "That's why it's important you learn to use the powers you have. If you don't, you could not only hurt yourself but also someone else. You have to learn to control it, as I think you just found out."

"Tarsus, I don't think I can do this. I don't know if I can handle it." Pip looked around the stall and went to one of the corners and slid to the floor. He put his head between his knees, and Tarsus could hear him taking deep breaths. In a muffled voice, he continued, "I guess, to tell the truth, I'm scared."

Tarsus merely waited, knowing Pip wasn't done.

Pip looked into Tarsus's face. "I'm afraid I'll be taken away again, but next time, I won't come back." Silent tears streamed down his face.

Tarsus nudged Pip's hair lightly with his nose and said quietly, "No, Pip, that won't happen. I won't let it. That's the promise I made to you, remember? We're in this together, come good or ill. I'll not let anything happen to you."

Pip touched Tarsus on the nose, tears silently rolling down his cheeks.

*   *   *

King Lionel paced his throne room. *What am I going to do about my knights? I need to get a handle on things, especially the trouble between Sir Dwayne and Tarsus, before they do something I'll regret.* He considered placing a guard around the dragon. *No, that wouldn't work. He'd just frighten whoever he'd send, intimidate him into leaving.* He considered having Dwayne reassigned from guard duty to the kingdom's diplomatic missions, but knowing Dwayne and Bilby, the chief negotiator for Musk, as Lionel did, both would probably have fits, Bilby for not being consulted. He had his own guards anyway, so he thought that wouldn't work either. Dwayne being the captain of the guard knew his duty too well, to be by his king's side; plus, it'd be an affront to his honor and pride, which would make things much worse. He tapped his hands behind his back, trying to mull the problem over, but no matter what he thought of, it just wasn't the right thing. *What to do? What to do?* With a sigh, he realized nothing he did would be the right thing, so he made a kingly decision to do the only thing: calling Sir Edward.

When Sir Edward arrived, the king could see the knight was nervous. He came before the throne and bowed respectfully and then waited for his king's command.

Lionel figured if he had to do something neither of them liked, he might as well make it official, and so he waited patiently on his throne while the knight bowed. Lionel sighed heavily, cleared his throat, and then began, for the good of the kingdom, of course, "Sir Knight."

"Yes, sire," said Edward, bowing again respectfully. "What may I do for you?"

"I'd like to talk to you about a delicate matter if I could?" Lionel said. "I think your insight might be just the thing needed." He leaned forward from his chair, as if it were going to be whispered.

The knight looked perplexed. "Sire?"

Lionel smiled pleasantly at Edward and said, "I'd like your help. I need to keep an eye on things around here, and I think the best one to do it is you."

"Sire?" The knight looked at Lionel uncomprehending.

"I know you must have a lot of questions, so don't be shy. Ask away," said Lionel, waving his hand in a 'go ahead' gesture. "I know I do. I just don't know who to ask."

Sir Edward couldn't say anything. He really know what his lord was getting at. "Sire," he finally asked, "have you discussed whatever it is with Sir Dwayne? He'd probably serve you better."

"Ah . . . well . . . yes . . ." Lionel stammered, leaning back in his throne. He tapped on its arm, then sighed heavily, and blurted without preamble, "That is the delicate matter I wished to discuss with you, Edward."

Sir Edward's eyes grew wide. "Sir Dwayne, sire?"

"Yes," Lionel said. "I need you to keep an eye open at all times. Things haven't being going quite so well around here, if you've noticed."

Now Edward knew what his king wanted, realization dawning on him. His king wanted him to spy on his own guards and report back to him. Sir Dwayne? He didn't know how the king could ask it of him.

"Well," asked the king, fidgeting himself, "will you help me?"

"Sire," stammered the knight. "I'll always help if I can, but I don't understand why you want me to do such a thing."

Lionel sighed again, got down from the throne, and walked to the knight. "I know this is hard to understand, but I've got to do something, even if it seems wrong. You saw what happened with Dwayne in the courtyard with the young stable boy and the outcome with Tarsus, didn't you?"

"Yes, sire," answered Sir Edward cautiously, wondering where this was leading. He always knew the captain had been a hothead, but he'd always been very competent in his position. And his mastery of the sword and fighting skill was unmatched in the castle. That's one of the things which made him so formidable in battle and the reason he was captain of the King's Knights.

"Then you know why someone has to watch over things, so something like that doesn't happen again," said Lionel, putting an affectionate hand on the knight's shoulder.

Sir Edward didn't know what to say, especially after the affection the king rarely showed to anyone. He'd never seen the king do anyone like that.

"Sire," Sir Edward said, bowing slightly, "if I can, I shall. But I wish it to be known that I'll not dishonor myself or Sir Dwayne. This feels like spying to me and I'm not equipped for such a thing. I've a duty to you, my kingdom, and myself. I'll uphold those to the best of my ability as long as I live, and as long as you allow me to, but I'll not do anything that will dishonor them."

"Yes, yes," said Lionel. "I completely understand, and I agree. I'd never ask you to do anything dishonorable. By no means. I simply wish for you to inform me if anything unusual seems to be happening, that Sir Dwayne feels may not have to be told to me. I know he wouldn't withhold anything that would endanger myself or the kingdom, but he'd probably keep things close to his chest until he felt it was necessary to say something. That sort of thing has been happening far too much around here lately.'

"Also," continued Lionel, "there's something very delicate I wish you to do for me. It's almost in the form of a private matter."

Sir Edward cocked his head quizzically.

The king took another long breath and jumped right in by saying, "If you could, would you look in on Laura and Tarsus."

"Sire?" Now this was getting ridiculous, as far as the knight was concerned.

Lionel looked almost abashed. "I don't want you to think I don't trust Tarsus. I do. Very much so. But I don't know how much I can trust him with my daughter."

This time Sir Edward was completely confused. What he just said didn't make any sense. How could he trust the dragon, yet not trust him at the same time? "Sire, I'm not sure I understand. You can't have it both ways. You either do or don't trust the dragon? Wouldn't this come in the purview of Sir Dwayne as your sworn protector?"

Lionel took his time to answer, slowly weighing what he'd say. Finally, he told the knight what he was really concerned about. "Yes, Sir Dwayne's responsibilities do encompass the princess, but, the way things are, the way things stand between himself and Tarsus, I believe he shouldn't go near the dragon for a while if at all possible. And if he does, the way things are, you see, he may do something we both regret. So . . ."

"I understand, sire," said the knight, smiling, nodding, and holding up his hand, stopping Lionel from finishing. "I believe I understand completely."

Sir Edward thought a moment on what he'd seen himself in the past few days and had to agree with the king. It seemed Sir Dwayne had been keeping things to himself, either about Tarsus or the princess, the knight felt should have been brought to the king's attention. But it hadn't been Edward's place to say, it had been the captain of the King's Knight's to do it. When confronted by these observations, Edward had been ordered by Dwayne to keep his mouth shut and to mind his own station. Sir Dwayne had kept his own counsel, and from what the knight had seen, it hadn't done very well by him. But confronted as Edward was, by his king, there was only one thing to do.

Sir Edward made a decision. "Yes, sire, I agree. I shall watch, wait, and inform you if something were to happen."

King Lionel breathed a sigh of relief. "Thank you. I appreciate it. I was hoping I could count on you."

"You may always count on me, sire," said Sir Edward, bowing.

"Yes, thank you."

*　　*　　*

CHAPTER 12

Raulch showed up the next morning at Granston's small camp, true to his word, but he wasn't alone. He and three other Gnomes had come to escort him to Grundehl. Granston didn't know whether to be flattered or outraged: Grundehl apparently didn't think Raulch would be enough. Granston smiled at the thought of how nervous he must make the fat king. Raulch, of course, he'd known for centuries, but the others he couldn't place. They stopped just outside the ring of his fire and weren't in a talkative mood; by the looks of them, they were in more of a kill-the-traitor-who-came-back mood. The one closest to Raulch, a big, stocky Gnome who looked like he could chew nails, looked at Granston like he was a nail in a wall and was deciding whether to pluck it out and eat it. As the Gnome came nearer, he grinned a vicious grin, but said nothing.

The others looked no better. Each looked like they hadn't seen a razor or a bath in more than a month. They were hired thugs, nothing more, which wasn't surprising. Grundehl tended to surround himself with hired thugs, not the brightest of thugs either. Raulch was one of the few exceptions; he looked the part of a hulking thug, but in actuality was one of Grundehl's relatives, a lackey, not much of a distinction if you were to ask Granston, but no one had ever asked.

One Gnome, who'd been standing closest to Raulch when they walked out of the woods, slowly sauntered through the small camp as if he were on a Sunday brunch, checked in every nook and cranny, including Granston's bedroll and packs on the ground beside his horse. He made the wizard very nervous, his eyes showing he cared for only one thing: trouble. There were few beings who could shake Granston's confidence, but this one had the look of a fighter about him; muscles rippled and shifted everywhere as he walked, which told the Gnome wizard he could be more trouble than the rest. He wasn't very tall for a Gnome, but his bulk made up for his height, being as wide as an old tough oak tree. Granston watched him warily.

The other one, surprisingly, was a woman and not a Gnome. As she slowly walked towards him, he could see a very distinctive mark on her forearm, one which screamed more than words what she was: Assanti. For one of her race, she was slender of hip and lithe in form; most of her tribe tended to be of the opposite order, big-boned, mighty as a tree stump. Her black hair was very short, a style reserved almost exclusively for men; her jerkin was plain dark black with no adornments, allowing her arms free range of motion; her breeches were the same as her jerkin, plain black with no adornments; her footwear, the most odd of all, consisted of a lone piece of tough dried leather on her soles, strips of thong tied around her shins holding them on her feet. At first glance, she looked barefoot. Very unusual, but elegant when put together with the rest of her outfit. But he had to admit, this was the first of her race he'd seen who was a woman. She, like every one of her race, was bred to be one thing: an Assassin. By all accounts, very good ones. To be in the guild, you had to be. He knew he'd have to be very careful if the Assanti were involved with Grundehl. There was something definitely going on about which he needed more information. Granston narrowed his eyes watching her approach, there being only one reason for her to play escort like Raulch and his thugs.

"I'm flattered you thought you needed help to bring me in, Raulch, but, if you remember, I came here on my own," said Granston, slowly looking each up and down, trying not to react to what they were doing: surround and contain.

Raulch looked at his companions and then at Granston and gave an evil smile.

"What do you think is going to happen?" Granston asked.

"Oh, me know what's gonna happen, Gran. You gonna go in front of Grundehl, and he's gonna let me string you between two poles." Raulch laughed raucously.

Granston merely smiled. "We'll see. He may have something else to say about that." He turned to Raulch's companion nearest him and asked, "And what is it you'll get out of this?"

The Gnome didn't say anything; he merely stared.

Granston looked at Raulch again. "He doesn't talk much, does he?" he asked, indicating the thug with the huge muscles.

"Don't worry about Staub. He'll talk just fine when he have something to say," answered Raulch, looking at the squarish Gnome. "No more waiting," he suddenly barked. "Get things together. Grundehl be impatient to talk with you."

Granston stood up as straight as he could, looking Raulch in the eyes, anger flaring in his soul. Without warning, and without much effort, he threw a small knife-like dirk, known as a *shirken* into the throat of Raulch's silent friend.

Staub grabbed his throat, slowly toppling to the ground without getting a chance to say anything, whether he would have wanted to or not. Thick blood splattered at Raulch's feet before the man's body followed.

After that, time slowed down for the wizard and sped up for Raulch. Granston didn't give Raulch or his companions a chance to do anything. With a gesture, he literally stopped them in their tracks. He put his palm in the air and told the world around them to come to a stop. Well, not stop precisely, just slow down to a crawl. An hour, minutes of that hour, seconds of that hour, slowed to a fraction of a millisecond, slowed, then took a quick breath: enough of a breath for Granston to take as much time in his little bubble to do anything he wanted, including talk.

Granston slowly walked around Raulch, looking him over from head to foot. A moment later, he said, "Raulch, my friend, I've a few questions for you, and you're going to answer the best you can, or I'm going to do to you what I did to that flea-bitten Staub." He pointed to the body at his feet. Raulch's eyes narrowed, his temper rising. Granston watched and smiled knowing the hulking Gnome couldn't do a thing about it. His body was frozen in place as if the very air around him had turned to stone and planted him in the earth where he stood. He could hear Granston, but that was about all. He couldn't move a muscle, only listen and answer.

"What you want?" sneered Raulch.

"I was just about to ask you the same thing, Raulch, old friend," said Granston. "I came here on my own, and what do I get for my troubles? My own kind trying to kill me." He slowly walked around the frozen Gnome again. "Why did you do that, Raulch?" he hissed.

"Grundehl sent us to take care of problem," Raulch reluctantly answered.

That stunned Granston, and his mouth fell open in surprise. When he left, over a century ago, he thought there wasn't bad blood between himself and the king. Oh, there were hard feelings, but Granston thought eventually Grundehl would see the light and get over it. But apparently a century wasn't long enough. He'd agreed to the terms of the truce and left without a fight. Why should he hold a grudge for so long? "What problem, Raulch?" Granston asked, poking the giant in his chest.

Raulch strained with all his might to move even a finger, but after only a moment, he realized it was of no use. "The problem of you coming back," answered Raulch with gritted teeth.

Granston stepped close, sneering up into Raulch's face. "What do you mean? I left like I said I would."

"Yes, but you came back. You aren't supposed to come back. Was told by king you will not ever come back. When he heard you came back, he didn't like it. You seem to always cause problem," answered Raulch, his eyes narrowing to slits again.

Granston realized what the king's problem really was; a century ago, the Gnomes lost nearly a third of their numbers in a little skirmish with the Elves. He, Granston, was their general. In a brokered treaty, after the fighting stopped, between the Gnomes and the Elves, the Elves demanded Granston not be allowed to stay. In essence, he was banned from his own homeland. He'd kept that agreement, until now. He guessed the king thought it might happen again, which it was. He just didn't know it yet. He had a few surprises for the fat slob.

"This is what's going to happen, Raulch . . . ."

*   *   *

CHAPTER 13

P ip stretched and yawned.

The night before hadn't been a very good one. His nerves were shot, and his manners were taking the brunt of it. Tarsus had begun to teach him about being a wizard, and he began to bark his comments, or what he called, 'suggestions' to him, before an hour had elapsed. It was as if he were suddenly in a hurry for Pip to learn everything he needed to know. And that was about the time when Pip's manners had taken a turn for the worse. With everything that happened in the last couple of days, Pip didn't think he could go very long without exploding. He could well imagine what it was like for the princess to take instruction from this walking goat muncher, the experience doing nothing for his disposition. The explosion was coming; Pip could feel it, could see it, and felt no remorse for what would befall the lizard.

The princess, however, he felt much sympathy for. He had an advantage over her; she had to do everything in front of the whole castle, Pip didn't. Pip and Tarsus had taken their little instruction sessions to a clearing, north of the castle. Pip didn't know exactly how far away it was, because every morning they started out, it was before daylight, and Tarsus flew them both until the sun actually came above the horizon. It could have been ten miles or twenty. Tarsus told him he couldn't afford to have anyone see what they were doing or suspecting anything unusual. All anyone was supposed to know was they wanted to be alone with the other for a few hours, which in hindsight wasn't suspicious in itself, after all Pip took care of Tarsus through the day, he was the dragon's page.

"Pip . . . No! Like I showed you. If you try it that way, you might shove yourself to the next kingdom." Tarsus barked again at him.

Tarsus was trying to show Pip how to throw an object at an opponent, and all Pip was succeeding in doing was throwing himself to the ground. His aches and pains of being pummeled for the past half-hour was proof of that. Tarsus wanted him to concentrate on the object being thrown, pick it up, then toss it, or shove it where he wanted it to go. But every time Pip tried to pick it up, he raised himself off the ground instead of the object, and the object Tarsus wanted thrown wasn't slight. It was a bundle of rags and strips of leather tied in a ball that was almost as big as Pip was. Tarsus said it would represent a person. It didn't matter what the weight of the object was, the concentration of the wizard performing the act was what counted, according to Tarsus. It didn't matter how heavy an object was either, as long as the wizard had the power, which Pip did, and the concentration, which he was struggling with. Pip didn't seem to have the knack for it, at least not the way the barking dog wanted him to do it. He just couldn't.

"I'm trying!" Pip said heatedly, grinding his teeth. "Every time I try to pick it up, I pick myself up, like in the barn," Pip finished, getting more aggravated by the moment. "'Why can't I do it the other way?"

"Because, if you do it like you want, you might throw yourself instead of the ball," answered Tarsus, frustration showing in his voice as well. "Didn't the barn teach you anything? You did the same thing there as you have here. You first have to control the power, and then direct it. If you don't, you'll just go wild."

"But . . ."

"No! Just do it!" shouted Tarsus, aggravated.

Pip succumbed to his anger, finally, and did it Tarsus's way, which turned out to be the wrong way after all. His anger at constantly getting it wrong magnified his power, throwing himself, just as Tarsus said he would. Coming to rest, quite hard a hundred yards away, didn't go over well with the new wizard. Tarsus being right wasn't the way to win any awards right now. He needed the blasted dragon to be wrong.

Pip groaned, Tarsus standing over him. "Will you please listen now? You've got to control your anger. It's gonna get you killed if you don't. And me along with you." Tarsus shook his head, not knowing how to get through to the boy.

Pip groaned again. Tarsus talking about control! That was rich. When he couldn't control his own temper around Sir Dwayne! Now he knew why.

Pip slowly got up and rubbed his aching back, trying to shake off the impact. "Can I at least try it the other way? It's almost what you said. If I can't do it, we can try your way again?" Pip looked at the dragon pleadingly.

Tarsus gave up. Walking away, he said, "Fine, but if you land in the lake, I'm gonna let you drown."

The Lake? What was he talking about? "The Lake? But that's over five miles away."

"That's right. I hope you can swim,." Tarsus said sarcastically.

Pip shook his head. He knew he could do this. He knew he could do anything that walking belt could teach him. He simply had to figure it out on his own. Rubbing his back, walking towards the giant ball of twine and straw, he gathered his courage. He started again; this time not wanting to pick it up first, he simply 'willed' it to go where he wanted. He felt it was like kicking it—aiming wasn't necessarily the problem—first there, then not, that kinda thing, the other way was like pushing it—sort of—he couldn't seem to get his mind wrapped around that way of thinking. You wouldn't pick up a wagon to throw it, or a tree, unless you were a giant, and he definitely wasn't a giant. All Tarsus had to do was pick it up in his mouth and fling it with his strong neck. Pip had to do it another way. When he thought of it . . . thought turned into deed; *whoosh!* The ball flashed by Tarsus's nose, straight towards the tree Pip had 'kicked' it at. The resounding crack and tree splitting nearly in half after impact told Tarsus it had been hurtled with tremendous force.

Pip stood where he was with a grin on his face.

Tarsus just looked at the split tree not saying anything.

"It worked! I knew it!" Pip exclaimed. He was almost jumping with excitement. "I didn't know if I could or not, but I knew the other way wasn't working for me. I knew it."

Tarsus shook his head. Apparently he had to find a different way to teach this young wizard. Pip had a different way of thinking than most. Maybe it was due to his age. Maybe it was due to the way he was brought up in the stables by Mulch; either way, if he didn't come up with some form of teaching that Pip could understand, he'd end up being the one to do all the fighting when the time came; come it would, no doubt. Granston wouldn't stay away forever. Tarsus knew it was just a matter of time before he showed up, and this time, it wouldn't just be between himself and the little Gnome. As long as Pip was around, which he would be, Tarsus didn't know whether he could keep his promise to keep him safe if he didn't know some magic to protect himself. Inside, Pip was a dangerous mage, maybe the most dangerous one who ever lived. Tarsus could see the power growing in him day by day. If he couldn't control that power, he'd find out exactly how so many wizards before him wound up dead. It wasn't merely the lack of training, but lack of control. Magic was a wondrous and very dangerous aspect of becoming a wizard, but lack of control of the power could kill a new wizard as surely as not knowing how to defend oneself; which was the main reason for these little sessions. It was important for Pip to realize that, to gain control.

"Let's go back, Pip," said Tarsus. "I think we've been gone long enough. I know you need as much instruction as I can give you, but we need to keep these little training sessions as quiet as possible. We've too many people watching our every move for us not to be careful."

Pip nodded. His grin still split his face from ear to ear, still a little flustered over what he'd accomplished. Without saying a word, he simply climbed onto Tarsus's saddle which was slung between two of the dragon's back ridges. When he got on, he marveled over the design of the amazing saddle. Tarsus had instructed Pip on how to make it, one of the many tasks the dragon had Pip perform those many days the princess had been training. One of many chores in which Tarsus wanted to keep a secret.

When Tarsus jumped into the air and spread his wings, the sensation of flying took all of those memories away. Pip found he loved the sensation of being high off the ground, not having ground beneath his feet, soaring like an eagle over the countryside; it was one of the most enjoyable things he could possibly think of doing. If he were never to land and be subjected to Mulch's demands, it would be too soon.

Wind whipping in Pip's face, hair streaming behind, Tarsus craned his long neck to regard his young passenger. Watching the young man enjoy what he took as a natural part of who he was, turned his somber mood around. If someone as innocent as Pip could marvel, and be delighted at what was a natural thing as flying, then Tarsus realized there was hope for them all. As he turned back, his own grin took over. *Thank you, Pip. You've renewed my own faith.*

Maybe we can come out of this with both of our skins intact.

* * *

CHAPTER 14

Granston leisurely strolled through the pines and oaks of the Gnome Mountain Range, heading, in no great hurry to the mouth of the cave which marked the entrance to the Gnome Kingdom. Beside him were the three who'd come to 'escort' him to Grundehl. He wanted to take his time and reflect on his success of not being brought to the fat king in chains, or on a burial litter. Plus, he wanted answers. He no longer worried about his escorts. With a gesture, he let them move again and then put them under his influence, changing their loyalties to him so he'd get the answers he wanted. Since their talk at his camp, he and they had come to an understanding: he wouldn't obliterate them, if they'd sing like song-birds.

The day was beautiful and bright, somewhat cold to his way of thinking, he'd been used to the moderate climate of Musk, snow showing on the mountain's peak. As they walked, he asked a few pointed questions, especially to the Assanti. He'd never talked to one of her kind before and was curious why she was there, besides the obvious, of course. Granston looked the woman over from head to toe, slowly assessing her whole frame: she wore no adornments to speak of, just a clasp on her left wrist, more a manacle than a piece of jewellery; her lithe form moved in a sensual and provocative way, but also conveyed an element of the dangerous, like a mountain cat, sleek but always ready to pounce; her legs and feet were most assuredly those of a woman, but as she moved, the muscles along her thighs and shins could be clearly seen rippling through them. He was coming to admire her form and grace of movement.

Granston thought her to be the perfect vision of what a woman should be, no matter not being a Gnome.

"What's your name?" asked Granston, sidling up beside her, his staff thumping on the frozen ground. His fingers tightened convulsively on the wood of the Staff, anticipating her words.

Not looking at the wizard, the Assanti said simply, "Marvelo."

"Why are you and the guild associating yourselves with the Gnomes, Marvelo?"

"I don't know," she answered, shrugging. "I simply go where the master tells me to go."

Granston thought a moment, scratching his chin. "Do you care?" he asked.

Marvelo looked his way then and said as if she were telling him the sky was blue, "No."

"You aren't curious at all?"

"No. It's not my place to know." She looked away, her eyes going back to the trail ahead.

Granston frowned; his influence wasn't going to get him anywhere with her apparently. He turned to Raulch. "What about you? Do you know why Grundehl has brought the guild into the kingdom?"

Raulch didn't say anything, simply shrugged his massive shoulders and kept walking.

Granston looked at the broad-chested Gnome beside Raulch and asked him, "And what about you, do you know why?"

The broad shouldered one shook his head not saying anything either. He just looked at the ground in front of his feet.

Granston swore to himself in frustration. This was getting him nowhere. He decided the only thing he could do was wait and watch. He'd have to get his answers from the fat slob.

Two hours later, his escort brought him to the mouth of the cave. At first glance, he couldn't see anything, just a cliff face with lichen growing on the rock. But upon closer inspection, and Raulch knowing exactly where to go, the cave mouth materialized, seemingly out of the rock itself. The opening was a dark and lightless maw that threatened to swallow any unsuspecting person. Raulch stopped before going inside. Granston was about to ask him why when the answer was given to him without asking: a lone Gnome, the ugliest, Granston could remember seeing, came traipsing out of the cave with a torch in his small fist. Granston cringed back a pace. The small Gnome, seeing him, smiled a wickedly ugly smile, showing rotten teeth and bleeding gums. His nose, misshapen and twisted, ran with mucus, dripping with every movement of his pale head. He was horrid. The little thing didn't seem to bother Raulch in the least. Raulch waved at the fellow, turned to his companions—Granston and the two following—and simply turned back. The misshapen Gnome grinned his horrible grin without saying a word and preceded them into the cave. Raulch gestured and followed.

Cringing himself, not particularly happy about going inside the dark opening, Granston reluctantly moved to follow. Inside, the cave was dark as pitch and just as cold as the bare rock which made up the mountain. Shivering, he walked inside. The glow from the misbegotten Gnome's torch was the only source of light he found. It was as if the world had gone black. After only a few minutes, he was totally disoriented and confused as to which way they'd entered. The echoes of their footfalls came back softly as the group continued in single file through the cave.

Granston thought they may have walked a hundred yards or so, when the light stopped ahead of him and took a sharp right turn. In that instant, the cave became totally black. He couldn't make out his hand before his nose. In fear, he shouted, "What's going on?"

Just as he shouted, a dozen torches flickered into being. The sudden flare of light blinding him for a moment, he couldn't see who had done what or where he was. When his eyes adjusted, only a moment longer, he saw a troop of Gnomes in front of him. The Gnome in the lead was Speck, a hundred years ago, the champion of a thousand fights in the arena. He was a killer, plain and simple; he spotted Granston almost immediately, standing between Assanti and Raulch, and gave a wicked smile, but said nothing. Another of the many Gnomes Granston wished had died.

Granston nodded to the killer, not showing fear. Speck didn't acknowledge him but simply stared.

Raulch looked at the Gnome and said, "We got him." He pointed unnecessarily to Granston. "Where's Grundehl?"

Speck gestured to the massive door behind him, still not saying anything. The door, which was made of granite, lined with oak timbers, hadn't been immediately visible. The flare of the torches had kept Granston from noticing it. Speck stepped to one side, gesturing again for them to enter, his smile growing wider, firmly expecting Granston to be put to the lash or even killed when he got before their king.

Granston smirked at the killer, knowing full well what he was thinking. We'll see.

The doors were slowly opened and the party walked into the hall of Gnomes, followed closely by Speck and his cronies. Granston smirked when first seeing the hall, the big open area adorned and outfitted with all the trappings of a throne room. Only an ignorant Gnome would call it such, however; for one thing, it didn't really look like a throne room, for another, it was simply a huge cave. No matter how you dress it up, with spiral columns of fine wrought stonework, a giant mural depicting the lives of Gnomes across the expansive walls, it was still a cave, a cave carved into a mountain so far back in the Gnome Mountain Range he didn't think he could have found it without help. And this was the first time he'd ever seen this particular cave. Over a century ago, the king of the Gnomes used a small outcropping of stone, overhanging the entrance to the catacombs of the Gnome city, to entertain his guests. He'd never have allowed anyone to enter the kingdom under any circumstances, for they fear they'd find their homes and kill its people. Gnomes tended to be secretive, which was about to change, although Grundehl didn't know it yet.

Granston saw in front of him a giant outcropping of granite formed into a seat. Sitting on it as if it were a throne made of diamonds and emeralds was the fat slob himself: Grundehl. His gross body folded into the 'chair' as if he were molded into it. At any minute, Granston expected the flabby king to roll off into the floor creating a giant puddle of goo. The sight of the so-called king wasn't something he ever thought he'd see again or wanted to. He hadn't changed in all the years he'd been gone. Grundehl was one of the foulest being in the five kingdoms, fear being his driving force. He was afraid of anything he couldn't control, and from the look in his eyes, Granston knew he feared being in the same room as him. As Granston approached the granite throne, Grundehl cringed, his body jerking as if with palsy, and his eyes widened to the size of plates. *That's good. That's very good, you fat slob. You should be very afraid of me.* The wizard smiled at the sight.

Granston was behind Raulch as the little group trouped in the hall. Standing in front of Grundehl, the fat monarch grinned with feigned glee. "Oh, Granston, come back. Why?" he demanded.

A gargantuan figure standing to the right of Grundehl chuckled at the king's greeting. Granston couldn't recall ever having seen him before.

Up until that moment, Raulch had been the biggest Gnome he'd ever seen, but the figure didn't quite look like a Gnome. His facial features were too flat, and he was too tall by half. Granston stared at him but said nothing. *I wonder what this is all about. And who in the five kingdoms is the big one by the slob's side?*

While he waited for Grundehl to say something else, Granston took the opportunity to look around. There were a few things he couldn't remember ever being around the Gnome's king. One of which was the amount of followers surrounding him. As far as he saw, he could tell there were over fifty, and not all of them were Gnomes. Not only was the amount strange—Gnomes didn't like to be surrounded by anyone, even if it were other Gnomes—he noticed there were more Assanti present: Assassins from the Guild. Now, this is strange. I wonder what's going on? Who are these people? Granston could understand sending one Assanti with Raulch to take him out, but not this many constantly being around the king. This was very unusual indeed.

Being secretive was the norm for Gnomes, hiding in plain sight was their advantage, no one in the outside world really seeing them. If they were noticed, people thought them to be Dwarfs, or even Elves, and no one believed anymore. It was one of the reasons he'd been able to pose as an adviser to the idiot Lionel for so many years. How could a short, slightly portly, little fellow like him be a 'fairy-tale' Gnome? So having so many non-Gnomish people in or around the Gnome Kingdom was very unusual. What if word got out about them? Would anyone really believe? How could Grundehl take the chance?

"What you want, Granston?" Grundehl barked, shaking Granston back to reality. "I tell Raulch bring you in chains. Why you not in them?" Grundehl said, looking at Raulch, his face twisting into a sneer. "The way you ran off, I not think you be seen again."

"Still haven't learned human speech very well, have you?" asked Granston. "I'd have thought it would've been easier for you by now. It's been how many years? A hundred? Can't you learn anything?" Granston saw he'd angered the king and smiled. It was good to know he could still get to the fat one. "And I didn't run off. We had an agreement. I thought it worked well."

"Why you here?" roared Grundehl, showing his anger now. "Me no care. Me only care why you here and what you want."

Still smiling, Granston said mockingly, "Me need help."

Grundehl scowled leaning closer. "Why? You not been here since you stab us in back. Kill my army. Why I listen to you?"

The tension in the hall rose perceptibly. The guild members shuffled their feet, nervous energy ratcheting up, halberds rattling as hands gripped sword hilts, one wrong word from either of them and violence would surely erupt. Granston smiled again. "Because if you don't, the giant lizard will find out where you're at, and when that happens, you'll probably all die."

Grundehl leaned back on the rock and sneered. "Big Lizard gone forever. I saw. You got rid of him. Then you leave. How he come back?"

Granston could see that he was getting to the fat slob now. He had to keep up the pressure. He'd figured out, not long after Raulch and his henchmen had come for him that to get what he wanted, he'd have to make plans revolving around that blasted lizard. Tarsus was the Gnomes' biggest fear, even after centuries of not seeing him. The lizard had caused the death of hundreds of Gnomes. Every Gnome alive today had been touched by him in one way or another, whole bloodlines eradicated and families decimated. Tarsus was the key. He had to work that angle.

"He's come back, Grundehl. I don't know how. I thought I'd got rid of him forever. I was wrong."

Grundehl didn't think it funny now, and his temper cooled down to a glacial freeze, but he didn't say anything, just stared at Granston. After a moment, the king pointed to the giant standing next to him. "This Traub. He gonna take you to a room where you stay till I call. Me gonna talk with everyone about what to do."

Granston smiled. He knew he had already won.

*   *   *

CHAPTER 15

Tarsus had to tell Lionel about Pip. He just didn't know how to do it. He hadn't truly lied to Lionel, but, like Lionel had said before, he hadn't told him the whole truth either. He just couldn't get out of the habit of not telling everything he knew. For Tarsus, that was one of his weakest points. He just couldn't talk openly of what he had in his mind or what was happening around him. He held knowledge too close to his chest for too long. When they finally came to light, he usually got burned for his efforts. He hoped Lionel would understand.

Tarsus slowly walked towards the stable doors. He was trying to form the right words in his head to spring his confessions to Lionel when Mulch came up to him. "Master Tarsus?"

Tarsus blinked in surprise and froze. He hadn't expected to see the stable master this time of day. Usually, Mulch was on errands of his own, it was unusual to say the least. Tarsus bowed his head acknowledging his presence and said, "Yes, Stable Master. What can I do for you?"

"No need for that "master" stuff, Tarsus. I'm but a stable hand, like the rest around here. I just have the distinction and honor of being in charge of these lazy louts." He smiled. "As you well know by now with having Pip around you so much."

Tarsus had to smile. He knew how any human could, at times, be somewhat slow in their duties, especially when something interesting was going on. He bobbed his head to Mulch in understanding. "Nevertheless, you're more the master than I. What can I do for you?"

Mulch was what he was and knew it. He bowed slightly and then went on. "It looks to me as if you have something on your mind. For the past half-hour, you've been wandering around as if you've lost something and don't know how to find it. Can I do something to help?"

It was very intuitive of the man to pick up on Tarsus's mood. He was impressed despite himself. After a slight pause, he said, "I don't know if you could help or not. I merely find myself in a place where I don't like, yet constantly find myself going back to. And I can't find how to stop the wheel from turning." Tarsus blew a small flame from his nostrils to show his frustration.

Mulch nodded and then grinned. "I'm going to give you a little bit of advice, if I may," said Mulch. "If you want to get to a better place, the best place to start the journey is from the beginning, not from the end." He looked at the dragon sideways, quirking a slight smile.

Tarsus blinked at the stable master. Surprisingly, the dragon realized he was right. Tarsus smiled broadly at Mulch and then bowed to him in thanks. "You're right, Stable Master, and I should stop feeling sorry for myself while I'm at it," said Tarsus. "Maybe then I'd have thought of the obvious instead of being reminded of it by you. I'm in your debt, and thank you." He gave back the smile Mulch generously displayed.

"You don't owe me a thing, Master Tarsus," Mulch said, shaking his head. "You owe yourself the truth. Me, I care for my king, my kingdom, and these smelly stables that have saved my life more times than I could ever have time to tell anyone. And personally, I don't care who knows, who, or what, I am. I do what comes naturally, and that's after living more than half my life doing the wrong things." Mulch looked down at his feet, blushing slightly. This was apparently the most he'd said in a long time, and he didn't know what to do now it was over. After a moment though, he coughed and said, "Well, I better be on my way," and then did just that. He went to do whatever he did.

Tarsus shook his head with wonder watching the faithful caretaker leave. The wonder of finding someone who knew who, and what, he was, in a world full of fools looking for something they couldn't even name, made him sure there was hope left even for himself.

Turning back to the stable doors, Tarsus knew what to do and decided not to stall any longer. Mulch was right; he needed to start at the beginning, not the end. And the beginning was at the head of the kingdom. He headed towards the castle to request an audience with the king.

*   *   *

With lumbering steps and head held high, Tarsus headed towards the castle proper, making not a few of the citizens of Musk scurry for cover along the way. The looks on the faces of the townsfolk said a lot for what Tarsus was doing. They'd never seen a dragon until recently, and here one was thundering down its streets heading for the castle. He could've flown, of course, but it seemed pointless when he only had a few hundred yards to travel. Plus, he was thinking of the town when he decided on his little trek, the wind off his wings could be very fierce, thrusting up and down to get lift for his massive body. If a poor fellow walking home from the fields happened to be under those drafts, he could find himself flying in the air like a bolt from a crossbow. He'd seen other dragons in his time fly over villages that weren't prepared, and the roof damage alone looked like a small whirlwind had stormed through. So, the next best thing was for him to walk, or thump, as the case may be. He just hoped his tail didn't catch an unsuspecting citizen by surprise. But he couldn't help but grin at the looks he was getting from the people watching him stomp by their shops and homes. When he finally came in sight of the portcullis to the castle, two guardsmen were warily eyeing his approach. Before he got to them however, one stopped his progress about thirty yards away with, "Halt!" The guard held up a spear barring him from going any farther. Then, he asked, "What do you want, Master Dragon?"

Tarsus looked at the man and his spear and said in a not too friendly voice, "That's not your business, young man. All you need to know is I wish to talk with King Lionel."

"Why?" asked the guard, suspiciously, pointing his spear at Tarsus.

"I've told you already," Tarsus eyed the spear leveled at him and said in a huff, smoke rising from his mouth, "that's not for you to know." He looked up to the castle walls and saw men racing to get into position for possible trouble. He'd clearly heard metal scraping metal as they armed themselves. He turned back to the lone guard in front of him and smiled wickedly, eyeing the man up and down, saying in a not-unpleasant tone, "Please send for your superior so I may make a formal request to see the king."

The guard, Tarsus didn't know his name and didn't care, looked at the dragon as if he'd grown two heads. "Why should I?" he said sneeringly. "We've orders from the sarge to keep everyone out. No exceptions. Just because you've been making noise around here doesn't mean we have to jump when you say, frog." He stuck his chin and his spear up. His chin saying, 'Beat it'; his spear saying, "If you don't, I'll make you."

Tarsus was tired of this. He hadn't done anything to deserve this treatment, at least not today; besides, he'd asked nicely. In a move faster than seemed possible for such a large animal, Tarsus put his nose right next to the guardsman's, just as he'd done Pip. It had a wondrous effect, stopped the guard cold. The man looked as if he was going to lose his dinner all over the front of his jerkin. "Get your superior, this moment, Sergeant, or I'm going to have fried guard on a spike." A puff of smoke chuffed out of his right nostril to emphasize his words. The man's face went even paler, sweat popping out on his face and forehead. "Now!" Tarsus barked when he hadn't immediately moved. That did the trick! The man sped off without another word or a look behind. Tarsus nodded, setting down to wait.

Tarsus didn't have to wait long. In a few minutes, another guard came out of the portcullis. Tarsus assumed it was the sergeant. He was a slight man with a few missing front teeth and a head of hair looking as if it hadn't been washed or combed in some time. And his features looked very familiar; if Tarsus hadn't known better, he'd have said this was a relative of the guardsman who he'd sent scurrying away. It was hard to tell though, everyone wore the same uniform, the only difference with this guy was a small red patch on his left sleeve.

"What do you want?" the sergeant said, sticking out his chin like the other fellow.

Does everyone have an attitude in this place? I'm getting tired of it. "Ask the other guard," growled Tarsus, his last nerve becoming frayed. "I'm getting very tired of repeating myself. And tired of people like you." Smoke rose freely from the chimney that was Tarsus's nose.

Weighing his options, seeing the smoke rise in the air, the sergeant decided it may not be a good idea to antagonize the dragon any more than he already had. He, of course, knew why the dragon had come, but he wanted to see how far he could push the animal before things got really ugly. And by the looks of it, he couldn't go very far. Sir Dwayne had ordered everyone to push the dragon into doing something stupid, so he'd be considered dangerous and would be thrown out of the kingdom.

Sir Dwayne said that it just hadn't happened yet. It would of course, Tarsus was an animal after all and animals could never be tamed for long. But maybe, the sergeant decided, taking another look at the smoke floating above the dragon's head, this wouldn't be the right time to do it. Instead, he cleared his voice and said, "Why do you want to see the king? He's busy. He doesn't have the time for petty grievances. Come back some other time."

Tarsus had heard from Princess Laura that humans tended to get along better with one another if they'd become close. Meaning, she'd said, friendly. Well, he figured it was time for some friendliness on his part. His front paw unceremoniously slammed the sergeant to the ground, closely pinning him to the earth. His nose touched the pinned man's, and he said in a conversational voice, "All I wanted was for someone to pass on a simple request. If you haven't noticed, I can't fit through this or any other door to the castle." Tarsus gestured with his head at the portcullis.

The sergeant blanched, which was understandable, the other guards on the wall not waiting for the outcome of the scene below. Tarsus didn't take his eyes off the man under his foot. He simply heard them flee, throwing down their arms in fear. He smiled a very toothy smile. So much for bravery.

Tarsus asked the sergeant, still in a conversational voice, "Can you deliver my message? It's a very simple one. Do you need to write it down on parchment before delivering it?"

The sergeant shook his head, not saying anything, which was all right with Tarsus. All he needed was for the man to do what was asked. He released the pinned man, watching as he slowly made his way to his feet. As he turned to go inside, Tarsus said politely, "Thank you." The sergeant, Tarsus never got his name either, stopped, but didn't turn around. "Please inform whoever it is I shall be in the stables waiting for a reply." The man nodded, with his head down, watching only his feet, continuing inside.

That wasn't as hard as I thought it would be. Maybe there's something to this friendship after all. Tarsus nodded, thinking he'd done well. He lumbered back to the stables again, not too worried about what the people might say about his passage the second time through the city, his thoughts returning to Lionel and how he was going to begin telling the truth. The answer he was hoping for didn't come, but some*one* did. He got a visitor he wasn't really surprised to see.

Sir Dwayne stepped out of the shadows of the stables as Tarsus approached. When the portcullis incident reached the ears of the knight, he didn't let any time lapse before he was confronting the dragon. Just another day in his life.

"Dragon!" the knight said with contempt in his voice, one hand on the hilt of his sword.

"Why do you continue to harass my people?"

"Why do your men constantly feel I'm a threat?" countered Tarsus, letting heat come into his voice also. "If you wouldn't let your own prejudice run over to your men, we wouldn't be in this situation right now."

"Don't make this about me, dragon. Why are your accosting the gate guards?" Dwayne demanded, his voice rising. "Answer my question!"

"Answer mine," countered Tarsus.

Just as frustration from both of them was about to bubble over, Princess Laura showed up. She seemed to be in the right place at the wrong time, as far as Sir Dwayne was concerned. Sir Dwayne was feeling as if the monster had some kind of guardian watching over him. And Tarsus felt he couldn't go on like this much longer. Even Princess Laura couldn't stop the bloodshed sure to happen when they both snapped. No matter each promising to try to get along.

"What's going on?" asked the princess, the hackles on her own neck going up. This wasn't right. Something was up between the two. "What's the trouble?"

Sir Dwayne bowed to Laura saying, "Your Highness, there's no trouble," and without saying anything else, he turned and walked away.

Laura looked at Tarsus. "Well?"

Tarsus bowed his head and said, "Your Highness, no trouble," and without another word, he turned and lumbered away in the opposite direction, leaving her standing alone watching them both.

All the princess could do was shake her head. *This has got to stop. Both of them are too proud to admit they're alike in many ways. And if this goes much longer, there's going to be bloodshed. Whether Father and I want it or not.*

*   *   *

Tarsus walked away from Laura and didn't like it. He didn't want to keep anything from her, especially anything to do with Pip. Pip, the kid who could barely get out of bed before noon. Pip, the kid who could easily throw a boulder a mile in the air and who will eventually be around the princess daily. It couldn't be helped, Pip was, technically, his page, and eventually training sessions would clash between the two, and Tarsus would be forced to train them both at the same time. And he couldn't exactly do that if the princess knew nothing of Pip's power. *Blast! I've got to figure this out, before my imagination gets away from me. I have to tell Lionel about Pip.* And, just like that, almost before the thought was out of his head, Lionel was there. Well, the king's personal aid was there to announce Lionel.

Tarsus turned to look at the stable doors. *That was quick. I expected to wait until morning at the least.* The man who came in was definitely *not* King Lionel. Whirle was his name, which definitely suited the man. He was a whirl of activity, bustling in as if he were the one going to take control of any situation. He bustled up to Tarsus and said in a quick, precise voice, "Master Dragon, our king shall be with you in a moment. I came first to ensure you would be alone. Majesty didn't know whether you'd want anyone to hear your conversation. By the way, what does it pertain to? I'll inform Our Majesty before he gets here, so he'll be prepared." Whirle stopped talking and immediately expected an answer, but the dragon never got the chance. Whirle continued as if an answer wasn't needed or expected, even after asking the question; the whole time, he was walking around Tarsus poking into every corner, behind bales of hay, piles of oat sacks. "Come, come, Master Dragon, what's it about? What? What? I don't have all night." He stopped poking around long enough to look into Tarsus's face, expecting an answer again. But, then again, before Tarsus could answer, a 'harrumph' came from the doors. Tarsus's neck snaked above Whirle to find Lionel standing behind him. Tarsus started to move his huge body to maneuver around the aid, to face the monarch, when yet again, Whirle twirled around to the king like a crazed squirrel, his speech sounding like chittering from that self-same crazed animal, fast and choppy, "Sire. You've come too soon. Yes, you have. You were too fast. I never got an answer from Master Tarsus about what he wanted to talk to you about. I never got it. Maybe he'll tell you. Maybe. Yes. There's no one here but him as far as I can see. You came too soon. I don't know. I'll go now. I'll go look outside. Make sure you're alone. Yes. Yes. That's what I'll do. You can see he's alone." He bustled around both of them as if no one was there, as if he were talking to himself. "You go ahead, sire. I'll be outside." And just like that, he was out.

"Sire?" Tarsus inquired, a look of puzzlement on his face, tilting his head slightly, watching the strange little man go out the doors.

Lionel had yet to say anything. Seeing Whirle bustling around him and Tarsus and then leaving, his smile broke his face in half. "That, my friend, is a man who's never let me down, and never changes. He's been that way since I was a little boy. At one time I thought he was crazy. I realized, however, he's just hyper. He's been one of my most trusted castle servants for many years. And if you hadn't noticed, I never said a word while he was here. I don't think I could have gotten a word in anyway." He still smiled thinking of the little man. It said a lot. He still, after all these years, had warm and friendly memories of Whirle. After a moment of wool-gathering, Lionel turned back to Tarsus and asked, "What can I do for you, Master Tarsus?"

Tarsus bowed to Lionel, a smile breaking his own face. "Thank you, sire, for seeing me."

Lionel bobbed his head to Tarsus, acknowledging him also. "That's not a problem. But do us all a favor: next time, try to get a message to me without causing my guards to have seizures. If you don't, we're going to run out of guards who will want to be around you."

"Yes, sire, but, if you could hear the full story, I got nothing but grief from the fellow at the portcullis. And I did ask nicely to see you." Tarsus smiled a toothy smile at him.

"Yes, I know. There were a lot of witnesses. You tend to make a lot of noise. It attracts attention by the bucket full,." Lionel said, smiling a little himself.

Tarsus nodded, his smile fading. Now was the time. "OK," Tarsus took a deep breath and said, "I'll try to do this quickly, sire, but I haven't figured out how to start."

Lionel looked at the dragon hard. *This doesn't sound good. I may need to be sitting for this.* Lionel said, sighing himself, "Sounds important. Is it?".

Tarsus only nodded. Lionel sighed again. "Well then, just start where it's easiest," suggested Lionel. "We can go from there."

Tarsus smiled at him, thanking him for his thought. It was a good idea. When he finally began talking, his voice started out weak, but, as he got going, his voice picked up in strength, and by the time he got around to saying anything about Pip, he was reminded of memorable Whirle. He was trying to get it all out before his audience lost his temper and exploded.

"Pip?" exclaimed Lionel. "What do you mean?"

Tarsus took a deep breath and dived in to the deep end of the pond. He knew this wasn't going to be easy. "Sire, I didn't tell you the whole truth."

Lionel laughed. "You think I don't know that? If you recall, I've stated something to that effect before?"

Oh yes, Tarsus remembered. How could he forget? The day he'd made a magical promise, the day Sir Dwayne nearly killed Pip, and the same day both of their lives changed forever. "Yes, sire. I know. And you were right."

Lionel nodded. *Oh yes, since he got here, he hadn't been forthcoming at all.*

Tarsus nodded himself. He thought a moment before going on and then said, "My biggest fault is that I haven't trusted anyone in centuries, sire, and when you get right down to it, my whole life has been like that. Unless, of course you were a dragon. Call it prejudice if you like, but I don't think so. I say that because five thousand years ago, or thereabouts, I met a dragon by the name of Maug I didn't trust at all." Tarsus stopped for a moment, and just as Lionel had done, his face showed he was remembering long ago. His eyes were flat and shiny, and his ears perked up like he was hearing a dragon's roar. Then he shook like a dog, snapping himself out of his reverie. He looked at the king and continued. "The point is, I don't trust anyone easily, and that failing has got me into trouble more times than I care to count. I keep things too close to my chest till it's too late. Until no one can help."

"Now that I can believe,' "said Lionel, looking for a place to sit. He circled Tarsus like Whirle, looking in corners and the closest stables.

Tarsus watched Lionel and wondered what he was doing. One moment he'd been listening to him shaking his head or nodding as he talked, and then he was like Whirle, looking in every corner, in every stable he could get open, and acting like he'd lost something. "Sire, is something wrong? Are you looking for something?"

Lionel kept looking as he answered, "For a stool or a pail, so I can sit. If this is going to take a while, I better sit before I fall over. My feet are sore, and my legs are killing me. When you get to be my age, you find you can't stand all day without something giving out. Twenty years ago, I'd just be getting my second wind, but now," he gestured with his hand like he was swatting a fly, "I'm usually in bed by this time, and I have a busy day tomorrow. King stuff, you know."

"Ah, yes. I understand, sire. If you'll look in the third stall on the left, you'll find a small three-legged stool." Tarsus smiled. A king hunting a stool so he wouldn't have to sit on the floor. This was definitely a strange day indeed.

When Lionel came back with the small stool and carefully sat down, sighing with relief, Tarsus said, "Sire, if I may ask, why are you in here without your guards?" Tarsus looked towards the stable doors, knowing his knights were just outside.

"Because I do trust," Lionel said simply, looking into the dragon's face, never flinching.

Tarsus bowed. "Thank you, sire."

"Keep going, Tarsus." Lionel again gestured with his hand. 'Get on with it'. "What's this about Pip?"

Tarsus sat down, a small cloud of dust puffing up from under his backside. Lionel coughed slightly and then fanned his hands in front of his face to dispel it, but didn't say anything. He just watched Tarsus try to begin again. After another moment, "Sire, I guess I better start to trust someone. I can't do this alone any longer. Like I said, I haven't been able to trust anyone for a long time. It's hard for me to admit it, but I need help."

"Tarsus, what does this have to do with the boy?" Lionel asked again, his patience running out.

"Please, sire, I'll get there. I'm just trying to figure out how to do it. Talking around it might help me. Plus, I don't think you're gonna like it."

"Go ahead. Just don't take all night about it."

"Yes, sire." Tarsus thought a moment more, his large cliff-like eyebrows rising and falling as he was thinking. Maybe if I started at the beginning of my life? No, that would take all night. What he needed to do was start where it mattered to Pip. Well, nothing for it. "Sire, I need to tell you a few things about myself so you'll understand what I'm going to tell you. I need to tell you part of my life story, so you'll understand how I came to be here, but that will take a while, and I don't want to complicate it, so for now, I'll start with what you'll need to know about Pip, OK?" He was trying to make this as easy as he could, but he was afraid he'd complicate it instead.

Lionel stopped him. "Whoa! Slow down a little, Tarsus. Just start with Pip. Later, we can get to the rest. If I don't understand, I'll stop you. Then we can get to the specifics, OK?'

Tarsus hung his head and took another deep breath. "Yes, sire. You're right. Let's start again." He took a breath once more and then asked, "Sire, what do you know about dragons?"

"Not much really," said Lionel. "Until you showed up, I don't think I really believed in dragons. All the stories I'd ever heard, fairy tales I guess you'd call them—" he wiggled his fingers to emphasize all of the nonsense stories people had made up about their kind. "—they never came close to how you really are."

Tarsus bowed. "Thank you, sire. I've heard most of those stories myself. They're mostly crap. I hope I haven't dispelled all of your dreams about us?" Tarsus smiled, and he saw Lionel smile back, shaking his head. "Well, one thing all those tales never even hinted about was how dragons can sense the use of magic or the ones who can tap into that magic, or more precisely, the ability to use that magic." Tarsus looked into Lionel's face, hoping for understanding. "Do you see, sire? I know who will be able to tap into magic and become a wizard. Even if they don't yet know themselves. When I first saw Pip in the stable, I knew he was such a person. The ability is very strong in him."

Lionel cringed, hanging his head on his breastbone. *My worst fear came to life.* Looking up again, staring at Tarsus, wringing his hands, he asked, "Why didn't you say anything? To him or to me?"

Tarsus shook his head. "Trust. I didn't trust anyone enough to say. I'd just gotten here with Laura and been accosted by Dwayne, I didn't think you'd want anything else on your plate. I don't know. I could say a lot of things in my defense, but it all boils down to trust. I was surprised to find anyone who had so much power. After I talked to him, I realized he was just a kid, and he didn't know himself. So how could I trust even him with the knowledge?" Tarsus shrugged his massive shoulders, looking at Lionel with pleading eyes. "Do you think he'd believe me if I told him he was a wizard? Would you have? I'd just gotten here. So, who could I trust? All I could do was wait and watch."

"I see," said Lionel. "And what did you expect to get from him?" Lionel's voice rose slightly, his anger coming to a boil.

"I don't really know that either. But the longer I was around the lad, the more I knew I had to help him."

"Help him? How," asked Lionel, his anger now showing. "By lying to him, and me, and Laura, about something so important?"

"I seem to go right back to the same thing.; I don't know, sire. Maybe help him survive the next thousand years," said Tarsus. "Maybe just the next few. Teach him enough of the power so he doesn't kill himself, or someone else accidentally."

Lionel's anger cooled a little. *A thousand years?* "Wait a minute." He held up his open palm to stop Tarsus. "What are you talking about? A thousand years? What do you mean?"

"Sire," Tarsus said, leaning down slightly to come face to face with Lionel, "how old do you think I am?"

That question took the king by surprise. "I don't know," admitted Lionel. "I hadn't thought about it. All I know is what the stories have said, and you've already said most of that's crap. But from what I remember, a dragon can live for thousands of years."

"This is one of the things the stories get right." Tarsus nodded. "Dragons can live for many thousands of years. The oldest one I personally met was nearly ten thousand years old. To us, that's middle age."

"Holy Mother," breathed Lionel softly. "What does that make you?" He looked at the dragon in a new light. Could he really be thousands of years old? Lionel shook his head not truly believing. "Why is it a dragon can live so long? And you said wizards can live for just as long or longer? What makes that possible? How is it . . ."

"Whoa! Whoa! Please, sire." Tarsus said, stopping the monarch. The questions were coming too fast. He didn't know where to start answering them. "Sire, I'll answer what I can. Please, give me a chance." He saw Lionel calm down a bit and went on. "A wizard *can* live for thousands of years. The more powerful the wizard, the longer he tends to live, and they can live longer than you can imagine. I don't know if they could die from a natural death as you. In essence, they're almost immortal. I don't know why, but that's usually the way it works. It probably has something to do with the nature of magic, and Pip has the potential to be one of the most powerful ever born."

Tarsus thought a moment and said to answer another of his many questions, "Dragons are as wizards, sire, but it has something to do with the nature of magic. Because dragons are part of magic, by our very nature, we can live very long lives. I'm more than five thousand years old, sire. I'm very young compared to most dragons."

Lionel's mouth fell open in astonishment.

Tarsus continued, "But I'm old compared to the lives of you humans and most other races. I've lived for it seems enough life for three dragons, but I can't say all the years on me have been worth it. I've made many mistakes in my long life and probably will make many more. I do know one thing," his voice rose slightly trying to emphasize his point to Lionel, "Pip and I are linked in a very special way. Because of what happened with Sir Dwayne, I've made a promise to Pip that I'll keep with my life. If he were to die, I'll die with him."

Lionel was shocked for the second time that night. He looked at Tarsus with soft eyes, not with pity, but with understanding and empathy, his mouth opening and shutting again with a snap. After a moment, he asked, "Why didn't you come to me, Tarsus? I could have at least given you advice on how to handle the matter. Why did you ever think you could do this alone?"

Tarsus hung his head in embarrassment. In a soft voice, he said, "That's my worst failing and shame, sire. I don't trust anyone enough to ask for help. How could I? And another thing, I didn't know what it would take to keep Pip alive. How could I ask anyone to take such a risk? But that wasn't the worst part." He looked up into Lionel's eyes. "The worst wasn't knowing how powerful he could and would become. When it came down to it, as a wizard, I didn't think he'd be able to protect himself and the kingdom, as a wizard, without my help."

That got the king's attention in a hurry. He jumped from his stool and confronted the dragon with eyes blazing. "What do you mean, Tarsus? Why the kingdom? What does my kingdom have to do with it?"

"I'm afraid, sire, that's my fault." Tarsus never took his eyes from Lionel's. "Do you recall what I wanted when I got here?"

"Yes, to help my daughter."

"True, that's one of the reasons I wanted to stay, but not the reason I was originally here for. Do you recall?" asked Tarsus, cocking his head.

Lionel thought a moment and then grimaced, remembering, "Granston!"

"Yes, the Gnome, Granston." Tarsus grimaced, nodding his head. "He's why I'm here in the first place. Eventually, he'll return. He knows I'm here, and I'll be a temptation he'll not be able to refuse. He'll come here and kill me." Tarsus snorted fire. "But I intend to kill him first.'

Pip and the princess were simply excuses for me to stay. I could just as easily left to look for him. To make some form of restitution for what

I did so many years ago, I chose to stay and see what I could do to help. But, as always, I've almost waited too long to seek help myself.

"Please, sire," pleaded Tarsus, coming to the end of his long oration, "If you have to blame anyone for this mess, it's me. I'll gladly do any penitence you wish. Pip couldn't have known what was ahead of him. He still doesn't. I've shown him a few things, but he's got a lot more to learn. I just hope he has the strength to survive it. It will test his metal to the ultimate, and it will be very long and dangerous to him and the ones around him. If I can't teach him control, he could easily destroy your whole kingdom in a peak of anger."

Lionel's face blanched.

Tarsus nodded. "Yes. He easily could. The day Laura's tirade nearly got Pip skewered by Sir Dwayne was the first time he'd experienced any power. It usually shows up in the person in the form of anger. No one seems to understand why, but that's the way of it."

"Is that the reason you spun such a giant story of you picking him up in the air?" asked Lionel.

"One reason." Tarsus nodded. "But another was because if Pip had been angry with the knight instead of frightened, I don't think Dwayne would still be in one piece today. It had to be diffused. Not everything I said that day was a pile of manure, I can assure you. I can make a few things happen. I just can't do what Pip can."

Lionel held up his hands stopping Tarsus. "That's enough for now, I think. I believe I understand a lot. Too much. But I needed to know, and I thank you for finally coming forward." Lionel stretched, yawned, and then said to Tarsus, "I'm not happy with you, Master Tarsus, but I think I understand. But from now on, I need to know what's going on and how you plan to handle this? You may be surprised what I can do to help."

"Yes, sire," Tarsus said, bobbing his head. "I'm sorry I haven't been more forthright with you. I really didn't mean to cause so many problems."

Lionel looked at the dragon and said simply, "We all make mistakes, Tarsus. That's what makes us all mortals. Apparently, even dragons." He turned towards the doors, and then he looked over his shoulder on the way out. "We'll have more time later to talk about these problems." Then he left the stables.

*   *   *

CHAPTER 16

P ip slowly opened his eyes, and what he saw made him groan. Sir
Dwayne was standing over him with the tip of a sword pressed to
his throat. The grin on the knight's face told Pip everything. From
the first time, to this, Pip had a feeling this was what Sir Dwayne had
been waiting for. He knew he shouldn't have gone to bed so early. Every
time he did, he tended to oversleep and usually got into trouble for it. It
looked like this was no exception, although he didn't have any idea what
could have caused the knight to come and get him again. He thought
Princess Laura and Tarsus had taken care of any misunderstandings.
*Looks like they didn't do a very good job of it. I'm gonna have a long talk
with the lizard if I get out of this with my skin intact.*

"Don't move," Sir Dwayne growled. "I'll not give you the chance to
do anything."

Pip didn't think he could have moved. His heart was racing, his
breath came in shallow little spurts, and sweat was popping out all over
his body. He was more frightened now than when the knight had first
trussed him up like a hog to the slaughter all those weeks ago. The back
of Pip's head was pressed against the straw of the loft so hard trying to
get away from the sword point, it made an impression in the hay. His
Adam's apple bobbed like a cork in a stream, he could feel the knight's
blade scraping small pieces of skin off the tender side of his neck. This
was definitely not how he wanted to start shaving.

"Slowly turn over, boy," Sir Dwayne ordered.

"I thought you didn't want me to move," said Pip.

The knight pushed the sword a little farther down, drawing a small drop of blood and a grunt from Pip's, which apparently suited the knight just fine, his grin looking more like a cat playing with a caught mouse. "Watch your tongue, boy," he growled.

Pip knew immediately he shouldn't have said anything. This was no time for smart remarks. He slowly put his hands up and said, "OK, OK. I'm sorry. What do you want?"

"Do what I told you. Slowly turn over," said Sir Dwayne. "I'm going to tie your hands behind you."

Pip only nodded this time. He figured his mouth had already cost him too much blood and skin. He slowly did what he was told, and within minutes, the knight had roughly bound his hands to the small of his back and was jerked to his feet. With iron fingers clamping his arm, Sir Dwayne hissed in his ear, "Now, we're going in front of the king, and I'll be vindicated in what I did the last time I had to 'fetch' you."

"I doubt that," said a small rumble behind Pip and the knight.

Sir Dwayne froze. His hands clamped spastically down on Pip's arm. Pip didn't seem to notice the pain. His attention was focused on Tarsus's voice behind them. "I told Lionel you wouldn't hurt Pip again, Knight. That wasn't a boast," said the dragon. "If you don't let the lad go, you'll not leave this stable in one piece."

"And you, dragon, will not leave without hurt yourself," said another voice behind Tarsus.

Tarsus snorted, a slim stream of smoke billowing from his nostrils. A snort of derision. And with that trailing smoke, came the point of a spear poking Tarsus's neck.

Tarsus craned his neck slightly, very slowly, to find Sir Hook holding a spear, just under his left ear flap. He wasn't smiling as Sir Dwayne was.

"And you, Sir Hook, will leave like Sir Dwayne, in pieces," another voice behind him said. Sir Hook felt a sword point planted firmly in the middle of his own back. He stiffened, and as Tarsus had done, the knight looked over his shoulder very slowly to find Princess Laura, in full training armor, holding a sword, one which had a slight blue tinge to it.

"And this will not happen in my stable," said a voice Pip could never forget. Mulch pressed a pitchfork into the back of a woman he didn't know, who had a glowing blue sword. A woman he didn't recognize. He didn't have the slightest idea what was going on or why in the two hells this was happening, but whatever the reason, no one was going to shed blood in his stables. And with Master Tarsus involved, he didn't want his stables burned to the ground either. In all the years as the king's stableman, he'd not lost a horse, or tackle, or anything to fire, and he wasn't about to start now.

Tarsus began to laugh. "Now what do we do?"

"All of you set your weapons on the ground, except you Great Lizard, and walk outside," an authoritative voice said behind all of them.

Everyone groaned and took a peak over their shoulders. That voice was the one in which none of them wanted to hear, except maybe Sir Dwayne. He'd plans on taking Pip in front of the owner of it, King Lionel.

Lionel didn't look pleased at all.

No one moved.

"Now!" roared the king.

Lionel had been ready for anything, at least he thought he had, but he'd definitely not been ready for what Sir Edward told him. And when he'd arrived at the stables, the sight of his most trusted vassals engaging in this ridiculous endeavor was beyond his capacity of understanding. And apparently his orders as a king were only suggestions, which above all the foolishness going on, angered him more than anything. He'd specifically issued orders for all of them to try and get along. They didn't necessarily have to like it, or each other, but they knew full well they had to do it. And his daughter appeared to be one of the worst. He was greatly disappointed. He firmly expected his daughter, Laura, not to go against his orders or wishes. He'd indulged her nonsensical whim of becoming a king's knight, mainly because of what he felt he owed Tarsus, for bringing her back to him, for what the dragon had done for the kingdom, of ensuring the perpetuation of an heir. That alone was worth more than his own life, but this . . . this wasn't worth all of his many generosities he'd shown him. Nothing was worth that. And there was definitely nothing worth the life of all of his vassals. He wasn't going to let a moment of anger and stupidity cause his kingdom to crumble. He knew this would do it. From the inside, not the out. The king and the kingdom needed to be whole and hearty: incidents such as what was occurring would have crumbled the trust of his people, therefore his kingdom. That would never do.

"Out! All of you! Out now!" roared Lionel. "We'll settle all of this right now. I'm tired of such nonsense happening in my kingdom."

Lionel was definitely not a happy monarch. All of his most trusted subjects had decided they could no longer get along, which included his own daughter. Lionel knew without the help of Sir Edward, he probably wouldn't have known this kind of thing was even happening. Sir Edward had come to him, well, ran to him, out of breath, and informed his liege lord Sir Dwayne had been seen near the stables with sword in hand. He didn't feel whatever was going to happen would be good. So, the only thing he could do was inform the king and bide the consequences of his actions. Naturally, Lionel did what any good king would when confronted with such news: ordered the stables surrounded by his guardsmen. If he had to, he was going to knock some sense into all the idiots involved. What he saw when he finally arrived was a totally different picture than the one painted.

Lionel watched as all of them, including the princess, come trooping out of the stable, the opposite way they'd went in. Mulch, Laura, Sir Hook, Tarsus, and finally, Sir Dwayne, pushing the bound Pip in front of him.

Lionel looked at Sir Dwayne and pointed to Pip. In a very un-Lionel-like voice, he said, "Release him."

"Sire, you . . ."

That was as far as he got. Lionel cut him off by almost spitting at Sir Dwayne, "Now, Knight! I didn't agree to treat this young lad like a criminal. As long as I'm king, neither will you. Release him! Now!"

Sir Dwayne nodded, unceremoniously cutting Pip's bonds, pushing him away. His scowl told everyone what he really thought of the idea of letting the boy go. Pip staggered and would have fallen if not for, surprisingly, Princess Laura. She'd slowly moved closer to Tarsus when her father was confronting the knight. As Pip was shoved, she moved quickly to stop his headlong plunge. Pip thanked her with a smile. She smiled back and nodded.

Tarsus snaked his head between them and asked Pip, "Are you all right ?"

"Yea, I think so," answered Pip, rubbing his wrists where the ropes had bound him. "He didn't get a chance to do anything to me. He'd just got to me when you showed up. Thanks."

"I'm sorry, Pip. I didn't mean for this to happen again."

"Not your fault, you big lizard," Pip said, affectionately putting his hand on the dragon's nose. "You can't watch me all day and all night, and

I'm sure not gonna sleep with you. You take up too much of that small stall for me to be safe." Pip smiled. He knew the dragon was taking this harder than he was. "You'd probably roll on top of me, and then where would I be?" But Pip knew he was feeling guilt. He felt guilty himself for not being more careful. It wasn't all Tarsus's fault. "You can't do everything you know," he finished, giving Tarsus another pat and smile.

Tarsus nodded and a slight smile spread across his face. Pip knew they'd talk about it later, however, when they were alone.

Laura put her hand on Pip's forearm and then Tarsus' cheek to get their attention. She then nodded her head towards what she was looking at. What Tarsus saw made him shiver. This was definitely not playing out as he'd planned. While the three were having their private little moment, the things going on around them had gone unnoticed. Lionel had surrounded the stables with his guardsmen; all of them, over a hundred, from what Tarsus could estimate, were holding swords or cocked bows. And in front of them all was the king with his fists planted firmly on his hips.

"That's enough!" Lionel roared. "No one move! I've had enough! You will listen!" He could barely contain his anger. "All of you," pointed Lionel to the line, "are to stay where you are."

Laura took a step forward and began to say something to her father. "Father . . ."

A very unmistakable sound met her ears that froze her in her tracks, the sound of bows being cocked, swords coming out of their scabbards, and feet stomping down on hard packed ground: an unmistakable readiness of violence from a hundred soldiers.

"I said, don't move," Lionel ordered. The look on his face told Laura this was no time for platitudes or apologies. Maybe later, if there was a later, but not now. "As you see," continued the king, "there are others under my authority who do what they're told. If you don't believe, look around. The guards you see before you will shoot the next person who talks or moves without permission." He looked at Laura and emphasized what he'd said with, "Anyone."

Laura froze. She neither moved back to stand next to Pip and Tarsus or said another word. Her lip trembled with fear, sweat flowing down her cheeks. She realized her father had had enough of what he thought of as 'foolishness and stupidity'. *I've never seen him like this before. I hope he doesn't think I caused this? Or Tarsus? If he would just give me a chance to explain, I could possibly do something to help. I'd say Sir Dwayne started this, and not just today.*

Pip rubbed his wrists, standing next to Tarsus. He was hoping he got out of this one without his head being put on the chopping block, although he didn't know why he may have been in trouble again, Lionel didn't look too happy. The king's arms-men didn't look as if they were going to a county fair either. It didn't look too good.

Tarsus merely waited. The smells coming to him from the people around especially Lionel told him everything he needed to know. Violence was in the air, the smells confirming it. He most definitely didn't want this to get any uglier, so he sat down to wait for the outcome, his tail slowly wagging back and forth; he looked like the family dog waiting for its owner to give him permission to eat.

Lionel looked at each in turn, frowning at the ones he was most disappointed in: Mulch, Sir Hook, Laura, Tarsus, and Sir Dwayne. Pip he felt was the one person in all this who'd been thrown in the middle. Pip couldn't have possibly foreseen what was going to happen to him. To him, Lionel simply looked over without showing too much emotion. He hadn't forgotten what Tarsus told him only hours before about the lad, which still didn't please him, but he couldn't in all honesty blame the young man for what was happening. At some future point, he'd have to confront the issue, and the boy, but not just yet. But Tarsus, sitting next to the lad like he'd nothing to worry about, was another matter. He'd already made it clear to the dragon he wasn't pleased with his actions or his reasons for not informing him sooner what was truly going on. Twice in one day for the dragon was too much. Twice in one day for anyone was too much. Now he had to decide what to do about this mess. Lionel took a deep breath and began—one by one was the way to take care of this—at the beginning. "Mulch, my old friend," he said to the stable master, "could you please explain to me how you got caught up in this foolishness?"

Mulch bowed, acknowledging his king. "Your Majesty. I don't know what's transpired other than finding a female holding a sword to the back of Sir Hook, and I knew I couldn't allow one of our knights to be skewered as on a spit. And also, Your Majesty, I knew if things, as it were, was to get out of hand, Master Tarsus may have decided to fire the stables along with whoever he may consider responsible. I couldn't allow that to happen either." Mulch's voice rose when he talked about his beloved stables. "I've never lost a stable or horse to a fire in all the time I've been here and I wasn't going to start. The only way I could see to try and stop it was to get in among them." He bowed again, stopped. That was Mulch, straight to the point.

"I see," said Lionel, shaking his head. It seemed he couldn't fault Mulch either for what he believed he could do to stop this kind of violence. He then looked at the princess. "And you, my daughter? What was your excuse for getting caught in this?"

Mulch's face blanched, realizing who he'd been holding a pitchfork against: Princess Laura. A strangled noise came from him, which didn't go unnoticed by her. She then bowed to her father, but before addressing the king's question, she looked at Mulch. "I don't blame you, Master Stableman. Don't think twice on what you've done here. You were doing your duty, no matter to whom you were threatening. I thank you for your diligence." Then she turned to her father and said, "Father, Your Majesty, I, like Master Mulch, found Sir Hook, with a spear, threatening Tarsus. I couldn't stand there and do nothing. I felt, as Mulch had, it was my duty to try and stop what was happening." She bowed again, finished for the moment.

"I see," said Lionel again. "And you, Sir Hook? I suppose you thought it was your duty to get involved also?"

"Yes, sire. And no, sire," said Sir Hook, bowing to his king.

"Now you sound like Master Tarsus, Sir Hook," said Lionel. "Has he been giving you lessons? How can it be yes and no?"

"Sire, I knew beyond doubt I had to get involved with the incident developing with the dragon and Sir Dwayne," Sir Hook began. "Yes, it was, and is my duty, to protect anyone in need of help, but also, no, sire, Sir Dwayne had already given me an order to be vigilant in my duties today. He'd given me orders to watch the dragon, and if necessary, for me to step in and take charge. He felt things may come to a head between himself and the dragon when he went after the lad. So, no, sire, I'd been given an order to get involved as you say, with all of this. I shall always follow orders from my superiors, sire. Always. And always, My King."

"I see," said Lionel again. "It appears a different picture is coming into view than the one I'd expected to see." Lionel looked at Tarsus. "And you, Master Tarsus? What do you have to say?"

Without hesitation, Tarsus said in a firm voice, "I've told you, and everyone here, I'll not allow the knight to harm Pip again. It was no boast on my part." He stopped, and then dipped his head to Lionel.

"So I see," said Lionel gesturing to the stables. He shook his head and sighed. It looked like this wasn't going to be easy. He had to get more of an answer than duty or honor. At least Tarsus' answer had been straight to the point. He looked at the knight, his first among many. "And you, Sir Dwayne? Do you have an explanation for going against my orders?"

The knight bowed like the rest and then said in just as strong a voice as Tarsus, "I haven't gone against your orders, sire. My duty was clear on this, and it calls for me to protect you, the princess, and my kingdom. After hearing about the lad, I felt I had to take steps to perform that duty. I don't regret what I've done." He bowed again.

The king frowned. "And what was it you'd heard, Sir Knight?"

Sir Dwayne knew not to hesitate, not only was the king in no mood, it wasn't his nature. When his king asked the question, he answered. "The lad isn't as the dragon has said. He's a wizard, and it's my duty to protect you and the kingdom against such a one as he."

"Where did you hear such a thing?" asked Lionel.

"From the dragon's own mouth, sire," answered the knight.

A shock ran through the group. All of them looked at Pip and then Tarsus. The kid, a wizard? And the dragon knew about it, all this time.

"And when did you hear him say this?" asked Lionel, almost dreading the answer.

"Not two hours hence, sire."

"Where?"

"Just outside these very stables, sire, when he was talking with you."

Another gasp went out from the crowd. This time, however, the king could clearly hear the surrounding guardsmen gasp as well. "I see," said Lionel softly, hanging his head. *This is what I was afraid of. This is definitely getting out of hand.*

Lionel knew this wasn't good. Not only was his most trusted vassals about to do harm against one another, but one of the few men he trusted more than anyone had been eavesdropping. The guardsmen around them wouldn't, or couldn't, forget such a lapse in judgment. And he didn't know if the trust destroyed this night between his captain and them could ever be mended. Plus, the trust he'd had for Sir Dwayne would be even harder to mend.

"Explain yourself, Knight," Lionel barked.

"Sire?" said Sir Dwayne, not fully understanding.

"My vassals don't eavesdrop," said Lionel. "I'm most disappointed. I don't have to explain myself to you or anyone, but you do."

"Sire, I didn't intentionally stop to hear what was being said between yourself and the dragon. I . . ."

Lionel stopped him by holding up his hand, palm forward. "That's enough of that. You will no longer refer to Master Tarsus as 'dragon', or 'monster', or anything else but his name, Tarsus. You've lost that right. And I'll not allow Tarsus to denigrate you," Lionel looked at Tarsus, "Clear?"

Tarsus and Sir Dwayne looked at each other with scowls on their faces and then back to the king. In unison, they bowed to him, acknowledging the rebuke.

"Sire," said Sir Dwayne, bobbing his head, although he didn't show it, he wasn't happy about it.

"Continue," Dwayne's king ordered.

"Sire, as I said, I didn't intentionally try to hear what was said between you two. I simply didn't say anything to stop you. My intention was to talk to you about guard posts on the parapets of the castle, but as I passed the stables on the way to the castle, I heard voices. One of which was the dr . . . Tarsus, sire." The king's eyebrows went up at the knight's near mistake. He went on. "Anything having to do with Tarsus has to be known. But when I found out it was you who had been talking to him, I quickly turned to leave. If it had been anyone else, I would have intentionally stayed, no matter it being wrong to do. I don't trust Master Tarsus," he sneered the name, making it known to everyone he didn't think highly of Tarsus. "As I turned to leave, I heard the name of Pip, by you, sire, that's what stopped me. I couldn't move. I found myself wondering why you'd be discussing the boy. That's when I stayed, sire. Tarsus," he turned to the dragon, "said the boy was a mage. Although all this time he'd said he wasn't. He hadn't informed you because he didn't know how to tell you. He wasn't sure about his powers or what he could do, but he knew he could no longer keep it to himself. The lad was getting stronger every day, eventually someone would find out and it would be out anyway. That, sire, is when I knew I'd be vindicated in what had to be done. My duty was clear." He stopped, apparently finished. He simply watched the king, waiting for what would happen, as the rest did.

Lionel didn't say anything for a moment. He could understand what Sir Dwayne had gone through and what his dilemma was about:

not listening to his king's private conversation, and what his duty told him to do about the lie Tarsus had told him. But his mistake, the king realized, was in not listening to the whole conversation, and not coming to him about it. Lionel wasn't perfect by any means, no one was, but he did realize when he needed help. That was the reason for advisers and vassals with utmost honesty. Lionel began again. "I can't condone all of your actions this night, Sir Dwayne, other than your unfailing devotion to your duty. But I can't have knights in my guard who take it among themselves to cause such an uproar without the express permission of myself. I wish you would have come to me with this. I would have gladly told you what had been said and what I felt could have been done about it, and I would have counseled you on your duty to your king and kingdom." Lionel paced back and forth, his hands clasped behind his back. After a couple turns up and down the line-up, he found himself back in front of the knight. "You've been one of my closest confidants for most of my life, but what you've done tonight has made you unseemly. So, my dilemma is what I should do about it." Lionel hung his head, wishing he didn't have to do this. His emotions were rising and falling so fast, you could see his facial muscles twitch like a belly-dancer at a gypsy fair. He was only a few paces from the knight when he asked, "What do you think I should do, Sir Knight?"

No one moved. Tarsus and the rest seemed to hold their breath, waiting to see what would happen between the king and his knight. This was very unusual. A king didn't usually ask one of his retainers such a question. Especially one who'd done what he had; this wasn't a usual case.

Pip gulped. He hadn't realized he'd been holding his breath in anticipation.

The guardsmen around them never relaxed; if anything it seemed they tensed for action when Lionel got nearer to Sir Dwayne. Tensions were running high. If Sir Dwayne made any move that could be considered harmful, he'd never get a chance to say otherwise.

"Sire," said Sir Dwayne, bowing to his king, "I'm yours to command."

"I hope so," said Lionel. "Normally, we'd be doing this in the throne room, but since you seem to like having an audience, we'll do it here. I don't like what you make me do, but it seems you give me no choice." For a moment, Lionel couldn't go on. To postpone what he knew wouldn't go over very well, he turned to the others in the line. "Don't think Sir

Dwayne is the only one in trouble here." He pointed to each in turn. "All of you have a finger in this, and I'll get to you in a moment." He turned back to the knight. "Sir Knight, since you can't seem to take orders from me any longer, I feel you can't give them to anyone either. From this point on, until I feel you can do what is expected of you, you're no longer the captain of the king's knights."

Sir Dwayne didn't say anything. He stood facing his king's judgment with his head held high. "Sire."

"Also," continued Lionel, "to teach you how to take orders, even from someone you don't care for, and hopefully teach you some humility, from this day forward, you shall be page to young Pip."

Another gasp went up from everyone present. But no one made more of a sound than Pip himself. "What!" He nearly choked, thinking of Sir Dwayne being around him every day. Pip clapped a hand over his mouth, not meaning to say anything. Had that really come from him?

Lionel quickly held his hand up to the guardsmen to stop them from letting loose a barrage of arrows at the boy. "That's all right, Pip. I understand. When this is over, I'll give you some suggestions on how to handle your new page."

No one laughed. This wasn't a laughing matter. In front of hundreds of people, King Lionel had torn down a man who'd spent his whole life in the service of his king.

Lionel faced the knight again. "Do you disagree with my judgment, Dwayne?" He consciously didn't use his honorific. From this point on, he wouldn't need it, until otherwise told.

"I'm yours to command, sire. As always," he said, bowing again. His face showed no emotion, a blank canvas. But inside, he was humiliated, gritting his teeth and nodding.

"Good. Now then," Lionel turned to Tarsus. "You, Master Dragon. I've been very patient with you, because of my gratitude, but that only goes so far. You've done nothing to help the situation between yourself and Dwayne, although I've asked you to keep your actions to a minimum, to just get along. My daughter has constantly come to your aid, but that only goes so far as well. And it appears, you've corrupted her to your ways." Lionel walked in front of the dragon. "From this point on, you'll keep to the stable area, unless you're teaching Laura or Pip. I don't really understand why I'm giving you this concession. If I had a big enough dungeon, you'd probably be going there instead, if nothing else, to cool your wings for a year or two. You wouldn't miss that much time, since all you have now is time. But I keep my promises to my daughter, even if they don't make much sense." Lionel stared at the dragon. "If you go anywhere without my permission, you'll be thrown out of my kingdom. Is this clear?"

Tarsus bowed his head, not saying anything.

"Good." Lionel then turned to Laura. Before she could say anything, he held up his hand to stop her. "Not yet, daughter, I'll get to you in a moment." Then without any further words, he turned to Sir Hook. "You, Sir Hook, I can understand. You were doing what you were ordered to do. But that doesn't excuse you for not using your own judgment. Your honor and duty should have insisted on it. At the very least, asking your superior why he couldn't come to his king. I wish you'd have come to me with what Dwayne had ordered you to do. It would have caused much less of a fuss."

Sir Hook bowed. "Yes, sire."

"You, Sir Hook, will walk the parapet on guard duty until further notice. Maybe with the time on your hands, you'll remember who you're really duty bound to."

"Yes, sire." The knight bowed, not saying anything else.

"Mulch, my friend," Lionel said, turning to the stable master. "You, I give the worst task of all. I hope you'll forgive me?"

"Your Majesty," said Mulch, bowing as the rest had done.

"You, I order to do what you've always done: keep your eyes and ears open. You've never done anything else and I'm very satisfied with what you're doing. Now what you have to do is keep your eyes and ears open on what happens around this giant lizard." He pointed to Tarsus and grinned slightly to take some of the sting off his voice. Mulch bowed again. "And now, the hardest of all." He turned back to his daughter Laura. He shook his head and pursed his lips, thinking on how to begin.

Laura simply waited like the rest. She didn't quite know what to do. This was the first time she'd seen her father in such a fury. She hadn't thought he could get so mad. It wasn't in his nature. Apparently, however, she didn't know him as she'd thought.

"You, my daughter," began Lionel, "should have known better than anyone in this line. I've indulged your every whim since your mother left us. Everyone knows it. Your obsession with becoming a knight I've also indulged." He reached out and lovingly caressed Laura's cheek, taking in her beautiful blue eyes, so much like her mother's. He loved her so much.

But even she could wear down on his patience, this was one of those times. He let his hand fall to his side and then stepped back. "You, my daughter, I'll punish like all the others. I should never have pampered you like I have all these years, maybe if I'd punished you sooner, you wouldn't have felt it necessary to run away in the first place. I love you, Laura. So, therefore, you'll not be allowed to go near the stable area unless I give you my express permission. You may be trained by Tarsus in the training yard, but that's as far as you can go."

"Yes, Father. Sire," Laura said meekly, half-bowing, half-curtsying. "I'm sorry."

"You, above all, should have known not to get involved with this foolishness. No matter the reason." He looked sternly at her until she nodded. "Good. Very good. Now, Pip," he said, turning to the boy.

"Sire," Pip said, bowing.

"When all of these troublemakers are gone, I'll need to talk with you in the throne room. Please come as soon as you can."

"Yes, sire," Pip said, not understanding why the king would want to see him this late in the evening, especially after all that happened in the past few hours. He's probably going to kick him out of the kingdom, and he didn't want anybody to see or hear him do it. Throwing out a dragon was one thing, throwing out a budding wizard was something best done in private.

Lionel looked to the line of 'troublemakers' as he called them and said, "That's all. You have your orders. They'll start tomorrow. And Dwayne," he looked to the former knight, "you won't need a sword. Leave it in your quarters."

"Yes, sire," Dwayne said, bowing. He walked off, his steps echoing in the darkness. As he passed the line of guards, two of them fell in beside him. They weren't honor guards, they were babysitters, and everyone knew it.

Lionel turned to the rest of the guardsmen and said, "All of you have heard and seen what has happened here. Spread the word. It's your job, all of you, to make sure these orders are carried out. Do you understand?"

"Sire," a giant cheer went out.

"Good. Now. Sir Edward, please come forward," King Lionel formerly announced.

Sir Edward was one of the many guards the king had put around the stables. He didn't feel there was any great need for him to be near the king when he arrived. He'd melted in among the other men as he was told to do. His duty was clear, to protect his king and kingdom at all costs. If that meant firing on his own, then that would happen. But when he'd informed the king on what he'd seen near the stables, he was only performing a service, nothing more: duty. He wondered what the king would want, stepping forward and bowing formally. "Sire."

"Sir Edward, from this point on, you're the captain of the King's Guard. Normally, it would go to the second, but apparently, Sir Hook will be too busy to take the position." Lionel looked to Sir Hook standing in line with the others. "Do you accept?"

Sir Edward bowed low and then said, "I do, Your Majesty. But I have to admit, the person who is most qualified for the job is still Sir Dwayne."

"That's all right, Knight. I'll gladly help you through the rough parts. All you have to do is not be afraid to ask for help."

"Yes, sire." Sir Edward said nodding.

"Pip, please come when you can. I'll be waiting." Lionel then turned without waiting for a reply and headed for the castle.

*   *   *

CHAPTER 17

When Lionel and his guardsmen had gone, Tarsus was the only one left in front of the stables. The rest of the group who'd so enraged their king was long gone. They'd slowly wandered off after Dwayne was escorted to his quarters. He watched also as Pip turned without saying a word and went back to the stables. Tarsus figured he was going to put on the rest of his clothes, couldn't be seen in the presence of royalty in his undershirt. Tarsus watched but said nothing. He knew exactly how the young lad felt; he'd been in his shoes many times over the centuries. Although Pip wasn't the cause of the trouble, Lionel knew as well as he, Pip would be the one to end it. Tarsus just hoped Lionel didn't throw him out of the kingdom. With a sigh, he sat down to wait. One spot was as good as the next. After a few moments, Pip came through the stable doors, fully dressed, head down, shuffling his feet in the general direction of the castle, not looking at the dragon as he walked by. Tarsus understood, watching until he couldn't see him any longer. He needed to talk to Pip after he talked to the king to find out what he was said, and what the king had wanted of him. This mess tonight was definitely not what he'd planned. Actually, he didn't have a plan, but this was definitely not one he'd have chosen. This was going to make it very hard to train Pip, not to mention the princess. But, the cat was out of the barn now, nothing for it. He had to go with the hand that was dealt. *How in the world does this always happen to me? I've got to learn to keep out of trouble. If I don't I'll never be able to protect Pip. I'll never survive to help him. Blazes! The magic won't let us survive.*

All he could do was wait and brood.

*   *   *

Oh Boy! This wasn't what Pip wanted. What was he going to do? Tarsus had been trying to teach him how to control the power, but he still didn't really know what he was doing. Tarsus was constantly harping on control. "You have to control what you do. If you don't, you could very easily kill yourself and everyone around you." But that didn't teach him *how* to do it. It was frustrating. He'd just recently learned he was a wizard. How could he learn control over a power he didn't understand? Maybe Sir Dwayne's right. *Maybe I do need to be locked away for everyone's safety.*

After the king finished with those he'd called 'the troublemakers' and asked Pip to join him in the throne room, Pip went directly to his bed in the loft to finish dressing. When he'd gone to his bed earlier, he'd taken off all of his clothes except his short clothes. He didn't have enough in the way of garments to sleep in, as well as work in them. A nightshirt, or sleeping shirt, was never given to him by Mulch. In the heat, he slept almost nude; in the cold, he'd burrowed into the straw so he wouldn't freeze to death. When the knight had come for him, he'd only his short clothes on. The knight had given him just enough time to slip on a short leather jerkin before tying his hands behind him. He didn't have a special set of clothes appropriate enough for seeing a king in his court. All the ones he did have were for working in, and around, the stables. He didn't seem to have the choice in very much tonight: no choice in what Sir Dwayne had done to him, no choice in what King Lionel had done, and no choice about what he had to wear to see the king. So, he put on his best face, the only clothes he had, the cleanest of two leather jerkins he owned, a pair of heavy trousers that bore holes in each knee, and his only pair of shoes, an ankle-high, soft deer skins that flopped when he walked. He sighed, crawled down the ladder, hit the straw-covered floor, and put the first foot forward to meet the king. His heart raced, sweat beading on his forehead, and his knees shaking, as he shuffled his way to the gates.

"Halt!" said a gruff voice at the gate. "What do you want?"

"I'm Pip from the stables. The king told me to come see him as soon as I could," explained Pip in a halting voice. "He told me he'd be waiting."

"Stay where you are, boy," ordered the guard. "It's late and I doubt very much the king would want to see you anyway. I don't know what game you play, but get back to where you belong before I teach you your place." The guard turned his back on Pip and resumed his vigilance around the portcullis, ignoring him. Apparently he was one of the few guards who hadn't been at the stables.

Pip didn't go away as he was told, he simply stood and waited. He didn't know what he was waiting for, but he knew the king had told him to come to the castle as soon as possible, and he had to get in there somehow. He stood where he was and tried to think of another way inside. The notion of following the same route Princess Laura had the night she ran off seemed like a very bad idea indeed, that would surely get him strung up, if tonight had taught him anything, plus, a journey like that would be too much for his nerves right now. Especially considering what happened. His mind wasn't working too well at the moment. All he could think of was Sir Dwayne coming to the stables in the morning to work as his page. His page! Sir Dwayne as a page, that would take a lot of getting used to. Why in the world would the king do something like that to one of his best men? He wondered if it had anything to do with him. He hoped not. Sir Dwayne scared him to death. Pip knew he wouldn't last two minutes if the knight decided to kill him. The only thing that prevented him from doing it the two times he'd had him was the knight's own personal reasons, not just out of duty.

In his reverie, he didn't notice the guard come up to him. He was lost in his thoughts and feelings of what he'd gone through in the past couple of hours. Grabbing his arm in a firm grip was the only thing that brought Pip out of himself. "Move, I say," shouted the guard. With a whimper, Pip was shoved in the direction of the stables. As he hit the ground, his mind registered what happened to him only after hearing someone shout, "That's enough!"

The portcullis guard turned to find his sergeant staring at him: Kitsch. "What's going on?" he asked. "Why did you throw that young lad to the ground, Morley?" He stood with his fists cocked on his hips, scowling as he watched Pip slowly pick himself up and rub his knee with a grimy hand.

"This boy said something about coming to see the king, Sarge. It's got to be some kind of game he's playing." Morley explained. "Do you really think the king would want to see a waif like him? And even if he did, do you think he'd see him at night?"

"Fine, but you didn't have to rough the lad up." The sergeant looked at Pip and scowled again. Then he asked, "What's this about, lad? Who are you?"

Pip rubbed his knee again where he'd scraped it from his fall. "My name's Pip. I'm from the stables. King Lionel told me to come see him as soon as I could. He said he'd be waiting for me."

"Pip, you say?" the sergeant asked.

"Yes," answered Pip.

The sergeant bowed to him then. Pip could hear an audible groan, and then, "If you'll follow me, Pip, I'll show you to the throne room. King Lionel is waiting."

Morley could only stand watching the strange scene with his mouth hanging open. Before Sergeant Kitsch escorted Pip away, he turned to Morley and said, "I'll deal with you when I get back. King Lionel just informed me of young Master Pip's summons to the castle. I was on my way to inform you and the others to watch out for the lad, when what did I see? You," he pointed his finger at Morley, "beating up on the very lad you were to admit to the castle." He didn't look very happy. Morley looked as if he could be sick at any moment.

Kitsch asked Pip, "Are you all right, lad?"

"Yes, fine. Thank you."

"Please, follow me." Kitsch turned and walked inside.

Pip had been living and working around the castle for as long as he could remember, but in all that time, he'd never actually set foot inside it until now. Mulch, of course, visited the castle many times over the years, but in those cases, he never let anyone accompany him. And as far as he knew, Mulch would never have let him go anyway. Through a maze of corridors and steps, Kitsch wound his way up from the portcullis to the throne room. Along every hall and niche hung numerous tapestries depicting scenes of violence and lovely landscapes; Pip was almost overwhelmed. Also there were suits of armor standing upright on pedestals that towered over anyone who stood beside them. Pip was in awe of everything. The sheer grandness of the castle itself nearly left him speechless.

Kitsch smiled at Pip. Every so often he'd look back to see the boy's face light up as he swiveled his head trying to look at everything at once. Torches spaced along the walls lit as many tapestries as not, smoke lazily floating upward towards breathing holes in the ceiling. "You've never been in the castle proper, have you, lad?"

"No, Sir Kitsch. This is the first time," answered Pip.

"My name is Kitsch, lad. I'm no knight. Not everyone you see guarding the king is a knight,." he explained, not unkindly.

"Sorry. I didn't know. To someone like me, everyone with a sword is a knight."

Kitsch smiled and shook his head. "I'm more than happy to guard our king and castle, without becoming a knight. It's my duty, just as it's theirs, and it's my pleasure."

Pip nodded.

"Try not to be too disappointed. Some of us do want to become knights, but the training is long and arduous. Some make it and some don't. I for one think if you can use a sword, and competent, you don't need the title to go along." Kitsch touched the sword hanging in the scabbard at his hip.

"But I thought everyone wanted to be a knight," asked Pip.

"No, lad," smiled Kitsch. "I'm perfectly content to be a guard at the castle."

After a few more twists and turns on their journey, they entered a long corridor ending in a set of ornately carved wooden doors nearly fifteen feet tall. Standing on each side were two guards holding spears. As Kitsch and Pip approached, both crossed spears barring their passage. The guard on the left said, "Halt! No one's permitted into the throne room."

Kitsch said to the door guard, "King Lionel is waiting for the lad inside." He indicated Pip with a hand on his shoulder.

The guard looked down at Pip and asked, "What's your name?"

"Pip," said Pip squeakily.

"Ah," said the guard on the right. "Majesty has been expecting you." Both lifted the spears out of the way, and the guard on the left opened one of the doors. "If you would, sire is waiting."

Kitsch didn't move. Pip looked at him. "No, Pip. It was my job to get you here, that's all. You go on alone."

"But . . ." protested Pip.

"It's all right, lad. There's nothing to fear. His Majesty merely wishes to talk."

Pip nodded. "Thank you for your help."

Kitsch nodded and smiled.

Pip entered the throne room. With a small click, the giant door slid shut behind him.

*   *   *

CHAPTER 18

Lionel was waiting for Pip as he entered the throne room. After the door clicked shut, Lionel stood from the throne and walked towards the young man. Between them was nearly fifty feet of granite floor sparkling with torch light, as if the light refused to be absorbed and extinguished. Twinkling stars in the earth at his feet, rather the night sky over his head. Pip was entranced by it. As he and Lionel moved closer to one another, he'd glance down once in a while to see a dim distorted shadow of himself reflected back. Lionel watched him and smiled. The floor always fascinated him too. Even in this day of wonders, he marveled at the beauty and craftsmanship in his great-grandfather's accomplishment.

As Pip got nearer, step by step, Lionel couldn't help but notice the clothes the lad wore, or lack thereof. He reminded Lionel of the many street waifs he'd seen in other kingdoms he'd visited. There were a few in his own, of course, but not as many as one would think for a kingdom of his size. Lionel prided himself on getting as many of them off the streets as he could. He fostered a housing program so many could get off the streets, putting them to work earning a modest living instead of having to steal, some of them watching the outer boundaries of the kingdom looking for signs of trouble. But in all he did, he couldn't keep up, and he couldn't help them all. Seeing Pip's trousers looking as if they'd been picked up from a garbage heap only made his memories stronger. Pip's jerkin was too short for his slender frame, his shirt not reaching to his wrists, his pants having holes in the knees, the only thing half-way presentable was his soft leather shoes, he did notice they slapped the ground at every step he took though. Although thread-worn and used, they were clean.

As Pip got closer, he knew what the king was looking at by the scowl on his face, and he immediately blushed with embarrassment. He'd just as soon come nude or in his small clothes. Pip bowed to Lionel within ten feet of him. "Sire." He was still blushing. "Please forgive me. I know my clothes aren't worth an audience with you, but they're all I have. Mulch has yet to give me new this season."

"No worries, Pip. We can do something about that later," said Lionel, waving away Pip's explanation, clothes being the least of his problems at the moment. "Come, let's sit for a short while so we can talk." Lionel gestured to the throne. Pip noticed there wasn't another chair, the only one being the throne itself. Pip was shocked when the king sat on one of the lower steps instead. Lionel gestured again, but this time for Pip to sit next to him. Afterwards, for a time, neither spoke. Lionel watched Pip, as he craned his neck trying to see everything at once in the hall. Lionel smiled watching him and then his thoughts returned to why he'd asked the youth to come and he sobered.

"Pip, lad, do you have any idea why I asked you here?"

"No, sire," answered Pip, shaking his head.

"Well, to put it bluntly, Tarsus."

"Tarsus, sire?" Pip said, not understanding.

"Yes. Tarsus and I had a chat just a short while before the stupidity at the stables. I think you may have guessed that by what Dwayne said." Lionel watched Pip for any sign of power, for anything hinting he could do the things Tarsus said he could. All he saw however was a confused and scared boy who didn't know what was going on, or why he was in the middle of it. He almost felt sorry for the lad. But for the sake of his kingdom and his Laura, he had to be strong himself and do his own duty. "Tarsus told me a few things today that didn't make me happy."

Pip didn't say anything, gulping, waiting for the worst. *Well, looks like this is it. He'll probably send me away. I guess I messed up bad. Mulch always said I'd been nothing but trouble.*

"Tarsus told me you're a mage, a wizard or sorcerer, after he'd told us otherwise."

Pip looked down at his feet instead of at the king. He was afraid of what he might find in his eyes: Anger? Disgust? Disappointment? Fear? He didn't know. He could only nod.

"He also said you didn't know it yourself until he told you. Is that true?"

"Yes, sire," Pip said in a small voice. "Until I floated in the air in the stables, the day I was so angry at Tarsus, I didn't know anything. I wish I still didn't." *Here we go. Now he'll tell me I can't stay.*

Lionel took a deep breath and then said, "I can't blame you for what happened, Pip. You didn't ask for what you've become. But I can ask you why you didn't come to me or even Sir Dwayne? We could have offered advice, if nothing else." He stopped, watching the boy's reaction. What he saw was the same thing he'd seen a few moments before, nothing more: a frightened youth who didn't know what to do. "That was your duty, just as it was for Sir Dwayne to say something about his conscience. It's not been the first time this night I've been disappointed with one of my subjects. But when it comes down to it, I don't really know what to do with you."

Pip wasn't very shocked to hear the king had been disappointed. It mirrored his own thoughts just moments ago. But Pip was shocked to hear King Lionel say he didn't know what to do with him. What did he mean? Didn't know what to do? He could do anything he wanted, he was the king. His king. He could throw him out into the world without a backward glance, lock him away in the dungeons to never see the light of day, have him skewered on a pike and placed in the courtyard for everyone to see, as a warning to future wizards; he was the king, his word was law. "Sire? You can do anything you want with me. You're the king."

Lionel took another deep breath and said, "Yes, I'm the king of Musk, but technically speaking, you're not one of my subjects."

Pip looked at him askance, shocked. "Not?"

"No, Pip." Lionel shook his head. "I gave up that right as your king when you became a wizard, or sorcerer. Under our laws, you're a sovereign person, subject to no laws but your own. To live as you choose, go where you wish, and do as you see fit from this day forth." Lionel spread his hands in a gesture of helplessness.

Pip was stunned. He couldn't say anything; for one, he didn't know what it meant he was a sovereign person; for another, he wouldn't know how to live on his own. He had many dreams of wandering the world, getting out on his own, living where there was no rules, doing what he wanted, when he wanted, how he wanted, especially after one of Mulch's thumping's, but it was only a dream. For his whole life, this had been his home, the thought of leaving terrified him.

"There's another problem also," Lionel continued, seeing the blank stare and shocked expression on the youth's face. "One of the biggest, but not the least, is one wrong word or gesture from you, whether accidental or not, you could destroy my entire kingdom. I have to think of the safety of my daughter above all else. She'll be the next ruler of Musk, because there's no other. I've no sons, no heirs but her." Lionel saw from the boy's expression the prospect of leveling the kingdom terrified him, which was a good thing. By all that was Holy, it scared Lionel too. Pip's face was a mask of misery, and then Lionel began to understand a few other matters. With an intuitive leap, he asked, "Hasn't Tarsus told you any of this?"

"No, sire," Pip said with tears brimming in his eyes. "I've just recently learned I was a wizard or sorcerer or whatever you want to call it. Sir Dwayne trussed me up like a chicken, twice, Mulch has been avoiding me for reasons I can't understand, and Princess Laura has taken to watching me as if I'd stolen something of value she means to get back. And now, you tell me you're *not* my king any longer." Tears streaked his cheeks as he said the last. "Tarsus has been telling me I need to learn control, but he doesn't explain very well how to get control or why I need it. Now, I guess I know." He shook silently as his tears flowed freely.

"There's one other thing, Pip," said Lionel, regretting what he had to say and do to the boy. "If I know Tarsus, and I think I do by now, the big lizard hasn't told you his part in all this."

Pip looked up at Lionel, his eyes pools of moisture. In a hitching voice, he asked, "What does he have to do in all this? If it hadn't been for him, I might have already done something stupid with this power. He's been trying to help me."

"Yes, he has. I don't doubt that." Lionel placed a reassuring hand on Pip's shoulder. "And he's probably the only one who can help you. I've never heard of another wizard anywhere near here. For that matter, I've never heard of a dragon being around here before Tarsus showed up on my doorstep. But, Tarsus, if you haven't noticed, tends to keep things to himself, sometimes, need-to-know things."

"I've noticed, sire," Pip said, bobbing his head in agreement, drying his eyes with the sleeve of his shirt.

"Well, you have a problem just as I do."

"Which is what, sire?" asked Pip. *Just what I need, another problem.*

"Granston."

"You mean your adviser, sire?" Pip's eyes widened. "What about him?"

"You did know why Tarsus is here, don't you?" asked Lionel.

Pip nodded.

"You know what Tarsus said about him?" Lionel watched Pip nod again. "He's a wizard too. A powerful one from what Tarsus said." Lionel shook his head in disgust. "I feel like a fool because of him, so I owe Tarsus. If not for that big scaly critter, I may not have a kingdom now, or I might be dead. Granston's the one who put Tarsus in that spell, or cocoon, or sleep, or whatever for so many centuries. Tarsus considers him an enemy. And himself bait." Lionel clasped his hands, wringing them as if he'd something on them he needed to get off. "From what he's told me, Granston will be back, and he'll want revenge. And you," he looked at Pip, "and my kingdom will be in his way." Lionel stood up and walked about ten feet away, turning back to look at Pip sitting on the throne's steps. "If what I understand is right, if something were to happen to him, the same thing would also happen to you. So, you have to learn to defend yourself, which puts my kingdom in the line of fire and Laura in danger."

Pip hid his face in his hands. *Great! Just great!* Pip ran his hands through his unruly hair and came to a very unpleasant decision. Looking up at Lionel, he said, "Then I'll have to leave."

"Can you?" countered Lionel quickly.

"What do you mean?" asked Pip narrowing his eyes. His mood had shifted to one of weariness, all thoughts of tears gone. "If my staying puts Princess Laura and your kingdom in danger, then I have to leave."

"But can you leave without Tarsus?" Lionel clarified.

"He's part of the problem, sire." Pip jumped up to face the king squarely. "He'll have to go with me. We'll go as far away as we can so no harm can come here. Besides, I need him, just as you said, he has to teach me to control this inside of me."

"And there lies the worst of my problems, Pip," said Lionel, looking sour himself. "He either won't go, or he can't."

"How so?"

"He made a promise . . ." Lionel said, scowling. ". . . And I agreed to it."

Pip looked stricken. He cocked his head enquiringly.

"Teaching Laura to be a king's knight."

Pip threw up his hands. "That cold-blooded lizard!"

*   *   *

Pip slowly made his way back to the stables. *How did this happen? How did I go from a stable boy to a wizard with no idea how to stay alive? My life was so much simpler without the lizard.* Pip's thoughts kept him from noticing that self-same lizard waiting for him. Pip's head was down, and he wasn't watching where he was going. He'd walked to the stables so many times, by the same path, his feet seemed to know the way without any conscious thought. Tarsus, seeing Pip's demeanor, didn't disturb him. He simply stepped in front of the boy. Pip didn't notice either the dragon's movement or his bulk in front of him until Tarsus sat down. Pip walked right into Tarsus's broad chest. *That* finally got his attention. With a start, Pip came awake, looking at the scaly mound that miraculously appeared in front of him. Then he looked up into the face of the dragon, him looking down. Pip said nothing, opening and closing his mouth like a fish out of water. After a moment, however, tears streamed down his cheeks, his throat tightened up, strangling noises bubbled through his nose. His crying was the thing that told Tarsus more than words could, Lionel told Pip certain truths as he'd seen them, and now Tarsus had to explain why he'd kept those truths to himself.

"Oh, Pip," Tarsus said softly, "it's not as bad as you might think. And I won't leave you. You're not in this alone." As gently as he could, Tarsus steered Pip towards the stable with his nose, nudging him in the direction of his own stall. This was no time for the lad to be alone. Pip didn't resist, nor pushed the dragon away, nor rail at him, which wouldn't have surprised the dragon.

Pip couldn't say anything, his thoughts occupied with events which effectively left him on his own and without a home. Lionel had said, "You're a sovereign person. You can do whatever you choose. I'm not your king. I'm not your king. Not your king. Not." He went where Tarsus steered him and found himself slowly sliding down one of the walls in a stall, until his backside met the ground.

For over two hours, Pip said and did nothing, while Tarsus watched over him. By degrees, his tears dried and his head fell to his shoulder, his exhaustion plain. Any time now Tarsus knew he'd be asleep. He leaned close and softly as he could said, "I'm sorry, Pip. I can only guess what

Lionel said to you. When you're ready, we'll talk about it." He gently nudged Pip's cheek with his long slender nose.

Pip listlessly nodded, saying nothing. In moments, he was asleep, leaving Tarsus worried.

*   *   *

CHAPTER 19

Granston's patience was wearing thin. For the past eight days, he'd been locked up in a small room without much light and little enough food. And for all his vaulted power, no matter how many times he tried, he could do nothing about getting out. Magic wouldn't work. His magic wouldn't work. He was stuck in an enchanted cage with no way out he could find, for the moment.

Twice a day, a small sliding panel in the door was opened and food shoved in, and twice a day without fail, he tried to confront his captors. Each time, however, the effort was wasted, and each time, he tried magic and nothing happened. He could see no way out. He could only wait. It didn't sit well.

When he'd arrived at the hall of the Gnomes with the Assanti Assassins and the Gnome idiot Raulch, his plan had been simple: encourage, cajole, or ensorcell the whole Gnome Kingdom to confront and then kill that blasted lizard Tarsus. After the confrontation at his little campsite, Granston wasn't going to take any chances of Grundehl saying no. Before leaving, he'd made a few adjustments to Raulch's loyalties, along of course with his helpers; but apparently that hadn't worked as well as he'd planned. Only twice since being put in this cage had he even seen Raulch, and both times was for him to deliver his meals, not a word or comment had been exchanged. The suggestions he used on Raulch and his cronies had apparently been washed away, or they had indeed worked, yet had been turned against him.

Grundehl had done his homework when it came to this cage, or someone did it for him. Whichever the case, it had the intended effect: capture and contain. Grundehl had been very smart not to let anyone near him, and Granston knew the king of the Gnomes wasn't very smart, which fact alone led him to believe the king had his own adviser, an adviser who was a wizard. Granston knew eventually he'd have the chance to meet this adviser, the one actually pulling Grundehl's strings, but for now, all he could do was wait.

He had many problems to tackle before he could even consider the giant lizard. He'd get to them, oh yes, he would.

*   *   *

CHAPTER 20

Pip came out of his funk the next morning. He still wasn't his old self, but he at least answered questions put to him. At one point through the night, Tarsus almost called for a healer. Slipping down the wall and falling asleep, tears streaking his cheeks, Pip didn't stir until the sun shone fully on the stable doors. Usually he would have been up and moving seeing to his many chores long before the sun made its birth in the sky. But Tarsus knew Pip needed time, not a healer, only time would heal what was ailing the lad. The news Lionel laid at his feet had been too much emotionally. Tarsus knew he could only wait and watch and help to ensure Pip came through this without any permanent damage. As Pip finally stirred, Tarsus was there by his side.

Pip's eyes opened.

Tarsus leaned close.

Pip blinked and then like a babe, he knuckled his eyes trying to shake off his heavy sleep.

Tarsus asked quietly, "Are you all right, Pip?"

For a moment, Pip said nothing. He ran his hand through his unruly mop of hair, wiped his face, and then knuckled his eyes again. "I guess so." He smiled.

"What happened, Pip? Can you tell me?" asked the dragon.

Pip's face fell, but he did answer. "I don't know yet if I can talk about it. I don't know what to do."

"What did Lionel say to you? Can I help?"

Pip didn't say anything, tears pooling in his eyes again.

Tarsus' emotional state wasn't the best at the moment either. He knew as long as Pip was hurting, he'd hurt as well. All he could do was be there for the lad and help him through whatever the king had said. "You're not alone, Pip. As long as I'm alive, you'll never be alone. If I can help, I will."

Pip could only nod.

"When you're ready, I'll be here," said the dragon.

Pip couldn't speak, his throat was shut tight with emotion. He realized Tarsus would be there to help him after all, after being so angry at the dragon last night. He'd been an idiot. What happened to him and was still happening wasn't Tarsus's fault. Tarsus hadn't made him a wizard. The gods did. If he was to be angry with anyone, it was them he needed to scream at.

Tarsus nudged Pip again to reassure him and then slowly lumbered out of the stall. When he did, he ran into the former knight, Dwayne. He was standing just to the side of the stall, waiting for something Tarsus knew not what. The dragon stopped in his tracks and looked at Dwayne askance. "Can I help you?"

Dwayne seemed fairly chipper this morning considering what happened the night before. Without any animosity in his voice, he answered, "You may, Sir Dragon. I'm looking for young Pip. I'm to report to him every morning for orders. Have you seen him?" He stood with his hands clasped behind his back in a relaxed manner and a slight smile spread across his face. The sight of a smile alone on the knight's face almost undid Tarsus altogether. Usually, the man was stoic and uncompromising, hard-featured, and never smiled. His clothes were that of a simple working-class man, just off to the fields, or stables: a simple soft leather breeches, tan boots, shirt of what looked like suede with a matching belt around his waist which sported a dirk, not his usual sword. And if Tarsus wasn't mistaken, he was enjoying himself immensely, which in turn made the dragon very leery.

Tarsus sat down and frowned at the man. "You're awfully cheerful this morning, Knight."

"I'm Knight no longer, Master Tarsus. This is the will of my king, and I'll not gainsay him. If I'm to be page to young Pip, I'll do so with my whole heart, as I've done everything in my life," the former knight answered.

Tarsus's mouth fell open in astonishment.

Dwayne simply smiled and then asked again, "Have you seen Pip, Master Dragon?"

Tarsus shook his head to clear it and then answered, "Yes, but if you would, can you leave him alone for a while. King Lionel delivered some unsettling news to him last night, and he hasn't taken it very well."

"Oh?" Dwayne asked. "Is there anything I can do to help?"

Tarsus eyed the ex-knight suspiciously. "No, I don't think so. He just needs time," said Tarsus. "I think you know how the king can be?" He inclined his head.

"I see," said Dwayne. "Well, then, if I can't do anything for him, or get my orders from young Pip, is there anything I can do for you?"

Tarsus was taken aback. He didn't know quite what to make of the former knight's attitude change. Just the night before, he was more than willing to see Pip and himself spitted over an open fire; now, he was more than willing to see Pip's laundry done properly. It wasn't just baffling, it was eerie. Plus, he was willing to do whatever he could to help.

Finally, Tarsus said, "I don't really know. By now, Pip's usually working in or about the stables. I usually don't have much for him to do until the princess trains, or he does. Pip still works with the stable master, Mulch. Why don't you see if he needs help with anything."

Dwayne bowed, smiled, turned, and left without saying a word. Tarsus watched him go and could only shake his head in bafflement. When the ex-knight walked away, Pip came out of the stall, slowly making his way to a bucket sitting next to the stall door. Without thinking he plunged his head and face into the pail. After a moment, he came up with a splutter and gasp, water streaming from his face and cheeks. Tarsus thought he looked slightly better afterwards. His face was still pale, his eyes sporting bags under them, but his color had improved from moments ago. He seemed to be trying to shake off his lethargy from the night before.

"Are you better, Pip?" asked Tarsus, watching the youth closely.

Pip lifted his head to look at the dragon, at first not saying anything, but after looking around like he was searching for something, he finally said, "What?"

"Are you better?" Tarsus asked again.

Pip bobbed his head, running his hand through his soggy hair, flinging water over his head. "Yea, I think so. I still don't know what to do yet, but I think I can handle it now."

"Handle what, Pip? What did Lionel say to you?"

"That he's not my king," answered Pip with a downcast look. Without saying anything else, leaving Tarsus speechless, he turned and walked towards the back of the stable.

✱   ✱   ✱

Laura was looking for Tarsus. Lionel, her father, had decreed she couldn't be anywhere near the stables unless he'd specifically given his permission. But he also said she could still be trained by Tarsus in the practice yard, yet Tarsus wasn't there, so there was a gray area for her to work from. She'd not be disobeying her king; she'd be doing exactly what he'd told her she could do. She couldn't train unless Tarsus was there to help her—he was late—she had to find the big lizard to get things started. Usually Tarsus was on time for her sessions. He hated tardiness, but today, he hadn't shown up, so she had to go fetch him herself. And she wasn't about to lose an opportunity to find out what was going on. She figured it was her duty to find out what the lizard had been doing and why he wasn't where he was supposed to be. Tit-for-Tat.

Like all plans, things didn't quite go as she thought. As her hand reached to open the stable doors, a very familiar voice spoke behind her. It was shades of last night all over again. Her heart nearly stopped, along with her hand reaching for the door.

"Can I help you, Princess?" asked Dwayne.

Laura turned to confront the former Knight. "I don't know if you can or not, Sir Dwayne."

Dwayne frowned at the princess. She knew as well as everyone what had befallen him. This blatant disrespect was uncalled for, even from her. "I'd have expected that from the dragon, my lady, not from you," rebuked Dwayne, his eyes going flat. "But even he didn't do so when we spoke this morning."

Laura looked crestfallen as soon as the words came out of her mouth. Dwayne was right. He didn't deserve that. "Please, forgive me," apologized Laura. "The past couple of days have done nothing for my manners. Father was right to rebuke me in front of the whole kingdom." She bowed to the ex-knight.

For a moment, Dwayne said nothing, and then with a nod of his head, he said, "Yes, your father is very wise at times."

This surprised Laura, given the fact he was stripped of his title and position by him. The surprise must have shown on her face, for Dwayne said, "I see you're surprised. Don't be. Your father's not as stupid as people think. For him to be king, he can't be."

Laura looked at Dwayne squarely. "How can you not hate him for what he's done to you?"

"Hate? My lady?" answered Dwayne with a puzzled expression, "How can I hate your father? I've never hated him. He's my king, and he's done nothing to me. I find myself without position and page to young wizard Pip because of my own actions, not because of your father. And I'll not have you, or anyone else, gainsay his decisions," Dwayne finished with his voice rising in anger.

Laura's mouth fell open in astonishment. She was beginning to see one of the reasons why he'd been chosen for the position of captain of the King's Knights, but his actions towards Tarsus and Pip also showed her reasons why it was taken away. The whole affair baffled her. From the moment Tarsus had entered the castle grounds, Dwayne had done nothing but antagonize him and degrade him, poor Pip the one in the middle of it all.

Dwayne smiled at Laura's reaction. "Why are you shocked, my lady? I've never blamed anyone for my actions. They were wholly my own. What I've done and continue to do is for my king and kingdom. If those actions haven't had the outcome I wished, fault can only be put on me, no one else. I don't regret what I've done. If given the chance, I'd do the same thing without hesitation."

Before Laura could say anything else, Dwayne continued, but in a different direction. "And you haven't answered my initial question, Princess. What are you doing here? If memory serves, you cannot be here." He crossed his arms and waited for a reply.

That stumped her for the moment. She'd thought to distract him into forgetting why he'd stopped her in the first place. She thought it had worked, apparently not. "I can go where I choose," Laura said quickly.

"No, Your Highness," Dwayne disagreed. "You can only go where your father allows you to go."

Laura was trying to think fast, but before she could say anything, the doors swung wide and Pip came out of the stables.

When he saw both of them standing by the door, Pip seriously thought about turning around and going back the way he came. But he was face to face with Laura and the knight, although a little intimidated by Dwayne, he didn't want to look like a coward. He looked at them and his throat tightened slightly, not saying anything, he didn't know what to say.

Dwayne was the first to do something. Even in an awkward moment as this, his training saw him through. He bowed to Pip and said, "Hello, wizard. Is there anything I can do for you?"

Pip's mouth fell open in surprise. This was the last thing he expected, or wanted, especially from him. King Lionel told him to order Dwayne to do anything: be firm, but fair. If he had any trouble out of the ex-knight, to get word to him through the palace guards and he'd see to his punishment. But after all the things that happened and what the king told him, actually doing, was a different matter. Pip was frozen with indecision.

Laura saw Pip's dilemma and stepped in to help. Maybe she could distract Dwayne and put his attention back on her. She looked at Dwayne and said, "You can go find Tarsus. I need to train today, and I can't seem to find him."

Pip breathed a sigh of relief, looking Laura's way and grinned. For the moment, Dwayne's attention wasn't on him. *Thank you, Princess. I won't forget this.*

Dwayne looked at the princess and repeated, "Princess, you're not to be here."

Pip realized what Dwayne meant, as if he were truly waking up. His mouth opened in a surprised expression. "Princess Laura, King Lionel said last night you couldn't be at the stables. You better go before you get into trouble." He looked at the princess like Lionel may come around a corner at any moment.

Laura looked sternly at Pip. How could he say something like that when she'd just saved him from an embarrassing moment? Laura was stunned. Even Pip? She could almost understand Dwayne trying to send her away, but Pip?

And that's when another's voice gave his two coins worth. "You must leave, Your Highness."

All three turned to see Sir Hook standing with sword in hand, just feet away. Apparently while Laura, Pip, and Dwayne were busy, Sir Hook had simply walked up. Dwayne was stunned, upset with himself, as no one had been able to get that close to him without his hearing since his training days, many years ago. This business with the dragon and wizard had distracted him too much to admit. *It would serve me right to have my innards handed to me on a plate.*

Pip jumped slightly, his nerves not being what they had days earlier. Laura stopped talking and hung her head. What could she really say?

And that, of course, was when the great lizard showed his huge head: literally.

Tarsus snaked his head around the corner of the stable and said, "Princess, you must leave. Your father would not be happy about you being here."

"That's true, Your Highness, you must leave," said Mulch right behind Dwayne. "Your father is not the kind of man to take this lightly. You must leave."

Laura covered her face with her hand. *This is just great. Who else is going to show up? This is becoming another scene like last night.*

And just like that, as if her thoughts were deeds, a very familiar voice all of them knew chimed in, "You're quite right. All of you. I'm not very happy with her right now."

Everyone turned with a small jump to see Lionel standing not twenty paces from them. The only difference between now and the scene last night was he wasn't surrounded by a hundred guardsmen. Pip was very grateful.

All of them immediately lined up and bowed to their king.

Sir Hook put his sword away and bowed again when Lionel's eyes wandered to him.

Dwayne simply smiled.

Tarsus inclined his head.

Mulch bowed and covered his face with his hand.

Pip bowed deeply to Lionel when his eyes roamed towards him and sheepishly grinned.

Laura cleared her throat when her father's stern gaze got to her and asked, "Father, what are you doing here?"

"This is my kingdom, child. I can go where I choose," he answered without humor. "More importantly, what are you doing here? I forbade you to come anywhere near here without my permission if I remember correctly." Lionel looked at each in line. "As I believe all of these gentle beings have told you." He gazed at his daughter sternly.

No one spoke or moved. A collective hush came over them all.

"Why, Laura?" asked Lionel, not receiving an immediate answer from his daughter.

"I came to find Tarsus, Father," she finally answered, after sighing loudly. "He was late for our training session, and I was concerned. Tarsus is usually never late for anything. So, I came to help if there was anything amiss."

"I see," said Lionel. "And why didn't you come to me so I could do something?" Lionel knew he was putting her on the spot, which was unheard of, especially in front of his other subjects—usually this sort of thing was done in the throne room with no witnesses—but he was very tired of his orders not being obeyed. Laura being his daughter was no excuse for this sort of thing happening. Lionel waited for an answer along with the rest.

Laura didn't say anything. She just looked at him.

"That's what I thought," said Lionel. He knew his daughter very well after all these years, so he knew what was going on. "You just couldn't keep out of things, could you? Well, this time is going to be different. Go back to the practice field and wait there. I'll honor my promise for Tarsus to train you for the guards, but you'll do it now with an escort at your side to make sure you go only where I tell you. Is that understood?'

Laura still didn't say anything, but her expression said it loud and clear. She wasn't happy about having babysitters.

Pip watched the outcome without comment. There really wasn't much he could say about Lionel's decision. From Pip's standpoint, Laura didn't have much of a chance against a face to face confrontation with her father, especially when he was pissed off.

"And the rest of you? What's going on?" asked Lionel. He looked at each in turn. "We don't want to have a repeat of last night, do we? I've had about enough foolishness."

Dwayne immediately spoke up. "No, sire. Nothing like that was happening."

"Good. So why is everyone standing around?"

"We were just going over the day's agenda, sire," Tarsus said quickly to forestall anyone else saying something they would all regret. "I was about to ask Pip if he'd like to get something to eat," he looked at Pip and then back at Lionel, "and see what he'd planned for today until his training began again later. And I wanted to know if Dwayne was going to join him." He looked at Dwayne.

Lionel turned to Pip. "And what are you doing today, lad? Have you taken my advice about my wayward Dwayne yet?" He looked at Dwayne and smiled broadly.

Pip took a deep breath and then said, "No, sire. This is the first I've seen of him today. I haven't had the chance to do much of anything yet." He looked at Tarsus, then at the princess, and then back at the king. "But one of the many things I need to do is clean the stalls. With my other chores with Tarsus," he snuck a peek at the lizard, "I'm a little behind."

Lionel grinned knowingly. He understood. "Yes, I imagine you are. But don't worry about the stalls. I believe Dwayne would be more than willing to take care of those for you." Lionel pointedly looked at the man with a grin. "Wouldn't you, Dwayne?"

"Yes, sire. It would be my pleasure," answered Dwayne with a smile of his own.

"Good. I'm glad." Lionel caught Pip's look of gratitude and grinned. "That should free up some time for you, Pip. Maybe you could find some time later today to come see me so we can talk some more."

"Yes, sire." He bowed.

"Don't get in any hurry. There's no rush. Do what you need to do. I'll see you later today. OK?" Lionel said, smiling at him.

"Thank you, sire," said Pip, bowing to him again. "I'll be there."

"Good. Now then, don't you all have places to go and work to do?" Lionel looked them all over sternly.

In chorus, each bowed and said, "Yes, sire."

No one moved.

"Well," said Lionel.

They all went their separate way. Fast.

*   *   *

CHAPTER 21

Granston still smiled, even after five weeks in the Gnome Kingdom. In those five weeks, he'd had many meetings with Grundehl about the return of Tarsus and what could be done about him. Also in those five weeks, he'd found out a few things about the circumstances surrounding Grundehl. One of which was Grundehl was definitely afraid of him. He decided he could use that to get what he'd come for. At every meeting, there were Gnome guards, including the giant flat-faced Traub, and as many as five Assanti Assassins. At one such meeting, not three days gone, the woman Assanti was present, Marvelo. She didn't say anything the whole time, but Granston got the distinct feeling she never took her eyes off him. In some strange way, other than the fact he had changed her loyalties along with Raulch and the others, she was drawn to him, just as he was drawn to her. After the meeting, he barely saw her, but he never forgot the feeling that came over him when she'd left the room. He missed her presence. He missed her, which was very strange indeed. He'd never had feelings towards anyone before. The whole encounter with the king and his allies was strange considering the nature of Gnomes, but this feeling was very unnerving. Throughout this whole five weeks, he never once used magic and found he didn't miss it. He was confident from what he'd heard and seen that he could get what he wanted without it. The other thing which convinced Granston of his success: Grundehl was not a smart Gnome by any stretch of the imagination, and the flunkies surrounding him told Granston much the same thing. Squabbles and fights among his followers were common, and they'd been escalating.

Raulch was seen often throughout the weeks, and he learned a few things from him. The suggestions he'd used on the Gnome and his cronies were still working, which gave Granston many opportunities to find out exactly what he wanted to know. But the main thing was why were the Assanti allies of the Gnomes? Why not the Trolls? Or Wild Fairies? Or even the wyverns, the slower, smaller, stupider cousins of the dragons? Raulch informed him the Assassins had come to Grundehl, not the other way around, apparently they'd been decimated even more than the Gnomes, not by the lumbering lizard, but by Trolls and fairy folk. They just wanted to belong somewhere they could be useful. Useful? The guild? They were only useful for one thing. Granston knew a load of claptrap when he heard one. No matter what they said to the Gnomes or how they convinced the king, they had other plans, one's which benefited only them. It was only a matter of time before he found the real reason.

The room Grundehl put him in wasn't a fancy inn's accommodations, but it was quite adequate. It wasn't the same cage he'd been locked in when he first arrived either. Not ten days after being locked up, he'd finally had a chance to use his influence on Marvelo, the Assanti, to campaign on his behalf. She convinced Grundehl's 'adviser' he could be manipulated if he had better accommodations. Crude, but effective on his part. Now, he was given a choice of foods to eat and a very well-stocked personal facility to use. When he'd first met the fat king, he thought he'd be put in a cell, but all the talk and bluster from Grundehl was just that, empty words. Oh, the great slob was definitely upset, but he knew enough not to irritate a wizard, which was a plus in Granston's favor.

This day was looking as if it would be like all the others before it—breakfast, short walk, lunch, meeting with the Gnome king in the great hall, supper, another short meeting with the slob, short break, and then retire to his room—do it all again the next day. But that was about to stop. He'd planned his own surprise for Grundehl today. His plan was going to be slightly different than the one his 'host' had been accustomed. He was impatient to deal with the lizard without many more delays. Time to get his affairs in order so the real work could begin.

As expected, a quiet knock came at his door just past daybreak. He knew it was daybreak from the morning sun streaming through his window. It appeared, when these caverns had been hewn out of solid rock, the craftsmen had the foresight to create sleeping chambers in an East facing cliff at the edge of the giant mountain range. Grundehl and his adviser had been kind enough to supply him with one. Granston opened the door to find the female Assanti Assassin Marvelo waiting outside. He was startled to see her. "Ah, you," he said, quickly getting a hold on his emotions.

The Assanti bowed slightly, but said nothing.

"Shall we go?" asked Granston, motioning to her.

She just watched him, not moving.

Granston took the time to look her over from head to foot. Besides her pale coloring and short stature like a Gnome, she was human in appearance. She had classic feminine bone structure and close cropped black hair, the only flaw being a small scar under her right eye. The clothes she wore was and wasn't anything he was familiar with: britches made of light durable brown fabric, shin high leather boots, a short metal fringed light tunic, and crossed double swords strapped to her back. On her wrist she wore a bracelet made of silver and fine filigrees of gold that intertwined like a snake slithering across a water's surface. In an overall sense of mobility, she looked as if she could run for a week without stopping to sleep or eat, and her eyes had the predatory look one would expect from a caged animal. Watching her, emotions were going through him he didn't understand. Joy? Fear? Joy at seeing her again? Of talking with her again? Of being rejected by her? Of having feelings for her? He didn't know. But watching her watch him, she must have the same feelings, her eyes never left his, as if seeking something in them he knew not what.

"I presume you're here to escort me to breakfast?" he asked finally.

She simply nodded, nothing more.

"Let's go." Granston closed the door and walked past the Assanti, firmly expecting her to follow.

She did.

*   *   *

After breakfast, Granston was shown into the so-called throne room again, and just as always Grundehl was slouching in it. His fat body oozed sweat and stink. The smell nearly gagged him the first time he smelled it. He was forced to use a masking spell so he wouldn't throw up. He guessed one could get used to anything after a time. It seemed to only bother him and no one else. Crinkling his nose, he figured out why the known realms referred to Gnomes as filthy animals. It wasn't one of his race's most enduring traits, and definitely nothing to be proud of. As he got closer to the king, he heard some very loud muttering. Grundehl was in a discussion with someone he hadn't seen before. When he and the Assanti woman got to them, they both suddenly stopped talking.

"Don't stop on my account, gentlemen," Granston said, watching Grundehl and the other mutterer.

Grundehl looked at Granston and grinned an evil grin.

The newcomer slowly turned to face Granston, but said nothing, looking the Gnome wizard over from head to toe, his expression never changing.

Granston found his throat tighten. He couldn't utter a word, his eyes bulging from his head in recognition. He knew this person after all. He knew him very well. For more than two centuries, however, he'd thought him dead. Apparently his demise had been grossly exaggerated.

"Hello, wizard. I believe I haven't seen you for a while," said Bappa, an evil twinkle in his eye.

"You could say that, Bappa," answered Granston, nervously watching Grundehl's companion. "I'd heard you died when Garcon invaded your lands nearly two centuries ago."

Bappa laughed uproariously. "Yes, that was a great jest. Garcon and the whole world never saw that coming. Or this I suppose." The Dryad's laughter stopped suddenly and he sneered at Granston.

"No, I guess not,." Granston said, taking a small nervous step backward.

"You know, Bappa?" asked Grundehl, looking from one to the other.

"Oh, yes," answered Bappa, smiling again and nodding at the fat king. "We go way back, him and I."

"This good. We can do many things. We can," said the Gnome king smiling, showing his crooked yellowish teeth. "We can all get lizard."

"Oh yes, I believe we can. But first," Bappa said turning to Granston, "how do you like my guild?"

Granston was astonished, his mouth fell open in surprise. He never would have figured this. "But you're not Assanti!." he exclaimed. "How did you get them to follow you?"

"That's a long story, my friend. Let's just say the Assassins you see today are the only one's alive, and leave it at that, shall we." Bappa smiled a mysterious smile at Granston that left him with a foul taste in his mouth. Granston knew Bappa had never been known to form any kind of lasting relationships. His association with the Guild, its leader, could only be another ploy on his part for something else. Granston had to ferret out what that was and quick, before it got himself killed. He could care less about the Gnomes or the Assanti, but his hide was worth saving.

The only ones left alive. Interesting. Very interesting.

"We need kill giant lizard. We need talk," said Grundehl, impatient to get going.

"Yes, we will, dear King," Bappa agreed smiling. "But first I think we need to talk about us."

✱   ✱   ✱

CHAPTER 22

P ip woke in a strange place, screaming. The dream he had wasn't pleasant, but it was very familiar. He'd been having the same one for the past two weeks almost every night. And every night, it ended the same; Tarsus dying in agony, at the hands of his worst enemy, Granston. A cold sweat popped out on his forehead, his hands shaking as he reached to wipe the moisture away. He stood with his hands over his face to catch his breath and take stock of his surroundings, gradually calming himself so his heart wouldn't feel like jumping out of his chest. With the pounding, however, came the realization he knew without question he was alive, if not scared out of his mind. Better to be scared and embarrassed then dead at the hands of a mad Gnome wizard.

Pip got out of bed and walked to a window looking down on the practice field. At this time of night, he could barely make out the forms of the many posts set into the ground used for sword practice. The many other blunt training swords, padded spikes, and wrapped arrows for the crossbows couldn't be seen for the shadows of the night. He shook his head in wonder, not for the night, a natural occurrence of any day, but for the view from the window. It was strange to get out of a real bed. The wonder of walking to a window with a view was something he wasn't completely used to either. For as long as he could remember, he'd been sleeping in the hay loft over the stables, which had a window of sorts, a wide door opening for hay to be passed in, which had a view of the corrals below. Seeing the horses below wasn't exactly exciting when you were around them every day. When King Lionel had suggested he use one of the many rooms in the castle, he nearly declined the offer. Lionel had seen his hesitation and pointed out, with his new status as a wizard and sovereign person, he had diplomatic status, whatever that was, and the use of the room came with that status, for as long as he wished to stay. With a slight breeze whipping his hair cooling his brow, he smiled to himself remembering the look on Mulch's face when he told the stableman he'd be leaving for the castle. For that alone he was grateful he agreed to the king's generous offer. But life in the castle was not as grand as he'd imagined it to be growing up outside the walls. In the past weeks, he'd learned a great deal about castle life and the difference between the ruling class and the servant class: the difference being a gulf too wide to cross without snapping support lines that held the kingdom together. He didn't know if he'd ever get used to it. And now whether he liked it or not, he was one among the ruling class. He found he didn't care for it very much. This brought the realization of just how much difference there was between Princess Laura and himself. He was born in squalor, found and raised by an honorable stableman. She's the heir to a throne, lavished all her life with everything she could ever want. One could not be more different from the other, which brought him back full circle to the difference in his dreams for the past two weeks. He never used to have nightmares; now, every night he woke, screaming of blood, Granston slaughtering Tarsus. A nightmare indeed. Tarsus was not only his mentor, teacher, and friend, but the only reason for who and what he was. Without Tarsus's help and guidance, he'd probably be dead by now, trying to cope with a strange power he never wanted and not being able to control. One wrong gesture, word, or comment in the wrong place could be fatal to anyone around him, including himself. He had to talk to the big lizard. Pip didn't know what to do. He hoped Tarsus could shed a little light on it. Maybe he'd have a way to stop the nightmares.

*   *   *

Pip headed out of his room and down the great stairs going straight for one of the many side doors into the castle. He never liked using the front doors. They reminded him of pomp and circumstance and kings and princesses, and he didn't want someone to open the doors for him. They were made of massive hard wood that took four guards to swing open just a few feet. And it seemed people were always watching to see who would come out, so to avoid any staring by members of the palace and the servants, he used a side door. Besides, one of the side doors went straight on the practice field, which was the perfect spot to avoid any unnecessary contact. No one really cared who was sparing because everyone did. He had to find Tarsus and ask him about his nightmares. If anyone could tell him what was going on, it had to be him. But, like all of his plans, he headed for the door and came face to face with Dwayne. Pip came to a sudden stop and sighed. He really wasn't interested in dealing with the former knight. He went out of his way to stay out of his way. But, from the look on Dwayne's face this morning, he wasn't going to have much of a choice. So, to keep the king happy and things running as smooth as possible, he met the ex-knight head on to get it over with. Pip put a smile on his face and said, "Hello, Sir Dwayne. What can I do for you?"

Dwayne bowed, then smiling, as always, said, "Morning, Pip. As you know, I'm no longer a knight. Please feel free to call me Dwayne."

"I'll always know you as a knight, Sir Dwayne," said Pip. "No matter what anyone says. Just because the king says you're no longer a knight doesn't take away the fact you've spent your entire life as one. I won't either."

"Yes, Pip," said Dwayne patiently. "We've had this conversation before. But no matter what you think, I'm nothing more than your page now, as my king has decreed."

"My page," said Pip with a groan. "My page. Can't you have a talk with King Lionel and apologize, or maybe do something else to make up for what happened?"

Dwayne looked at Pip but said nothing. He'd done just that not seven days before. His honor had come away from the experience a little more bruised. The reception his king gave him was very frosty indeed. The king's words still echoed in his head. 'I don't believe you've learned what you need to learn yet, Dwayne. Your job now is to take care of young Pip to the best of your abilities. Don't worry about anything else unless I tell you. When I feel you've done that, I'll consider something else for you to do. Do you understand?' His king was trying to teach him a lesson. He just didn't comprehend what it was yet, and until he did, his job was to take care of the young wizard he once tried to kill. "You know, young wizard, I've done everything I've been ordered to do by my king. So I'm doing now. I'm page to you until told otherwise. So," he sighed himself, "what can I do for you?"

Pip took a deep breath trying to calm down. This was ridiculous. He heard the same answer every time from the man. He supposed he better give the same answer to him again. With another sigh, he said, "Mulch may have something for you to do, I don't. Go, see if you can find him."

This time, however, Dwayne had other ideas. Instead of turning to go to the stables, Dwayne shook his head. "No, I think I should stay with you today, Master Pip. I've been falling down on my duties these last couple weeks and I believe it's time for me to make sure you're cared for."

Pip was frightened by the prospect of being around Sir Dwayne more than a couple minutes. If he could, he'd stop it from happening. "No! That's not necessary," he said quickly. "I'm just going to find Tarsus. He'll make sure I'm OK. You can go ahead and help Mulch."

"That's fine. I haven't seen Master Tarsus in a few days myself. Maybe he'll be able to tell me how to handle you." He looked at Pip sternly. "Plus," went on Dwayne without a pause, "I need to get out more and find out how things are going with Sir Hook. I haven't had time doing so many chores for Mulch. It'll do both of us some good I think to get out. You haven't been out for a few days yourself, so I think we could make a day of it. Don't you?" Dwayne smiled at Pip and gestured for him to go ahead and he'd follow.

Pip groaned. He couldn't think of a way to stop Sir Dwayne from going along. "Really, you don't have to. I'll be all right." Pip tried to reassure the ex-knight, trying once more to get him to help Mulch.

"Yes, I know. I'll make sure of it." Dwayne gestured again for Pip to proceed.

Pip hung his head in defeat. *Fine. Maybe he'll get bored and go away on his own.*

They both walked towards the side door leading to the practice fields, Pip as nervous as he'd ever been. It was a wonder his knees weren't knocking. Dwayne never once left his side. It was a very strange feeling to be escorted. The feeling that most described the situation was Dwayne keeping an eye on him to make sure he didn't do something magical and hurt anyone. The one thing missing from the picture was Dwayne's sword. The only reason he didn't have it was King Lionel's decree that forbade him to carry it. This was more like being a prisoner again, except, of course, Dwayne didn't have him hogtied to a pole, but he was still being paraded in front of the whole kingdom. Pip tried to keep a good face on the whole situation, but it was tough. As both passed through the side doors into the practice field, Princess Laura stopped them as they left the last step. Pip groaned inside. Laura was the last person he wanted to see. Ever since moving into the castle, he'd tried to avoid the princess as much as possible. Not from fear: he had nothing to fear from her; she'd done nothing but try to help him, ever since he'd first found out he was a wizard; no, it was from embarrassment. How could she look at him and not think him a coward. He'd been hiding behind someone from the beginning, herself included. He didn't even know how to protect himself, having to rely on others. Tarsus, mainly. That was one of the main reasons he needed to get this magic stuff right. Not the only reason, of course, but the main one. Plus, he didn't want to die from hanging, sword, or magic, and seeing the princess reminded him of not being able to do that.

Laura stood in front of Pip and waited.

Pip didn't say anything, just watched her watching him. She was wearing her practice clothes—light brown britches, soft brown boots, brown tunic and shirt, and a practice sword strapped to her back—from what Tarsus told him. The magical sword he'd given her, she didn't use for practice, although practice wouldn't have scratched it in any way. All together she looked impressively dangerous and lovely.

Finally, "Hello, Pip."

"Hello, Princess," he said, bowing.

Dwayne bowed also and said smiling, "Your Highness. It's always good to see you."

Laura nodded to Dwayne, and then turned her attention back to Pip. "I hope you're finding the room to your liking, Pip?"

"It's fine, thank you, Princess. King Lionel was very kind in offering to let me use it."

"Kindness had nothing to do with it, Pip. Your becoming a wizard gave you the right. The laws governing the kingdom gave you the right. Father was simply following the law."

Pip shuffled his feet slightly thinking of King Lionel being forced to do anything against his wishes. "I'm grateful anyway, Princess," said Pip. "No one's ever done something like that before. Except Mulch, of course. But that was a different situation."

"Yes, I suppose it was," Laura said, her eyes softening.

Dwayne was watching the two spar. He couldn't quite figure out who had the upper hand: Pip or the princess. But he did know it wasn't going anywhere. He wanted to spank Laura and shake Pip. Small talk between them didn't work.

Pip asked Laura, "Have you seen Tarsus? I need to talk to him."

"I saw him for a moment at first light, but not since then. I assume he's at, or near, the stables."

"Yeah, that's what I thought too. I was hoping to get lucky and find him here so I wouldn't have to go all the way down there." Pip just shook his head. "Oh well. Thank you."

Laura nodded, and then before Pip could move, she did something very unexpected. She slowly put her hand up and cupped Pip's left cheek with her right hand. "You need to take better care of yourself. You look too pale."

The touch startled Pip. He stiffened, frozen in place. Looking into her lovely blue-gray eyes, he found his voice enough to softly say, "I'll try."

Laura looked startled herself, her hand slowly leaving his cheek. With one last look, she slowly turned and walked away.

Pip watched her go without saying anything.

Dwayne thought he saw tears in the princess's eyes as she turned to leave.

*   *   *

Tarsus wasn't in a good mood. For the past two hours, he'd been waiting for Pip. Usually he wasn't late when it came to his training sessions, but since he'd moved out of the stables, it seemed he was preoccupied with other matters. His mind and spirit split in two. Tarsus knew if Pip didn't get his head back together, he'd end up on the wrong end of a Gnome pike, or worse, a wizard's killing spell. Pip's training was progressing well, and he needed the lad to be focused and alert, distractions would get them both killed. Whatever happened to one, happened to the other, so Tarsus supposed it was time for some friendly intervention. He harrumphed, bared his teeth, and then turned to stalk out of his stall. That's when Pip walked through the door.

"Where have you been, Pip?" asked Tarsus, not worrying about the niceties of saying 'good morning'. He wasn't in the mood for anything but answers.

Pip froze, rooted to the spot, standing just inside the dragon's stall. He gulped. He'd seen the big lizard like this before and he wasn't to be messed with when he was in this state of mind. Pip thought he was ready to go another round with Sir Dwayne. Pip said as fast as he could, "I've been looking for you."

Tarsus rose as far as he could in the cramped space of the stall and looked down his nose at the lad. "And why's that? Why were you looking for me, when you were supposed to be here this morning for training?" He bared his teeth.

Oh crap! "Training was this morning?" *Crap!*

"That's why I'm still here," answered Tarsus. "For a few minutes, I went to the fields, but you weren't there. So I came back. What's got into you?" Tarsus was literally fuming. Smoke rose from the slits of his nostrils.

That's when it got worse. Dwayne spoke up, "Why don't you calm down, Master Dragon?" Dwayne had been a few steps behind Pip as they entered the stables. When Pip entered the dragon's stall and was immediately accosted, freezing him in place, the ex-knight calmly walked between the two.

Tarsus's eyes blazed at the sight of someone coming between himself and his pupil. That someone being the ex-knight only made matters worse, poking his nose where it didn't belong. Tarsus whipped his head down lightning quick, his nose coming inches from the former knight's face. A small puff of smoke curled from his right nostril as he asked, "What business is this of yours, page?"

To Dwayne's credit, he never flinched. The sight of a dragon puffing smoke into his face mere inches away did nothing to break his composure. He answered the question without hurry. "None. As you've observed, I'm merely page to young Pip. But one of my many duties as page is to take care of him. Stopping you threatening him falls under that proviso."

Tarsus thought about that for a moment, chuffed smoke again from his nostrils, bowed his head, and then slowly moved from Pip and Dwayne and sat down.

Dwayne nodded. "Good. Now then, why don't you tell us what's wrong, Master Tarsus?"

Pip heaved a sigh of relief. "It's my fault I guess, not Tarsus." He looked at Dwayne and then at the dragon. "I'm sorry. I'd forgotten about training today. I've had other things on my mind."

"Pip," said Tarsus, taking a deep breath, frustrated. "That's the problem. That's been happening more and more lately. What's causing it? There has to be a reason. You've been like this since the moment you moved out of the stables."

Pip covered his face with his hands and slowly sat down, not even moving to a wall, just sitting by the doors of the stall. After dropping his hands, he looked at Tarsus and in astonishment the dragon saw not the easygoing young man he'd been training, but a mere boy afraid of what's waiting for him in the dark.

Dwayne went to Pip with sympathy written in his voice, clasped the young man's shoulder, and said, "Go ahead, lad, tell us. Even I don't wish to see you like this."

Tarsus looked to Dwayne with suspicion. "Getting soft, Knight? Not too long ago you wanted Pip strung up."

The former knight said evenly, "As long as I'm with young Pip, I'll do what I can for him. That includes comfort. Duty demands it."

"Duty! Bah! At times, you don't know the meaning of the word. Only when it's convenient for you." Tarsus stared at Dwayne with contempt. "Pip doesn't need duty right now. He needs help from someone who actually cares for him. He just has to tell us what kind."

Dwayne started to respond, but Pip cut him off. "Stop it, both of you. No matter it is duty or something else, I do need help. I just don't know what kind myself. Or if anyone can help me."

Tarsus snaked his head down to the young man looking at him closely. "What's wrong, Pip? What's made you like this?"

"I don't know what it is, Tarsus," said Pip with watery eyes. "All I know is I've been having nightmares for the past couple of weeks. Since the first night I moved to the castle. They're all I can think about. They terrify me." He covered his face again.

"Nightmares?" asked Dwayne. "What kind of nightmares?"

"Full of death," Pip said through his fingers.

"But they can't hurt you, lad. A dream can't hurt you," said Dwayne. "You have . . ."

Tarsus stopped him by saying, "Wait! Dreams can be serious." Tarsus jerked up straight.

Dwayne looked at Tarsus as if he had two heads.

"Don't look so surprised, page," Tarsus said sarcastically.

Pip looked up in shock.

Tarsus looked at Pip. "Yes, they can be serious for one such as you."

"What do you mean? One such as me?"

Dwayne just shook his head.

"For wizards, Pip. For wizards. They're nothing to be messed with. You should have come to me sooner." Tarsus shook his head in disgust. This was one more example of Pip not having his head on straight.

"I thought they were dreams, scary dreams, but nothing that could hurt me," said Pip. "Just as Sir Dwayne said. But even then I guess I knew better, they didn't feel right. They don't feel the same as a dream that can't hurt you. Every time I have one, they feel real somehow. As if it's already happened and I was remembering."

Tarsus heard the distress in the boy's voice and nudged Pip's head gently with his nose. He then asked, "Can you tell us about them?"

Pip nodded. "Yeah, but they scare me."

"I know. But we need to know what you've seen. I need to know," said Tarsus. "Let me see if it really is a dream, or something else."

"What do you mean?" asked Dwayne. "Something else? What could they be but dreams?"

Tarsus looked at Pip and Dwayne and sighed. "You know, why don't we get some fresh air? I'll tell both of you what I know, but I don't want to do it here." He looked around the stall, knowing there were too many ears around that could hear what he had to say. *I'd just as soon not have everyone know our business. And a few of the things, I have to tell them may get the locals fired up for hanging. Ours. I think it's time for some privacy.*

Pip scrubbed his face with his hands and nodded. Dwayne simply moved out of the stall to wait for the dragon to lead the way. Dwayne shrugged. One place was as good as another to him. But, if it got the dragon to talking, no matter. He waited patiently for the dragon and Pip.

Tarsus lumbered out of the stall and headed for the doors. He was tired of keeping secrets from the people who he cared for. Pip needed to know everything he could tell him to survive, and this was just one of the many things he needed to teach the lad. Dwayne didn't really need to hear anything, but from the determined look on the knight's face, Tarsus doubted he could have persuaded the man not to go wherever Pip was going. So, the best thing to do was start talking, no matter the ex-knight was present. No time like the present.

Tarsus headed out the stables at an even pace. Normally, he would have put Pip on his back and flown to an isolated spot and talked things over. But this was a different situation. For one thing, Dwayne was with them. Tarsus didn't think the knight would react well to a dragon ride, so that was out. For another, he was trying to stall a bit to get his thoughts in order, and walking through the yard and the grounds of the stables and castle was the perfect way to do it. There were too many ears around for anything close to privacy. They weren't going far, just a few hundred yards. Tarsus figured a good spot would be the running stream just south of the stable area. It was where the stables got fresh water every day for the horses and other animals and where Pip usually bathed. Not too far away, but far enough.

Pip knew exactly where they were headed. It didn't matter much to him. He just wanted answers. The last two weeks had changed his thinking about being a wizard. He didn't know whether he could do it any longer, especially if he had to deal with any more nightmares. The visions scared him too much. He'd had bad dreams before, but these felt too real for his liking.

As plans went, it was a good one, but as a working plan, it went about the way all of them did. Tarsus was usually pretty good about planning ahead, and the idea of discussing Pip's nightmares in the stables wasn't going to work. Anyone passing by his stall may have been spooked hearing what Tarsus needed to say. The stream was the only place he could think of for a bit of privacy. Everything was going well, just a few short yards from the water's edge, when his acute hearing told him someone was following them. He stopped to let Pip and the knight catch up and then took a quick peek over his shoulder. As Tarsus peeked, Dwayne caught the direction he was looking and stopped in his tracks. He wasn't stupid; he knew something was up. And that's when the plan went to pieces, as plans go.

"Hi, boys. What are you doing?" asked Laura, smiling at them.

Tarsus growled, shaking his head. He should have known. Her smell alone, if nothing else, should have given the princess away.

Laura had calmly walked a ways behind the three as they left the stables. Her father said she couldn't be near them, or the corrals, without his permission, but nothing was said about the stream behind the corrals. Asking Lionel for his permission to take a stroll, she'd calmly walked the trail leading to the stream.

Pip looked at Laura and nodded, his face a mask of misery.

"Your Highness," said Dwayne, bowing, "I believe you aren't to be here without your father's permission."

"True," answered Laura, still smiling. "He knows exactly where I am, however. He told me I could come down this way." Laura looked at Tarsus. "I can't just stay in the castle all my life and train, can I? Or wait there until something happens. Every once in a while I need a little fresh air and different scenery." She looked around at the trees and grass and took a deep breath and then looked back at Dwayne.

Tarsus looked at Laura with suspicion. "And just so happens you came to watch the stream flow by and listen to the water gurgle?"

"Something like that," she answered still smiling.

"With your armor on?" asked Dwayne with raised eyebrows.

"This isn't armor. It's practice clothes," argued Laura.

"Uh huh."

"Plus," Laura winked at Pip, "it helps if one of the wall guards spots you traipsing down here."

"Uh huh."

Pip looked into Laura's lovely face and finally smiled. He looked at Tarsus and said, "At least she's honest about it."

Tarsus and Dwayne both said at the same time, "She better be."

Tarsus looked at Dwayne and bowed.

Dwayne bowed back.

Laura scowled at both.

Pip said to Laura, "I'm glad you're here."

Laura smiled. "So am I, Pip."

Tarsus exhaled smoke in the princess's direction and asked, "Why do you care where we go, Princess?"

Laura answered to Pip instead of the dragon or Dwayne, "You know, Pip, I normally wouldn't care one way or the other what you do, but the look on your face when I saw you and Dwayne go through the fields made me worry. You looked as if you'd sick up at any minute."

Pip looked as if he might sick up now. "I looked that bad?"

"About like you do now," confirmed Laura.

Pip nodded. "It's the way I feel."

"Why?"

Dwayne spoke up. "We were about to find out when you interrupted us. That's why we're here. We thought a little privacy was best."

Without hearing an answer, Pip walked the few remaining yards to the bank of the stream and sat down on a boulder protruding over the water. He took a slow deep breath to calm himself and then looked at Tarsus. "Go ahead. Tell me. What's wrong with me?"

Laura was startled. "Wrong? Is there something wrong with Pip?"

Tarsus looked at Pip and then at Laura. Pip saw he was reluctant to say anything with her present, but Pip just smiled. "It's all right. She has just as much at stake in this as the rest of us. Maybe more. Go ahead."

Tarsus looked unconvinced, but he went ahead with his explanation anyway. He took a position to the left of Pip, looking down at the water streaming by and a good view of the lad's face to gauge his reactions. He then looked at Dwayne and said, "You're wrong, Sir Knight. Dreams can be very dangerous."

Laura was shocked. "Dreams? What do you mean dreams? Is this what all the tensions about?"

"Yes, Your Highness," answered Dwayne. "Young Pip has been having nightmares these past weeks. Lord Dragon yonder thinks they may harm him." He scowled at the thought.

Tarsus scowled back at the ex-knight. "I know they can," the dragon spat.

Pip spoke up. "How? They're only dreams, aren't they?"

Tarsus sighed. "Before I say anything, tell us what the dreams are about?"

Pip shuddered thinking of the nightmares. He looked at Tarsus and shook his head. "Just as I've said, they're about blood and death: terrible things."

Dwayne went to Pip and put a hand on his shoulder. "Go ahead, lad, say the rest. We're all here to help."

"They're dreams of all of you dying," Pip said reluctantly, looking at each in turn. "But they're only bad dreams, right?" He stared at Tarsus for reassurance.

Tarsus shook his head. "It depends on the circumstances, Pip, if they can really hurt you. Normally, a dream is just that, a dream, be it bad or good, but for wizards, your dreams can be very dangerous."

"Dangerous? How?" asked Laura. "Bad dreams or not, dreams can't hurt you."

"That's what I told him," said Dwayne. "Dreams can't hurt him."

"For special people like Pip, namely wizards or sorcerers, dreams can be a road to their minds." Tarsus looked at Pip closely, trying to gauge his reactions. "And if you can attack a wizard's mind, you can control the wizard. Dreams can make it possible for an adept to hurt or even kill the wizard." The dragon looked at Dwayne. "And then there are the dreams of a wizard and some sorcerers that are glimpses into the future. A foretelling of things to come,." explained Tarsus.

"Bah!" scoffed Dwayne. "Dreams are just dreams. The young lad may indeed be a wizard, which it took me a while to believe, but now you tell me he may be able to predict the future."

Laura was also skeptical. She twisted her lip into such an accurate mimicry of Dwayne's, Pip actually laughed. Tarsus, however, found no amusement in it. "No, I'm not telling you any such thing. I'm just informing you of the possibilities when it comes to dreaming. But, for now, let's get back to what the dreams are about," said Tarsus to Pip. He wanted very much to hear about his dreams. "Can you tell us, Pip?"

Pip looked up at Tarsus and nodded. He then looked again at the slow moving stream, and with unshed tears filling his eyes, he let the water tell his story. One moment the water was moving slowly by his dangling feet, and then it visibly slowed further until it stood still in front of them, shimmering like a mirror. In the middle of the mirror formed a very familiar shape: Tarsus.

Laura looked at the stream and gasped. Tarsus was looking back at her. Well, another Tarsus. *Not* the Tarsus on the bank, but another in the mirrored water.

"Holy Horde Mother!" That from Tarsus. The one sitting next to Pip.

"This is what I see in my nightmares," explained Pip. "I didn't know I could show you until just now."

"Neither did I," Tarsus said. "This is something new."

Dwayne, standing by the boy's side, put his hand on his shoulder and gripped it firmly. From the moment he'd been told Pip was a wizard, he'd scoffed and disavowed all, even after he'd heard the words from his king's mouth. Now, he truly believed. What the boy was doing had never been done before as far as he could remember hearing. He gave another quick squeeze to Pip's shoulder, encouraging him and trying to convey he wasn't alone and then removed his hand.

Pip seemed not to notice the touch; his focus was on the 'mirror' in the stream. All of the viewers focused their attention on the stream, watching scenes from Pip's mind slowly play out.

The scene of Tarsus changed to Granston, the court adviser, standing over the bloody remains of a man in armor. The crest of Musk was seen clearly on the man's breastplate. Granston reaches down to lift the knight's visor to see his face, when he stops suddenly with a jolt. In the helmet of armor is not the face of a man, but the face of a woman: Princess Laura.

Laura gasped.

The scene shifts again to see a blue lightning bolt slam to the ground right in front of the castle's gates, flinging its protectors away like leaves in a storm. Afterwards, what is left is three bloody guards kneeling over a fallen comrade, with heads bowed. A closer view shows clearly the fallen comrade as the king of Musk, King Lionel dead in front of the gates to his own castle.

"No!" whispered Laura in horror. "No!"

The next scene in the shimmering water is of Pip with raised hands commanding the heavens to blast Granston with his own lightning: the look on the mirrored Pip's face is of horror and loss.

A shift in scene shows a grossly fat Gnome shouting excitedly to an unknown woman to do something; the scene shifts to reveal Pip having his throat cut from behind.

The next scene, that of the mirrored Tarsus screaming in agony, dying, while Granston gloats; whatever happens to one will happen to the other.

The last scene before the stream starts flowing again was of Sir Dwayne battling the unknown woman who had murdered the other Pip.

Pip looked up when the water continued its journey. With tears flowing freely, he said, "That's why I've been a little distracted lately. Every night I watch you all die. I don't know if I can do it anymore."

A hush fell over the four except for Pip's silent sobs. Laura was the first to come to her senses and realize the hurt these dreams were actually causing him. She went to him and folded him into her arms. There was no shame in this, for she remembered not long ago being comforted by her father as nightmares invaded her own sleep. She could relate very well with how Pip was trying to come to terms with them. For a few moments, Pip sobbed silently on Laura's shoulder, but only a few moments. Pip realized who was watching and self-consciously straightened up, quickly wiping the tears from his cheeks with the knuckles of his hands.

Pip looked at Laura and said, "Thank you, Princess. I guess I just needed to get those out."

Laura slowly lifted her hand and cupped Pip's cheek tenderly, just as she'd done no more than a half hour ago. "No problem, Pip."

Tarsus leaned to Pip and nudged the same cheek lightly with his nose. "Know this, Pip, your fate and mine are linked until each of us pass from this Earth. From what you've shown us and told us about these nightmares, I think I know what they are: revelations."

Laura was the first to speak, shocked. "Revelations? What are those?"

Dwayne said," 'What are you saying?"

Pip groaned, covering his face with his hands.

Tarsus finished, looking at Dwayne again. "They can be either good or ill in nature. Some wizards have dreams such as these their whole lives and none come true. Others, every one they have is a foretelling of things to come."

Laura asked excitedly, "Can you tell which is which?"

"No," said Tarsus, shaking his head. "But I do know if they're revelations of things to come, they'll happen within the next few hours, days, or weeks, and one thing in those dreams must come true for it to be an actual foresight."

"Can it be fought?" Dwayne asked with gritted teeth.

"Yes, it can. But only if you see it coming, Sir Knight."

"So, what do we do?" asked the princess, her hand unselfconsciously gripping Pip's shoulder.

"We should wait and help Pip prepare. That's all we can do,." said Tarsus, watching Pip.

Pip gulped, uncovering his face. "Prepare for what?" he asked.

Tarsus looked at Pip and grinned. It was a very evil grin. "You have to tell me, Pip. They're your dreams, after all." Then Tarsus looked at Dwayne and the princess. "No matter who hears, know this, I'll not let Pip be alone in this matter. What he faces, I face."

Laura and Dwayne both bowed to the dragon.

*　　*　　*

CHAPTER 23

Granston, Bappa, and of course, Grundehl came to an agreement. It wasn't exactly a treaty, more of an understanding. The main point being to kill the damn lizard Tarsus. If truth be known, it was the only agreement that mattered between them. The lizard had been a thorn in the side of the Gnomes for far too many years, notwithstanding the time he'd spent in the 'Bubble of Time' Granston put him in. Whole generations of Gnomes had been wiped out by that damnable lizard. The Assanti, hurt almost as much, although not by Tarsus, wanted to take a fight to where it would do the most good. Bappa wanted to lead his Assanti to greatness, word to spread throughout the kingdoms of the use he made of his Assassins in the coming fight, paving the way to getting everything he wanted. Granston didn't care about any of it. His only interest was killing that damnable Tarsus before all the races of the world got caught in the middle of a war, becoming extinct in the process. Granston also knew he couldn't wholly trust Grundehl to put what was left of the Gnome race into an all out battle, and if he didn't, the destruction of Tarsus wasn't a certainty. Grundehl had to put as much into the fight as the rest, or it just wouldn't work.

Bappa may not know it, but he was the wizard's secret weapon against the Gnome king if he refused. Granston knew too much about the Dryad for him to say no. Three hundred years of keeping quiet should be worth something, no matter his people thinking him dead. *Bappa, my dear friend, you've finally met your fate.*

Granston fully intended for Grundehl to die in the war to ensure the outcome of the lizard's death. Along the way, he was going to use the Assanti to take over the kingdom of Gnomes, right along with the kingdom of humans. In just a few short days, the war began.

*   *   *

CHAPTER 24

Pip's next few days were in some respects rougher than the previous two weeks. He was never left alone for more than a few minutes except for the nights he was alone in his room. His nightmares continued, with the worst coming last night. In it, not only did everyone he know die horribly, but the Kingdom of Musk was wiped off the map: burning, destruction, and killing. He woke up screaming again. And to make matters worse, his training sessions with Tarsus included two extra faces: Dwayne and Princess Laura. With the added stress of dealing with his nightmares at night, now he had to deal with not looking like an idiot in front of Laura. He'd had enough of that lately, thank you.

This morning was no exception to having an audience, but there was one major difference, Tarsus and Dwayne started their rivalry again. Since Dwayne had been stripped of his title as knight by King Lionel, Tarsus and he hadn't been at each other's throat, being a page mellowing the former knight, and giving him a heart to boot. It was as if fighting among each other no longer mattered to them. But now for some unknown reason, all of a sudden, it did. Whatever they were arguing about, it was getting heated and loud, Pip wanting nothing to do with it. As they went at each other, he slowly walked off to watch the sword practice. Sir Hook and Laura were going through training routines. He leaned casually against a wall to watch and looked back once to see if the argument between the knight and dragon had ended and saw it didn't. He sighed. *They were doing so well. I hope they can get back to* that soon. Maybe they'll remember why they're here in the first place. He sighed again, turning back to Laura and Hook.

*   *   *

"The lad needs more, dragon," exploded Dwayne. "What if his magic can't save him?"

"The lad has a name, page. And so do I," growled Tarsus right back.

Dwayne took a deep breath to calm down. "I apologize, Lord Tarsus. I tend to speak before I think. That's a failing of mine. I don't mean to offend." He bowed to Tarsus. "But my argument stands," he said straightening up. "Pip needs more than magic. You need to teach him sword craft also."

"You know I can't," argued Tarsus, turning his back on Dwayne and starting to lumber away. "I can't teach the princess and Pip, and keep up with his magic lessons too. There's not enough time in the day. I'm only one dragon after all."

Dwayne stopped Tarsus from going anywhere by stomping on his tail. It didn't hurt, but it was annoying. Annoying enough to get the big lizard's attention, which was the point. Tarsus snaked his head back to growl, "Don't do that. You know it only irritates me." He puffed smoke into Dwayne's face to emphasize the fact.

The ex-knight waved the smoke away with a hand and growled back, "And you know the smoke thing irritates me." He cocked his fists on his hips. "You must do this. You, yourself, have said Pip needs every advantage in the fight surely to come. This will give him that chance."

Tarsus just shook his head. "No! I can't! You know this!" Tarsus was beginning to get very angry at having to go over this again. The man just wouldn't listen. His stubborn pride was getting in the way. "I can't go back on my word to the princess. She comes first, whether I like it or not, that's why I'm concentrating Pip's training on magic."

"Yes, I've heard this before, but my argument still stands. You wouldn't be going back on your word. You'd just be teaching more than one student at a time."

Tarsus sighed and sat down, this getting tiresome. "You know that wouldn't work either. Pip is too far behind Laura. She's advanced well beyond the beginning stages of swordsmanship. Her time for the trials is almost here."

"Sir Dragon, you must." Dwayne wouldn't let it go.

Tarsus sighed heavily again. He looked down at Dwayne and said, "If you think it's so important, why don't you teach him?"

Dwayne sighed heavily himself then. "And you know I can't. My king has forbidden me to pick up my sword until he thinks me worthy. I can't go against my lord."

"Then we have a problem, don't we?" said Tarsus.

"Did I hear you had a problem?" asked Lionel behind them. "What problem is that?"

Both Tarsus and Dwayne stopped arguing, turned quickly to face Lionel, and bowed. Neither had heard the monarch as he'd come up from behind. That surprised Tarsus, for his hearing was far superior to humans, which showed just how distracted he was. And Dwayne was upset for letting his guard down so badly, no one should have been able to do what Lionel had just done.

"I see you're surprised to see me," commented Lionel, a slight smile playing across his lips. "You shouldn't be. You're surrounded by my walls after all." He gestured to the walls.

Tarsus grinned at the king, shaking his massive head. "No, not surprised, sire. Just distracted with affairs."

"I see." Lionel grinned at them both, cocking his head. "And would that distraction have anything to do with a problem you have?"

Dwayne spoke up. "Yes, sire, it does."

"That's a shame." Lionel looked around the fields slowly. There was a lot of activity going on for this early in the morning. At least a dozen knights were going through sword practice. Lionel scowled seeing Laura practicing with Sir Hook, but didn't comment. He saw a few using a grappling hook on an outside wall for scaling practice, even knights on horseback jousting by the lists at the far end of the fields. It seemed nearly all the remaining knights were here doing something. "I see a lot going on this morning. Is there something happening I need to know about?" Lionel looked back at Tarsus and Dwayne, cocking his head inquisitively again.

"No, sire," answered Tarsus. "Just the usual morning exercises. There's just more people doing it these days."

"I see," said Lionel, nodding. "And where's Pip? Should he not be here also?"

"He's right here . . ." Dwayne turned to where Pip was only a moment before and found the spot empty. He looked around, but didn't at first find him. "He was here a moment ago. I don't know where he went, sire."

"You should keep an eye on the lad, Dwayne. That's your job as page you know. To make sure he's all right and to see to his needs. He may be important to us all one day."

"Yes, sire. I'm trying."

"Well, apparently you're not doing too well." Lionel looked around as both Tarsus and Dwayne were doing. He was the one who spotted the lad off to the left of the sword practice area, leaning against an outer wall, watching Laura and Sir Hook go through practice drills. "Young Pip seems to be very interested in swordplay. I wonder why?" Lionel scowled at the boy, who was paying more than his share of attention to Laura.

"Ah, yes, sire," said Dwayne. "He seems to be."

Watching the boy for a moment, seeing him so interested in the exercise, Lionel asked, "Has he done any swordplay on his own? Seems to me he might benefit from it."

Tarsus sighed yet again. *Not Lionel too?* "No, sire, he hasn't. He's been too busy learning magic."

"I see," commented Lionel for a third time. "But it doesn't look as if he's very busy right now." He pointed to Pip leaning against the wall with all his attention focused on his daughter.

"Yes, sire," answered Dwayne before Tarsus could. "He moved there, I believe, because of the discussion Tarsus and I were having."

"Yes, I heard," Lionel said. "That's when I interrupted you two I believe. So, I ask you again, what's the problem?"

Tarsus made it out to be nothing. "Nothing to worry about, sire. It think we have it handled."

Dwayne disagreed. "No, we haven't, Lord Dragon. Our arg . . . discussion still stands."

Dwayne moved to stand in front of Tarsus before he could try and get away.

Lionel could smell something fishy between them. "What's the argument? Maybe I can help." He looked between the two. "You know, I can still be of use. I've told you before, if you need anything, just ask. You never know what can be done."

Tarsus looked dubious.

Lionel looked straight into Tarsus's face. "Is there anything I need to know, Tarsus?" he asked. "You've kept me abreast of things with yon Pip and my daughter, haven't you? You haven't left anything out of your reports? Something you're not telling me perhaps?"

"No, sire. Nothing like that. You know everything Dwayne and I do."

Lionel stared at him not saying anything.

"Truly, sire. You know everything we do. There have been no more secrets."

"Yes, sire," Dwayne agreed, coming to the dragon's aid. "There have been no more secrets. But . . ."

"But . . ." Lionel's voice went up slightly, thinking of something that could be wrong and them not having the courage to tell him.

"But I believe more could be done for Pip," said Dwayne, looking at Tarsus.

"Such as?" Lionel asked.

Tarsus interjected. "I can't!"

"Can't what? What's going on?" asked Lionel, showing a little bit of anger and frustration himself. "Talk," Lionel ordered.

Dwayne spat it out fast. He knew if he didn't do it quick, he'd lose his nerve. "I think Pip should learn the sword, sire."

The king thought a moment, turned to Tarsus, nodded, and said, "That's not a bad idea."

"But I can't teach him," growled Tarsus, spreading his wings to stretch some kinks.

"Why not?"

"I don't have the time, sire. I can't teach both your daughter and Pip." Tarsus blew a plume of steam from his nostrils in frustration.

"Why not? I believe you could teach both." Lionel spread his hands, gesturing to Pip.

"Normally, yes. But the time for the knight's trials is close for Laura. She needs more intense training so she'll be able to pass them." Tarsus saw Lionel flinch with the mention of his daughter and trials. She'd have to fight to go through them, the thought scared him to death. "She needs my attention more than ever when I have her for training. And I'll not break my promise to her. And Pip . . ." This is where he sighed heavily again. "Although I love him like my own flesh and blood, Pip didn't start with Laura and would have to start from the beginning. She is too far advanced to have a beginner with her." He gave Dwayne a cold stare. "Although Dwayne knows this, he still insists on Pip being trained." He looked back to Lionel. "I wouldn't do justice to Pip if I started to teach him now. That's why I've been concentrating on his magic."

Tarsus looked down on Lionel and chuffed, smoke billowing from his nostrils. "Dwayne is just being stubborn about it." He looked at the ex-knight. "That's what we've been discussing, sire." He looked at Lionel again, gritting his teeth. "And that's why I asked him to do it." Tarsus looked at the ex-knight. "But he keeps saying he can't either."

Lionel turned to Dwayne as well. "No, he can't, Sir Dragon." The look he gave Dwayne was one of determination. He wouldn't relent until the man learned the humility he so desperately needed. Lionel turned back. "What about another? Why can't another knight do it?"

Dwayne bowed his head. "No, sire, they can't either." He saw the bewildered look on his king's face and continued, "All of your knights are subject to your laws, sire." Lionel nodded his agreement. "Therefore, if one teaches Pip the sword, he'll be in violation of helping me pick one up again, and I'm not to pick one up until you deem me worthy. Anyone who helps me suffers the same fate as me, be it punishment from the lash or banishment or even death as my lord decrees." Dwayne bowed to Lionel. "None will take that chance, and I wouldn't ask it of them."

Tarsus stared at the king quizzically. "The same fate?"

Lionel nodded. "Yes. Why do you think we have very few criminals in our kingdom, and no one helps the ones we have?"

"Then we have the same problem, don't we?" asked Tarsus.

"No, I don't think you do,." Lionel corrected, smiling. "I'll do it."

"You, sire?" asked Dwayne surprised.

"You, sire?" said the same from Tarsus. "Can you even use a sword?"

"I don't know," Lionel mocked Tarsus. "Which end has the point?"

Tarsus stuck his nose cat quick down to Lionel. He was nose to nose with the monarch. "That's not funny, sire." He puffed smoke from one nostril.

Lionel coughed. He didn't back away from the dragon as most people would. He just waved the smoke away with one hand and grinned at Dwayne. "He doesn't have much of a sense of humor, does he?"

"Not that I've seen, sire. No." Dwayne answered.

Tarsus stepped back and sighed. Then he sat down heavily.

"But he does sigh a lot," said Dwayne, a grin showing on his face.

"Yes, I've noticed that." Lionel grinned also.

Tarsus just looked both, wondering which would be better roasted than baked, when Lionel did something he wholly didn't expect: going to a sword rack and picking a sword. Tarsus stretched his neck down to him again and cocked his head quizzically, wondering what the monarch thought he was doing.

Lionel smiled but said nothing. The sword he finally settled on was more of a rapier than broadsword. It was just as long as a broadsword, suitable for swinging and chopping when necessary, but thin enough and balanced enough for close action like a rapier. Ripostes and parries wouldn't be a problem. He swung it a few experimental times to test its balance and then grunted in satisfaction. He looked at Tarsus and grinned. "Let's see what I remember, shall we?"

Normally, Lionel wore a red-rimmed robe and short gold crown in front of his subjects, but today, he was dressed very differently. Tarsus hadn't noticed until just now. He had on a pair of very tough tan breeches, short leather boots, a jerkin of tan hide that matched his boots, and a wide belt that helped with the look of the outfit. All in all, it complemented his form very well. It wasn't very often the king got to relax; running a kingdom wasn't a job one could take time off from. It was a non-stop position for life. But Lionel knew traipsing around the training field with his crown and robes flapping in the breeze would only distract his knights from their training, in which they needed all their concentration. He looked at Dwayne. "I give you permission, my friend, to pick up a very dull training blade so I can teach yon dragon, I haven't always been a king. At one time, I wasn't too bad at this."

Dwayne didn't move. "Sire, I'm sorry, but I can't. I'll not fight you even in practice, sire. I'm not worthy as of yet to do such a thing." He bowed to Lionel.

"Why? I'm giving you permission to pick one up." Lionel looked at the man sternly. "I'm getting very tired of not having my commands obeyed, Dwayne."

"I'm obeying your orders, sire." Dwayne bowed his head even lower to his king. "Until I'm released by you from this command, I'll never lift another sword, be it practice or not. I'll gladly die for the sake of my king and kingdom without having picked one up. Until I'm worthy in your eyes, I can't do it, and I will not. Honor dictates it so. My king decreed it."

"I see," said Lionel calming down a bit. "I guess it's my fault for that. But Dwayne," Lionel looked into the face of the ex-knight, "I've never been ashamed of you. Disappointed, yes, but never ashamed. You'll find your way back, I've no doubt." He put his hand on Dwayne's arm. "Why do you think I put this punishment on you?"

"To teach me a lesson, sire."

Lionel nodded and then asked, "Do you know what that is?"

Dwayne looked straight into his king's eyes and said without emotion, "No, sire. I simply know I'm no longer what I was."

Lionel looked crestfallen. "That's why I did it. You're not the man I once knew. When you find him again, I'll see him worthy, for I greatly miss him." He turned from Dwayne to Tarsus. "Let's see if someone else will help, shall we?" Lionel turned to the sword practice behind him, leaving Dwayne to ponder what had been said to him, and Tarsus wondering if the king of Musk hadn't simply lost his mind.

In a few short strides, Lionel was standing in front of the knights. He wanted Sir Hook or Sir GuWayne to do him the honor of a practice session. Both men, however, were busy. And he noticed Sir Hook's opponent was his daughter. Apparently, Hook hadn't forgotten Laura's drubbing she'd given him the last time. He looked as if he were trying to take her head off. But it did look as if he'd learned one valuable lesson: a pretty face in battle makes only for a pretty opponent. Sir GuWayne, making an example of an upstart newcomer. Reports he'd been given about the young man in contest with the formal knight hadn't been good. He'd been reprimanded more than once for excessive force, in the field and off. The only thing he knew was violence when it came to the king's subjects, from what Lionel was seeing, GuWayne was teaching him what violence really was.

Pip's mind was focused so much on Laura, he never noticed King Lionel until he was standing in front of him blocking his view of the princess. He nodded to the king. Pip noticed he didn't nod back. *Now what have I done?* He stared at Pip as if he wanted to put him on a spit.

Lionel turned from Pip and waited. Sir Hook and Laura finished as he watched. Laura blocked a tremendous blow coming straight for her head and returned one of her own to the knight's gut with her foot to gain distance. As Sir Hook held his stomach, Laura called a halt, bowing to each other, each coming away from the match sweaty and winded, but unharmed.

Laura noticed her father, standing in front of Pip and to the side of Tarsus and Dwayne. She smiled at him, but he didn't return it. Lionel spoke first, "Laura, may I have a moment with Sir Hook?"

Laura nodded, bewilderment in her eyes.

Sir Hook bowed to his king. "Yes, sire," he said, still breathing heavily, "May I do something for you?"

"Yes, Sir Knight. How would you like to spar with me?" Lionel held up the practice sword and saluted his knight.

Hook stared at his king without saying anything for a moment. Then, he said, "I'm sorry, sire. I cannot. I cannot and will not go against my liege lord."

"Explain," demanded Lionel. "How would you be going against me if we sparred?"

"Sire, as knights, we can't help anyone involved in a punishment set down by the crown. Just as the citizens of the kingdom can't. You, yourself are directly responsible for the punishment of the former Sir Dwayne. We're specifically commanded to not let him pick up a sword until you felt he was worthy to do so again. Sparring with you would be a direct violation of your law, since you're directly involved in his punishment. I cannot, sire. I'm sorry." Hook bowed to Lionel again.

Lionel scowled at the man. "I see."

"I think we still have a problem, sire," said Tarsus, sarcastically.

Lionel turned his scowl on Tarsus.

"Maybe I can help," said Laura coming up to her father, as winded as Sir Hook. "I'm usually pretty good about solving them. What's the problem?"

Tarsus chuckled.

Laura stuck her tongue out at him.

"Very mature, Your Highness," Dwayne told her afterward.

Lionel stepped between the two before anyone else could say something that could start a war. "I need a sparring partner to prove a point to the lizard here," he indicated Tarsus.

Tarsus stuck his tongue out at the king.

"Very mature yourself, Master Dragon," pointed out Pip. "Did you learn that from the princess?"

All of them turned to stare at Pip. Laura's stare especially hurting Pip. No one spoke.

Pip held his palms out in surrender. *Whoa! Sorry.*

Lionel stepped in again. He quickly turned back to Laura. "Like I said, I need a sparring partner for a few minutes."

Laura looked at her father with suspicion. "You, Father? I didn't know you knew how."

"Even you, Daughter?" Lionel shook his head in disgust. "Doesn't anyone understand I haven't always been on the throne? I inherited it. When I was young, I went through the trials myself."

"You? The trials? Why didn't you ever tell me? Did mother know?"

"Laura, your mother knew everything about me. And when she left us," Lionel bowed his head remembering his wife's last night before her death, "there was no need for you to know."

"But, sire," jumped in Dwayne. "How long has it been since you picked up a sword?"

"Well, you got me there." Lionel looked at the sword in his hand. Shook his head. "It's been a while. Since ascending the throne, the kingdom took precedence over everything else. But," he shrugged. "I think it's like riding a horse. Once you learn, you never truly forget." He lifted the sword for emphasis.

Looking at her father with her mouth open in amazement, Laura realized he was serious. This was very unusual. First, he never showed any interest in the blade as far as she could remember; second, he absolutely forbade her from picking the craft up; and now, third, he wanted a sparring partner of his own. This was turning out to be a very educational day indeed. Maybe if she did it? "OK, Father, how about me?"

"What about you?" Lionel asked bewildered.

"I'll spar with you," explained Laura, smiling, pointing to the sword in her father's hand.

"You?" Lionel said, shocked.

"That's not a bad idea," said Tarsus, thinking out loud. "I don't think anyone else is going to do it." Tarsus looked at the faces of the knights surrounding them.

No one in the small group had noticed, but everyone on the fields had stopped what they were doing to watch their king and princess.

Lionel looked about him, every one of his knights shaking their heads. *Blast! Looks like I may not have a choice.*

"Father, since I haven't gone through the trials, I'm not officially under the rules of the knighthood. If you need a sparring partner and no one else will do it, I'm more than happy to spar with you." Laura smiled, her mischievousness showing. "I'm a member of your kingdom, of course, but I'm foremost your daughter. So, I think I'm your only real choice."

Lionel thought a moment and then reluctantly nodded. "I think so too. I may not like it, which I don't, but there it is."

Laura nodded, looking at Dwayne and Tarsus.

"This should be interesting," Tarsus choked out, laughing.

*   *   *

CHAPTER 25

E veryone on the fields watched as father and daughter prepared to square off. Laura felt as if she were walking out to face Sir Hook again. In that match, she had more at stake; now, she was better prepared, far better, but the stakes seemed to be just as high, not for her, but for her father. In all the years, she'd known and loved him, there was still more to learn.

The crowd of onlookers made a circle around them so the spectacle coming could be plainly seen by all. Lionel wondered what he'd gotten himself into. He'd only wanted a sparring session, not this. Oh, he had to admit, even to himself, he wanted to make a fool of Tarsus for his snide remarks, but he most assuredly didn't want to take it out on his daughter. Lionel knew there was going to have to be ground rules for this little exhibition fight, or it would be cancelled. Laura was the most important person in the kingdom, and she couldn't be harmed. And he sure as blazes wasn't going to be the one to do it.

Lionel stepped into the ring of onlookers, inside Tarsus, Dwayne, and Pip alongside Laura, waiting for him. When he approached, he said, "Before we do this, we have to have some ground rules."

"Then you need to find another partner, Father," said Laura immediately.

"This is only sparring, not combat," Lionel said heatedly.

"All fighting is combat, Father, sparring or not," Laura pointed out just as heatedly. "I've been taught to give everything to every training session, including sparring. That's the fastest way to learn from your mistakes. After a few bruises and broken bones, you tend not make the same mistakes twice. The only allowance, we'll be using very dull swords. They may not cut, but they'll break bones and bruise." Her face was set like stone.

"Very well, daughter," Lionel agreed with gritted teeth. "Apparently you don't want to listen. It seems I'll be teaching two lessons today." He turned on his heels, walked twenty paces away, turned, and waited. He figured he'd taken more than enough back talk from his upstart of a daughter, time to be a parent.

Tarsus watched the king walk away, then leaned to Laura, and said, "You haven't learned a very fundamental lesson, Princess, but I think you're about to."

"And what would that be?" shot back Laura, watching her father.

"When to keep your mouth shut." Tarsus indicated Lionel waiting for her. "I hope you're ready."

Laura gulped and looked at her father standing in the middle of the knights. His jaw was set and his stance indicated he was ready. Laura took a deep breath and shook her head. *I hate it when the lizard's right. I may have provoked father too far this time.*

Laura slowly walked to her father, coming to stand ten feet from him, saluting with her sword. As the blade came up to her nose obscuring her view for a second, Lionel didn't hesitate, striking with the back of his hand across her left cheek. The move was fast and unexpected.

Tarsus looked at Dwayne and grinned. Pip's mouth fell open as most of the other onlookers did. Dwayne didn't say anything, only watched and shook his head.

Laura went to the ground like a sack of grain. Not giving her any time to react, or come to her feet, Lionel advanced, lifting his sword as if to strike again. Laura saw the move, brought up her own to block the supposed downward blow, unprepared for a boot to her left side instead. The resounding impact of the boot took the wind out of her and sent her reeling. Two unexpected maneuvers right from the start put Laura off her game, exactly as Lionel wanted. Not a good way to begin. But to her credit, as the blow rolled her away from Lionel, she used the momentum to get to her feet. She was winded and hurting in the first thirty seconds, but she was up and facing him again.

Lionel didn't wait. He took two steps to begin an offensive series of thrusts and parries to cut Laura down quick. His style was fast, precise, and to the point. Laura was hard-pressed to keep his sword from clubbing her and breaking something important.

Dwayne watched with avid interest. In the first part of Lionel's training so many years before, his father, King Roderick, was just like any protective parent, and he didn't want anything to happen to his only heir to the throne, but, just as Laura was doing to him now, he'd already done to his own father. He was willful, rebellious, and stubborn to the point of insubordination. Lionel wanted to learn every style of fighting and every weapon so he could defend himself and his family if that time ever came. Two seasons of training and almost thirty broken bones later, his sword arm alone being broken three times, Lionel passed the trials with merciless ease. He'd become that which he'd always wanted: a sword master. No one knew this fact, for when Lionel had to take the throne after the death of his father at thirty-two, he'd forsaken the blade and the knight's training for the sake of his kingdom. Now, nearly twenty years and twenty-five extra pounds later, he was proving to himself he could still defend his kingdom and teach a valuable lesson in the process.

Lionel stepped in close and brought his sword up to slash downwards on Laura's head. Laura stepped to the side and brought her sword up to block. When she did, Lionel hit her again across the face with the back of his hand. She reeled away spitting blood. At this point, she realized her father was taking this very seriously, the talk of her not wanting any quarter or giving none had been just plain stupid on her part. Tarsus was right, she'd have to learn to keep her mouth shut and not let her pride or her anger get in her way. Lionel didn't wait. He followed through, taking two quick steps kicking at her. Laura saw it coming, dodging the blow, and then dropped to one knee, extending her other leg to trip the incoming king, which got her another boot to the thigh.

Howling in pain, she rolled as far as she could to get some distance between them. It worked, but true to his style, Lionel advanced again; however, Laura didn't retreat. She unexpectedly rolled back under the incoming king, and when he was in position, she kicked out and connected with his stomach. As Lionel doubled over, she kneed him in the nose. The impact wasn't enough to end the contest, but it stunned him enough for her to jump to her feet. Blood dripped from Lionel's nose as he advanced again.

As the contest continued, for it was not sparring no matter what anyone said, Lionel knew he couldn't keep this kind of pace up. Not only was he out of shape, but he hadn't used a sword of any kind in many years. In the end, he knew Laura would best him when it came to stamina. Whether older people wanted to admit it or not, youth did have some advantages. He advanced faster this time, and he had planned to kick the blade from his daughter's hand and end this as quickly as possible. But, like all plans, they tended to go astray. This time when he advanced, instead of back-pedaling, Laura advanced also, immediately going on the offensive. She'd been right, after receiving a few blows, she tended not to repeat the same mistake twice. Slash downward, parry from Lionel; thrust from Lionel, parry from Laura; a midair swipe for the king's mid-section, a side step to avoid it. For a few moments, it went back and forth: strike and block, strike and block.

Lionel didn't feel right about striking his own daughter, but, 'all out' was what she demanded, and he was getting tired of playing by someone else's rules. So, he gave her exactly what she wanted.

The next move ended the combat decisively in Lionel's favor. As Laura parried a thrust, she overcompensated just enough for Lionel to pivot on his left foot, strike her with his left elbow in the nose, and link elbows to throw her over his right hip to the ground. When she landed, Tarsus heard distinctly the wind whoosh from her lungs. Lionel immediately planted a foot on her chest and lifted her chin with his sword. As quietly as he could, bar the heavy breathing, he asked her, "Do you yield?"

Laura looked up from under her father's boot and grimaced. In his eyes, she saw something she'd never seen: anger, and it was directed at her. The thought of him actually using such a maneuver on an opponent and then see him kill that opponent was very unnerving to the princess. Laura slowly put her hands up and whispered, "I yield, Father."

As the princess brought her hands up, Lionel saw fear in her eyes. Seeing that fear, all the anger in him fell away. He slowly released Laura, helping her to her feet. When she was upright and puffing like a bellows, as he was, he turned to the onlookers around him. In a voice which was tired and used up for the moment, he scratchily said, "I think my time with you today is at an end. Thank you for the spar."

Every knight on the fields went to one knee and bowed their heads to him. No one spoke.

Lionel then stepped back to his daughter and said, "We'll talk later if you like, when you clean up. You probably have a few questions."

"Thank you, Father." She bowed to him.

Lionel turned to Tarsus, Dwayne, and Pip. "Pip, I'd like to talk to you also. Come see me when you can." He nodded to him.

"Yes, sire," said Pip, still amazed at what he'd just witnessed. He bowed to the monarch as he left the fields.

"I knew that would be interesting," said Tarsus smiling, watching Lionel walk away.

*   *   *

In his chambers an hour later, Lionel waited for his daughter. On reflection, he couldn't say that was a sparring session, more an exhibition of power on his part. He was ashamed. He'd told himself many years ago he'd never do to his own child what his father had done to him; today, he'd broken that promise. King Roderick had drummed a fighting lesson into him so severely he'd been bedridden for two weeks. Lionel swore he wouldn't teach that lesson to his own offspring, and yet, here he was repeating the past. He had decided after this little episode to explain a few things to his daughter and try to clear the air between them at the same time. It was long overdue.

A knock came at his door. He expected it to be Laura. He took a deep breath and said, "Come." He was surprised, however, when Dwayne entered.

The ex-knight came forward a few feet, stopped, and then bowed. He didn't immediately say anything, seeming to look the king over from head to toe. Lionel got the distinct impression he was assessing the damage done by the spar, which wasn't visible. Lionel sustained very little real damage from Laura. His stomach felt like a bag of mush where she'd kicked him, but Laura wasn't strong enough to do any permanent damage. Her strength was her youth and agility in matches, not brute force. Finally, he said, "That was quite a show you put on, sire."

"Quite," said Lionel disgustedly.

Dwayne didn't comment on that. He simply looked at Lionel as if he wanted to say something totally different. Then he said, "The princess will be here shortly."

Lionel looked Dwayne over this time. He didn't seem any different than the man he'd seen on the fields with the dragon, but he got the distinct impression he was different. Dwayne had been his personal bodyguard, friend, and sometime mentor for more years than he cared to admit, but since Tarsus had arrived, he'd changed fundamentally. His demeanor and actions over the past months hadn't been the same as the man he'd admired, respected, and loved for all those years. That's why he'd put him in a position of page to a person he'd have considered being of a lesser and unimportant status. The person he'd known for so many years wouldn't have been as petty as the person who emerged when the dragon first came. Maybe his one-time mentor was finally realizing the change and coming to understand. He hoped so for his sake. He sorely missed his friend. In bewilderment, Lionel asked, "Is this the reason for your unexpected visit, Dwayne? To announce the arrival of my daughter?"

"Yes, sire," answered the ex-knight. He bowed again, turned, and left the room.

Lionel shook his head. *Maybe there's hope for you yet, Dwayne. I pray that is so. I sorely need your council.* A moment later, another knock came. "Come." This time it was Laura who walked in. She was none the worse for wear, her nose slightly swollen from being hit a few times, a cut over her left eye, and a noticeable limp on her left side, but, she was whole and well for all that. Upon seeing him, she didn't say anything, just sped up until she literally flung herself into his arms.

Lionel caught her and held her tight. This was a very surprising welcome. He'd wanted to hold her and comfort her so many times over the years since her mother had left them. Sobs escaped her lips as she choked out, "I love you, Daddy." He held her tighter with tears leaking from the corner of his own eyes.

"Oh, my Laura. I love you so much. Your mother would be so proud of you."

They held each other for the longest of times, then slowly let each other go, and wiped their tears. Laura had so many questions she didn't know where to start. Lionel beat her to it, however, by saying, "Can you hold off on the questions for now, Laura? I know you have a lot of them. Pip will be here shortly, and I'd like for you to be here when he comes. I may need your help to talk to him."

Laura nodded. "All right. But I don't know why you'd want me here. I think he'd do anything for you." She turned away for a moment, her tears stopping, needing an excuse to wipe them from her cheeks. As she did, she looked for something to drink. Usually, Lionel kept a water jug at hand or a pitcher of juice. Laura knew her father wasn't much of a drinker, so he kept an alternative at hand. On a stand by his only window looking out at his small walled city was what she wanted. She poured a glass for herself and then one for the king. As she drank, she wondered just why he'd kept so many things to himself, and if there were more surprises to come. "Don't think I'm not going to ask you all the questions in my head, Father. When Pip leaves, you and I may be up all night." She smiled. He affectionately smiled back. He didn't doubt it for a second.

Speaking of the young lad, Lionel's mind went back to Pip. He thought as much about the boy as Laura did, that he'd probably do just about anything for him, but, as a wizard, he didn't have to do anything at all. That frightened Lionel badly. Thank the gods the lad didn't have an evil nature. That thought brought back the point he was going to pitch to Pip: he'd have to fight Granston, who according to Tarsus, was a very evil wizard indeed. Lionel didn't have the right to ask it of him, but with Laura supporting him, maybe Pip would see the situation and agree to help. Plus, he had to convince the young wizard to be taught sword craft by a king. *What in the two hells was I thinking?*

When Pip arrived, fifteen minutes later, Lionel was walking the floors. He was as nervous as any mouse around a room full of cats. How was he possibly going to convince Pip to train with a sword? And him the teacher? A small knock came at the door. Lionel took a deep breath to calm himself, looked at Laura for courage, and then said, "Come." Pip entered all right, but on the heels of Sir GuWayne, which was a surprise. No one was expected but Pip. Laura smiled at the young man, Pip grinned back. Before either could speak, GuWayne said, "Sire, we may have a problem."

Lionel looked at the knight sternly and came to full attention. His nervousness vanished with the thought there might be some kind of trouble. "What problem? What's going on? Why didn't Hook come to me with this problem?"

"Sire, Sir Hook sent me to inform you. Master Tarsus and he are assessing the problem."

"Well," Lionel said anxiously. "What is it? What's the problem?"

"Sire, there's a Dwarf, Elf, and a human at the gates of the city. Sentries say the Elf has urgent news for our king," GuWayne explained.

"What news?"

"I know not, sire."

Pip said, "I guess that's what Hook and Tarsus went to find out."

Lionel looked at Laura. "We better see what's going on."

Laura nodded.

Lionel looked at Pip and said, "I'm sorry, Pip, looks like we'll have to talk another time."

"That's all right, sire. Your duties come before me." He bowed.

"Lead the way, Sir Knight. Let's find out who's come to call." Lionel gestured for the knight to go ahead.

GuWayne bowed, turned, and headed out the door.

Pip sighed in relief. This news of strangers coming to call was a godsend for him. He hadn't been looking forward to the talk Lionel wanted to have. It seemed every time he talked with the king, he heard bad news, usually about himself. With the strangers coming, the heat was off for the moment. *This should be interesting. No one said I couldn't go too.*

On his way from his chambers to the south gate of the city, Lionel didn't say a word. His thoughts centered on not only who may be at his gates wanting to impart urgent information, but also on what had transpired on the fields. The ones at the gates could be anyone. He had many informants throughout not only his kingdom but the other four main kingdoms as well. War was always at the back of his mind, although peace between his neighbors had lasted for decades. Other concerns, however, were taking most of his thoughts. The contest between himself and Laura had disturbed him greatly; he'd let his temper get the best of him, nearly injuring Laura. When he was young and foolish, his temper had gotten him into much trouble, but he'd learned to control it. At least he thought he had. Most of the people in the kingdom who were around then to witness his royal personage fly into fits of temper were either long gone or dead. Dwayne was one of the few exceptions. His father had always said his temper would be his undoing and eventually cause him great pain; today, it nearly had. Nowadays he was more than content to be considered the 'Kingly Bungler'. He had ears, often hearing the jokes told about him throughout the castle and the city, but turned a deaf ear to them. He'd much rather be a simpleton king than known as a tyrant. His people were healthy and happy and that's what mattered to him. Now, however, he was being forced to climb out of his 'bungler' stage and didn't care for it.

At the south gate, Lionel and his companions found a very motley crew indeed. Tarsus, Dwayne, Sir Hook, an Elf, a Dwarf, and a very grubby human were discussing quite pleasantly the downfall of his kingdom.

When the Dwarf spotted Lionel, however, he stopped talking, pointed, and began laughing. Sir Hook and Dwayne took offense to it. Hook went so far as to draw his sword to chop the little fellow in half. Lionel yelled for him to stop. "That's enough, Sir Knight." He looked at the Dwarf. "This fellow is simply slow in the head. One has to make allowances."

Sir Hook lowered his sword, but didn't immediately sheath it. The rest of the onlookers gaped at the little man and the king facing each other.

The Dwarf rumbled, "True. But this slow head of mine pulled your slow bottom out of a few fires, didn't it?" He laughed even harder.

"Once," corrected Lionel. "If Dwellin hadn't been there, if I recall, you'd have joined me." Lionel was smiling broadly at the Dwarf.

Tarsus huffed.

"Oh, shut up, you big lizard. Your butt has been pulled out a few times, too." The Dwarf whipped his head around to stare at Tarsus.

Tarsus huffed again, but didn't say anything.

Pip stared at the Elf in amazement. He'd heard of the fairy folk, but had never seen one until now. The Dwarf was another thing all together. He'd seen one of his kinds many years before in the city. Mulch had to get supplies from the store house in town, and one of the grubbiest little people he'd ever seen had been there wiping down a small pony with an oil cloth. He hadn't said anything, but Mulch had commented to the warehouse man he shouldn't have been allowed there. At the time he'd wondered what he'd meant, maybe after all these years he was going to find out.

The Elf joined in. "Both of you shut up." He looked at Lionel. "When was the last time you were out and about, you old Lion?"

Lionel grabbed his stomach and shook it like he was shaking a jellied roll. "Too long apparently." He too laughed. "This thief," he pointed to the Dwarf, "told me you'd died in the Forest of Eld. Something about a staff, or tree limb, or some such. I didn't think it worth traveling after that." He smiled at both of them.

The Elf scowled at the Dwarf. "You told the Lion I was dead?" He looked at Lionel. "My staff is nothing to be sneered at. It has great power when needed. To acquire it took many years in the Forest of Eld." He scowled again at the Dwarf. "If not for the necessity of coming here, I'd attend to your mouth myself."

The Dwarf frowned. "I, as you know, didn't know you lived through the fall. I was busy at the time trying to keep my hide on, just as you were, before you took the plunge."

Laura jumped in before the Elf could respond. "Do you know these people, Father?"

The Dwarf turned his attention to Laura, walking to her, looking her up and down quite forwardly. He looked back to Lionel. "Is this little Lo?"

Lionel smiled and nodded.

The Dwarf whistled. "I am getting old." Apparently he'd known Laura years before.

The Elf bowed to Laura. "Forgive the demented little guy, my lady, his mouth is quite loose."

"I'll show you *loose*, you . . ."

Lionel and Tarsus both jumped in. "No!"

The Dwarf stopped, but just barely. Tarsus said then, "I think it's time we go somewhere and talk. I think Little Lo," he indicated Laura with his head, "may explode if we don't."

Laura glared at him.

I guess father has some surprises left after all.

✱   ✱   ✱

Lionel studied his three visitors closely. The Dwarf, Gimble, he'd known for most of his life. The little fellow wasn't very refined or courteous, but he trusted him with his life. Like the Dwarf said, he'd saved Lionel's bacon more than once from the fire. The Elf, Muriel, Lionel would've gladly laid down his life for. Far too many times the Elf had saved not only his life, but also the lives of all the royal family. Seeing them both was a relief and a disappointment. Although knowing they were still alive was the relief because he hadn't seen them in many years, it was a disappointment because when they showed up, trouble wasn't far behind. Trouble seemed to follow them like a cat follows a mouse. The human, Lionel didn't know. But, if he had anything to do with Gimble and Muriel, it definitely wasn't a good sign. The man's name was Dura, Dura the Assassin, from the Assanti Assassin guild; unusual in itself, the

Assanti weren't human. They were human in appearance but that was as far as the resemblance went. If he got into the guild, he was a very dangerous man, which made Lionel very nervous indeed.

To accommodate everyone, and because Tarsus couldn't fit inside the castle, the fields were emptied and one corner was made ready. A canvas tarp was stretched to form a pavilion, and food and drink were brought out. There was a lot of drink: ale and wine being the main beverages.

"Father, maybe you can introduce us now," said the princess, looking over the newcomers.

Lionel smiled. "I suppose I can, although I don't know why anyone would want to be introduced to such scoundrels."

"Father!" Laura was scandalized by Lionel's bad manners.

Gimble laughed uproariously, nearly falling out of his chair. His glass of mead rocked so hard in his hand that the contents sloshed all over the tabletop. Muriel, on the other hand, stood and saluted the king for his 'kind' words.

Lionel continued, nonetheless, "If you must know, the little fellow laughing so hard is Gimble, a Dwarf of immense self worth." The Dwarf didn't stop laughing. "And the Elf," Lionel indicated, "is Muriel, a creature of fate."

Muriel smiled and made another flourished bow.

Tarsus snorted.

"Fate?" Laura asked.

"It seems," Lionel explained, looking at the Elf slantwise, "when trouble's about to befall me, he's fated to arrive."

The Elf bowed again. "I think it has more to do with the witch than actual fate."

"Witch?" piped Pip, staring at Lionel.

Lionel looked at Pip. "That's a story for another time."

Laura was intrigued. *Father does have more secrets. How interesting!*

Tarsus leaned down and eyed Gimble. "Would you shut up?" The Dwarf had yet to stop laughing. Tarsus fully expected the little man to have a heart seizure at any moment. That's when Gimble finally fell off the chair.

Tarsus looked at Muriel. "Can't you do something with him? I think he's gotten worse."

The Elf shrugged, watching the grimy Dwarf rolling on the ground.

Pip watched Tarsus closely. Although he seemed to be enjoying the banter, he never fully relaxed, his eyes constantly moving to the human who'd accompanied the Dwarf and Elf. Pip couldn't quite place it, but there was something not right about the man. Tarsus must have felt it too, which made Pip all the more leery.

Laura smiled at the byplay between the four friends, for as surely as she sat among them, they were friends. It was almost impossible, since Tarsus had been asleep for centuries, but there it was. "Master Tarsus, how is it you know these two? I don't believe I quite understand. You were put in your sleep, according to you, centuries ago."

Muriel stared at Tarsus, surprise in his face. "Sleep?"

Tarsus shook his head. "It's a long story. Let's just say I've been away for a while, shall we?"

"Away? You've been gone!" Muriel exclaimed. "I searched for you for a hundred years, you old lizard. I thought the Gnome had finally gotten rid of you."

Tarsus snorted. "He very nearly did. He put me in a dream for a few centuries, that's all."

"All," squawked Gimble, coming off the floor, sitting again at the table and chuckling.

"The last time I saw you, you were flying straight at the big Gnome with the crown, more a Dwarf than a Gnome, and he wasn't very happy to have you come to call."

Laura held up her hands to stop the banter. "Hold it! Wait!" Everyone in the tent stopped and watched her. "Do you mean to tell us, you," she pointed at Muriel and Gimble, "and Master Tarsus have known each other for centuries?'

Muriel went into laughter then. It was Gimble's turn to answer. "My lady," he bowed mockingly at Laura, his smile splitting nearly his whole face, "you have the wrong of it. It may not seem so, but Master Tarsus is but a pup compared to Muriel and myself."

"What do you mean?" asked Pip.

Gimble looked at Pip and scowled. Before he could answer, however, Muriel cut in. "What my companion is trying to say, boy, is that Gimble is much older than the dragon. He and Tarsus have known each other longer than this little village popped into existence."

Lionel spoke looking at the dragon, "Yon Master Tarsus seems to have gotten around." He eyed the dragon with suspicion, pointedly directing his next comment at Tarsus. "And it seems he has a lot yet he hasn't told us about."

Muriel nodded enthusiastically. "Oh yes, our friend with the scales has a lot of things he doesn't talk about."

Pip stared at the Dwarf. "But," he squeaked out, "that would mean . . ."

Tarsus chuffed again. "Yeah, but don't let that fool you," Tarsus inclined his head to Gimble, "this grubby Dwarf may be older, but he's certainly not any wiser." He eyed the Dwarf as if he were a tasty snack. "He's gotten into as many scrapes as I have over the centuries." He turned to Muriel. "Just as this one has, if you counted up the number of times I had to pull both of their tails out of the fire, we'd be just about even. They aren't saints by any stretch."

"True," said Gimble. He looked at Lionel with a glint in his eye. "Neither is Lion here. Have you ever told your lovely daughter the story of how you and your Ely ran away and nearly got yourself strung up?"

Laura swung her head to Lionel. Lionel blanched. "That," said Lionel, "is not for this meeting. There may never be time for that."

Gimble guffawed. "I bet."

Laura asked, "Father?'

Lionel shook his head, sweat beading on his forehead, knowing he'd never hear the end of this. He knew he should have just heard what needed to be said by the trio and kicked them out the gates again. But . . . they were not only old friends but people he could trust when arrows started flying. And Tarsus? Knowing the two and traveling with them for a time wasn't surprising either; now that the cat was prowling, it was too late to call him back.

Dwayne stood back and watched as the four friends renewed their friendship. He should have been a part of the reunion, but his station as a page forbade him to do so. He contentedly stood behind Pip watching for any sign he may need a helping hand.

Dwayne's silence wasn't lost on the Dwarf. He noticed Dwayne lurking in the shadows, and he couldn't help saying, "Why are you not joining us, you great galoot of a knight? Have you forgotten the drubbing you received from me the last time we met?" He laughed again, but only for a moment. "Do you not want another try at me?"

Dwayne didn't say anything, merely looked at Lionel for permission to speak. It wasn't the job of a page to do anything but be attentive to his charge, not be an active participant in a meeting like this. Lionel nodded his assent.

"I'm performing my duties, Master Dwarf. Nothing else is required of me."

"Duties?" The Dwarf looked at Lionel. "What's going on?" He turned back to Dwayne. "What are you talking about? And by the way, why aren't you in your armor? Doesn't it fit any more?"

Dwayne looked at Lionel again, but this time, it was Pip who came to his aid. "His armor fits him fine. He just doesn't wear it any longer. He's helping me for the time being."

Muriel watched the exchange between Dwayne and Gimble without saying anything, but hearing Pip, he held back no longer. "And who are you? You're nothing but a boy. Why are you sitting among your betters?"

Tarsus' temper had been rising since coming to this little meeting, Muriel with his holier-than-thou attitude brought it to the surface. "That's enough, Elf. You may be the rightful holder of the stick, or twig, or meat grabber, or whatever you want to call the thing, but it doesn't give you the right to accuse anyone of anything." He chuffed loudly and smoke billowed from his right nostril. "Don't think you're any better than the lowliest dung carrier in this city."

Muriel jumped to his feet. "My staff of power and station in life has everything to do with who I am, dragon! Who are you to tell me otherwise?" His temper was showing like Tarsus. "Do not presume to put me in 'my' place. I know my place and duties."

Lionel jumped to his feet. "That's enough! From both of you. We're not here to argue but to find out exactly what you," he pointed to Muriel and then Gimble, heat rising in his own voice, "have to tell me. Why are you here?"

Time to get to the meat of the problem.

Muriel and Tarsus stared at each other a moment longer, and then the Elf sat down again.

Tarsus chuffed loudly, but kept quiet.

Gimble watched the two friends with interest, before Muriel sat down. He chuckled to himself seeing the two renew their friendship after so many centuries. He knew they'd be OK. Tempers always flared when they were around each other. To start, Gimble pointed to the one person in the tent no one knew, the scruffy human who had accompanied the Dwarf and Elf to Musk. "He's why we came, Lion. You need to talk to this person and find out why his people intend to destroy your kingdom."

Tarsus eyed the dirty human. "I don't believe I've ever seen him before."

Before Gimble could answer, the human did, "I can speak for myself, dragon."

"Good," rumbled Tarsus, putting himself nose to nose with the man, lightning quick, just as he'd done to Dwayne those many months before. "And if you call me dragon again, I'll show you what one can do." He chuffed a billow of smoke into the man's face, his temper still simmering from his and Muriel's harsh words. No one stopped him. Apparently, Tarsus was speaking for the whole group. He grinned realizing it.

"Please, I beg your forgiveness," said the man, although still showing no emotion. He acted as if a dragon threatened him every day. He was either very brave or crazy as a loon. He bowed to Tarsus. "My name is Dura. I'm an Assassin from the Assanti guild."

"Assassin?" exclaimed Laura. "But you're not an Assanti."

"No, my lady," said Dura, looking at the princess. "I'm not." He looked at each of the others in turn, resting his gaze on Lionel. "I've already told my traveling companions some of my tale." He indicated Muriel and Gimble. "But I've not told them all. Suffice it to say I no longer wish to be associated with the Assassins and leave it at that."

"Then why are you here?" Laura asked.

Everyone turned to the scruffy man who was supposedly an Assanti Assassin. His demeanor hadn't changed since walking into the city or the tent, and he'd yet to say a word about why he'd come with Gimble and Muriel. Laura was getting more out of him than anyone had. From hooded eyebrows and underneath scraggly hair, he looked up. "You need to run. Your kingdom will come to an end when Grundehl and his army arrive."

"By the Horde Mother!" Tarsus swore.

Lionel demanded of Tarsus, "Do you know what he's talking about?"

Tarsus only stared at the man.

Muriel blanched and then spoke up himself, "You don't know what's in store for your kingdom, Lion. You may want to leave before he gets here."

"When who gets here?" asked Laura. "You keep talking about someone showing up and trying to kill us and our kingdom, but no one has yet to say who this person is."

Dura looked the princess in the eyes and said, "Grundehl."

Pip squeaked out, "Who's Grundehl?"

Tarsus explained. "He's the king of the Gnomes, Pip. For centuries now, his people have been trying to put me in an early grave. On one occasion, he nearly succeeded. His people and I've had a very bad relationship ever since." Tarsus snorted.

Lionel asked, "And why's that?"

Muriel chuckled. "How long has the lizard been here?"

"For a couple months now," said Laura. "He's been helping me train."

Muriel turned to Tarsus. "Still keeping secrets, I see."

Lionel stood up, anger bubbling in his eyes. "Secrets, Tarsus. I thought that was over with?"

Tarsus sighed. "They are, sire. I've told you everything you've wanted to know. I didn't think you wanted my life history. You'd be a very old man if I told you everything that happened to me over the many years of my life. This is simply one of the many things that did."

Lionel sat back down. He calmed enough to realize Tarsus was right. "Well, I guess you have a point. I can't exactly expect you to tell me everything that happened to you. But you better tell us something." He sighed and blew out a breath. "What's this about?"

Tarsus also sighed again. He was getting very good at it. "Grundehl feels I may have killed a few of his followers."

Muriel chuckled again. "A few?"

Gimble laughed outright. "A few thousand."

Tarsus stared at the Dwarf. "They were trying to kill me."

"And I suppose you had nothing to do with that?" asked Laura.

Tarsus turned his gaze on her. "Not really." He chuffed. "I was simply defending myself."

Muriel laughed again.

"OK. OK. That's enough," said Lionel. "I think we get the point. You and they have a history. But what does that have to do with my kingdom?"

Gimble spoke up again. He looked at Lionel. "And where do you think the dragon is now, Lion? Huh?"

"Blast!"

"Yup," said the Dwarf, nodding his head and grinning.

"And what do you think he's coming here for?" asked Muriel.

"Blast!" said Laura.

"That's why you better run if you can, Lion. I don't think you'll want the whole Gnome race on your front porch." Muriel pounded the table top for emphasis. "And if they have a wizard with them, you better beat it soon."

Sir Hook didn't take too kindly to that. For the whole of the meeting, Hook and his guards were among them, but silent. When faced with running or dying in defense of the kingdom, he could keep quiet no longer. "We don't run from a fight. I'll not abandon my kingdom or its people. There's no honor in it."

"No one is going anywhere," Lionel said heatedly. "My kingdom will not be abandoned no matter who threatens it."

"Then you're a fool," stated Dura. "You can't hope to win over Grundehl and his wizard. You'll all die."

That got all their attentions. "What wizard?" asked Laura. She, like Hook and everyone else, couldn't and wouldn't let Musk die.

Pip choked. A wizard? A wizard was coming to Musk to kill them all? He wasn't ready to face a wizard yet. He didn't know if he'd ever be ready.

Dura's eyes glazed over and said, "A wizard with the power over the very ground itself. One who can make anyone he chooses do anything. I know not where he came from, but I knew I couldn't stay and watch my people become his puppets."

Sir Hook said contemptuously, "We aren't cowards as you are."

In the blink of an eye, Dura threw a knife at Hook. But in that instant, Pip had seen him do it before the knife actually left his hand, a picture flashing in front of his eyes. Just inches away from the knight's throat, the knife stopped in mid-air. Hook's eyes widened to the size of saucers. Silence descended from the onlookers as Pip casually got up from his chair and plucked the knife from the air, turning his attention on Dura.

The look on the Assassin's face was one of surprise. When he saw the knife stop, he immediately turned to flee the tent, but he had nowhere to go; the tent changed in mid-stride to walls, solid, three-feet thick stone walls. He came to an abrupt stop seeing he was trapped. Hanging his head in defeat, he turned back to his captors.

The boy was the one he faced. "I think this is yours?" Pip held the knife out to him. Dura didn't take it.

Dwayne immediately put himself in front of his king, shielding him with his body. Laura slowly rose from her seat and walked to Pip, putting a hand on his shoulder, whispering quietly, "I think that's enough, Pip. Sir Hook can take it from here." She reached around and took the knife from his limp hand and slid it in the belt of her jerkin, looking around finding the walls gone and the tent returned to normal. She saw Lionel and Tarsus watching her just as everyone else was. Tarsus was nodding his head and her father taking deep breaths to calm down. When she turned back to Pip, she saw his attention was solely on her. She smiled. "Come on," she said, taking his hand, "let's go get some air, away from all this. Shall we? I think I've had enough."

Pip nodded, but didn't say anything.

Laura led him out of the tent and slowly walked him towards the nearest exit of the fields. Maybe a nice walk would do the trick. It sure couldn't hurt. Pip let Laura slowly lead him away, not seeming to mind at all.

Sir Hook indeed took it from the boy. He immediately went to Dura and forced him back in the chair with himself standing guard, a short sword in the knight's hand, dangling just inches from the man's throat.

Dwayne watched Pip and Laura leave the tent, not moving from his place in front of Lionel. He knew he should have helped Pip instead of his king, but ingrained reflexes had taken over. He looked back at Lionel. Seeing he was all right, Dwayne slowly moved to follow his young charge. Lionel called him back. "No, Dwayne. Let them go. I think I may need you here."

Dwayne looked at the princess and Pip once more, not liking leaving the boy, but knowing his duty for the moment was with his king. Turning to Lionel, he bowed. "Yes, sire."

Lionel nodded and then turned his attention to Dura. "I think you better start talking. If you don't, I may have to give you to our own wizard." He nodded in the direction Pip had taken and smiled a very evil smile. "He may be young, as you've seen, but I think he could get you talking like a parrot." His smile got even broader. "Or," Lionel made as if to reconsider, "I could just give you to the big lizard behind us. He loves roasted coward."

Dura blanched. He knew when he was beaten. That's why he got out of the Gnome kingdom when he did. He didn't come here to die. He spread his hands in acceptance. "Very well, what do you wish to know?"

Lionel said, "To begin with, who's this wizard you mentioned?"

"I don't know where he came from, but he's supposedly a Gnome like Grundehl. Although he doesn't act like one," Dura sneered.

"Do you know his name?" asked Tarsus, thin wisps of smoke rising from his nostrils.

"Granston," said Dura with a snarl. "He gets closer to the king of the Gnomes by the day. But he's not there for the king. He wants something from the kingdom no one's yet to figure out. And the main thing he is obsessed with is killing you,." Dura sneered at Tarsus, spittle spraying from his lips.

Tarsus snorted smoke and then turned to Lionel. "Didn't I tell you he'd come? Pip must be ready."

*   *   *

CHAPTER 26

P ip walked placidly beside Princess Laura. He didn't know where she was taking him, but he didn't care. Pip found as long as the princess was near, he tended to be calmer and more focused. He didn't quite understand whether it was due to how he felt about her or whether it was because she was near. Either way, he knew he'd never tell her. And he certainly could never tell Tarsus or Dwayne. The ex-knight would have the hardest time accepting the fact a low born was stuck on the princess, and the king would definitely have him thrown out of the kingdom. So, even though his heart soared being around her, his heart ached because he could never voice it. Pip wondered if all wizards went through something similar or just him.

Laura watched Pip closely as she walked him out of the fields. He seemed calm and collected, in total control of himself. In the tent, the knife incident with Dura had been a complete surprise to her. She never realized Pip could do something like that. She'd been told more times than she cared to admit he'd been training with Tarsus with magic, but to actually see it was putting a whole new perspective on the subject; until that moment, she didn't really believe. She'd seen Pip at the stream show her, Dwayne and Tarsus his dreams in the water, but that hadn't felt like magic. She'd convinced herself afterwards, Tarsus had done it and not Pip. But, seeing the knife thrown by Dura stop in mid-air put a whole other perspective on things. Now, she couldn't not believe. And with that belief came worry, not only for her father and the kingdom, but for Pip himself. Over the past months, she'd come to realize she cared for him perhaps more than she should. Watching him, she wondered if he could really fight Granston and come out alive.

Granston, a wizard! The little shuffling man had always made her nervous, for reasons she couldn't even name, now she supposed she knew why. She shivered at the thought.

Pip was young, according to Tarsus, in the ways of magic. He may not be able to handle such a contest. Laura wondered herself about the fight coming, if she'd be ready. Her trials for knighthood were fast approaching, and she doubted if she'd be ready for those, let alone this scared young man. If a war came to the kingdom like Muriel and Gimble and this Dura said it was, she couldn't do anything about it, maybe no one could. Pip and Tarsus was the only hope of fighting off an army of Gnomes. The knights and guards of the kingdom would give a good accounting of themselves, of course, but they had no hope of defeating an entire army. Musk hadn't had a regular army in many decades. It wasn't needed. Shivering at the thought of fighting and bloodshed to come, she hoped Pip and Tarsus would help them.

"Pip?" Laura looked at the young man and couldn't help but wonder about his power. "What can you really do with your power?"

"What do you mean?" asked Pip, looking at the princess quizzically.

"That was amazing what you did at the tent. Can you always do something like that?"

Pip looked at the princess uncomprehending. "What did I do?" asked Pip.

Laura watched Pip closely, stopping their walk with a light touch on his arm, then peering into his eyes. His face showed a blank expression, as if he'd just woken up from a long sleep. "Don't you remember what happened?"

"Remember?" Pip stared at Laura blankly.

"Do you remember anything from today, Pip?"

Pip nodded slowly. "Yes, of course. I remember talking to you and your father in his rooms. Then three people showed up at the gates: an Elf, a Dwarf, and a human. We talked to them. Now we're taking a walk." Pip looked at Laura sideways with a puzzled frown on his face. "Isn't this what you wanted?"

"Is that all you remember?" Laura asked, looking deeply into his blue eyes, Laura's eyebrows rising with concern. She couldn't tell if there was anything wrong with him other than the fact of him not remembering what happened. That scared her. Why didn't he remember? She slowly cupped his cheek and stroked his face. "Pip?" she said softly.

Pip shook himself like a dog, seeming to come back from some faraway place. Blinking furiously, he really saw, she thought for the first time, who was standing in front of him. "Princess?" He looked at Laura and started to blush. "Where are we going?"

Laura dropped her hand from his cheek. "Are you all right?" she asked.

Pip nodded. "Where are we going?" he asked again.

Laura smiled, linking her arm in his and said, "Oh, nowhere in particular, just taking a nice walk. Is that OK with you?"

Pip looked at her arm linked in his and sheepishly grinned. He nodded. He was afraid if he said anything he'd look like a fool.

They kept walking.

Laura knew she had to tell Tarsus when there was time. For now, however, there was time for her and Pip to take a walk together. One never knew what tomorrow would bring. One had to grab times like this and hold on.

*   *   *

Muriel stared at Lionel. "Who's the boy, Lion?"

Tarsus answered instead of Lionel. "He's a wizard, Elf. You'd think that to be obvious from what you saw."

"He's a wizard?" Muriel cocked an eyebrow at the dragon. "I thought you stopped that knife from skewering the knight." He looked at Sir Hook and then back at Tarsus. "What's wrong with him? He looked as if he didn't know what he was doing?"

Tarsus snorted. "He probably didn't. Young wizards have that problem."

"Wait!" roared Gimble, coming to his feet. "Do you mean he's just now found out he's a wizard?"

"Not this instant, no, but not long ago. I've been instructing him?" said Tarsus, eyeing the Dwarf. "You know how it is?"

Gimble flopped down in his chair, arms going limp, and face going slack. "By the gods, dragon!" He quietly said. "Why didn't you tell us?" He looked up into Tarsus' face. "Have you gone mad? Do you realize what that boy could have done?"

Tarsus didn't say anything.

Dwayne finally came to life. Without having permission, he asked, "What's going on? Is there something we should know?"

"I don't know, you big galoot," said Muriel sarcastically. "Did you know that boy could have killed all of us in this tent without remembering doing it?" Muriel wiped his face with his hand and then slowly lowered his hand to his sword and clenched it. "If I'd known about the boy before we came, I don't think I'd have come through the gates."

Lionel asked, "What's going on? What's wrong?"

"Wait a minute," said Gimble, pointing at Tarsus, "You didn't tell the Lion about this, did you?" He shook his head, "I should have known."

Tarsus still didn't say anything. He looked at everyone and everything besides the Dwarf.

"Oh, boy. That's what I thought." Gimble shook his head again. "I should've turned around the moment you walked up to the gate." The Dwarf shook his finger at Tarsus in anger. "You haven't changed a bit, you overgrown lizard. Still keeping secrets and holding information close to your chest." He grunted, wiping his face.

"That's enough!" roared Lionel, jumping to his feet. "I want answers, Tarsus. Didn't we just go through this a moment ago? No more secrets. What's going on? What haven't you told us about Pip?'

Tarsus didn't have to say anything, Muriel explained. "Lion, you best get that lad out of your kingdom. He's very dangerous. If what I've heard so far, or more to the point, not heard from Tarsus, the boy hasn't yet changed. And that's very bad." Muriel stared at Tarsus with a grim look on his face.

"Changed? Changed how?" asked Dwayne again without permission.

The Dwarf took up the narrative. "Well, let's see." He put a finger to his nose and spoke as if reciting from a text. "A young wizard, not necessarily young in body, but young in the ways of magic, has to go through a change in mind before that wizard can master the art of wizardry. If such change doesn't occur, that wizard may become unstable and volatile. That wizard can, in an instant, destroy, without realizing, that which he is near."

"What does that mean? That which he is near?"

Gimble grimaced and said through gritted teeth, "He can destroy everything and everyone around him, Lion." He took a deep breath to calm down a bit. "He can, with but a thought, release his magic all

279

at once, and anything and anyone around him will be destroyed. And he won't remember doing it. The more powerful the wizard, the more devastating the destruction."

Lionel looked at Tarsus, his eyes going wide with horror. "Is this true?"

Tarsus snorted. He stared at the Dwarf as if he were sizing up his next meal, and then looked at Lionel again. "Yes, sire. It is."

"By the gods!" Dwayne whispered. "I knew I was right about the boy." He saw Lionel's face darken with anger and then with fear.

Tarsus blew a thin stream of flame across the tent. Tempers were starting to rise, and he needed to calm things down a bit. It did the trick. The tent became quiet as Tarsus looked at each in turn. He focused his attention on Lionel. "That will not happen, sire. I've taken steps to prevent any unfocused magic from destroying your kingdom or anyone near Pip."

"Explain," said Lionel with gritted teeth. "I thought we had an agreement you'd no longer keep secrets?"

"We do, sire. I haven't kept anything from you." He stared at Dwayne with open hostility. "And you're wrong about Pip, Knight. He wouldn't do what you think."

Lionel asked, "And what did you do?"

"I've already told you, sire. The magical bond we share will prevent such a tragedy."

"The bond?" asked Dwayne. "You mean the promise you made with young Pip to share his fate?"

"Yes, the promise." snapped Tarsus. "But it's not just a promise. It's a magical contract between him and me that can't be broken. Whatever happens to him will befall me. This shared bond will prevent a volatile nature from coming to the surface."

"By the Lord Follower!" swore Muriel, gripping the table, his fingers going white. "Please tell me you didn't pledge yourself to him, dragon."

"I did," answered Tarsus simply.

"Then you're as mad as he," said Gimble. "Such a pledge can only be broken by the death of one or the other, and if you pledged the fate of the other, then nothing can change the fate each shares." He stared at Tarsus like his life depended on the dragon denying what he'd done. "No pledge of this kind has been attempted in eons. Records of such have been kept of all pledges since the time of Tannin. And that didn't end well." Gimble pounded the tabletop with a fist.

"Tannin was a different matter," snorted Tarsus. "This is a totally different situation."

"How so?" asked Lionel worriedly. "Who's Tannin?"

Gimble explained, "Tannin was the grand dragon of his age. Nearly seven millennium ago, he bonded with a human wizard, much as Tarsus has done. But his wizard went insane with power. To prevent him from destroying every kingdom he went to, Tannin was forced to confront him. The magical strain of Tannin trying to keep the wizard alive and also stopping his conquest of the world killed them both, but not before destroying half a continent."

Muriel finished. "The wizard Tannin bonded with had just gone through the change. His chances of survival were much higher than if he hadn't. But Tarsus here," he motioned to Tarsus, "hasn't waited for the boy to go through the change. And if he's gone through it, the dragon never knew." He stared at Tarsus. "And that, to me, is highly unlikely. Dragons can sense the change in a new wizard before they even know it themselves."

"Tarsus?" inquired Lionel. "Is this also true?"

Tarsus didn't say anything at first. His thoughts went back to the night he was woken up by Pip screaming in his sleep. After rushing to his young charge's bed, he found Pip woven into a cowl of magic. In just moments, as Tarsus watched, the cowl disappeared, but not before Pip screamed out Laura's name. He'd been dreaming of Laura in danger. Pip talked about the nightmare the next morning, but hadn't said anything about the cowl of magic. From what Tarsus gathered, he didn't remember doing it. He'd apparently been trying to protect the princess, contain the magic, so it wouldn't do harm to her. The cowl, the key. In that cowl, the change usually takes place for a wizard. For a minute, or an hour, it didn't matter, for all wizards, the stronger the cowl, the quicker the change, the most powerful wizards emerge. Although the magic emitting from the cowl was no stronger than any Tarsus had ever sensed, Tarsus felt he'd changed in a totally fundamental way, benefiting not only himself, but those around him. A shiver went through the dragon thinking of Pip turning to the dark side of magic. A sorcerer, or wizard as most call them, can become intoxicated with the power they wield. If that happens, they tend to go insane with that power. Unspeakable horrors could very easily be unleashed by such a wizard. Tannin's wizard he'd bonded to was just such a wizard. The magic drove him insane, Tannin paying the ultimate price stopping him. Tarsus shivered, looking around the tent at the faces of the others, and then told what happened that night, and with the telling, he found he couldn't doubt the change in Pip, nor doubt his power. Pip was potentially the most dangerous wizard alive, probably the most dangerous wizard ever born.

"By the gods!" Dwayne swore. "And he's with Princess Laura."

"And he'll do nothing to her, Knight. He wouldn't. Pip doesn't have an evil bone in his body." He looked at the king. "Please, sire. I'd never put Laura in danger, and neither would Pip. What these two haven't told you," he looked to Muriel and Gimble, giving them an evil stare, "is that for something like that to happen, Pip must first have that trait in him. That's to say, if Pip were naturally evil-minded, that trait would be amplified from the change. You've been around the lad quite a bit in the past months, have you not? Have you noticed that kind of behavior from him?"

Lionel didn't say anything. He simply looked as if he were thinking about all that had been said. Then he noticeably relaxed, said, "No. You're right. Pip has never shown anything but reticence, and sometimes boredom, from his magical studies." He shook his head. "No, I can't believe he'd harm my Laura. Or anyone else for that matter."

Tarsus gave a sigh. "Yes, sire. He's shown those things and more. And that's what's made me believe he didn't know what was happening with Dura, here. He has a natural aptitude for magic. He can control it even if he knows what he's doing or not." Tarsus shook his head. "No, I believe Pip will be a very powerful wizard." He looked at Dwayne and said sternly, "And he'll not be evil."

"For your sake and ours, Master Tarsus, I hope you're right," said Dwayne. "For I'll not let anyone harm my princess. Even if I have to kill my own charge." Without permission or an answer from Tarsus, he stood and strolled out of the tent.

Lionel didn't stop him from leaving. Dwayne knew his duty as surely as he did by assigning it to him. He was headed to wherever Pip and his daughter were. He turned back to Muriel, Gimble, Tarsus, and the other knights in the tent. "From this point on, Sir Hook, you'll double the guards around the walls of the castle, and sentries will be posted at every entrance to the city. Anyone approaching will be stopped and held for questioning. No one will do harm here. Is this understood?"

"Yes, sire," said Hook, bowing. "And what do we do with this?" Hook had yet to release Dura, still holding the short sword to the man's throat.

He pulled the man's head back and yanked his hair for emphasis, putting the blade to his neck drawing a thin bead of blood.

Lionel simply said, "You know what to do. Put him where he'll not cause any problems."

"My pleasure, sire," said Hook, pulling Dura to his feet and walking him by the arm to the tent opening.

As the two left, Lionel turned back to Muriel. "Thank you for your timely intervention. Now what will you do?"

"I think we'll stick around a while longer and see what happens." Muriel decided, looking at Gimble. "You may need our aid."

Lionel nodded. "I thought so." He gave a sigh of relief. "And I thank you." He nodded to the Elf.

Muriel and Gimble nodded back. Gimble said to Tarsus, "And what about the boy, you lizard? Does he know what's happening? Have you even bothered to tell him what may become of him when this other wizard shows up on your doorstep? You better train the boy quickly if you haven't already started."

Tarsus nodded. "Yes, he knows. But he still has to be prepared for it. And since you came to give us the good news of him actually arriving, he'll need all the help he can get to be ready."

Lionel figured that was an excellent time to bring up the subject of training. With the actual coming of Granston, he may not have the time himself to train Pip. But Gimble or Muriel? "Speaking of Pip, Sir Dragon." He looked to his two 'guests'. "We may be in an excellent position to find a trainer."

Tarsus looked at Lionel as if he'd grown an extra nose. "You don't mean . . . ?"

"Oh, yes." Lionel nodded and smiled. "I may not have the time now."

Tarsus looked at Muriel and then Gimble. "I don't know, sire. He may not go for it. With someone he knows, he'd be a little more cooperative, I think. You he respects. I don't think he'd go for just anyone." Tarsus shook his head. "He just met these two."

Gimble slowly stood up and faced Tarsus. "What are you planning, you great bag of wind? I didn't come here so you can get my hide flayed from my body." He looked to Lionel. "And you, my kingly friend, are no better if you're scheming with the lizard here." Gimble cocked a thumb towards Tarsus. "Remember, we didn't have to come. We could've just killed the human and went on our merry way."

"And what would King Balsas have said to that?" Lionel cooed, eyeing the little Dwarf.

"Don't bring my king into this, Lion," stated Gimble heatedly. "There's no need in it."

"Oh, I think there's every need. What happened the last time you didn't come when there was trouble?" Lionel's eyebrows rose with the question to the Dwarf.

Gimble's face fell, and he slowly sank into his chair again. "I don't wish to think of it," he said in a small voice.

Muriel's curiosity got the better of him. "What happened, Lion? I haven't heard this tale. At times, yon Gimble can be very closed-mouthed indeed." He looked at Tarsus. "Just as this one can. It's very frustrating."

Lionel never took his gaze from Gimble when he answered, "Many years ago, yon Master Gimble, found out Musk was going to be invaded by Prado. He decided to do nothing about it, and his uncle, King Balsas, didn't take too kindly to having a relative of his shirk his duty. Master Gimble was sent to a very dark and dank mining community of outcast Dwarfs. This is the first I've seen of him since. That's why I was so surprised to see him at the gates."

"Well, well, well," said Muriel. "That must be why I found him wandering in the mountains of Yon a few years ago. He looked as if he hadn't seen the sun, or a bath, for a long time." Muriel scrunched his face to emphasize the smell that came from the Dwarf. "I cleaned him up, and we've been traveling together ever since. I never asked him why he was up there."

"Why not?" asked Lionel. "Didn't you ever wonder where he came from or why you hadn't seen him in a while?"

"Of course, I did. But it never came up until now. And besides," Muriel looked away and stared out the tent flap, "I have a few things I don't want to talk about either."

Lionel looked to Gimble again. "Did you leave without permission? Is that why the Elf found you the way you were?"

Gimble was shocked. "No! I left when I got word from the high council my time was up. I didn't think they'd ever let me out. I just started walking. I didn't care where I ended up, just so long as it wasn't back in the lost mine." He set his jaw and scowled at all of them, especially the Elf.

"Well, you're here now," said Lionel, "so you might as well make the best of it. If you don't at least listen to what I have to say, I'll send an envoy to Balsas and tell him where you are and what you've been up to. And that you won't help us again."

Gimble blanched. Then he nodded.

"Good," said Lionel. He looked at Tarsus. "I think we've found the answer to one of our problems, Tarsus."

"I think you may be right, sire. I just hope Pip sees it as a solution too."

CHAPTER 27

"A re you serious?" asked Pip. "I thought you were going to help me?"

Tarsus sighed. He knew he'd have problems convincing Pip to start sword training in the first place, but now, he had the added challenge of convincing him to take instruction from perfect strangers. Since Laura told him what happened right after leaving the tent, Tarsus now knew why Pip was so reluctant to train with them. Pip didn't remember what happened with Dura, just as Gimble had surmised. As far as the lad was concerned, these two just showed up to teach him the sword.

Muriel and Gimble both agreed to teach Pip sword play, with reservations on Tarsus's part and a lot of extortion on Lionel's. Balsas was brought up more than once to get Gimble in on the deal, and Muriel had to be threatened by Lionel with being thrown in the dungeon for bringing an Assassin into the kingdom who tried to murder one of his vassals. But through all of that, Pip was turning out to be the most stubborn and the one who needed convincing.

"Pip, you need more than magic," Tarsus said for possibly the tenth time. "How many times do I have to go over it?" Tarsus turned aside from Pip and lumbered outside. His stall at the moment seemed too cramped. For the past two hours, he'd been trying to get it through the thickhead of the boy he needed sword training, and he couldn't train him.

"Fine," agreed Pip, following the dragon outside. "But why can't you do it? You've been teaching the princess. Why can't you teach me too?"

"Pip," huffed Tarsus, smoke billowing from a nostril, "I've already gone over that with you. I don't have the time."

Pip was getting pretty frustrated with the lizard. He'd been arguing with him for the past two hours, and he wasn't having much luck. He'd just have to keep trying. "Sure you do. When we have magic lessons, we can take a few minutes to train with a sword. Either before we do the magic or after. It doesn't matter. Come on."

Tarsus sneered, which for a dragon wasn't easy to do. "A few minutes? It's taken me all the time I've been here, nearly every day, at least five hours a day, to get Laura where she is now. How long do you think it'll take for you to get to the same level she's at with only a few minutes a day?" He shook his giant head in disgust. "No, Pip. You need to be ready when Granston gets here. You need someone who will be there every day. And for a lot longer than a few minutes."

"So, why can't Sir Dwayne do it? He and I don't see eye-to-eye most times, and I think down deep he'd rather see me in chains in the dungeons, but at least I know him."

"You know why, Pip. He can't pick up a sword until Lionel tells him he can."

"Fine," Pip finally grumbled. "But why them? I don't know them."

Tarsus sighed again. He seemed to be doing a lot of that lately. "Pip, please. There's no one else. You have to be as ready as possible for Granston when he comes. We may not have much time."

Pip only stared at the dragon. *Why's this getting so complicated? Tarsus said he wouldn't abandon me, yet here he is passing me around like a plate of mutton to the next at the table. And not just one, two, who I don't know.*

At just that time, Dwayne walked up with the Elf and Dwarf, and just like that, things went from bad to worse. Dwayne bowed to Pip and nodded to Tarsus before saying, "Lord Dragon, the Elf has another problem." He indicated Muriel with a twitch of his head. He then turned to Pip with a disgusted look and said, "I'm sorry, young wizard, I'm not able to instruct you in the ways of the sword. For surely I'd do better than these two." He looked at Muriel and Gimble. "Instead, you're forced to have these strangers give you their limited knowledge."

Before Muriel or Gimble could dispute what the former knight was saying, Tarsus grumbled at the knight, "What problem? I thought we'd worked out the problems with the lessons?"

Pip was disgusted himself with this turn of events, another setback would probably send him over the edge. His edge had a very long drop indeed, not just for himself, if he took the plunge, everyone in the kingdom would take the plunge with him. And he was surprised by the former knight's apology. He'd always thought Dwayne hated him.

Dwayne pointed to Muriel. "I've no idea what the problem could be. He won't tell me. He said he'd only talk to you. So you better ask him yourself."

Before Tarsus could ask what the problem was, Muriel said, "I can't stay, Lord Dragon."

Tarsus looked suspiciously at the elf. "Why?"

Muriel looked down at the floor. His eyes wouldn't meet the dragon's. "Elder March is looking for me. I haven't been in our kingdom for a while, and I'm afraid he may come here and yank me out. So, before that can happen, I need to leave."

Tarsus had enough of excuses and whining from everyone. Steam rose from his nostrils and a small lick of flame blew out of his mouth. His eyes turned red, and his ears went flat on his head, and with a grumble, he huffed a stream of hot steam-like air into the Elf's face plastering his fine silvery hair back along the crown of his head. Muriel stepped back quickly before anything important could be singed and threw his hands over his face. Tarsus leaned close and spat angrily, "I've had enough! You'll begin instruction now!" To emphasize what he'd just commanded, he spat another cloud of steam into Muriel's face.

Muriel came away ashen-faced, nodding his agreement. Gimble, standing there through the whole exchange, said nothing, color slowly draining from his face.

Pip stood with his mouth open. This was the first time he'd seen Tarsus mad at anyone but himself, and it was the first time he'd seen the dragon actually blow fire. *I hope I never get him that mad at me. I guess all the other times we've disagreed was just an annoyance to him. Whew!*

Dwayne nodded his agreement. It's about time the big lizard showed some anger towards someone besides him. *It's nice to know I'm not the only one to get on his nerves.*

"Fine! Fine! I'll do it," said Muriel disgustedly. "But if Elder March comes for me, I'll be forced to leave."

"You mean run?," sneered Tarsus.

"Call it what you want, but I'll not be what he wants me to be."

"And what is that?"

"A puppet on a string."

"If that happens," huffed Tarsus, "I'll take care of it."

Muriel stomped away, his back straight and limp hair flowing behind. "Good luck." He looked at Gimble and Pip and motioned for them to follow. "Let's go have a lesson, boy, before the dragon has another fit."

Tarsus huffed again behind them as they left. His nerves to say the least were not the best. As he watched the trio troop away, he smiled. He could relate now to how Pip probably felt all these months being badgered by him. He snorted, turned, and then slowly walked back into the stable and his stall. He needed rest. Even a catnap would help him.

*   *   *

Dwayne didn't say anything after the little episode between Muriel and Tarsus; he simply followed behind Pip. His duty was clear; he needed to be wherever Pip was. He didn't trust the Elf or Dwarf to properly train the lad anyway, so this gave him a legitimate reason to go along. Plus, he intended to be with them the whole time, no matter how long it took to properly give Pip a fighting chance.

Before following Muriel, Pip looked at Tarsus and scowled, but didn't say anything. The way he was feeling, if he were to say something, it could very well come out as a fireball.

The trio headed to the training yard. When they arrived, Pip had a few words for them all. "I don't see why I need this. I'm learning magic, you know. And I know quite a bit already. If someone was to come at me, I'd just throw them across the kingdom or something."

Dwayne looked at Pip, his manor giving nothing away as to what he intended doing. Without warning or words between them, Muriel and Gimble had swords to Pip's throat, and Dwayne had stepped behind him holding a knife to his ribs. Pip froze. He never saw the actions of any of them. One second he was facing the trio, the next, each had a blade in their hands, pointing somewhere at him.

Dwayne said from behind, "That is why, Lord Wizard. If you're already dead, you can't do those things."

Pip gulped. Sweat beaded on his forehead. Touching Muriel's sword point against his neck, he gulped and said, "I see your point."

The next three weeks was no picnic for Pip. From dawn to dusk, and sometimes even beyond, he trained with a sword. Muriel and Gimble never gave in to his whining or wheedling when it came to practice. Under no circumstances was he not to train and under no circumstances was he to quit. Every day was the same, and every day was grueling. But every day he learned more than either of them imagined. Pip seemed to soak up sword play like he did magic, like a sponge. In the evening hours, Tarsus instructed him in the ways of magic. And after each day, he collapsed in his bed too exhausted to do anything but sleep. Muriel and Gimble turned out to have quite an exceptional arsenal hidden inside them when it came to sword craft. Some of the more colorful maneuvers they tried to show him didn't quite sink in, but basic fighting skills, Pip soaked up readily. In just a few short weeks, Muriel was confident Pip could take on any sword smith in the castle, and if not beat them, at least fight to a draw—which in the end was all that could be asked, it would keep him alive long enough for him to stand strong with his magic.

Dwayne wasn't too sure of the idea Pip could challenge any one of the knights and come out without a scratch, but he saw great potential in the lad. Although he didn't approve of the style of fighting or the methods the Elf and Dwarf taught, he did know a competent sword style when he saw one. On the finesse of sword play, Muriel was the one to go to; on the heavy lifting side, that's the chopping and stabbing side of the coin, Gimble was the one. Pip barely had time for a meal in those few short weeks, but also in those few weeks, he'd put on a few pounds of muscle. He was filling out nicely for a lad of his age and the difference wasn't going unnoticed by the princess. Although Laura didn't see very much of Pip in the weeks since his training began, she did get glimpses of him as he went from castle to training grounds every day and back. She didn't have much time herself to stop and notice very much, however; Tarsus kept her in training of her own for her trials with the knights. Her time was coming fast, and she was determined to be ready. Every day she'd seen Pip trudge to the grounds with Gimble or Muriel, she'd wondered if he'd eaten or Dwayne had made sure he was taking care of himself. She wasn't sure why she worried about the health of Pip or his welfare, but she was coming to realize she did.

On one of the many days in which Pip had been exhausted from his training and was slinking back into the castle with his head down and his eyes seemingly glazed over, Tarsus noticed a small bright blue glowing ball following behind the boy. This was the day he'd decided Pip wouldn't have to do magic lessons. For one thing, he himself was too weary to teach him, and for another, it looked as if Pip wouldn't be able to concentrate long enough to learn anything. To Pip, he didn't seem to realize anything was different, with seemingly no thought on his part, the glowing orb just followed behind. As Tarsus watched, it changed its shape from a glowing ball to a sword, to a dagger, to a lance, to a shield, and back again to a sword. Tarsus shook his head to try and clear away the image. It had to be a mirage. It had to be the strain from the past couple of weeks getting to him. But when he looked again, the orb was still behind Pip following him like a long lost puppy. He thought about calling to him and finding out what was going on, but after only a moment kept his mouth shut. He simply watched Pip go into the castle and not come out again.

"Aren't you going to find out what that was?" asked a voice from behind the dragon.

Tarsus nearly broke his neck whipping his head around. He eyed the man, but said nothing. Steam slowly rose from his nostrils and an acrid stench came from his mouth. When he saw who it was, he quickly gulped down the flame he'd almost shot into the king's face.

Lionel looked up at Tarsus and asked, "Something wrong?"

"Only you sneaking up on me, sire."

"Sorry," Lionel said, Tarsus doubting he really was. Lionel grinned slyly. "I didn't actually sneak up on you. I walked calmly to where you are now. You just didn't hear me do it."

"That's the definition of sneaking, sire."

"No, that's the definition of you not hearing me." Lionel grinned even broader.

Tarsus sighed. "True, sire. I suppose. But, please, don't do that very often. I may not realize who you are until you're roasted on your feet one of these days."

"Ah," said Lionel. "I'll try to remember that."

"Please." Tarsus looked back towards Pip, entering the castle, wondering again what he'd really seen.

Lionel waited for a moment longer, looking towards the same spot as Tarsus, and then asked his original question again. "Are you going to find out what that was?"

Tarsus looked down at Lionel and sighed again. "You saw?"

Lionel nodded. "Yes, I saw. I just don't know what to make of it. Is that normal?"

"Normal, sire? I don't think anything Pip's been doing is normal." He chuffed loudly.

"I see," said Lionel. "So what do you think it is?"

"I have no idea, sire." Tarsus shook his head.

"Excuse me." Lionel whipped his head up to Tarsus, his mouth hanging open in surprise.

Tarsus hung his head and took a deep breath. He turned to face Lionel squarely and sat down, looking down on the monarch. Tarsus said, "Sire, you have to know this before I say anything else about Pip. He's one of the most powerful wizards I've ever come across in my life. He's a very unusual case. The cowl that was around young Pip the night of his nightmares looked to be no more or less strong than any other a wizard develops when first acquiring his powers. It only lasted a moment. But the change in him was immediate and very strong. Usually, when a person finds out he's a wizard, or sorcerer, he or she tends to slowly build power over a few decades. In time, they come to understand how to handle what they've been given with a sense of rightness or wrongness. In that way, they learn how to control what they wield. Rightness tends toward the lower order of power, that is, they'll usually do remarkable feats of wonder with a flourish: lights, bells, whistles, and smoke going off where there's normally nothing to see or hear. Wrongness tends toward the bold and hearty: they're the show-off of the bunch. Not only will lights go off, but lightning will fall from a clear sky, the ground beneath their feet crumble and fissures swallow anything around them."

"And Pip?" Lionel gestured towards the castle doors Pip went through. "What's he? This wrongness you speak of or the rightness?" asked Lionel.

"Pip," said Tarsus, "is in a class all his own, tending toward both, but neither. Did Laura ever tell you about Pip having nightmares and how he showed us his dreams?"

Lionel nodded. "Yes. She said it took her breath away."

"She was right. It took mine away too. I was humbled before what I saw."

Lionel gazed at Tarsus in wonder. A dragon who'd been humbled. Pip must be a most remarkable wizard indeed.

"Such a feat shouldn't have been possible. In all my life, I've never heard of such a deed by anyone. And I've seen wizards do remarkable things in my life. Yet," Tarsus shook his head, "Pip makes them seem easy and unremarkable. His powers seem to come with great ease and no effort. He doesn't realize what he does nor how he does it. This glowing ball is just one example. In a hundred lifetimes, I doubt not he'll still be the greatest wizard alive. His power grows by the day, without any influence from any source I can discover." Tarsus looked at Lionel and grinned. "And that's one of the main reasons I've stayed with you and your kingdom. I neither had an obligation to you, nor to Laura, not really. I could've taken a couple night's rest and then been on my way. Normally, that's what I'd have done. But," he looked at the sky and shook his head, seeing Pip standing in front of him in the stables, "I sensed something in the air the moment I touched down outside your castle. I didn't know what it was, but I knew I had to find out. Pip was what I'd sensed. As I've told you, dragons can sense the presence of power, but we can't tell how much power is actually in a new wizard. We watch and wait. I don't regret pledging myself to your daughter, Your Majesty, but to put it as bluntly as you'd like, that was merely a means to an end. I regret that now, for I find myself in a place which I cherish. A place in which I've never felt like I do now. One in which I've found not only companionship, which I haven't known for too many centuries, but a place where if the gods are willing, I may call home for a time. But one thing I'll never regret is finding this remarkable wizard in among this most unlikely of places." Tarsus looked at Lionel again. "I'm sorry for the things I may have put you through, Your Majesty, but I had to know. I've had that same failing for as long as I've been alive. I've a need to find out that which I sense, that which eludes most people, an unquenchable desire to find out why I'm alive. It's caused me no end to my grief in the latter part of these centuries, but I can't help myself. Dragons by their very nature are inquisitive creatures, but I tend to take it to the extreme. And it's caused me to lose not only the only mate I've ever known, but my offspring as well." Tarsus stopped for a moment and then shook his head. He looked at Lionel with unshed tears in his beautiful eyes, emotions overflowing in him, "One day, it'll probably cost me my life. But I have to know. It's my nature and my curse. Since finding Pip, I hope to atone for some of my many mistakes. You've shown me nothing but kindness and gratitude while I've been here, except for Sir Dwayne, of course, and I don't blame him. Some of that can be put right back on my shoulders, I didn't exactly help the situation." He smiled wanly at Lionel. "But I'll tell you this, as long as Pip's here, I'll be here. And as long as I'm here, I'll not let this kingdom fade away to dust or be destroyed by one of my many mistakes. I can't change what I've done, nor do I wish to, but maybe I can give something back to those who've tried to help me." Tarsus's smile faded. "Over the next few centuries, I think it'll be very interesting being with Pip." He grinned again, but this time, it was an evil grin.

Lionel shook his head. "I'll never understand you, dragon." Lionel cocked his head and grinned himself. "But I do thank you for your aid and your friendship, no matter how you came to be here. I've a feeling you may come in handy in the next weeks."

*   *   *

Granston watched the city gates of Musk from a distance. His glass eye, which he'd enchanted, saw everything happening within the walls. That blasted lizard Tarsus had apparently made himself at home. He wheedled himself into the hearts and minds of everyone he met. It was always the same, no matter where he went; this time it would cost him. This time Granston had had enough of the lizard poking his nose into his business. The play king of Musk and his brat of a daughter were almost his when the lizard showed up, and he was forced to flee for his life. This time, however, would be different. After all the centuries, he'd get his chance to finally take care of the walking fish eater. All he had to do was get the army into the right position to strike. Not long now, just a few more hours. With the help of Bappa and Grundehl, he'd be rid of the infernal nuisance. Within days, the gnomes would be close enough to make the first move.

*   *   *

CHAPTER 28

Pip walked out of the castle and onto the practice field with Dwayne by his side as always. For the past two weeks, he'd been training with Muriel on the fine art of sword play; today, he was ready to take on an opponent. At least Muriel said he was. Pip didn't quite agree, but Gimble and Muriel both assured him he was able after just a few short weeks to try his hand at a contest. Dwayne didn't agree either, but then, Dwayne hadn't agreed with the Elf since he'd begun Pip's training. Before coming onto the fields, Dwayne had again, for the hundredth time, began to disagree with the Elf's methods. "You aren't ready, Pip. Two weeks isn't enough time for anyone to be competent enough for a spar."

Pip didn't say anything. He'd already said as much. He'd had this same conversation with the ex-knight too many times in the past couple of hours for his liking. He looked at Dwayne, sighed, and hung his head. He took a deep breath to calm himself and walked on.

Dwayne's main point for not wanting him to compete in any contest with swords was because of his own style of fighting. Pip tended to be reckless when it came to charging an opponent. In the many practice sessions he'd had with Gimble and Muriel, he'd been taught over and over to stand his ground and let his opponent come to him, not let the opponent goad him into doing something reckless, like rushing him. Rushing your opponent only makes him or her that much more difficult to defeat, because he or she is dictating what happens in the contest. True to his nature, time and again, Pip rushed his opponent.

What Pip hadn't told anyone was a few things he'd found out by accident himself. The first being he could see what was about to happen before his opponent actually did it, just as he did in the tent with Dura those few weeks ago. Dwayne had commented on more than one occasion he didn't know how Pip was coming along so fast with his training. Pip soaked up any instruction in just a few hours. What would've taken anyone else months to learn, Pip was doing in hours. His ability to see the outcome of an event helped him when Muriel or Gimble showed him a move with the sword. Pip simply replayed that lesson in his head over and over again until he could do it without thinking, the whole process taking only moments. It was as if everyone and everything around him stood still. The second was a surprise he'd hold off on until he knew it would make a grand statement. Although he wasn't very enthusiastic about doing a spar with anyone, he wasn't naive enough to believe he was an expert by any stretch of the imagination, he felt he could compete against anyone in the yard, just not yet.

Before Dwayne could say anything else to persuade him not to go through with the contest, Muriel walked up. "Are you ready, young Pip?"

Pip only nodded. He didn't feel especially talkative at the moment. He just wanted this to be over.

"Good." Muriel rubbed his hands together and grinned. "Let's pick your opponent, shall we?"

Gimble stood back from Pip, Dwayne, and Muriel and grinned. He'd planned to bet a few crowns of gold on Pip. He was confident the lad could take anybody in the yard. The boy was a natural. He just needed confidence in his own abilities. This was his chance to get it, and Gimble was about to make a bag full of coins on the outcome.

On the fields this morning were many of the regular knights that trained repeatedly. Sir Hook was in among the many in sword training; Sir GuWayne was doing what he did best, teaching another upstart a lesson in manners, and of course, Princess Laura was in among the sword play with Tarsus watching her every move.

Pip watched as Muriel walked among the knights and politely stopped them. "Hold!" He yelled, "Hold!"

Everyone turned to stare at the Elf. Harsh breathing could be heard from many who'd stopped what they were doing. The clanking of metal on metal or metal on somebody's flesh simply ceased. It was eerie and frightening. Apparently, everyone had been expecting it. Pip groaned. Tarsus had been talking. He'd warned everyone to be ready for something like this.

In the very back of the group of knights stood Lionel. Pip hadn't noticed the monarch until the knights stopped their activity and moved apart to clear a space among them. Not only was he to have a match with one of the knights, but it seemed he had to do it in front of the king as well. *Great! Just great. If there wasn't enough pressure.*

Muriel held up his hand and announced, "Please, can I have your attention? Young Master Pip needs an opponent for a little sparring. Do we have a volunteer?" He looked around the group of knights.

No one came forward. It wasn't that they were afraid to take on anyone, especially someone so young and inexperienced; it was that Pip was a wizard. Muriel felt the tension among the knights and nodded. "Yes, yes, I know. You think he'll use magic in his defense against you." He waved that away. "But I have it on good authority he'll not use magic." Still no one came forward. "I see," said Muriel. "Let me assure you, he'll go by the rules of sparring. In this, I give you my word. We simply want to see if he's ready. Of course, when it comes to the real thing, he'd use any means to take down his opponent, but for now, he'll use only his own strength and skill."

The knights looked around among themselves and two stepped forward. One was Sir GuWayne, and the other, to everyone's surprise, Princess Laura.

Pip gulped. He didn't want to go against the princess under any circumstances. His eyes bulged and sweat beaded on his brow. Tarsus in the background saw Pip's discomfort and chuffed.

In a strong voice so everyone in the yard could hear, Lionel yelled, "I'll do it."

Everyone looked at the king as he slowly made his way to stand in front of Muriel and Pip. Sir Hook came to stand by his side and said, "No, sire. I can't let you. You're too important to the kingdom. Nothing can happen to you, not even by accident."

Lionel grinned. "And you're too important to the kingdom as well, Knight. If something were to happen in the next few days, I'd need all of my knights in defense of the city and castle. I shall do it."

Laura stepped forward and gently laid a hand on her father's arm. "No, Father. You can't do a foolish thing like this. Against me you proved not only your worth, but your command of your knights. Against Pip you'd prove nothing." She looked at Pip and grimaced at seeing his reaction to her words.

Pip hung his head, but said nothing. She was right. His worth was nothing compared to the king's.

Lionel saw how much anguish this was causing his daughter and smiled for her. "Pip wouldn't hurt me, Daughter. I have confidence in that." He looked at Pip to confirm his thoughts.

Pip stepped forward and bowed. He didn't want to fight either of the monarchs. "Sire, please, don't do this. I'd gladly give my life for either of you. I don't wish this."

Lionel walked to Pip and put his hand on the lad's shoulder. "I know, Pip, but I'll not let you go against any on my knights, and especially not against my daughter. I've been watching you for the past few weeks as everyone else has, and I can see great potential in you. Let's make a deal, shall we?"

Pip stood watching the king. "What, sire?"

"If at any time the spar goes too far, we call it quits." Lionel squeezed Pip's shoulder.

Pip looked at Tarsus in the back. He was ginning. He nodded his head in approval and flapped his great wings.

Pip thought for a moment and then bowed again. "Yes, sire. Thank you. It'd be an honor to spar with you."

"Good," said Lionel, slapping his shoulder. "But, let's get this clear, shall we, no magic on your part, right?"

"No, sire. None," answered Pip. "But, is it the same rules as everyone else has in a spar? Do we give it our all?'

Lionel thought a moment and then said, "That's up to you. I'll give no quarter if that's what you mean. Apparently, that's how it's done around here." He looked around the fields at his knights and saw them all nod in agreement.

Pip thought a moment himself. "Fine, sire. I just don't wish to hurt you, or you me. The only thing I ask is if at any time you feel the contest should end, you make it plain to me, and everyone around us." He indicated the circle of knights. "I don't wish to have my head put on a pike, or strung up like a hog to slaughter." He smiled sheepishly, looking to the ex-knight, rubbing his throat, remembering Dwayne's rope nearly choking him all those months ago.

Dwayne, standing close to Tarsus, hung his head in shame. Although the thought hurt him, he knew if necessary, he'd without question, do it again.

Lionel saw the look on his friend's face and grimaced. But there was nothing for it. Now, however, "OK." he said turning back to Pip. "Agreed." Lionel then looked at his knights. "Hear this. Do nothing until I order it. Even if you feel I'm going down in defeat, do nothing!" He repeated. "This will be an honorable combat." He faced Pip again, spreading his hands to show Pip he had no ill will.

Pip nodded and bowed for a third time. "Thank you, sire."

"OK. Let's do it." Lionel walked to the sword line and picked a small rapier-like sword that fit his hand. He swung it a few times to get its balance and then faced Pip. While he was doing this, a circle formed around them both, making a ring, made up of knights and guardsmen and whoever else was available. He shook his head. This is going to be interesting. *I hope I didn't get in over my head.*

Pip simply stood facing the king, waiting, not having a sword.

Lionel noticed Pip was without a weapon and said, "Are you not going to choose a weapon, lad? I'll not fight you without one."

Pip grinned. "Yes, sire. I already have one." In a slow deliberate motion, Pip reached behind his right hip and seemingly grabbed something out of thin air. When his hand came back into view, he was holding a blue-tinged rapier-like sword, much like Lionel's, except the steel going into the hilt was thicker and broader, flaring out like a fan.

"By the gods!" swore Dwayne behind Pip. "Where did that come from?"

Tarsus snorted flame. *This is new also. Apparently Pip has a few surprises of his own.*

Sir Hook came to stand in front of Lionel. "Foul from the start," he said, holding up his sword in defense of his king. "You swore no magic."

Pip's grin dropped away. "It's not," said Pip. "It's simply a sword."

The knights stepped closer to their king, Laura noticing this getting out of hand. "Wait!" she cried, holding her hands up high, stepping forward. She looked at Pip. "Can I see the sword, Pip?"

"Yes, please," said Pip, holding out the sword to her, hilt first. "It's only a sword."

Laura took the sword and inspected every inch. True to his word, it was only a sword. She went as far as thumping the blade tip against the ground, having no give, made of metal as all swords were. The only thing she could really say that was unusual about it was the fact it had a blue tinge to the metal. And of course it was as blunt as a tree stump. She looked at Pip and asked, "It's not sharp. How did you do that?"

Pip looked at her and shook his head. "I don't know. All I know is that I don't need it to be sharp for practice."

Laura handed it back to him. "Can you make it sharp?"

Pip shrugged his shoulders. "I don't know. Probably. But I don't need it to be right now."

Laura looked at Lionel. "It's just a sword, Father, like he says. Blunt like all the others."

Lionel nodded. He looked at Sir Hook. "It's all right. No harm done."

Hook reluctantly nodded and backed away. The others did the same. The circle formed around the two again, giving them plenty of room to maneuver.

Pip and Lionel faced one another. Pip said, "Forgive me, sire, if I don't bow or salute you. I saw what happened when Laura did that." He grinned.

Lionel grinned also. Out of the corner of his eye, he saw Hook blush. He was remembering Laura's and his contest as well. At least the lad learns. Lionel came forward with his sword held high to guard his face.

When it finally did start, the contest only lasted minutes. Although to Lionel and Pip it seemed an eternity.

Pip came forward the same as Lionel, with his guard up. A hush fell on the crowd of onlookers as the two came together. The first blow went to Lionel, with a swing and a thump, their swords clashed, making each of their arms strain with the resounding clang. With a grunt, Pip sidestepped and swung for Lionel's side, too slow, the sword missed and kept traveling. Lionel didn't let up; when the sword flashed by his side, he rushed Pip. He did to Pip the same thing he did with Laura. He wasn't letting Pip get his barring or his breath.

With every passing moment, Pip and Lionel found each a match for the other. Slash, parry, riposte, charge, swing, thrust. Back and forth each went until their breathing could be clearly heard by everyone.

Lionel stepped in close to slap Pip across the face, but surprisingly, when he did, Pip had already moved. Instead of hitting Pip's cheek, Lionel found himself slapping at nothing but air. His momentum took him a few paces away, and when he turned back, Pip ducked underneath his sword and punched him in the mid-section with all his strength. In a whoosh, Lionel lost all his breath, and in that instant, Pip seized the opportunity to knee the monarch in the nose as he doubled over. As Lionel came violently back up to a standing position, Pip was holding his sword to Lionel's throat. There was no time for the king to do anything but wait and see if Pip would end the match.

In a breathy wheeze, Pip asked, "Do you . . . yield?'

Lionel slowly brought his sword up and with deliberate movements, threw it to the ground. "I yield," said the king to Pip. "With honor, I yield."

A gasp went out from the onlookers. "By the Horde Mother!" Tarsus swore in the background. "I never would have thought it possible," came the reply from the front of the crowd. "Yes!" came Gimble's voice clearly.

Pip took his sword from Lionel's throat and stepped back. When he did, he almost collapsed in a heap at Lionel's feet. His breathing was fast, and his eyes watered. He just managed to fall on his backside, instead of his face, when he finally did collapse. Looking up, breathing heavily, he said, shakily, "I hope I never have to do that again. You nearly made me have a heart seizure."

Lionel extended his hand to help Pip up and grinned. "I hope you and I are always this polite to each other. My stomach feels like a bag of mush." He rubbed his gut with his other hand.

Pip grabbed his hand and was hauled to his feet. "I think I need to sit down somewhere, sire, before I collapse again." He looked at Lionel sheepishly. "I'm sorry, sire. I didn't mean to hurt you."

"Nonsense! I was definitely trying to hurt you." Lionel grinned at Pip again, still massaging his stomach. "That's the rules, right?"

Laura came to Pip and put a hand on his arm and smiled. Lionel looked at her as if he didn't know who she was. Dwayne didn't say anything, just watched Pip's reaction. Pip simply looked at the princess's hand, not knowing what to do. Before he could think of an answer, however, saving him from a more awkward moment than it already was, a horn sounded from behind them.

No one moved for a moment. All noise ceased. You could have heard a pin drop in the training area. A guard on the wall broke the silence, shouting, "*Someone standing outside the south gates. Looks like former adviser.*"

That's when all hell broke loose. Lionel shouted to his knights to go to arms. Laura shouted orders for a regiment to head to the gates to protect the citizens. Sir Hook could be seen standing guard over his king. Dwayne frantically looked for Pip to protect. In the melee that started after the cry, he'd lost sight of the young wizard. It was a mad scramble of bodies and horses to do their duties. Utter chaos reigned around the king. Knights began grabbing for their swords and scabbards, pages ran to and fro running messages to their charges, and horses could be heard in a panic from grooms trying to saddle them all at once. And the loudest thing commanding Pip's attention was Tarsus bugling at the top of his lungs. Pip realized Tarsus was sounding a cry of anguish and fury. In only a moment, Tarsus could be seen jumping into the air heading with all possible haste to the south gates and confronting his worst enemy.

"No!" shouted Pip, but it was too late. There was no way for Tarsus to hear him. He looked around in the stream of people for the princess but didn't find her. Apparently, she'd gone with the rest of the knights after the alarm had been sounded. Although she wasn't officially a knight, she felt it was her right and duty to be with them when the dung hit the cart.

"No!" Pip shouted again, seeing only white in front of his eyes.

With that one word, he found himself standing in front of the south gate.

Dwayne saw the flash of light and instinctively threw King Lionel to the ground for protection. When his eyes cleared from the glare, he found Lionel lying underneath him and Sir Hook hovering over them both. Dwayne jumped to his feet, looking around to be sure nothing was threatening his king, and then helped Lionel to his feet. He asked excitedly, "What happened?" He looked amidst the chaos of activity and then asked quietly, "Where's Pip?"

Pip staggered. He looked around and saw he'd somehow moved from the fields to the south gates. *What the blazes is going on?* And with that he heard another of Tarsus's bugles, this time coming from above his head and to the right. He looked up and saw the dragon just getting to the gates. He then realized it didn't matter how he'd gotten where he was, he had to find a way to stop the big lummox from doing something he'd later regret, namely try and attack Granston on his own. Pip thought quickly and decided the best way to do that was to throw something at him. It just so happened, the only thing lying close by were two small two-wheeled wagons used to haul hay and dung into and out of the stables and streets of the city. Pip grinned. This was the first thing Tarsus ever taught him to do. He opened himself to the magic, picked up the cart, and with a shove, flung the cart towards Tarsus.

Like a rock from a sling, the cart rocketed straight towards the dragon.

Tarsus, in his anger, didn't at first see the dung heap heading his way. But a split second before impact, realization sank in and he took the only action open to him: he cremated the cart to ash. In a blinding flash of light, Pip sent the other cart on the heels of the first. Tarsus avoided that one and in a mid-air display of nimbleness, flamed that cart as well. That definitely got the dragon's attention. He wasn't so red-eyed angry as to allow those missiles to impact the ground and possibly kill one of the inhabitants of the city. Tarsus looked towards the ground and found Pip waving his arms like a lunatic. Tarsus snorted and blew a stream of fire before calming enough to land gracefully before the youth.

Pip looked into the dragon's eyes and said breathlessly, "What are you doing? You can't fight him all by yourself."

"What?!" yelled Tarsus. "Are you the one who threw those carts at me?"

Pip nodded. "There's no time now. What are you doing?"

"I'm going to have a little talk with the Gnome on our doorstep." Tarsus growled.

"No, you're not." stated Pip. "You can't just rush out there and start a fight. That's what he wants."

"And that's what I want." Tarsus snorted, prancing like a horse on parade, not able to stay still. "You know how I feel."

"Yes, I do. But if you do that, you'll just get yourself killed."

Tarsus snorted and animatedly stomped his front feet into the dirt. "I must do this, Pip. I have to have some kind of satisfaction from killing him."

"And why do you think he's all by himself?" asked Pip heatedly. "Do you actually think he'd come here by himself and ask you to give up? Roll over and be dead?" Pip looked at the dragon pleadingly. *Think, you big lummox!*

That stopped Tarsus. In his anger, he hadn't taken the time to really think this through. After a moment of clearly seeing what he was doing and why Pip had stopped him, Tarsus shook his great head, calming down. "No. No, he wouldn't." He looked Pip in the eye and said more confidently, "No. He wouldn't do that. You're right. He'd want me to see how much he's gained from me not being around for so many centuries. He'd rub it in. Make sure I knew he was better."

Pip nodded, taking a calming breath himself, patting Tarsus on the nose. "That's the sense I get too." He looked around and saw the knights arriving from the fields. In the lead was Sir Hook, Princess Laura, and Dwayne. Each was riding their mounts for all they were worth. As they approached, they slowed long enough to dismount. Laura was shocked to see Pip. She indicated the young wizard to Dwayne and said, "How did you get here?"

Pip shrugged. "Don't know, really. I just needed to stop the flying leather purse here from doing something stupid." He indicated Tarsus with his head. "But that's not to worry about now. We need to go see who's come to call."

Tarsus narrowed his eyes at Pip for his comment, but answered his other query. "It's Granston, all right. He's standing about thirty yards from the gates. No one else around I could see."

"Fine," said Pip. "Are you calmed down enough to see what he's really up to?"

Tarsus took a deep breath. "Yes. I think so."

"Good," said Laura joining them. "I want to go with you. I need to see him too."

Dwayne had something to say about that. "No, Princess. You'll stay here. If you like, you may watch from the wall, but it's too dangerous for you out there."

"But . . ."

Dwayne was adamant. "No!"

This time Dwayne couldn't be swayed. And then Lionel arrived with Sir GuWayne. When he jumped from his charger, he pointed to Laura, but said to Hook, "You'll not let the princess out of your sight. And she'll go nowhere near Granston. Is that clear?"

Sir Hook nodded and bowed.

"Father!" pleaded Laura.

"No! You'll not!" Lionel said heatedly. "You're more important than I'll ever be, and you'll not be put in jeopardy if I can help it."

"You can't keep me out of this for long, Father. When the army shows itself, you'll need all the fighters you can get." Laura stared at her father with fire in her blue eyes.

Thinking he must at all costs keep Laura safe, Lionel looked away and didn't answer. When the time came for him to make such a decision, he hoped it would be much later in the future. And he prayed to the gods that day never came.

Tarsus broke the awkward moment between the two monarchs by asking, "Where's Muriel?'

Dwayne answered. "He's yet to show up." He looked around as the others did.

"Well, we can't keep waiting," said Pip. "We need to do something about Granston soon. We need to go out there and confront him before his army arrives." He saw the king watching and amended his statement. "Well, before his army shows itself anyways."

Dwayne asked the dragon, "Why do you want the Elf, Lord Tarsus?"

Tarsus looked at the former knight and said as simply as he could, "Because he's the best I've ever seen with a bow. Elves are renowned for their accuracy with the long bow, and he's the best at it. I've never seen him miss where he aims."

Sir Hook was skeptical. "Never?"

"Never!" Tarsus exclaimed adamantly. "In a thousand years, I've never seen anyone as accurate. No one."

Dwayne was secretly impressed. "OK."

"Sire," said Tarsus, "when he shows up, put him somewhere he can do the most good. I'm going to have a talk with our guest." He looked at Pip. "Alone."

"No way,." Pip said. "If you go out there by yourself, he'll have a perfect opportunity to attack. You'll need some help. I'm the wizard, remember?"

"Pip, I need you to watch with the princess and the rest. You'll know if I need help. I've dealt with him before."

"Yes, dragon, you did," said Gimble, coming up behind them. "But if I remember the story correctly, that didn't turn out too good for you."

Tarsus swung his head to face the Dwarf. "Where have you been? And where's Muriel?"

"Never mind that now. Why go out alone?" the Dwarf asked.

Tarsus sighed. "Because I don't want the Gnome to know about Pip until he has to. As far as I know, he doesn't know a thing about him. And I want it to stay that way until the time comes." He looked at Pip again and nodded.

Pip thought a moment, nodding. "Makes sense." He looked at Laura for confirmation. "I think."

Laura reluctantly nodded her agreement, as did Lionel.

Tarsus swung to the gates. "All right then, let's do it."

With a nod from Lionel, the gates swung wide to let Tarsus walk out to face the former king's adviser.

Everyone dashed to the walls and the nearest ladder. Pip was waiting for them when they got there. Another flash of white light preceded his arrival. While looking out at the Gnome and Tarsus facing him, Pip said in a whisper, "I hope he knows what he's doing?"

CHAPTER 29

Granston waited patiently outside the gates to the city. His first inclination after arriving was to attack and keep them occupied until Grundehl got there with the rest of the Gnome army and the Assanti. But upon further reflection, he decided it was best if he took on the giant lizard by himself. He really didn't trust the king of the Gnomes to do what was necessary. He'd taken care of Tarsus once before, and he could do it again. In the centuries since he'd been imprisoned, he knew he couldn't have changed very much. When the lizard got his mad on, he was sure he'd do something stupid and then the end would be inevitable. So, the best thing for him to do was stand and wait. It didn't take but a few minutes before an alarm sounded and all hells broke loose in the city. Granston smiled. It wouldn't be long. And, sure enough, no more than a couple minutes later, the gates swung wide and the blasted lizard walked out to face him.

Granston smiled again. This was going better than he first thought. It seemed no one was with Tarsus. Looked like no one had the guts to face him but the lizard. Good. This shouldn't take long at all. He had other more important things he needed to be doing anyway. Taking care of the lizard was just one of the many errands he needed to accomplish before the day was done. Although he was glad to be finally over with this nonsense, he couldn't help but enjoy the show.

With a grin, he said to Tarsus, "Hello, lizard. We meet again."

*   *   *

"Hello, lizard. We meet again."

Tarsus looked around before answering. "Hello, Gnome. I see you've come back so I can finish what I started so long ago."

Granston laughed. "Did you have a nice nap?"

Tarsus blew a small stream of flame. "It was very restful, thank you."

What's going on? He should have attacked me by now. What's changed in the lizard? Granston wearily looked about him. This was definitely not what he'd expected. *Now what? The blasted lizard changed his tactics?*

"Where's the play king, lizard? Did you gobble him up like a dinner appetizer?" Granston laughed at his own humor. "Or did you just woo him with your serpentine ways?"

Tarsus snorted. "Did you miss him? Did you come here for a reunion, wizard? Did you think he'd welcome you with open arms? He knows what you are now, and he's ready."

Granston laughed again. "Ready or not, lizard, it'll do no good. I'll see him soon enough. Just like the play king's daughter, neither will get away."

Every fiber in his body told Tarsus to attack the little Gnome. He'd done a lot of damage to the monster the last time they'd gone against one another. Tarsus also knew, however, he had to find out what the Gnome was doing. By now the petty man should have attacked with everything he had. Then in an intuitive leap, Tarsus knew the wizard was stalling for time. Apparently, his army wasn't quite ready. Tarsus grinned.

Granston saw Tarsus grin and began to worry. The lizard had apparently figured out he was trying to stall. *I never said he was stupid.*

That's when Tarsus took advantage of the petty little Gnome's tactics. In only an instant, Tarsus sprang into the air and let fly a blast of fire that would have roasted a full-grown cow.

*   *   *

Pip watched the whole exchange from the city walls, alongside Princess Laura and Dwayne. From what Tarsus had told him of the many times he'd defended himself against the Gnome wizard, Granston should have attacked the moment he had Tarsus in his sights. But something wasn't what it should have been. Pip watched Tarsus and his enemy banter for a few moments, and then suddenly, a wicked grin spread across the dragon's mouth. Pip realized, as did Tarsus, he's stalling for time.

From the dragon, a fast and furious attack came without warning.

Granston waited for the fire to reach him and merely shook the attack off like someone waving away a pesky insect. Then he smiled and waited for the dragon's next move. Let's see what he's come up with now.

Banking high in the air after unleashing his blast, Tarsus realized fire alone wouldn't do the trick. Swooping back, Tarsus folded his wings in front of his body and was going to use his momentum to scoop the wizard up in the air. The Gnome was craftier than he'd expected. In a swirl of dust and a blinding flash of light, Granston disappeared before he could touch him.

Tarsus was left with nothing but empty air and nowhere to search.

*   *   *

Pip pounded his fists on the top of the wall. "Blast!" He looked at Laura and said, "Looks like we'll need something else."

Laura nodded. "You're probably right."

Just as Laura turned to make a comment to Dwayne, a blinding flash of light caught the corner of her eye.

*   *   *

Tarsus swung around in a graceful arch and saw nothing of the Gnome. He knew that wasn't the only time he'd show himself. He was waiting for his army to come and bail his little butt out of the fire he started, the same as last time. As Tarsus flew over the city gates, he saw Lionel had indeed taken his advise and positioned Muriel in a very good spot to do major damage if he got the chance. He nodded to himself. Good. The next pass showed him a lot of things were going on, especially on the walls and towers. In all, he counted well over a hundred knights scattered about taking defensive positions. He nodded to himself again, at least some were using their heads. The defenses needed to be as fortified as possible if they hoped to come through this with little or no casualties. Tarsus also noticed Pip was nowhere to be seen, which was surprising. If there was one thing he could count on, it was Pip to be in the middle of anything bad. He had the nasty habit of finding trouble. He shook his head remembering all the times he'd seen Pip try and stay out of trouble just to get himself into worse trouble than when it started; now he was nowhere to be found.

Out of the corner of his eye, the dragon saw a blinding flash of white light and with it, felt a weight between his shoulder blades. At first, he thought Granston had launched another attack and then realized it to be a very familiar weight. Pip had appeared and was riding him as if they were on a scouting run. Tarsus looked over his shoulder and grinned. In a loud voice, so Pip could hear, he bellowed, "Nice of you to join the fun."

Pip bellowed back, "Didn't want you to have all of it."

"You're getting pretty good at that, you know."

"What? Showing up when I'm not wanted?"

"No. Traveling."

"What?"

Tarsus shook his head. His throat was beginning to tire from so much shouting. "I'll tell you when we get to the ground. I'm tired of yelling."

Pip said in a clear and unstrained voice, "Why? I can hear you fine."

Tarsus did a double take in mid-air. The unintentional movement nearly threw Pip off his back. Tarsus yelled, "How can I hear you so well?"

Pip covered his ears. "Not so loud. I can hear you fine. I got tired of yelling myself. I should have thought of this months ago." He grinned.

Tarsus looked back at him, not grinning. "You need to start telling me when you're going to try something new."

Pip nodded. Then with a queer look on his face said, "I didn't know I could do it, until just now."

Tarsus was shocked. But he was also learning Pip could do a lot of things other wizards couldn't. Tarsus had always suspected Pip was going to be one of the most powerful wizards ever born, but this was a major discovery. He was turning out to be one of a kind. However, there was no time for this now. He needed to get back to the business at hand. "If you see Granston, just tell me. We need to know what he's going to do next."

Pip nodded.

*   *   *

Laura was dumbfounded. Where had Pip gone? Just a moment before he'd been standing beside her and Dwayne, watching as Granston and

Tarsus took shots at each other, and now, gone. Simply gone. "Where did Pip go?" Laura said more to herself than anyone around her.

Unexpectedly, Dwayne answered, pointing skyward, "He's with Lord Tarsus, my lady."

Laura looked and sure enough, Pip was riding on the dragon's back, as if he'd always been there. Laura looked at the ex-knight. "How did he get there? Just a moment ago, he was standing next to me."

"I know not, Princess. But just before he vanished, I saw a blinding flash of white light, just as we all did in the fields before this started."

Laura nodded. "I did too, but I didn't think anything of it." Laura looked skyward again, shaking her head, sighing. "He's gonna have to learn not to do that."

Dwayne grunted.

*   *   *

Grundehl and his Gnome army showed up just as Tarsus tried to scoop Granston in the air. When he saw the blasted lizard, he nearly did exactly what Granston had wanted: attack. Killing him would almost be too good for the creature. But more level heads prevailed. Bappa grabbed his pudgy arm and stopped him from a rampage that would have caused everything they'd worked for to go south. This wasn't the time for heated decisions and perhaps getting killed in the process. "No! We cannot. Not yet." Bappa told the fat king. "We have to let this play out. If we have any hope of killing the lizard, we must first let the wizard tire him out." He dropped Grundehl's arm.

Grundehl snarled, "Why? I kill now."

"Yes, and get us all killed with him,." Bappa sneered right back. "You know the plan. We have to work together to get this done, or it isn't going to work at all."

Grundehl looked out from the trees again and watched as Tarsus slowly circled the field around the walls of the city. His snarl told Bappa he couldn't be trusted to do anything they'd planned. "I wait! But not long. I must kill lizard. He been thorn in side for many centuries. Will not let him go now."

Bappa nodded. "We have to get ready for the next part. Tell the army to spread out and keep a watch for Granston."

Grundehl looked at Tarsus high above and snarled, drool dripping from his lips, and then snorted a wad of snot on the ground. Turning, he headed back to tell his army.

Bappa watched the fat monarch of the Gnomes waddle away and gulp air. *You better know what you're doing, wizard. The walking cesspool isn't cooperating. You better do something fast.* He then turned and followed Grundehl. He had things to do himself.

*   *   *

CHAPTER 30

When Tarsus walked out of the city gates, Lionel was stunned to see his former adviser standing outside. He never truly believed he'd ever see the little man again, since hearing what he was from Tarsus. What he wanted from his kingdom was intolerable. But what stunned him even more was the shuffling fellow using magic. In all the years the man had been by his side, he hadn't showed any inclination towards such a thing. He owed Tarsus a debt of gratitude, and, more importantly, an apology for not believing him. For all the talk, he'd secretly hoped the dragon had been wrong. Now, seeing it with his own eyes, he couldn't deny Granston, his so-called friend of more than twenty years, was a wizard.

Lionel looked for Dwayne. At first, through the chaos, he couldn't see him, then, when the dust settled, he found the knight high on the wall next to Laura. He slowly nodded. Yes, that was proper, Laura being far more important than he. His eyes teared thinking of his Laura unprotected in a fight for her life. He knew what had to be done.

With a start, Lionel felt a hand on his arm. Turning quickly, he saw Sir Hook holding on to him with a grim expression on his face. "Sire, we must see to the dragon." The knight pointed to the dragon flying over the walls of the keep. "He's alone, fighting for the kingdom."

Lionel put a reassuring smile on his face and said, "No, Knight, he's not alone."

Hook let go of the king's arm and bowed. "Yes, sire."

Lionel got his breath and spoke sharply, "Tell someone to bring me Dwayne."

"Right away, sire." Hook turned and bellowed for GuWayne.

Lionel knew what had to be done, this not being a time to show weakness on his part. His pride and honor be hanged. His daughter was the most important thing in this kingdom and it was his duty and honor to see she stayed safe. He knew what he had to do, and by all the gods of hells, he was going to do it.

*   *   *

Bappa gathered his Assassins. It was time to kill the Knights of Musk. That was the sole reason Granston and he made a deal. Otherwise, he'd never have given the vile Gnome the time of day. Two centuries ago, the Dryad and the little Gnome wizard had gathered another army to dethrone his own king. But in a fit of rage, for a slight Bappa knew nothing about, Granston betrayed him. In the battle that ensued, Bappa faked his own death in a grand display of pyrotechnics, which allowed him to flee. For two centuries, he'd been waiting for the chance at revenge, now, after all, he'd get it. Bappa didn't particularly like aligning himself with the Gnome coward, but to gain control of Grundehl's army, what he'd planned from the beginning, he was willing to do much worse. The plan they'd devised to win this confrontation was bold, the whole thing hinging on Bappa and his crew getting rid of their worst opposition: the knights. The only other deviation to the plan was for Raulch, who wasn't an Assassin, to take out the king. Granston wanted nothing to do with it, pointing out that ever since he'd been found out by that blasted lizard, and had to flee, he was more interested in taking care of him than taking out the play king. So, one of the main jobs Bappa had was getting the big Gnome freak into the castle proper so he could do his job. *Oh well, maybe he'll come back without a head. I hate the big lummox. He's always watching me. It makes my skin crawl. Once this is over, I'll kill Granston, the weasel. Maybe have Marvelo do it. He'd never suspect her, getting his revenge and the gnome army at the same time.*

Marvelo, the woman in question, was one of only a handful to have ever made it into the Assassins guild and would have the privilege of taking out the commander of the knights. She was the best person for the job. Bappa, of course, would never tell her, or the rest of his men, but he felt she had the best opportunity to get close enough. Her ability to track and get close to an unsuspecting target was bar none the best he'd ever witnessed, including himself. If there was a way for it to be done, she'd find it.

There were so few of the guild left. After the many wars and skirmishes over the centuries, fighting for land to grow families and farms, and the many hunts to feed starving families, the losses taken by them had been monstrous. The biggest monster to take its toll on the clan had been a lizard like Tarsus. The only good lizard was a dead lizard. Its attacks over the centuries had been devastating. The deaths of nearly two out of three guild members killed in the last four centuries could be blamed on that monster. It was time the guild and the Gnome race got a little payback; taking out this kingdom of robbers, land barons, killers, and people who'd harbour fugitive slimy dragons, would be a great start for recompense.

*   *   *

Granston watched as Bappa gathered his Assassins. He didn't trust the low-life as far as he could throw him, without magic of course, but he could be very useful. He needed the twit to get into the castle to take care of the little incidental side matters. It mattered not whether any of them came out alive; he didn't need them after this war was over. Besides, his overall plan was to kill anyone left. Grundehl, that great bag of filth, was the worst king the Gnomes could've possibly had, and Bappa, the Dryad, was just as disgusting. Granston knew he should have killed him two centuries ago. If he hadn't needed them as fodder for the war, he'd have stayed around Musk and taken care of his problems by himself. But time was not a luxury he wanted to squander any longer. If he'd waited around this stupid kingdom for his chance to attack, he'd have been here a thousand years, which wasn't a prospect he cared to contemplate. This backwater little no-nothing kingdom wasn't worth any more of his time or effort. The reason he stayed to see the little twit of a king on the throne was he needed men for the campaign he really wanted to wage: the conquest of the Gnome lands and the Troll borders. Getting rid of the play king would've been nothing more than a simple poison that couldn't have been traced to him. Then he could've manipulated the little squirt of a girl to do anything he wanted. A few staged fights on the border and a plan to take out the Trolls, and it would've been done. Then he could've easily taken out the whining brat of a queen the same way he'd taken the king. Tarsus, that damnable lizard, had put all of his many years of sniveling and whining to naught. He'd come up with this war to compensate for the trouble the lizard had caused. Grundehl and Bappa were a means to an end, that's all.

Concealing himself from Bappa, Granston watched as he gave orders to the guild. He couldn't afford to have a weakling like Bappa do anything that wasn't in the plan. He needed all of the players to do their part and die like they were intended to. Raulch, that detestable giant Gnome, was the worst of the lot and the one target he wished to be rid of the most. His strength and stupid loyalty to Grundehl made him the most dangerous of his adversaries in his army of puppets. His main purpose was to die; by sending him after the king, who'd be guarded more thoroughly than anyone, ensured it. The only part of the plan he really didn't care for was sending Marvelo to take out the knight. Bappa and Marvelo herself had assured him she was the only one of the guild who had the remotest shot at doing it. But, after spending so many nights with her, he wanted to keep her for himself, the one hitch in the plan that could bring it down. He needed to figure out a way to keep the girl and still kill the knight. There was still time.

The guild and its so few members moved out, Granston chuckling softly. After today, he'd be free to concentrate his every waking moment on his plans of conquest, and there was no one who could stop him.

*　　*　　*

Lionel watched as the others did. Laura stood by his side with an anxious look on her face. He didn't know if it was for the dragon or for young Pip, and he didn't care at the moment. He too feared for them. His knights were spread as thin as he could allow for protection of not only the city but its people, the guards among them. The whole city was as prepared for a battle as could be expected. Lionel knew the odds of coming out of this wasn't very good, but his kingdom was at risk and he and his knights, with the help of Tarsus and an untried boy wizard, were the only things standing between an army of Gnomes and a murderous wizard. A wizard he hadn't even known was a wizard. For as many as twenty years, Granston had been his most trusted adviser and friend, to find he'd been trying to take over his kingdom and possibly kill him had been the most humiliating moment of his life. How could he have not seen the signs? So the only thing left to do was take care of that which had to be done. In all those years, the only true friend he'd had was Dwayne. Throughout his reign, Dwayne had been the one who'd stood by his side, even in the most trying of times; he'd wronged the knight. It wasn't Dwayne who needed humility, but himself. And he was going to rectify that right now.

While watching atop the wall for any signs of the coming army, as the rest of the kingdom, Dwayne came to him as ordered. He bowed and said, "Yes, sire. You wanted to see me?"

"Yes, Dwayne, I did," said Lionel. "I'll not waste your time or mine this day, so I say to you plain and in front of my daughter and other knights, I'm sorry." He bowed to him.

"Sire?" Dwayne said, puzzled.

Lionel looked at Dwayne sadly and grimaced. "I've done you wrong, my friend. I'm the one among us who needs a lesson in humility, not you. In all the years, you've been by my side. You've never been anything but yourself. I should have realized that long ago. You've done nothing in these past months except do your duty to your kingdom and to your king. From this day forth, I give you back all the things that are rightfully yours." He bowed again to the knight. "Sir Dwayne."

Dwayne watched his king bow to him and was saddened. "No, sire, you've nothing to give back, nothing to apologize for." Dwayne shook his head. "You're my lord and king. I can't accept that which I haven't earned." He went to one knee in front of Lionel and bowed his head.

Lionel was dumbstruck. Out of the corner of his eye, he could see Laura's jaw drop open in surprise. "Explain," commanded Lionel. "I've given you back that which you've earned many times over. Something I should've never taken away."

"No, sire," Dwayne said again. He looked up into his king's face. "In all the years I've been by your side, I've never known you to judge anyone who didn't deserve it. You haven't taken anything from me I haven't thrown away myself."

"Get up, Knight. It's unseemly for you to be in front of your king like this,." commanded Lionel.

Dwayne didn't move. "No, sire," he said yet again. "It's never unseemly for one to lower himself to his betters." He raised his hand to silence his king before he could say anything else, for he could see it on his face. "Please, sire. In these months with young Pip, I've learned you've been right, not wrong, about me. I've learned I truly am not the man I once was. Until I can find that man and feel whole again, I can't be your knight. It's not you who must find me worthy, but myself who must." He lowered his head again.

Lionel was dumbstruck. It was Laura who came to her father's rescue, however. She put a hand on Lionel's arm to stop him from answering and asked the knight instead, "Dwayne, what are you saying? Why aren't you worthy? You're the most honorable of men."

Dwayne looked to his princess. "No, Your Highness, I'm not. My king was right about me from the beginning. I've lost myself over the years. In my arrogance, I'd thought I could never be brought down. Especially by a mere boy." Surprisingly, unshed tears could be seen in his eyes. "But I've found in those same months, that mere boy, was only trying to find himself too. And I nearly took all that away. Without the help of Master Tarsus, no thanks to myself, he'd have been found guilty of nothing more than trying to survive with something he doesn't understand. I've striven to emulate his courage and strength. So, until I do, I can't go back to that which I'm not worthy of having. Honor dictates it so."

Lionel put his hand on Dwayne's shoulder and gently squeezed. "Do you not yet realize, if you can come to such a conclusion about yourself, you are worthy."

"No, sire. I'm not,." he said, yet again, looking up at Lionel. "I thank you for your words, and your friendship, if I'm allowed to say such things, but you're wrong. I'm not the man I once was, that realization has taken something fundamentally away from me. You can't give back that which I myself have lost. Until I find it again, I'll remain page to young Master Pip. It's nothing I don't deserve."

Lionel nodded. He then looked at the knights around him and his daughter and said, "Then let it be known, Dwayne may be page to Master Pip, but he's also knight to the Kingdom of Musk."

Everyone, including the princess, bowed to their king, acknowledging what had been said.

Lionel looked at Dwayne again. "Whether you feel worthy or not, you're still knight of my army. And I've never been more proud of you than I am right now. You've all the rights and privileges of any knight

318

in this kingdom, including wearing your sword and taking your rightful place as leader." He nodded again. "Now, rise, we have work to do."

Dwayne came slowly to his feet and bowed deeply to his king. "Thank you, sire. But I can't lead. I'll gladly stay with Pip. And I can't use a sword until I'm worthy again. That's my oath and vow. I thank you."

Lionel nodded again. "Yes, I thought you might feel that way. But my order still stands. When you're ready."

*　　*　　*

Tarsus and Pip circled the area around the city wall for over an hour and didn't find anything. Apparently Granston had wanted only to intimidate them before doing whatever it was he came to do. It was like a cat toying with a mouse before having dinner. And it didn't sit very well with either of them. "What do you want to do now?" asked Pip.

"I don't know," said Tarsus. "The only thing we can do is wait."

Tarsus circled again and then landed within the city walls. When they got on the ground, Laura and Lionel were waiting for them.

Laura asked, "Well?"

Tarsus shook his head. "Nothing."

Pip sighed. "It's as if he didn't want to do anything but announce his coming. We don't understand it."

Lionel swore to himself. "Master Tarsus, you better go make a few rounds around the kingdom. I don't know if it'll do any good, but we need to know when or if an army comes to the gates, and from which direction."

Tarsus nodded. "You're right, sire." Tarsus looked at Pip. "You coming?"

Pip shook his head. "No, I think I better stay on the ground. If fighting starts, you'll probably be the one to start it, and I'm in reserve, remember?"

Tarsus took to the air again. Pip looked at Laura and sighed again. "Now what?"

Laura only shook her head. "I don't know. The only thing for sure is we can't do anything till Granston does. Or until we find the army headed our way."

Pip smiled back. "Guess you're right. But it makes for a long and frustrating day."

"That's the way it goes, I guess." Laura looked Pip over carefully and then said, "Pip, where's your sword?"

Pip automatically looked down at his hip, but, of course, there was nothing there. With anyone else, a sword would be dangling from a scabbard, Pip didn't seem to be carrying anything, not even a dirk. Pip looked at the princess and said sheepishly, "Well, I don't really know."

"You don't know? Why don't you? Just a few hours ago you seemed to grab it out of thin air. Where does it go?" Laura asked, looking at Pip's hip.

Pip shrugged. "Well, I don't really know that either."

Laura shook her head. "For a wizard, you don't really know a whole lot, do you?"

"Not really," said Pip. "I'm flying by the seat of my dragon, I guess." He grinned broadly.

Laura looked stunned. Then she too laughed.

Ten minutes later, no one was laughing.

*　　*　　*

CHAPTER 31

Grundehl and his army attacked the south gates of the city with a swarm of Gnomes. Gnomes scrambled out of the trees screaming with rage, charging to the gates with murder in their eyes; ladders, grappling hooks, and siege engines, they intended to get over the walls one way or another.

"Here we go," said a guard on the walls. "Looks like they're tired of waiting."

Laura looked at the mass of Gnomes and groaned. Nothing like this had ever happened to their kingdom before, and she was afraid they may not come out alive. Just watching such an army storm towards the city was enough to make her fear for the kingdom. She prayed to the gods Pip could do something to help them. If not for him, she feared they may not come out of this in one piece. She looked at Pip and sighed. "I'm sorry, Pip. I wish this wasn't happening. But my father and I are gonna need your help. The People of Musk are gonna need your help."

Pip nodded and vanished in a flash of light.

Laura quickly covered her eyes. *I wish he'd stop doing that!* She looked around and found Dwayne standing before her. "We have to make sure father is safe, Dwayne. Come on."

Dwayne quickly went into action. With a nod, he turned and headed for the last place he'd seen his king, but Lionel wasn't there. Just moments before, he'd seen Lionel surrounded by Sir Hook and at least fifteen guards of the castle.

Laura shouted, "Where is he?"

Dwayne had no answer. He and she both looked around the chaos before them and couldn't immediately find the monarch. Just as Laura was about to panic, Sir GuWayne came running to her, "Your Highness, your father, the king, wishes to see you. He's moved to the west gate. He fears for the safety of the citizens."

Laura gulped. She had to find the way not to panic when things didn't go as expected, or she'd never make it through her trials, if her trials ever came.

*   *   *

Pip vanished in a flash of light. In an instant, he was standing in front of the horde of Gnomes coming towards the city gates. He didn't exactly know what he was going to do to stop the screaming things, but he knew he had to do something. Laura was counting on his help, and as far as he was concerned, he'd do anything to help her. He didn't know if Lionel would approve of him, but he knew now he had feelings for Laura other than friendship. He wasn't a monarch or a knight, even a duke, but he couldn't just give her up without fighting for her. Standing in front of the sea of Gnomes with murder in their eyes, he did the only thing he could think of: he threw a line of trees at them. One by one, cedars, elms, and firs came uprooted through the air and landed without any thought on as many of the horde as possible. The screams of the dying could be heard all over the field of battle. If Tarsus had wanted to keep his powers secret to fight only Granston, that time was long past and definitely out for the world to see. He couldn't stand aside any longer and watch the people of Musk die.

Apparently, Tarsus was of the same mind; as Pip threw trees at the rushing horde of Gnomes, the dragon came out of the sky and fried just as many with a blast of fire as he'd flattened with trees. With a tremendous bellow of flame, fire scorched the earth where he aimed; in it was heard the screams of dying Gnomes.

Pip looked at the swooping Tarsus and then back at the gates of the city. On top of the ramparts, along the wall was Sir GuWayne and perhaps a hundred guards clustered together fighting off Gnomes trying to swarm over the walls using ladders and grappling hooks. Pip saw what was happening and in a flash of light was standing under the ladders propped against the walls. With a thought and gesture, he commanded the wood to burst into flame. In a tremendous rush of magic, ladders, lines from the grappling hooks, and the Gnomes climbing them blazed with fire and death. In another flash of light, Pip disappeared and reappeared twenty feet away, atop the walls. With a push of magic, he threw the burning ladders from the walls to watch as they crashed to the ground, splintering into fiery fragments.

GuWayne saw what was happening and nodded in approval. It had been chaos and fighting since this had begun only moments before. The knight had never seen such wanton carnage.

In another flash of light, Pip appeared in front of the princess.

Laura screamed with shock. Then she realized who was staring at her and gulped. "Where did you come from?"

Pip shook his head. "Never mind, where's your father?"

Laura shook her head. "I don't know. GuWayne said he'd moved to the west gates. We were about to go look."

"No need," said Pip. "I'll find him. You and Dwayne stay here and help." Pip looked at Dwayne. "Make sure she's safe. I'll be back." And with that, without waiting for the page to answer, he flashed out again.

Laura uncovered her eyes and sighed heavily. "I wish he'd stop doing that."

Dwayne nodded. "At your word, Your Highness, there's still time to put him in a dungeon."

Laura looked stunned at the knight.

Dwayne shrugged. "I can always spank him instead."

*   *   *

Lionel headed for the west gates, by his side were Sir Hook and a hundred regular guards from the castle. He knew he had to fortify that part of the town or the Gnomes would simply swarm over the walls and take over. Just outside the gates was a giant elm that had been there for as long as the town. Its branches climbed to the sky in a majestic spread of wood and leaves, and in the summer, the shade from it as coveted as water in a desert. As he faced the gates, Gnomes were swarming over the walls in a flood, from that self-same tree. The guards patrolling that part of the city were already dead. A spear had run through the captain of the guards; a blade had been used to severe his head from the sergeant of the watch. It wasn't a pleasant sight. Blood and gore surrounded the area as the guards who were left battled for their lives.

Coming upon the grisly sight, Lionel had his troops fan out in an arch to confront the ones already in the city, try to stop the rest coming over the walls. He rushed ahead of his guards with his sword raised high, a scream of battle reached his ears he didn't immediately recognize as his own until he confronted the first of the invading Gnomes. In a slash of metal on metal, he met the Gnome and in mere seconds, had plunged his sword into the guts of his attacker. Without stopping his attack and without much regard for his own safety, Lionel met his second opponent. Slash, parry, strike, come back with a blow to the stomach, while his opponent was winded, slashed down with the blade to neatly strike off his head. As he went down, another took his place; so it went, for nearly thirty minutes. His guards and Sir Hook by his side caused just as much carnage as he, but they didn't stop, couldn't: slash, block, stab, thrust, cut down the foe in front of them, go to the next. On and on it went, blood and gore spattered everywhere, a never-ending feast of fighting and death. Just as Lionel was confronting his next foe, he'd lost count of the ones he'd dispatched, Pip appeared in front of him in a blinding shock of light.

Lionel nearly stumbled, confronting Pip instead of the Gnome intent on his death. But Pip was the one who dispatched the dirty Gnome. In a blink of an eye, Pip had seen what the Gnome had in mind for the king; he plucked the grimy creature from the ground and threw him over the wall. It was fear that drove his shove, as he pushed he grunted with the effort, the Gnome went sailing over the wall screaming. But the flood of foes didn't stop with the disappearance of one; in an eye blink, the space once again filled with another. Without thinking, Pip reached behind him and plucked his sword from the air; this time, the sword wasn't a dull piece of metal used for practice, but razor sharp and ready for action. As another Gnome faced him, he rolled with the swing of its axe heading for his head, ducked under, plunged his sword into its body, yanked it out, and then faced the next. By his side, Lionel faced his own opponent. On and on it went, foe after foe. Pip, like Lionel, wondered if this would ever end.

In a lull in the fighting, Pip turned to the king, breathing heavily, and asked, "Are you all right, sire? The princess said you'd moved. I came to help, to ask you to take shelter from all this. Let me and Tarsus do what we can. You're needed more than me."

Lionel looked at the lad for a moment saying nothing. In just a few short days, the difference in Pip was plain to him: his face had taken on a haunted look, his eyes sunk into his skull from not sleeping well, his face and manner suggesting he'd made a decision that he couldn't back down from, and his eyes shone with a light he'd never seen in him before; the coming of age. In a flash of insight, he saw what Pip the man would look like, and what he'd become. And in that sight saw more death than anyone could possibly want in ten lifetimes, let alone one. In a saddened rasp, Lionel said, "No, lad. I'm needed here right now. And you're wrong. You're as needed as I am. I'll fight with you. This is my kingdom after all. I'll not turn tail and run from a fight. My people wouldn't see it as prudence." He looked around at the many guards and knights fighting for their lives and the people they were sworn to protect and shook his head. "No, I'll fight and die with them if I must."

Pip could understand. He'd great admiration for the king and his kingdom and the knights of Musk. He could understand why Laura always wanted to be a part of it. Pip nodded. "I can relate to that. But I wish you wouldn't take so many chances. I need you to come out of this alive. Laura would never forgive me if you didn't."

Lionel smiled. "Neither would I." He then turned from Pip and plunged his sword into the next Gnome coming for him.

*　　*　　*

Tarsus circled the castle and the city, and when he thought it could help, he dived and made a run with his fiery breath. Although many of the Gnomes went down, there seemed to be a never-ending flood of them still coming. Granston must have searched the world over to find so many willing to die for his cause. As he swooped into another fight, he caught a glimpse of Granston down on the front line of the Gnome army. He appeared to be giving orders. Tarsus couldn't wait any longer for his chance to take the bloody wizard out, so with a bellow of fury and a blast of hot breath, he cleared a way towards the mad Gnome. His time had come and Tarsus wasn't about to waste the chance.

With another bellow of fire, Tarsus raced towards Granston, this madness gone on long enough, time for one of them to die. But as he came nearer, he saw he hadn't been fast enough to catch the little Gnome by surprise; instead, Granston turned, facing him with no apparent fear.

This was highly unusual. Something was wrong. He immediately tried to abort his dive, climb back up to the sky with giant strokes of his wings, but it was too late. He'd made a critical mistake. At the downbeat of his first wing stroke, Granston unleashed a powerful spell, sending the dragon careening off into the forest, looking like a falling rock coming from a blowing mountain of fire. Crashing into the trees wasn't the worst part of the spell, the worst being the impact from hitting the ground. A whoosh of air exploded from Tarsus as he hit, the force taking his breath and sight for a short time. A bellow of pain exploded from his mouth, stars literally dancing before his eyes.

Tarsus slowly came to his feet and groaned. He shook his head to clear the cobwebs and looked behind him; a trail of fallen trees, rock, shrubs, branches, and a trench of dirt stretched into the distance. He shook his head again. "Blast! That hurt," he groaned. "I bet that leaves a mark."

*   *   *

Pip heard a bellow of pain and felt the impact as Tarsus crashed through a stand of trees. The pain running through his body was near unbearable; he didn't know how he stayed on his feet or conscious. Then he realized Tarsus was still awake, his magic saving them both from passing out—what happened to one happened to the other. The roar of anger from Tarsus sent a shiver of fear into him. He jerked his head in the direction from which it had come, and in a blinding flash of light, he left the Gnome he was fighting standing alone.

Pip arrived in a clearing just outside the main gates to see Tarsus's smoking flesh careening headlong into the trees. "No!" he shouted with the force of a hurricane. With instinct alone, he slowed Tarsus's plunge with the wind from a cyclone. As clear as if he were standing by the dragon, he heard, "I bet that leaves a mark."

After Tarsus got to his feet, bellowed his anger at the heavens, and headed towards the Gnome wizard, Pip could control his rage no longer. He looked at Granston and snarled, "'You!"

*   *   *

Granston saw the flash of light in front of him and immediately put his hand to shield his sight. When his vision cleared enough to see what had caused the flash, he saw an amazing thing: a mere boy of perhaps fifteen, watching the lizard get up. Facing him, the kid screamed in a tremendous voice, "No!" Then he pointed to Granston and in an even angrier voice, shouted, "You!"

Granston couldn't believe his eyes, apparently a mere boy wanted to attack him. Looking at the boy and then at the lizard, he realized the kid had a fondness for the monster. Granston smiled an evil smile and started to laugh. He didn't know where the flash of light had come from or how the kid had shown up in the middle of it or what he had to do in all this, but he'd surely learn not to trifle with his betters. It was time for a lesson, to teach him to stay out of things that weren't his business.

With a negligent wave of his hand, Granston sent one of the many Gnomes at his disposal to kill the flea-ridden kid and get him off the field of battle. Then he turned his back and scanned the area where the dragon had landed. He knew that push of power couldn't have taken care of the walking purse, which was merely to get his attention. When he came out again, however, the lizard would find him waiting for the final fight.

*   *   *

Pip was stunned into silence, his anger for the moment gone. Granston had dismissed him with a wave of his spindly hand. He apparently didn't think a mere boy could do anything to hurt him or his plans. He saw the coward send a lackey to take care of a measly pest of a boy. Pip grinned. It was time for a lesson of his own, a lesson the ex-adviser wouldn't soon forget.

As the Gnome trotted near, Pip raised his hands as if surrendering.

The Gnome grinned evilly, no quarter was to be given to any human. He brought up his sword to take care of the sniveling brat as the wizard commanded once and for all.

Pip stopped him in his tracks: literally.

In an instant, he froze the Gnome where he was, in mid-stride, not two long paces away.

The smile on the face of the Gnome faded away in a heartbeat, and he sensed something very strange going on. He couldn't move. The only thing he could do was watch as the mere strapping of a kid came closer. Amazingly, the boy started whispering in his ear.

*   *   *

Granston jerked around at the sound of a thud. What he saw puzzled him. Marvelo had skewered a Gnome coming up from behind him with a knife in his hand. It looked as if he was going to strike at him with it in the back. Granston stared at Marvelo, slowly removing the sword from the body of the Gnome and then afterwards pointing to the kid standing in the field.

Granston looked at the kid still in the field, waving at him. He looked at the Gnome at Marvelo's feet and then back at the kid . . . then realized he'd sent that same man, dead at Marvelo's feet, to take care of the boy.

Wait a moment. The kid?

He looked at the dead Gnome and then the kid again.

The kid was still out there, alive.

Granston growled in anger.

*   *   *

Pip waved at the wizard. Then smiled. *Let's see what that does for him?*

*   *   *

Something was definitely not right about this kid. Granston had to find out what. And why had the Gnome he'd sent to kill the kid come back, without killing the kid, with murder on his mind. He looked at Marvelo and nodded, his signal to her to go do her part. He'd take care of the boy. This could work as an advantage to him. Maybe with this small distraction, it would be enough for her to get in the city.

Marvelo nodded, fading away into the crowd of Gnomes and other beings milling about.

Granston looked back at the boy.

The prattling boy waved again.

A snarl came to Granston's face as he walked slowly towards the kid on the field. Thirty paces from him, he stopped to really look at the lad.

He was merely a boy, not even shaving yet. He wore rugged but clean britches, a light shirt of vellum, and soft sand-colored boots, nothing special about the brat.

"Who are you, boy?" Granston snarled.

* * *

Pip watched the wizard as he came closer and noticed nothing particularly special about the Gnome. He was shorter than expected, but not overly so, and his clothes, although patched in spots, clean. A nice vest of black leather with plenty of front pockets bulged with unknown items as it swung slightly with his movements. His breeches went all the way to the ground, covering up what looked like a hard soled leather boot, and he had no sign of a limp or shuffle to his gait, as Laura had described to him. All in all, nothing to get excited about, and if Tarsus hadn't told him he was a Gnome, he wouldn't have ever guessed it.

When he got about thirty paces away, the wizard stopped and growled, "Who are you, boy?"

Pip bowed and grinned back at the Gnome and said, "My name is Pip."

"What are you doing here?" snarled Granston.

Pip didn't answer, he merely grinned at the wizard.

"What are you doing here?" asked the Gnome again. "What do you want? Do you have any idea what's going on?"

Pip smiled and nodded. "Oh, yes, I know. You're being an ass towards my friends."

Granston stood up straighter. *An ass? What was this?* "Leave, boy, before you get hurt. This is no place for sniveling brats like you." He waved his hand in Pip's direction, dismissing the very sight of him. "You should know not to mess with your betters."

Pip stopped smiling and took offense.

* * *

Laura was just as busy as any other knights of the Realm, dispatching more than her fair share of the Gnomes trying to overtake the city. At one time, she and Dwayne had defended their little plot of land from ten different attacks, her with the magical sword Tarsus had given her, and him with his bare hands and a flimsy knife, still refusing to pick up a sword. When things had been a little slow, she'd asked him, "Why don't you take your sword, Dwayne? You could use it right about now."

Dwayne had answered, "Because, until I'm worthy in my own mind, I'm not worthy to wield it for my king or my kingdom." Then he struck down another Gnome, slashing him across the throat.

Laura could only shrug, taking up the challenge of a human wielding a pike. In just a short period of time, Laura realized the Gnomes weren't alone in their takeover attempt. Some very unusual characters were scattered among the Gnomes, fighting just as ruthlessly, and some of them human. She gathered at least a few of them had to be the Assanti Assassins Muriel and Gimble had spoken of.

Clearing out the few remaining Gnomes and one lone human running in the opposite direction of the fighting, Laura headed again for the walls of the city. She had to find out what was going on. She'd heard a bellow of pain that could have only come from Tarsus just a few moments ago. She needed to find out if the great lizard was still among the living. As she climbed the walls, she heard another voice shout like a thunderstorm, "No!" Then a moment later, "You!" in a scream of fury.

She hastened her pace to look over the wall to see Pip standing out in the open confronting a Gnome headed in his direction. It wasn't the wizard Granston, but she'd no doubt what the man planned for him, but before he got to Pip, the Gnome simply froze in his tracks. Pip went to him and whispered something in his ear. After a moment, the Gnome simply turned around and headed back to the group surrounding Granston at the other end of the field. Pip nodded and then smiled. He then crossed his arms and planted his feet and looked as if he were waiting for something.

Laura shouted down to him. "Pip, what's going on?"

Pip didn't answer. He didn't even seem to have heard her. His mind was totally on the man returning to Granston. She looked to the other end of the field, as Pip was doing, and saw the Gnome returning holding his sword up as if to strike. From the wind blowing softly, she clearly heard a gasp from someone in the group. That's when she saw Granston and some other person, looked like a woman, point in Pip's direction.

Pip noticed the two watching him and waved at them, as if saying hello. This seemed to invoke a response in Granston that was unexpected. Granston began to walk slowly towards Pip, no one else with him, taking his time getting there. He seemed to be looking the situation over, weighing his options on what to do. Laura also noticed Pip doing the same thing, his expression never changing as he took in Granston walking out to him. When he arrived, neither spoke at first; they simply watched each other. Then Granston growled with gritted teeth, "Who are you, boy?"

Pip bowed and grinned and said, "My name is Pip."

"What are you doing here?" asked Granston.

Pip didn't answer. He just grinned at the Gnome.

After a moment, Granston asked the question again, "What are you doing here? What do you want? Do you have any idea what's going on here?"

Laura noticed Pip's expression as the wizard grilled him for answers, which he wasn't getting. The more Granston became angry at not receiving an answer, the more Pip seemed to like it. Then Pip said, as if he'd just thought about it, "Oh, yes, I know. You're being an ass to my friends."

Laura could see Granston visibly stiffen at Pip's comment. Then he said, "Leave, boy, before you get hurt. This is no place for sniveling brats like you." Then he waved his hand negligently at Pip, dismissing him. "You should know not to mess with your betters.'"

It was Pip's turn to stiffen then. Laura didn't think Pip thought it wise to dismiss him out of hand, that's, when things went south in a hurry. Although Laura saw what came next with her own eyes, she nearly discounted the whole thing. In the blink of an eye, and a flash of light, Pip moved only thirty feet ahead, just to the right of where Granston stood, and then threw a punch at the wizard's head that grazed his left jaw. With a yelp of pain and a growl of surprise, Granston pitched backwards and fell on his butt.

Holy Mother of all the gods!

*   *   *

Pip stood over the wizard and smiled. "Maybe you should go before I do something you'll regret later, old man."

*   *   *

Granston had been wholly unprepared for the blow the kid delivered. His fist hadn't connected solidly, but it did have enough force behind it to throw him to the ground. Granston wasn't too happy about the affair. He hadn't brought any bodyguards with him to this little meet-and-greet because he felt the kid didn't pose any threat. Him looking up at the youth from the ground told him otherwise. It was the first time in centuries anyone had laid a hand on him, and it would be the last. Granston rubbed his jaw where the kid had hit him. The kid looked down at him and said, "Maybe you should go before I do something you'll regret later, old man." This sent the wizard into a rage. To show the little twerp who the boss was and to get the little urchin out of his way so he could get back to business, Granston pushed enough power at the brat to move a fairly large boulder.

Nothing happened. The kid was still standing where he'd been since throwing the punch.

But . . . Granston knew that was impossible. He should've been sailing through the air head over tea kettle towards the nearest mud puddle.

Granston looked at his hands, nothing wrong there; he pushed again with power at the twerp.

Nothing!

He had enough of this game from the kid. Jumping to his feet and brushing dirt from his backside, he went to him, and from no more than a foot away pushed as much power at him as he could, which had no effect at all.

A look of understanding finally crossed the wizard's face. "Just who the blazes are you, kid?"

*   *   *

As Pip stood over the wizard, a force of power rolled over him. It wasn't a very big one, but if not for Tarsus showing him what to do when a force spell was aimed at him, he didn't think he could have just stood there. A few moments later, another force of power came at him. Now that one would've knocked him into the next kingdom if he would have let it. *Whew! Wonder if he'll get tired?*

Pip grinned down at the Gnome not saying or doing anything. Granston, however, Pip could see, was beginning to fume. *Now is when it's gonna get interesting, I think.*

Sure to his prediction, Granston pushed himself to his feet and with a determined air about him, came right to his chest and pushed with all his power; now *that* was the stuff.

As the wizard gained his feet and came up to him, Pip clenched his own power around himself and braced for the worst—good thing he did—that stuff would've surely taken his head off at the shoulder if allowed to connect.

Nothing happened. Pip could see realization dawn in the wizard's eyes just before he spat, "Just who the blazes are you, kid?"

*　　*　　*

Pip felt he'd had enough of this little Gnome trying to bully him around. It was his turn to make a statement. When Granston asked, "Just who the blazes are you, kid?" Pip decided to show him.

When Granston lowered his arms in anger at not getting the result he'd wanted, Pip directed a small bit of his own power at the Gnome. In a spectacular light show seen for ten miles around, Granston was shoved away.

*　　*　　*

For a few brief moments, fighting stopped as everyone turned to watch the lights in the sky. It was as if time had slowed to a crawl and everyone was trying to catch their breath. It wasn't just beautiful, but terrible to see.

*　　*　　*

Granston clenched his will just in time, power cascaded over him in a brilliant flash of light around him. The next thing he remembered was coming to in a trench some fifty yards from the edge of the clearing he'd confronted the boy in. All around him, trees smoked and branches were spread out from where they'd fallen, surrounding his landing spot. He looked like Tarsus coming out of the trench he'd put him in. A straight furrow of plowed earth marked his passage.

He shook his head to clear the cobwebs and slowly got his feet under himself, leveraging upright. He was wobbly, his head ached like a drummer beating a marching tune, and his hands were numb from clenching them, but altogether he was unharmed.

Blast! Blast! Blast! I didn't see that one coming. I need to find out where this kid wizard came from. And who he is. And fast!

*   *   *

Pip watched as Granston slowly made his way out of the trench. He didn't look too happy at the moment, which made Pip very happy. He was tired of not being taken seriously. He may have acted out of haste and in a bit of a huff, but that was no reason to be ignored. Upon first seeing the little wizard, and especially after talking with him, Pip knew the dragon was right; he was a bit of a snit.

Pip waved as he came back into the clearing with the other Gnomes.

*   *   *

Granston wasn't happy, not happy in the least. To make matters worse, the kid was waving at him again. And to rub salt into his wound, upon the breeze, he could hear laughter. He looked out at the city walls and saw the guards and knights laughing at his predicament. *We'll see about that!*

Granston again headed towards the upstart of a kid. Well, an up-start of a wizard. For anyone who could throw him around like a sack of rice was definitely not an ordinary person.

*   *   *

Pip watched Granston and grinned. This should be interesting. He waited patiently as the Gnome wizard walked within thirty paces of him again.

Granston said very mildly, "I see I've underestimated you, my young friend."

Pip bowed to his compliment. "Can I take it you'll go away now and leave me and my friends alone?"

Granston smirked. "No, I can't do that." He looked around at the fighting going on and shook his head. His eyes falling on the kid again, grinning, he said, "You see, there's the little matter of a certain flying lizard I need to take care of first."

Pip saw the snit watch the fighting and laugh about it and his eyes blazed with anger. "You don't have to worry about him," said Pip, gritting his teeth. "I'll keep him in line for the next thousand years. Or two thousand." Pip shrugged. "However long it is I'm alive. All you have to do is call off your dogs and we'll just name this a big misunderstanding." He indicated the dead and dying in the field. "Otherwise, I think it's going to get very unpleasant for you very soon."

Granston looked about again and smiled. "No misunderstanding about it. I meant to kill all of your people, and the lizard, and I won't stop until the job is done." With those words, he pushed a mountain of power at Pip.

Tarsus was the one who stopped it from reaching its intended target. Watching from his trench of earth and debris where he'd landed, he'd seen the two wizards confront each other, knowing it wouldn't be healthy for Pip. He had to do something, and quickly. With a groan and a tremendous down draft of his wings, he exploded from his position. In a flash of green, as he dived between the two wizards, Tarsus swatted the power back to Granston. A tremendous 'crack' sounded as the bolt connected with his pendulous tail. Immediately following, the dragon let loose a fiery counter that should have fried the little man where he stood. But, in the instant before the heat could reach him, Granston vanished.

Upon seeing Granston disappear, Pip flashed out of sight also.

Tarsus was left alone in the field, wondering if he'd killed them both.

*　　*　　*

Laura, Dwayne, Sir GuWayne, and nearly a dozen guards from the castle, along with Muriel, who'd snuck up to see the confrontation brewing between the two wizards, saw Pip flash out of existence right after Granston. Laura looked at Dwayne with her mouth hung open in surprise. "Where'd he go?"

Dwayne shook his head. "I know not. I've never seen such power."

Muriel spoke up then. "I don't know where the wizards have gone, but I do know we're not through with this war. Gnomes and humans alike are still dying in the streets of the city. Gimble is trying, with little success, with the help of a few of the kingdom's knights, to route them out." He looked at the princess. "Your father has taken a few of your fellow knights to the other side of the city to draw them out. We must help."

Laura, sweat beading on her forehead, nodded. "You're right."

Dwayne immediately headed down the ladder intending to help his king. Laura, however, stopped him. "No. Dwayne, stay and help Pip when he comes back."

"But I know not where he's gone, Your Highness," Dwayne shot back. "Or when he'll return. I must help my king if I can."

"We'll do that," Laura said, indicating Muriel and the others. "You pointed out, not too long ago I might add, that it was your duty to stay by Pip's side. Now it looks like you'll have to do just that." Laura stared at the ex-knight, not giving in to his worries or his complaints.

Dwayne couldn't argue with her logic. He didn't like the idea of staying behind, but there was no choice. He bowed to his princess. "Yes, Your Highness."

Laura knew what this cost the former knight. "Don't worry, I'll find father and make sure he's all right."

Dwayne nodded. All he could do now was wait.

*   *   *

Granston flashed out of existence right as the lizard spit fire in his direction. He knew he wouldn't have survived such a blast, and the only way to get out of its reach was to go where he knew none could follow. So, in a blink, and a flash of light, he sent himself back to the mountain stronghold he'd used when first forced to leave the castle. This was the only place where he knew no one could possibly go but him. Plus, he needed to get the Staff of Talsoun, and this provided the perfect opportunity to retrieve it. While stuck in his 'prison' in the Gnome Mountains, he'd kept the Staff with him at all times, not wanting anyone to get their hands on it even by mistake or carelessness on his part. When the army moved out, however, he didn't altogether trust Bappa and his ilk not to try and take it from him. Questions about the Staff had crept in to many of their conversations in those months. He couldn't keep lying to them about it. So, one night while he was alone, he'd 'flashed' to his retreat, stuck it in the cave, placing a protection spell on it, and 'flashed' out again. Although he knew the Staff couldn't be used for a major event for another few decades, the Staff was still a great talisman. He could do many other things with it.

Flashing into view at the entrance of the cave, Granston looked around. His many traps and snares to wreck havoc on any trespassers hadn't been tripped, so knew it was safe to enter. He walked slowly in, thinking of what had to be done next, what he had to do about that young wizard he'd faced. Just twenty paces into the cave he came upon his sleeping mats and a long low-slung platform he used for storage near the far wall. The cave wasn't much to look at, he admitted, he hadn't had much time over the years to spruce it up. Lionel had kept him fairly busy doing stupid mundane errands. The chances to burrow the opening farther into the face of the mountain never seemed to come. So he did what he could and called it quits. All he ever needed was a safe place in the eventuality of a fast retreat anyway. He just never thought it'd come so soon.

He stopped and surveyed his belongings: a few basic necessities sitting by a washstand, a soiled washcloth that should have been thrown out long ago, a straight razor and strapping leather, one lone bowl for eating, a knife made of a bone from an elk, and slightly used fur covers for his bed. Not much, but the basics of living. He knew he could always catch food when he needed, so he never stored any meat. A larder would've just been a waste of time, besides, since he didn't use this place often, any meat would've spoiled. Looking in the far corner, glowing in a pale blue color, stood the Staff of Talsoun. When he reached for it with a grin playing across his face and touched the polished wood, the glow faded and died. The spell he'd put on the Staff had ensured only he could touch it, so there was no fear about leaving it. He lifted the Staff up and with an inaudible sigh of relief turned for the cave mouth. Just as he was returning to the cave opening, a flash of bright light illuminated the area around him. Whipping his head in the direction of the flash, he came face to face with the wizard kid naming himself Pip.

"How the blazes did you follow me? That's impossible!" exclaimed Granston.

*   *   *

Pip grinned at Granston. "Nice place. Been here long?" and without saying anything else, he unleashed a push of power at the Gnome that would've knocked him cold if it had connected. Granston was far too wily for such a sneak attack, although surprised to see Pip, he was faster on the uptake.

In an instant, Granston threw a ball of power at Pip from the tip of the Staff he was holding. Pip deflected the power to the side, but only barely, it exploded just to the left of the Gnome wizard, destroying a rickety table. Then Pip knocked the Gnome back a pace with a power ball of his own. And to make the wizard regard him with more than contempt, Pip waved away the staff from his hand. In an instant, the staff flew back into the cave the wizard had just come out of, which took him by surprise, giving Pip the opportunity to push another ball of power at him. Just as the power left his hand, Granston disappeared in a flash of light. The power missed the wizard, but didn't miss the entrance to the cave. In a spectacular thunderstorm of power, the cave mouth imploded, blocking the entrance with thirty tons of granite and rock. The shifting of the rock on the mountain could be heard for hundreds of miles, as if the mountain had ripped itself up out of the very earth and taken a step to the west. Dust and debris rained down over an area the size of Musk, and the shockwave from it pitched Pip into the air.

Before he reached the ground, however, he was able to flash himself after Granston again.

*   *   *

Grundehl was fighting mad.

For the past couple of hours, his army had been losing. He'd lost nearly half of the Gnomes that had come with him, and he didn't want to lose many more. The pathetic wizard Granston had assured him to take out the city and the castle of Musk, all they had to do was kill the dragon; it wasn't working. That blasted dragon was still killing his army. The slaughter of his men on the field would be the second lose he'd known by the monster. He couldn't let that happen, not again. The stupid wizard Granston was doing nothing to help. He was to kill the flying nightmare. Where was he? Where was his support in taking down the one creature responsible for decimating the Gnome empire? No! This couldn't happen again. He'd waited too long for this opportunity to let it slip away. He had to do something quick.

Summoning his generals, Grundehl planned to take the fight straight to the enemy. Namely, he was planning to kill the monster himself and be done with it. But to do that, he first had to get rid of the one helping the dragon.

"Raulch!" barked Grundehl. "Raulch!"

Raulch came lumbering forward, waiting for the call to finally do something. "What you want me do?"

Grundehl reached out and grabbed the giant Gnome's neck with a meaty paw and brought Raulch eye to eye with him. As he stared into the dim one's face, he barked, "You kill king."

Raulch choked and spluttered, his hands clawing at Grundehl's trying to shake them loose. "Me? Why me?"

Grundehl shook the Gnome in his fist like he was shaking a tree, waiting for an acorn to fall out. "You kill king! You do now!" he barked at the hulking Gnome.

Slowly the air was leaving the giant's body, his windpipe was being crushed. Kicking and clutching at the fat king's hands in freight, gurgling, Raulch managed to get out, "Yes."

Grundehl let go and watched as the hulking Raulch coughed and spluttered, massaging his throat. "Go, now! King dead. No more war!"

With fear in his huge eyes, Raulch scrambled away, not wanting to end up dead for nothing. It was the last time anyone ever saw him.

*   *   *

Dwayne waited for Pip to reappear. It was all he could do. In the meantime helping where needed. After Princess Laura left, Dwayne was as jumpy as a toad on a hot rock. More times than not, Gnomes attempted to scale the wall, and Dwayne and a handful of guards were forced to dispatch them. Gnome after Gnome fell at the hands of the guards and Dwayne with his lone knife.

After nearly an hour, with the sound of screaming in his ears, he heard a noise behind him that didn't fit. While grappling with yet another Gnome who made it over the wall, instinct told him to turn around; which saved his life.

While blocking a sword thrust from the Gnome he was battling, he looked over his shoulder to see a woman coming towards his back with her own sword raised. Dwayne knew he'd only moments before this unknown assailant impaled him through the back. With a jerk of his hand on the sword hilt from his original opponent, he spun the Gnome in the direction of the woman coming from behind, the woman unintentionally killed Dwayne's opponent for him, impaling the Gnome instead of him.

Dwayne took two quick steps back from the woman holding the now dead Gnome. He knew from a quick glance she wasn't a Gnome: her shape wrong, her movements more fluid and graceful. Dwayne deduced she had to be one of the Assanti Assassins, and she gave him no time to think of anything else. Immediately after throwing the corpse from her, she attacked with a swiftness born of constant training; she giving no quarter, in the end, Dwayne forced to show none.

*   *   *

Lionel fought right along his knights in the streets of Musk. In the many alleyways and dark places throughout the city, Gnomes seemed to come out of the woodwork. As soon as he dispatched one opponent, another, or even two, took his place. There was seemingly a never-ending supply of Gnomes and even humans, who wanted to destroy what he and his family had built over the many generations. He was sickened and saddened at the amount of carnage flowing through his city. And he had no time to mourn the dead or dying. His knights were as brave and fearless as any king could've expected, and yet they weren't enough to slow the tide of death. Just as he thought it couldn't get any worse, a thunderous noise erupted overhead, then another, and moments later a third. With the noise came a rumble, shaking the buildings and ground underneath his feet, a ground quake; it would do more damage than the fighting. Thank the gods it didn't last long, only moments. He didn't know what caused the noise or the shaking, but with a sigh of relief, he continued down one of the many alleys of the city. Entering the gloomy place, a light gray fog? Mist? Rock? started falling from the sky. In moments everything around him was covered in the silky stuff. He swiped it from the sleeve of his long shirt, leaving a gray dusty smear.

Sir Hook, the only knight left at his side after nearly two solid hours of fighting, was hard-pressed to keep his kings back clear.

Lionel knew his many years of training with Dwayne was paying off, but he'd never been in a battle such as this, the years taking a toll on his stamina. He hadn't had to do so much strenuous activity in many years, and a short battle with any opponent was taxing on him. He was grateful the Gnomes hadn't been as expertly trained as his own knights, their strategy to hack and rend what was in front of them, making it easy for him and his troops to take them down in droves. The problem was the number of Gnomes being sacrificed for the fight, his men too few to keep going. By sheer volume, his kingdom would fall eventually.

Going through the alley, checking every conceivable hiding place he could for stragglers, Lionel ran right into the biggest Gnome he'd ever seen. The giant looked as if he hadn't had a decent night's sleep in months; his hair matted to his bulbous head, he knew not from the gray dust covering him or lack of cleanliness, his clothes hanging in tatters, his boots worn and about to fall off his misshapen feet. All in all he looked like how Lionel felt. Then he spoke with a guttural growl while hefting an ax. "Me kill play king now."

"Oh, boy. This don't look good," commented Lionel taking a step back, lifting his sword.

Sir Hook followed his king into the alley as quickly as he could. The Gnome he'd just dispatched being a little better at defending himself than the others he'd taken care of today, so it took him a few minutes longer than expected, and the gray fog coming from the sky hadn't helped him in the slightest. As he entered the alley, he saw the giant Gnome sprint towards Lionel howling with rage.

"Sire!" Hook screamed, running forward to help his king.

The Gnome charged Lionel howling with rage; then fell at Lionel's feet, face down in the gray covered dirt, an arrow protruding from the middle of his back.

Hook scanned ahead, charging to the rescue, only to come up short when seeing the hulking Gnome lying prone at his king's feet, dead. He looked at Lionel, but said nothing. Heaving with the effort to catch his breath, he watched as Muriel came striding forward.

Lionel looked up from the corpse to see Muriel holding a bow in a shooter's stance, just having released the arrow that fell the giant. As he stood with the bow, grayish flakes floating off his arm, Muriel walked to Lionel and looked down at the Gnome. "Big one, wasn't he?"

Lionel nodded, not able to say anything just yet.

Muriel nodded back. "You still haven't learned to stay out of trouble, have you?"

"I guess not," answered Lionel, heaving a sigh of relief.

*　　*　　*

Tarsus watched from high above the city. He saw clearly how the Gnomes, although very bad fighters, would eventually overwhelm the kingdom by sheer numbers. On and on he helped where he could, cutting down hundreds of screaming foes at a time. His strafing runs yielded many casualties, and many more unable to continue the fight. Grundehl had done an excellent job of brainwashing these poor creatures into doing his bidding. As many Gnomes were being killed in this conflict, it would take centuries to repopulate.

Tarsus was heartsick in the fact Musk would take generations of its own to do the same. Dozens of citizens had died today trying to save what they'd worked so hard in making. And the knights were dying right along with them. Although knights of the guard took as many as they could with them before they fell, they still couldn't compete against the sheer volume of Gnomes pouring into the streets. With each dive, Tarsus searched for Pip. After watching him and Granston disappear outside the gates, he had yet to find him again. His fear was Pip wasn't a match against the wily veteran wizard. But there was no sign of either. Tarsus knew the only way to save even a portion of the Kingdom of Musk, they needed Pip to literally drive away the enemy using any and all magic. He knew he wasn't dead, the magic binding them hadn't been severed, but he didn't know where to look for him either. Pip could be anywhere in the world, not just in the kingdom. A wizard who used 'flashing' to travel— most magicians or wizards call it translocation—didn't use it very often; it tended to be unreliable, unpredictable. One could not simply 'flash' thirty feet ahead. One could only leap great distances, say, a thousand miles. The wizard who used the technique could never duplicate the same travel twice. It was a sporadic and dangerous method, used only in an emergency. And yet, when Granston flashed, Pip flashed right behind him. It was as if he were chasing the gnome, which was impossible. Once a wizard disappeared from flashing, it wasn't possible for another wizard to follow him. You had to have a specific destination in mind before the trick even worked, and then it worked only half the time, usually sending you miles from your target destination, or overshooting it entirely. It took practice to get the slightest chance of accuracy right. Tarsus just hoped Pip didn't land up on the other side of the world trying to find the mad little Gnome. If he did, it may be far too late for anyone to help Lionel and the Kingdom of Musk.

*   *   *

Granston staggered as he popped back into reality. Although he got away from the young snot of a wizard, he'd thrown himself too far from the fight, with too much momentum. He wanted to land closer to the Gnome guards to have some little protection. He couldn't take on both the knights and this new wizard. He needed help. Overshooting his mark wouldn't get it for him. How was that kid doing that? It's impossible to follow after someone flashing.

And speak of a horde of devils, Pip popped out again, like a bad copper mark Granston couldn't lose.

*   *   *

Pip popped out with a flash of light and came face to face with Granston. He smiled, waved at him again, and then struck.

*   *   *

In a blinding flash of light, Granston popped onto the field of battle. Right on his heels, no more than three seconds later, Pip did the same, standing no more than thirty paces away. And each looked as if they'd been spit out by giants: torn, tattered, and in some spots bloody, the constant battling taking its toll, and each took no time in throwing power at the other. Showers of rock and dirt sprayed up from the blasts, either by missing their marks or being deflected by the other. It was turning out to be a monumental struggle by both of them. The very air was electrified with the total volume of power flowing from the two wizards. But when it came to power, Granston knew he was outclassed, and he was no match for this newcomer, just barely holding his own. If not for his inexperience, Granston knew this kid could have easily killed him. He'd never seen such power flowing out of a wizard before. Back and forth, back and forth, with no one coming out on top, the fight went between them. Eventually, however, something had to give. Granston tried over and over again to overwhelm Pip with shaking the ground under his feet, which Pip used an anchoring spell on himself to counteract the attacks. Neither could get the upper hand. The combatants around them tried to keep fighting but the power expelled was too much, no one could do anything but run for their lives. Back and forth the contest went until Pip stopped what he was doing and in a flash of light simply vanished.

Granston looked around bewildered, his upstart of a foe nowhere to be seen. His nerves were still crackling with juice, the muscles in his arms and back twitched anticipating throwing another powerball. "Where the hells are you, boy?" he screamed. "We aren't done yet!"

*   *   *

Dwayne fought for his life. In all the years he'd been a master of the blade, this woman was the first to push him to his limit. Back and forth they went, neither getting the upper hand: slash, parry, block, slash, parry, block. Through the fighting, Dwayne could see where ultimately one of them wouldn't walk out alive, as time wore on, he feared it would be him. Because of his pledge not to use a sword, the only weapon he had was a long knife. It definitely wasn't a sword, but it was more than a plain knife. It was becoming harder and harder to block her many moves with the sword she carried. More than a few times, he couldn't avoid being cut by her blade. Maneuvering the long knife, being shorter than a sword, put his hand and arm in the perfect position for her sword when she thrust in close and attacked. This woman was very good. She fought with the ferocity of long knowing she was the best. He didn't want to kill her if he could avoid it, but she was pushing not only his skill, but his patience to the limit.

Taking a quick breath, Dwayne asked, "Who are you? Why are you doing this?"

There was no reply. She neither smiled, laughed, frowned, nor did anything else. Her attention was wholly focused on her job, killing him. She was a consummate professional, and it showed in every line and form of her craft.

The worst part of it all, she didn't say anything. There was no bragging, boasting, or anything else, except grunts of exertion. In most fights, two opponents kept a dialogue open between them in case of a surrender, in this case, nothing. It was most disconcerting.

Dwayne sidestepped a thrust from her sword. Although it didn't cause the damage she'd wanted, it did slice another furrow down his arm. Blood slowly seeped down to his wrist, making it hard to keep a firm grip on his knife. He knew the end for one of them was close. He also knew if it didn't end quickly, he wouldn't be the one to walk away. After another parry from him and slash from her, Dwayne knew he had to do something, the time for compassion over. Another thrust from her turned the tide in his direction. In an unexpected move on Dwayne's part, he let the Assassin's thrust come in farther than she intended, and with a quick grab at her wrist, pulled her forward even more—overbalanced, outweighed, caught off guard—her own momentum drove his knife deep into her chest, piercing her heart, a single off balanced step having killed her.

Dwayne looked down at the fallen woman and sighed. She'd been a very good opponent. In another few moments, he didn't know whether he'd have been so lucky.

After it was over, as he stood over the body, Laura and his king, with Muriel and several others, including Sir Hook, showed up. Each was covered from head to toe in a grayish colored dust. Dwayne didn't know what it was, and he didn't ask. His attention was solely focused on the fact all of them were safe.

Laura looked at the bloody woman at his feet and asked, "What happened? Who's that?"

Dwayne gulped air, sighed, and while looking down on the woman said, "I know not, Your Highness. But I believe she's an Assanti Assassin." He looked at Laura. "And I think she specifically came to kill me."

Lionel asked, "How do you know this?"

"It's the way she did it, Sire. At no point did she engage anyone else. And she had plenty of opportunity."

Lionel nodded. "I see."

"Sounds like what happened to you, sire," put in Sir Hook, also glancing at the dead woman.

Dwayne's head snapped up and stared at Lionel. "You, sire? What happened?"

Laura answered. "Not to worry. Muriel took care of the problem."

Sir Hook answered his ex-captain's question. "A very big Gnome came after our king in one of the many alleys in the city. And he was after only one person." He pointed to Lionel.

Lionel said, "We don't know that, Sir Knight. But however it came about, I owe my life to Muriel." He looked at Muriel and smiled slightly. "Again."

Muriel bowed to him, dislodging some of the gray dust clinging to his hair.

"Either way I think we need to keep an eye on our king," said Dwayne. He sternly looked at Hook. "Don't you think?"

Hook blanched and stiffened. "I was."

Before Dwayne could reply, or ask about the gray dust on everyone, a roar came from outside the gates, a roar of pain.

*   *   *

CHAPTER 32

Tarsus watched as Pip disappeared from the fight in a flash of light. On more than one occasion while watching the two wizards sling power at each other, he thought about swooping in and helping; the longer he watched, however, the worse the idea became. If for one reason or another he was to attack Granston in the middle of one of Pip's power balls, he very well could come out of it with more than scorched pride. The amount of power being tossed around by the two wizards was enormous. Any distraction by anyone could cost them their lives, including himself. So, he waited. He wanted Granston to know who was going to end his life. He wanted to watch as the realization he was going to die by the very enemy he'd intended to kill, sink in.

"Where the hells are you, boy? We're not done yet!" screamed Granston, frantically looking for Pip.

Tarsus was thinking the same thing. What was that boy thinking? He can't run now. It's not his nature. And that's when Pip popped back into the fray, right behind the Gnome wizard.

Tarsus was astonished, no wizard in history, as far as he could remember, could translocate only yards. In years of practice, most could only do it for hundreds of miles, with great difficulty and with great pain. It tended to be a last ditch effort at escape. But . . . Pip had shown another new talent. *Impressive, kid. Very impressive.*

As Pip flashed behind Granston, the light from his trip was a dead giveaway. Granston spun to watch as Pip reached behind his back and pulled his sword. With a quick flurry of motion, no more than a split second, Granston disappeared, but not before Pip's sword sliced through the space he'd been standing in. With the speed of a god, eye blink quick, Pip was gone again, right after the Gnome.

Tarsus had never seen such wizardry. He'd never even heard of such a thing. And he most definitely didn't teach it to Pip. The young lad was learning on his own at a fantastic rate. Translocation was a feat not many wizards could do, and he was doing it with ease, accuracy, and skill.

Tarsus circled over the city keeping an eye out for his young charge. After more than a minute, he heard an explosion to the west. In the blink of an eye, he'd done a barrel roll and oriented himself in that direction. As he flew, he saw smoke and not ten strong beats of his wings brought him to the cause. Granston was flinging granite boulders the size of the castle at Pip. Only the gods knew where he was getting the things from. They were appearing from out of nowhere, but as the gray rocks headed towards Pip, they broke into giant dust storms. The resulting shock of the giant rocks coming apart in mid-air caused the sound. Pip broke them apart as fast as they were coming. When the rocks broke, a gray dust floated towards the ground. In mere moments, the sky was as gray as if clouds had covered the area.

*   *   *

Pip stood his ground watching the Gnome wizard throw rocks at him. Rocks! Big or small, they were only rocks. Tarsus taught him to do that quite a while ago. He smirked with disdain for the threat, a smile on his face for Granston, making dust out of them.

Afterwards when he saw Granston had given that up, Pip waved cheerily at the little man.

*   *   *

Granston was incensed. *How dare the brat be so bold. The kid is actually laughing and waving at me again.* It was intolerable.

*   *   *

Pip watched and smirked at the Gnome. *Now that was a tantrum. Not long now. It's about time for me to end this.* That's exactly what Pip did, but as Pip often found out, things don't always go quite to plan.

*   *   *

The war wasn't over yet. Tarsus knew if Pip didn't stop Granston soon, he'd wipe out the whole kingdom. But he also knew Granston wasn't the only one to worry about. Grundehl was still controlling his army of Gnomes, what was left of them. Although he'd taken out many of the foot soldiers, there were still a lot of them standing. A new push had begun at the main gates of the city, a veritable horde of Gnomes, wraiths, and humans were trying to break them down. Grundehl had been a very busy general, foot soldiers assailed the city in a swarm of bodies, chaos and bloody slaughter making their way to the gates. Tarsus knew he had to do something.

In a split second, he dived towards the horde, flame belching from his gullet. He passed no more than ten feet over the army's heads, the backlash of wind causing as much damage as his fiery breath. But they didn't stop their approach. He dived again, this time flying low enough to pluck ten or more from the ground with his back claws. As they screamed and raged with mad intent, his powerful wings took them hundreds of feet from in the air, where he let go.

The city guards cheered as Tarsus broiled their enemies, the sight awesome and loathsome. No good would come from this fight, Tarsus knew. But he couldn't stop it from happening. All he could do was help and hope nothing happened to his friends.

*   *   *

Pip flashed again; this time, however, he didn't go where Granston was. This time he knew he had to do something about the army attacking the city. In a blaze of light, he appeared almost in the middle of the Gnomes, just as abruptly, throwing them in every direction at once. There was chaos among the fighters. With blazing balls of power, just as Tarsus had taught him, he threw as many of the invaders into the air, screaming and wailing. It was as if a scythe had sown a harvest: a harvest of death. With each step, he gathered his power, shielding his own body like a blanket, making it slowly expand outward, in this way forcing the invaders back, step by step. No matter what they tried, no one could get through his defenses, his will keeping the energy strong and impenetrable. With tears streaking his cheeks, he kept the tide of Gnomes at a standstill. He knew it couldn't last long. He was tired from going after Granston, eventually his strength would give out, but maybe if he proved to them they could do nothing to get to the city, their will would break, and this would end.

*   *   *

Tarsus saw Pip flash into the middle of the army as he was coming back from another snatch and grab. Again he was amazed at what the kid could do. His powers were growing every day, a few of the tricks Tarsus had never seen before, watching as Pip slowly pushed the army away. A blue shimmering nimbus of color surrounded him and expanded as he gestured with his hands. It seemed to be a wall, or barricade, of force he was using to keep the Gnomes from advancing. As the horde touched the bubble, they were violently thrown away. But Tarsus knew the kid couldn't keep it up all day. Power took a lot of strength, and eventually giving out, he'd most likely die. The time to help had come; with a roar of fire, a giant down thrust of his wings, he plummeted towards Pip. At the last second before reaching him and his fight, Tarsus spotted Granston on a low hill not a hundred yards away. In an aerial display of maneuverability not seen for a hundred generations, Tarsus turned and headed instead towards his greatest enemy. As he drew near, he opened his jaws wide, to expel as much fiery breath as he could. His intention was to finally fry the little Gnome and rid the earth of a menace long overdue. Great gouts of flame expelled from his mouth as he reached the wizard, the furnace of heat enveloping the Gnome, surrounding him and incinerating the ground and trees near him in mere seconds. Climbing with mighty thrusts of his wings, after, he looked back to see Granston still standing on the knoll. Although he'd seen clearly he'd got the wizard, the fire hadn't touched him. A red nimbus of power slowly dissipated from the wizard; he'd used some kind of a shield, just as Pip was doing. Roaring with frustration and anger, Tarsus headed for Pip. He'd only one chance to help the young wizard. He couldn't afford to waste time on Granston again. Thrusting mightily with his wings, Tarsus dived, that's when his plan went into the crapper.

*   *   *

Granston also watched how the lizard plummeted to help the snot of a wizard. After being flash fried by the damn lizard, payback was in order.

In the blink of an eye, Granston shaped his power into the form of a spear and threw it at the plummeting lizard. Seconds later, as the scaly dragon came within an arm's length of the Gnomes and the boy wizard below him, the spear of power sank into the meaty part of his right shoulder. In a great roar of pain, he crashed to the earth, the spear piercing his flesh and causing him to lose control.

*   *   *

Great gouts of blood shot from the wound in Tarsus's shoulder. When he crashed into the field, among the Gnomes and humans fighting, the Gnomes saw it as a great opportunity to steal the life from him. Thrashing in agony, Tarsus defended himself as best as he could, but sword thrust upon sword thrust was shoved into his open wound, tearing and rending was now being done to him, instead of the other way around. Now he knew what it must have felt like for the one's he'd already sent to their makers. *I love you, Pip. I'm sorry.*

*   *   *

Pip watched helplessly as Tarsus screamed in agony. A split second later, he screamed as well. He'd been too distracted by repelling the Gnomes and fighting his own battles, to truly notice what had been going on above him. With the roar of pain from Tarsus, coupled with the pain he was feeling because of the shared magic between them, his mind went immediately white hot with rage. "No!" screamed Pip in a thunderous voice. The ground shook with the concussion of it.—"You will not!"

In the explosion of power that followed, Pip's mind went blank. He only saw one outcome, making sure his mentor and friend didn't die. What happens to one, happens to the other. As he flung gnomes in every conceivable direction, he made sure they'd never bother anyone again. In a concussion of rushing outflow of power, he set everyone and everything to blaze in a fiery furnace. Fire blossomed outwards in every direction, the heat blazing to such an intense degree, even rocks were showing signs of melting. A river of magma was rushing towards an inevitable explosion. He had to reach Tarsus. He couldn't, wouldn't, let him die in the dirt, his life's blood spilling out like a small river. With a shout of agony on his lips, and the pain of his mentor dying, Pip blazed with power. Gnomes, humans, Assanti, anyone, and everyone fried where they stood, and still he wasn't done. Through anger and frustration of not having prevented this from happening, he sent back to Granston a power spear of his own. As straight as any arrow ever fired from a bow, the shaft of blue light streaked towards the wizard. With all his heart, Pip willed the shaft to be buried in his chest.

*　　*　　*

Granston watched as the lizard writhed in agony upon the ground. His smile covered his whole face. He knew in just a few moments, the lizard would surely be done for and in just a few short moments, his worries would finally end, and the many centuries waiting for the death of the blasted lizard would be over. Over! He'd done it, without the help of the Gnome king. He'd done it! Him! He didn't need the slob of a king any longer, his usefulness finally at an end. Now, after the death of the lizard, he could finally take what was rightfully his, by right of birth, by right of being the most powerful force in the world. No one and nothing could stop him. He raised his fists in the air and crowed his triumph to the gods.

*　　*　　*

As Granston gloated and patted himself on the back, he'd not been the only one watching Tarsus die in agony. Grundehl, king of the Gnomes, had also been waiting for the right time to take care of unfinished business. He'd told the wizard to never come back to the kingdom of the Gnomes. He'd warned him he wouldn't come out alive if he did. And by the power of luck, Granston the wizard had returned. Luck for him, because Bappa, the leader of the Assanti, had to council him to use this as an excuse to finally kill the lizard. Granston was the only one who had the faintest chance to kill him. He'd been the one they could use to get rid of the worst enemy they'd ever known, the one being in all creation that had wiped out so many of their kind. Only after he'd been taken care of would they then take care of the wizard. Now the chance he'd been waiting for had come. The only way to kill a wizard as powerful as Granston would be to sneak up on him and plunge a knife between his ribs. And Grundehl was doing just that.

Granston gloated and capered about as if he'd killed twenty dragons with one spell, instead of one. His mind was as preoccupied as it would ever get. Grundehl didn't know where Raulch was. He'd not returned from killing the play king of this backwater kingdom, or he'd have sent him to do the dirty work. But, no matter, Grundehl could handle it.

Grundehl spoke very softly into the ear of the wizard before he struck. "You die now!"

*   *   *

Granston saw the upstart wizard throw a spear of his own and then heard a very familiar gravelly voice in his ear, "You die now!"

Without turning, he froze the king of the Gnomes in place, just as he'd done those few months before to Raulch in the campsite in the mountains. As he turned to face the king, he smiled ruefully.

Grundehl's eyes went wide with shock and freight, sweat beading on his sloping forehead and his paunchy stomach quivering.

"Not as easy as you imagined, hey Gnome?" asked Granston, turning to watch the kid's spear rocketing towards him and the king. "I've known from the start you wanted me dead. But I didn't think you'd have the guts to do it yourself. Raulch maybe, but not you. Now, however, you'll end your days in this world never seeing the end of the lizard or me."

Granston pitched the unmoving king of the Gnomes in front of Pip's power spear. In an instant of clarity and dread, Grundehl saw what was coming. The only sound he made was a moan of horror. When the spear hit him, he was torn in two, right through the middle, with the power meant for Granston. Gore and guts splattered everywhere.

Granston looked towards the snot of a wizard and waved cheerily at him and then disappeared in a flash of light.

*   *   *

Bappa watched as the bloated slob Grundehl walked behind Granston and prepared to stab him in the back. He smiled, knowing the outcome. He'd convinced the king of the Gnomes the only way to get rid of the lizard was to have Granston do his dirty work. The wizard would take the chance of not coming out of the fight alive. But Bappa had also convinced the despicable Gnome he was the one to take care of the wizard as well. As Grundehl made his way, with murder and madness in his eyes, to Granston, he saw the blue tinged spear of power come hurtling out of the distance. When Granston stopped time, in an instant, Bappa knew the king's time on the earth was over. In a flash, the wily wizard threw Grundehl in the path of the spear. He watched as the wizard waved cheerily to the snot of a boy and disappeared. In a tremendous flash of power, the spear exploded and Grundehl was no more, and Bappa knew the war was no more as well. Laughing hysterically, not caring if the Gnomes lived or died, his only worry for his few Assanti, he turned from the field of battle.

In the chaos that followed, knights traipsing in and out of the woods surrounding the city of Musk, rounding up stragglers, no one noticed one lone Dryad melt into the bark of a pine to escape. His fight may be over, but his war had only begun.

✱   ✱   ✱

Pip watched as the blue streak of power rushed towards the Gnome wizard. The end had finally come for the little man, he'd never bother anyone again. He hadn't really wanted to kill through any of this, but circumstances warranted the death of Granston and his whole army. He watched as the spear got nearer, and then he was shocked to see Granston throwing someone else in its path. *Blast!*

The cheery wave by Granston before he flashed out of existence sent Pip's blood to boiling again. He could see in his mind's eye where the little man had gone, but he couldn't follow, not now, not when Tarsus needed his help.

Pip scrambled as fast as he could to his friend's side. Upon reaching the dragon, Pip could see nothing but blood. He couldn't tell whether he was still alive. Tarsus lay unmoving in his own gore, pain flooding both of them. There was so much blood pouring from the wound in his shoulder, the ground was actually soggy with it. Going on instinct alone, Pip held his hand to the wound and willed it to stop bleeding, but nothing happened. Nothing. Blood poured from the wound and pooled around his knees.

No! No! You can't die! You can't! You have too much to show me. Hot tears streamed down his cheeks as he labored to staunch the river of blood. Pip started to shake, his arms going slack, his breath slowing. He could feel his own heart gradually losing beats, coming to a stop, along with Tarsus's. Then, without warning, Laura's hand clasped his shoulder. He looked up to see her weeping also, his pain hers. Lionel, Dwayne, and Muriel stood to one side watching and waiting, he could clearly hear Laura sobbing, and Lionel swearing as if he were a sailor come off the sea. For some reason, this gave him strength. Taking a gulp of air, he began again, determination in the set of his shoulders. He knew if all those around him were as concerned for Tarsus as he, he could do anything. Swiping the tears from his cheeks, he closed his eyes and concentrated with all he had. He used not only his head, but what was in his heart to start the power flowing . . . without warning, a blue flame sprang from his hands, surrounding Tarsus and his wound. *You can't die. You can't die. You have many centuries left to keep me out of trouble. Come on! Come on!*

A gasp came from behind him. He didn't know who'd done it, and he didn't care. But with the opening of his eyes, he saw the wound in the dragon's shoulder wasn't as deep as it once was. A moment longer, blood stopped flowing and the slash knitted itself to a small thin line. With a sigh of relief, tears streaming down his cheeks, weariness of the long day gripped him. With a groan of pain, Pip released his magic, knowing Tarsus would live.

That's when Pip slumped over and knew no more.

*   *   *

CHAPTER 33

P ip woke to the lovely sight of Princess Laura watching him. She wiped tears from her eyes before leaning down and kissing his cheek tenderly. He looked at her ragged clothes and blood-stained boots and sighed wearily asking, "What happened?"

Laura smiled and said quietly, "You passed out. We all feared for your safety."

Pip shook his head to clear his thinking a bit and then remembered with clarity: Tarsus! "Tarsus? Is he . . ." he said sitting up too quickly, groaning. "Is he all right?"

Laura pushed the young wizard back onto the bed. "He's fine. He'll be as good as ever because of you." Laura stared at him hard. "He owes you his life."

Pip shook his head. "No, I owe him. If it hadn't been for Tarsus trying to keep me alive, I'd have never made it. Granston nearly did me in." He smiled ruefully. "King Lionel?" he asked.

Laura smiled and sighed herself. "He's fine too. A little bruised and battered, but fine. Just as the rest of us are. We owe you much." She leaned down again, this time brushing his unruly hair from his forehead. "Sleep. We'll talk again later." She then got up from the edge of the bed and walked to the door of his chamber. As she was leaving, she looked back and grinned.

As the door closed out the sight of the princess, Pip realized just how much he actually cared for her and how much trouble he'd be in if the king found out. Hell, if Dwayne found out, he'd be in chains again. And with thoughts of Laura, Lionel, Dwayne, and Tarsus running through his head, he slowly drifted off to sleep. But it wasn't a very restful slumber; not two hours later, he awoke with a scream on his lips.

Granston would come again. And he wouldn't be happy about their last encounter. Trouble had just begun.

*   *   *

Pip woke again, this time alone in his chambers. He felt as if he'd been stomped on by a giant angry green lizard. He smiled thinking of Tarsus still going to be around giving him instruction. He lay in bed a moment savoring the thought of living through the fight with Granston and the many Gnomes. If it hadn't been for Tarsus helping him cope with being a wizard and teaching him so much, he knew he wouldn't have been able to survive. As he slowly got himself together, washed, done his necessaries, a knock came at his door. "Come," he said, wincing at his many aches.

Dwayne walked through the door and bowed. "Lord Wizard." He straightened and then looked Pip over quizzically. "You look fairly well from the last I saw of you. How do you feel?"

Pip grinned and said, "Like the great green monster rolled over top of me."

Dwayne bowed, nodded, and said, "Understandable."

"Please don't call me "Lord wizard," said Pip, watching Dwayne closely. "I'm not a lord by any stretch of the imagination, as you well know. And if it hadn't been for Tarsus, I may not have made it to wizard."

Dwayne nodded and then said, "I came to see if you'd care for something to eat."

"Yes, please," answered Pip enthusiastically. "My stomach feels like my throat's been cut." And, as if on cue, his stomach grumbled. He hurriedly finished dressing and followed Dwayne down the great staircase of the castle. He expected them to turn towards the dining hall, but instead, he headed to the side doors leading to the practice fields. Before Pip could ask, Dwayne said, "We'll be dining in the pavilion just off the fields. Everyone's there waiting."

"Everyone?" Pip asked, not understanding.

Dwayne nodded and kept walking, not saying anything else.

As they emerged outside, knights of the guard were lined up in front of the door. As he walked down the steps, they immediately went to attention and saluted him with their swords in the air. Pip saw Sir Hook and Sir GuWayne at the head of the line and nodded to each. Through a giant cheer, "Hail Pip! Hail Pip!" he walked slowly towards a pavilion that had been erected at one corner of the fields. He didn't know what to make of this. No one had ever cheered him before, chased him off maybe, but never cheered.

Dwayne grinned and gestured for him to keep walking. As they walked, Dwayne explained, "They're giving you a great honor. It doesn't happen often, Pip. They know if it hadn't been for yours and Lord Tarsus's efforts, no one would've survived."

Pip was embarrassed. His cheeks had a ruddy red glow when he finally made it to the tent where a long table had been set up filled to overflowing with food. At the head of the table sat King Lionel and Princess Laura. Along the far side of the table sat Gimble, who'd already filled his plate to overflowing, munching contentedly on a drumstick of some kind. It seemed the Dwarf waited for no one. Muriel, the Elf, sat beside him, watching Pip and Dwayne as they made their way to their chairs. Surprisingly, Tarsus was there also. He looked tired and worn, but for all that, healthy. He'd stuck his head through the tent opening so he could be with the group.

Pip rushed to him, ignoring everyone for the moment. "It's good to see you, Lord Dragon."

Tarsus dipped his head. "And you, Lord Wizard." He grinned at Pip and winked.

Pip shook his head. "Please, don't call me that. I'm not a lord. I'm a stable boy." He grinned at the dragon. "But I'm glad to see you," he finished, smiling, patting the dragon's nose affectionately.

Tarsus nodded again, only watching him. Then Pip turned to the table and feast.

Gimble grunted with his mouth full.

Muriel chuckled.

Lionel stood and addressed Pip. "Pip, we've a lot to discuss. I thought it would be easier for us to do it out here." He gestured at the tent, indicating Tarsus, everyone knowing why. "And I thought maybe you'd like something to eat while we did it." He indicated the table filled with food.

At the king's gesture, Pip's mouth started to water. He was as hungry as he'd ever been. "Thank you, sire, I am a bit hungry."

Lionel quirked his mouth in a lopsided grin. "You should be after three days."

Pip looked at Lionel startled. "Three days, sire?"

"Yes, that's how long you've been out. I can tell you, we all were a little bit worried about you. Tarsus and Laura especially." Lionel glanced at his daughter, his mouth quirking into a slight grin, or was it a grimace? Pip couldn't decide.

Tarsus snorted. "Well, I have to have someone clean my stall."

Gimble went into gales of laughter, nearly tipping his chair over.

Laura smiled at Pip as her cheeks took on a rosy glow like his.

Lionel gestured for him to sit, and as he did, Dwayne pulled up a chair as well. Pip started piling food on his plate. The more he got on it, the more he wanted. To not look like Gimble's kinfolk, he decided it would be OK to go back for seconds if needed. No need to make a pig of himself. He started eating and savoring the taste of eggs, bacon, fresh bread, greens, ham, and much more, washing it all down with a cup of mild spring wine. After finishing the plate, he belched quietly and sighed. And through the whole meal, although Lionel had said they'd a lot to talk about, yet no one said a word. When he was finished and debating about loading his plate up again, Lionel said in a rush, "Pip, I'd like for you to be our resident wizard."

That put a damper in Pip's hunger, forgetting about a second helping. *Resident wizard?*

Pip looked at Lionel but said nothing. Tarsus, however, did. "Pip, you should consider it. I don't know how you did some of the things out there on the field, but you seem to be very powerful. I thought you might be, the sense I got was very strong when I first met you. If you'll allow me, I'll teach you more."

Pip nodded at the dragon. "I'd like that very much, Tarsus. But, sire," he looked at Lionel again, "I don't think I want to be a wizard in residence."

Muriel said aghast. "Then you're mad. It's a great honor."

Lionel held up his hand to forestall any other outbursts from the Elf. "That's enough, Muriel." Lionel studied Pip and sighed. "May I ask why, lad? You're more than welcome to stay here as long as you wish, for I can't order you to stay. You're a free man and not under mine or anyone else's control. Remember, you're a sovereign person. And I don't know of any other way to thank you for what you've done for me and my kingdom."

Pip didn't at first say anything. He looked at the people around the table one by one, finally staring at Laura sitting by her father. His emotions for her was as strong as ever, but he felt something was missing. Not her feelings for him, and not his feelings for her, but he knew in his heart they'd never be together because of the separation of royalty and the common man. The gulf was too wide and feelings and traditions about that sort of thing too ingrained in the culture of the kingdom. He didn't know whether he could stand seeing her every day knowing he couldn't be with her. In the end, he didn't say anything of that. Looking at Lionel, he said, "You already have thanked me, sire. You did it the day you allowed me to use a room in the castle. That's all the thanks I need. Plus, I don't want to cause you or your kingdom any more trouble. When this all started, I did a lot of that. And that wasn't my intention."

Dwayne stood and cleared his throat. He looked as if he had something to say on that subject. The knight looked down at Pip and began. "I wish to apologize to you, wizard. I was wrong in my judgment of you." He bowed to Pip. "And if you stay, I'd like to stay with you as page. You may find I have a lot I could show you myself."

"But you need to go back to the knights," said Pip excitedly. "You don't have to be with me any longer. They need you more than I do."

"No, lad." Dwayne disagreed. "I can't go just yet. I'm not worthy."

Laura stood and heatedly said, "You are worthy. I'll hear nothing else from you about it! You're just being stubborn."

"No, Your Highness, I'm not. Until I'm worthy in my own mind, I can't go to the knights."

Lionel said, "And that's why you're needed in the knights, Dwayne. If you can recognize the failings in yourself and pass those lessons on to the ones who really need it, then you're as worthy as the rest of us. Plus," Lionel shook his head, "if you don't do something about GuWayne, we may not have very many new knights left. He's taken it upon himself to teach every new recruit the error of their ways."

The rest of the group chuckled. But it did no good.

Dwayne shrugged. "Be that as it may, sire. I can't."

"Very well, "said Lionel, slapping his palm on the table in frustration. "But you're too harsh on yourself. I've more faith in your judgment than I do in my own."

Dwayne bowed to his king. "Thank you, sire. But I'm content with my duties right now." He sat back down.

"So, what shall you do, lad?," asked Lionel, looking again at Pip. "You may stay as long as you like in the castle. The rooms are yours."

"Thank you, sire. I'd like to stay at least until Laura has gone through her trials." He smiled at the princess. "Then, I don't know. What I really want to know is what happened after I passed out on the field? What happened to Granston and his army?"

Muriel snorted. "That's the funny part in all this. After you took a nose dive on the field, the wizard disappeared and hasn't been seen since." He snorted again.

"And the army," said Gimble with his mouth half-full, "what was left of them, just melted away into the woods. I guess they didn't want anything to do with more fighting after they saw their leaders get killed."

"So, that's the end of it?" asked Pip. "We won?"

Tarsus snorted. "Won? I don't know about that, but we sure as blazes didn't lose. You can about bet the castle on the fact we haven't seen the last of Granston."

"That's just great." Pip shook his head, remembering his dream of the night past. "Now what?"

"We can only do one thing, Pip," said Dwayne. "Wait and see."

"Why don't we go after him and finish the job?" asked Pip quizzically.

"And where would we look?" asked Lionel. "It could take a hundred years to find where the little Gnome went to."

"What about his cave? We could start there," said Pip. "I'd rather finish what was started. I don't want to keep looking over my shoulder the next thousand years."

Tarsus huffed a steam of smoke out of one nostril. "What cave? What are you talking about?"

Pip took a deep breath before answering. "He's got a cave about five hundred miles or so from here. At least he used to have a cave. In the mountains to the north. That's where I followed him when we were fighting."

"Followed him? How did you do that?" asked Tarsus curiously.

Pip looked abashed. "I don't really know." He shrugged. "When he vanished off the field, I just knew where he was going. So, I followed him there."

Laura asked, "You said he used to have a cave? What happened? What was he doing?"

"Nothing really,." Pip answered Laura. "I caught him coming out of the cave with a walking staff. I didn't give him time to do much else than defend himself. He's too good for that. So, I said hello to him, which in hindsight wasn't very smart on my part, because it pissed him off."

As Gimble laughed, he choked out, "I bet."

Pip ignored the Dwarf and went on. "He tried to throw a punch at me with his Staff. When that didn't work, I yanked it out of his hand and threw it back into the cave and then threw my own back at him. But it didn't connect. He flashed before it got to him." He looked at Laura and grinned. "But the cave sure felt the blast. The wind was knocked out of me from the cave collapsing. And that's when I followed him again back here." Pip shrugged. "You know the rest."

Muriel suddenly became very interested. "What kind of staff?"

Pip shrugged. "I don't know. Just a wood staff."

"Describe it to me," Muriel said, leaning over the table towards Pip, very interested indeed.

Tarsus was staring at Muriel like the rest. Something was really eating the Elf. Lionel looked at him as curiously as the others. "What's the matter?"

Muriel flapped his hand at the king to hush him. "Please, Lion. This could be important."

Every eye turned to Pip. "I don't know what kind of wood it was made of, but it was carved with symbols along the base, and it had a small red jewel sitting at the top." Pip looked at the Elf and shrugged again. "It was kind of pretty, actually. It was shiny and glowed a little bit."

"Was the color it glowed red, too?" asked Muriel.

"I think so. But I didn't get too good a look at it. It all happened pretty fast. I just didn't like him throwing power at me with it, so I yanked it from him."

Muriel leaned back in his chair and an audible groan came from his lips.

Tarsus shook his head in denial and said, "No, Elf. It can't be. I know what you're thinking, and it's not possible. They were all destroyed millennium ago."

Muriel disagreed with the dragon. "No, dragon, you're wrong. I have one of them."

"What? The twig, or branch, or whatever it is you earned in the Great Forest of Eld?" Tarsus asked, skeptically. "It can't be."

Muriel said heatedly to Tarsus, "It is dragon. And it's not a twig or branch. It's one of the five. The elders have examined it and all agree. It's one of the original five."

Lionel jumped in then, trying to make sense out of what was being said. "Whoa! Whoa! Slow down. What are you two talking about? What five? What staff? What's going on?"

Tarsus sneered when he explained. "Sire, millennium ago, it's said, five staffs were created by the gods, at one time used by the five most powerful wizards of the age. Each had their own powers to command and each could do great or harmful things. But the most powerful, called the Staff of Talsoun, could only be used once every thousand years to cause great harm and destruction."

"Yes, and it's said by the old ones of the forest, the other four could counter the destruction of the fifth. That is, they could undo what harm had been done by the Staff of Talsoun," continued Muriel. "The old ones also said that Talsoun is the Staff that severed the earth in half during the Great Awakening."

"The Great Awakening?" asked Dwayne. "What's that?"

Tarsus snorted. "The Great Awakening of the dragons. It's myth and legend, nothing more."

"You don't know that dragon. Most myths or legends have their basis in facts," stated Muriel.

Tarsus just shook his head.

"What's the Great Awakening?" asked Pip, now becoming interested himself.

Gimble answered for Muriel. "The awakening of the dragon's ability to reason, lad. My people have a legend also concerning this. It's said by Dwarfs, at one time, dragons were imprisoned by the gods because they were wild animals that couldn't be controlled. To stop their terror upon the earth and to ensure the continuation of all the forms of life they'd striven to create, they had them entombed. The greatest wizard of that time bargained with the gods for their release. With the Staff of Talsoun, he opened a great chasm in the Earth and set them free."

"What was the bargain?" asked Laura.

Muriel answered, watching Laura's face for her reaction, "The dragons would get the ability to reason and think, and he'd get their undying loyalty until he died."

Every eye went to Tarsus. He said in a mocking voice, "That's nonsense. We're inherently magical in nature. We didn't come from the ground like rodents."

"OK," said Lionel. "Never mind for now. What happened to the Staffs?"

Muriel shook his head. "No one really knows. Over the hundreds of centuries, the Staffs were lost. Some old ones say they were handed down from generation to generation, others say the gods reclaimed them. And still others say they were hidden so no one could find them."

"But you found one," asked Dwayne. "How?"

"Pure luck, my friend, pure luck," Muriel said, smiling, looking at Gimble. "Without going into it now, let's just say I paid a high price for it. Many others who'd gone looking for it never came back."

Gimble nodded his agreement. "That's an understatement."

"The point being," continued Muriel, "is that I have one of them. It's my Staff of Power. It doesn't look quite like the one the young wizard describes, but it does have a small jewel on the top, a blue one."

"And?" asked Tarsus.

"And," said Muriel, staring at Tarsus, "if the Staff young Pip saw was the Staff of Talsoun, someone needs to go get it. We wouldn't want Granston to get his hands on it again, would we?"

*   *   *

EPILOGUE

Pip yawned and then grumbled, "Isn't this enough. I'm tired, wet, and hungry. Let's stop until morning or next week or next month.' He stumbled and almost fell.

Tarsus wasn't unsympathetic to the young man's plight. He knew Pip was exhausted, but he also knew he couldn't stop yet. A one-time victory over Granston didn't give any of them the right to let down their guard, and it most especially didn't give them the right to stop digging. It was a matter of time until the miserable Gnome came looking for revenge for what Pip and he had done to his army.

Pip stopped throwing the house size boulders, sighing, exhausted from the strain. Just north of the castle, no more than five hundred miles, a lonely mountain range roamed its way across the northern part of the continent, spires of snow-capped peaks and crags of jutting stone made their way majestically into the sky. Pip found himself marveling at the sight of such beauty as this, understanding the gods had a good day when they made these vistas. It's granite statement of defiance giving character to what would otherwise be a sprawling desert. And Tarsus was having Pip crumble it to dust, one house size boulder at a time. "That's enough! I'm wiped out."

Tarsus grunted. "Not quite. You need to finish this as quickly as you can. The next time we may not be so lucky."

Pip jerked his head to stare at the dragon. "What do you mean? We did it. Granston's gone."

Tarsus looked at Pip, cocking his head. "But for how long?"

Pip looked stunned. He hadn't thought about that. He only stared at Tarsus, not answering.

Tarsus nodded his head. "Me either. That's why we need to get this done."

"If I'd known I was coming back for the Staff, I wouldn't have pushed so hard," complained Pip, throwing another boulder out of the way.

"If I'd known the little wizard had the Staff, I don't think I would've jumped at killing him so hastily," countered Tarsus. "Muriel better be right about this. If his Staff of Power and Granston's are two of the original five, we can't leave it here, no matter how long it takes."

"Yeah, I guess you're right," said Pip, throwing still another boulder. "But can't you do some of this? I'm about to collapse." He slumped where he stood, heaving in great lungful of air.

"I'm doing my part, kid. I'm watching and instructing." Tarsus leaned close to Pip and peered menacingly into his eyes.

Pip only chuckled, wiping sweat from his brow. "You better do better than that. I've seen you with a mad-on, remember?"

Tarsus chuffed and drew back. After a moment, he gave in a little bit. "Take a rest. You do look a bit tired."

"Thanks," said Pip dryly. "You're too kind." He sat down where he was, not worrying about finding a soft spot. He took a grateful drink of mountain water and sighed heavily. Looking down at his grumbling stomach, he said, "I think I could use something to eat, too."

Not really listening to Pip, Tarsus said absently, "I'll go find us something to eat in a while. Right now is for digging that Staff out of the hole it's in." Tarsus nodded towards the cave mouth, now looking like a tunnel instead of a pile of rubble.

"Then what?" asked Pip, watching the dragon.

Tarsus didn't have an answer for that except, "We wait.'

*　　*　　*

CHARACTER AND DEFINITIONS

Pip—The stable boy who became a wizard.

Laura—Princess of Musk. Later a knight of the King's Guard.

Dwayne—Captain of the King's Knights until busted to page.

Lionel—King and ruler of Musk. Father to Princess Laura.

Whirle—Faithful lifelong servant to Lionel, king of Musk.

Balsas—King of the Dwarfs.

Shimmer—The wizard Granston was apprenticed to centuries before.

Granston—Lionel's adviser and wizard. Enemy to Tarsus.

Grundehl—Gnome king.

Gimble—Dwarf that showed up at the gates of Musk. Nephew to King
Balsas of the Dwarfs.

Muriel—Elf who showed up at the gates of Musk.

Elder March—Elder of the Elf race.

Assanti—A race of beings who resemble humans but are not. Their whole
lives revolve around the profession of being Assassins for hire.

Bappa—Leader of the Assanti Assassins.

Dhaka—A female Assanti Assassin.

Raulch—A giant Gnome. The muscle for the king of the Gnomes.

Dura—A human Assanti Assassin.

Tarsus—First dragon to ever enter the Kingdom of Musk. Was thought by most inhabitants of the kingdom to be nothing but legends.

Aranea—Mate to Tarsus that was killed by Granston many centuries ago.

Staff of Talsoun—One of five original staffs, supposedly made by the gods. It wields tremendous power, but can only be used once every thousand years for a mighty deed.

Staff of Power—One of five original staffs, found by Muriel in the Forest of Eld.

Translocation—Moving oneself from place to place with nothing but the power of your mind.

Fate—Even if not followed, it will drag you where it wants you to go.

Today's mighty oak is just yesterday's nut that held its ground.